D0481283

THE
GAUDÍ
KEY

THE
GAUDÍ
KEY

ESTEBAN MARTÍN

AND

ANDREU CARRANZA

Translated from the Spanish
by Lisa Dillman

wm

WILLIAM MORROW
An Imprint of HarperCollins*Publishers*

Originally published as *La Clave Gaudí* by Plaza y Janes in Spain in 2007.

Photograph credits:
Spires on page 173 © Damian Tully/Alamy
Cryptogram on page 320 © Eduard Solé

This book is a work of fiction. References to real people, events, establishments, organizations, or locales are intended only to provide a sense of authenticity, and are used fictitiously. All other characters, and all incidents and dialogue, are drawn from the author's imagination and are not to be construed as real.

THE GAUDÍ KEY. Copyright © 2007 by Esteban Martín and Andreu Carranza. Translation copyright © 2008 by Lisa Dillman. All rights reserved. Printed in the United States of America. No part of this book may be used or reproduced in any manner whatsoever without written permission except in the case of brief quotations embodied in critical articles and reviews. For information address HarperCollins Publishers, 10 East 53rd Street, New York, NY 10022.

HarperCollins books may be purchased for educational, business, or sales promotional use. For information please write: Special Markets Department, HarperCollins Publishers, 10 East 53rd Street, New York, NY 10022.

FIRST EDITION

Designed by Cassandra J. Pappas

Library of Congress Cataloging-in-Publication Data has been applied for.

ISBN 978-0-06-143491-4

08 09 10 11 12   OV/RRD   10 9 8 7 6 5 4 3 2 1

*The Temple of La Sagrada Família is a work that lies in the hands of
God and the will of the people . . .
Providence, with its holy designs, will bring it to completion.
The inside of the temple will be like a forest.*

—ANTONIO GAUDÍ

AUTHOR'S NOTE

Antonio Gaudí was born on June 25, 1852. Many consider Gaudí the father of the Gothic Modernist movement that swept Europe in the early part of the twentieth century, a movement that still influences many artists of all mediums today.

An ardent Catholic, Gaudí abandoned all secular work and devoted his life to Catholicism and his construction of La Sagrada Família, one of the world's most beloved architectural masterpieces.

On June 7, 1926, Antonio Gaudí was mysteriously run over by a tram in Barcelona. Because of his ragged attire and empty pockets, multiple cab drivers refused to pick him up for fear that he would be unable to pay the fare. He was eventually taken to a pauper's hospital. Nobody recognized the injured artist until his friends found him the next day. When they tried to move him into a respectable hospital, Gaudí refused, reportedly saying, "I belong here among the poor."

Gaudí died three days later on June 10, 1926, half of Barcelona mourning his death. He was buried in the midst of La Sagrada Família. Because he did not use blueprints for his unfinished masterpiece, but worked from instinct and his vivid imagination, which he felt was ordained by God, his fellow workers could not complete the cathedral. It is for this reason that Gaudí is known to many throughout the world as "God's architect."

THE
GAUDÍ
KEY

PART I

THE KNIGHT

1

BARCELONA

JUNE 6, 1926

I

T HAS TO look like an accident."

The masked man's voice was deep and ominous.

"It will," replied one of the two men standing before him. "Don't worry, Asmodeus."

They'd both arrived at the crypt at the exact time the man known as Asmodeus had commanded. Dressed in black, their heads bowed down respectfully, the pair approached the sculpted, black marble altar where Asmodeus stood, awaiting them.

The crypt was located under an ornate mansion known in Catalan as *Set Portes*—Seven Doors—and was illuminated by small candles protruding from fixtures embedded in the walls, their bluish flames casting a dim light throughout the centuries-old stone chamber. Asmodeus's figure was lit by the two candelabra hanging on either side of the altar. The flickering candles cast shadows that exaggerated the leather folds of the mask he wore, which resembled a muted and ancient version of a Venetian carnival mask. Asmodeus's face was completely hidden. In fact, none of the disciples in the Corbel had ever seen his face. It was their way. The identity of Asmodeus must never be revealed, even to them.

He gestured vaguely with his right hand, signaling one of the two men to speak.

"We've been trailing him for quite some time now, just as you ordered. The old man takes the same route every day. He leaves his studio at about five thirty each afternoon and heads for the church in Plaza San Felip Neri," the taller of the two men reported.

"That's quite a walk."

"He's old. He thinks it's good for his rheumatism," the other explained.

He was burlier than his companion and had a soft voice that seemed out of sync with his hard features. Despite their obvious physical differences, the two actually resembled each other. Asmodeus always maintained that the faces of those meant to serve the Dark One were always cast from the same mold.

"He walks down Gran Vía and crosses at Calle Bailén, by Plaza Tetuán, then takes Urquinaona and continues down Fontanella until he finally gets to Puerta del Angel. And from there he takes Calle Arcs, Plaza Nova, Calle Bisbe, Calle San Sever, and ends up at San Felip Neri." He glanced at his companion standing next to him, who nodded encouragement, so he continued.

"The old man stays in the chapel until it closes. Then he retraces his steps—"

The other one cut in. "But when he gets to Plaza Urquinaona, he stops at the kiosk to buy the evening paper, the *Veu de Catalunya*. Then he goes back to his studio."

"He doesn't get home until about ten," the other concluded.

If Asmodeus's face had been visible, they'd have seen his satisfied smile. They worked well, these two. Of all the members of the Corbel, he was right to choose them.

"Does he visit anyone?"

"Father Agustín Mas, in the San Felip Neri Church."

"His spiritual adviser," the other explained.

"I chose you two because you're the best. There can be no mistakes," Asmodeus intoned.

"Don't worry," the taller one said.

The other hesitated for a moment. Asmodeus took note.

"Is there a problem?"

"There's a boy."

"A *boy*?"

He nodded. "For the past few days he's been accompanied by a boy. He lives with him, in his studio. We checked."

"How long has this boy lived there?"

"A few months."

"A *few*?"

"Well, almost a year . . . eleven months."

"What's a boy doing living with him? Who is he?" Asmodeus's voice conveyed the frustration he felt at not having immediately been told about the existence of this boy.

As he waited for an answer, other men began to file into the room with military precision. They lined up several feet behind the two men standing before Asmodeus. They began reciting their traditional incantation. Their words blended into a low murmur, a hollow sound that slowly gained volume by sheer force of its repetition. Their chanting grew louder and louder. The time to begin the ceremony had arrived.

"What's a boy doing living with him?" Asmodeus repeated, almost whispering the question to himself.

"Some mornings they just wander around aimlessly, and then in the afternoon the boy goes with him to mass. I don't think we need to worry about it. We can—"

"No." Asmodeus cut him off. "Two accidents would raise suspicion."

"We'll take care of him. He's just a kid."

"Is he a relative?"

"We don't think so. The old man has lived alone ever since his niece died several years ago. He's a very strange man."

"Yes, very strange. His life is over, but tomorrow afternoon, you will deliver his soul to his god. And then you'll bring me the secret."

"Does he always carry it?" the stockier man asked.

"Always," Asmodeus confirmed. "He even sleeps with it. Kill him and bring me his secret. You won't have much time before a crowd gathers. No mistakes on this."

"Have faith in us. There won't be any."

"There better not be."

They both knew Asmodeus meant what he said. He would never forgive a mistake.

"*Dei Par. Dei Par.*"

The men who now filled the room chanted over and over. There were about twenty in all. The incantation intensified. What had begun with the solemnity of a prayer became a fervent mantra, invoking their worshipful phrase, "*Dei Par.*"

Asmodeus held his hand out to the two men standing before him, who each kissed the ring on his finger. Its onyx stone symbolized Asmodeus's power. The chanting took on frenzied, almost inhuman tones.

The men swayed in unison, surging back and forth like a wave, anointing themselves worthy—a ceremony performed by the brotherhood for centuries.

After speaking with Asmodeus, the two men left. Fueled by the importance of their mission, they moved quickly and with purpose. As they left the room, the dark figures closed in behind them. The celebrants cried out; some knelt, others lay prostrate on the floor.

"*Dei Par. Dei Par.*"

Asmodeus grinned behind his mask. Watching the scene before him reminded him of the many centuries of history the Corbel had amassed. Strict discipline and a strong sense of mission most assuredly prepared one's soul for the Dark One. The Corbel's was a history of absolute devotion.

After the ceremony had concluded, Asmodeus stood alone in the crypt once more. Finally, after so long, the secret would be in the possession of the Corbel. *The old man could have been the best,* Asmodeus thought to himself. He'd been given a chance, but you can't simultaneously serve God and the Dark One. Since childhood, the old man had spent his time studying ancient philosophy, along with the secret art of construction under the master builder. The Corbel had tried to tempt him back then, but he refused to join their brotherhood. It was then that the Corbel's sworn enemies, the Seven Knights of Moriah, took him under their wing. They made him a knight, and under the tutelage of their powerful patron, he went on to become the grand master, entrusted with the secret, finally becoming the keeper of the answer to the greatest enigma of all.

But the Corbel was vigilant, keeping track of his every move. The old man had received the gift, the revelation, and the order to finish the Great Work. The Corbel was there to stop him. Like Moses, the old man would never reach the promised land. There would be no promised land. Asmodeus knew how far the old man had come. He had worked his whole life for this one thing.

And it was on the verge of completion.

He'd drawn a map of his project, the compass points, the coordinates, the order of each structure, the exact combination of each symbol, the secret language itself. The Corbel had kept their distance for years, their spies informing Asmodeus of every step the old man took. The Corbel wouldn't interfere with his work. In fact, it helped him. Though the old man didn't know it, he was working for them, too. The Corbel knew, from the start, when and where the secret was handed over and what would happen if it all came to fruition. They just had to be patient and wait for the right time.

That time was now.

Now the old man must die.

"*Dei Par,*" Asmodeus thought. "*Equal gods.* Barcelona, the city of eternal duality. Founded by Hercules—the sun, the light, but also the moon—and Tanit, the darkness. The chosen city. *Dei Par.* The time has come. It's our turn now."

Asmodeus knew the vital importance of concealing his true identity. He was the only one with access to the secret passageways. After waiting a safe time, once he was sure he was alone, he'd change clothes and regain the façade of a distinguished gentleman. He left the premises draped in his dark cape, brandishing a cane in his left hand. Two of his personal bodyguards awaited him just outside. The chauffeur opened the door of the car parked at the curb. Asmodeus wanted to walk, and he motioned to communicate this to his bodyguards. But before he had taken more than a few steps, the sound of a scuffle abruptly stopped him. Shouting broke out. One bodyguard rushed into the street. The other approached him and said, "It's not safe for you to walk. This part of the city is very dangerous at this time of night. Sir, you must get in the car."

Barcelona is a treacherous city. But some nights he preferred to walk without his bodyguards, even if he knew it was reckless. This night was special. He needed to be alone, to feel the danger, losing himself in the shadows of his dark city, a city with a long and storied history of depravity and secrets. He needed to feel the power of this history, to think about old times, when he was only Bitru, no more than an ambitious youngster in the Corbel, hoping to one day become the new Asmodeus. That was the way it had been for centuries. Now another Bitru had taken his place, and one day another would ascend to become the new Asmodeus. To replace him. It was the order of things.

Before long, his silhouette disappeared into the night, leaving the meaningless street brawls of the lost behind him. At that late hour there was hardly anyone out walking in the stench of the Barceloneta port where he now found himself, just a few seedy prostitutes. He stopped in a darkened doorway, waited a few minutes, and donned his mask once more. He wanted to blend into the night as he really was, not as the gentleman he pretended to be. He made his way beneath the arcades. The air was still, breezeless. It was going to be a hot summer. Glancing over to the other side of the avenue, he saw the Lonja, the city's stock exchange. This part of Barcelona seemed a ghost town at that time of night. He'd just been enjoying the solitude when someone grabbed his arm.

"Hey, want a good time?"

He turned and yanked himself free. It was a hideous, filthy woman. She smelled, and her dress was a collection of rags wrapped tightly to her sagging body.

"Get off!"

Pointing to his mask, she stammered, "You so ugly you have to hide your face? No worries, I like perverts."

He debated killing her. But the revulsion that she provoked in him when he looked at her saved her life. He hurried off.

He cut down Calle Avinyó and, minutes later, stepped into Plaza Real.

He walked to the center of the plaza. Surrounded by palm trees and resting on a concrete foundation were two streetlamps with six arms each, their lanterns made of bronze, iron, and glass. He was flushed with energy, a mixture of anticipation at the events about to unfold and disgust for the deplorable woman whose life he had just spared. He contemplated the shape of the animal forged on one of the streetlamps, a coiled serpent.

"Crazy fool! What's so interesting about a lamppost?"

Asmodeus slowly turned and saw a swaying drunk. The drunkard stared back at him, paralyzed by fear.

Asmodeus's eyes were the last thing the poor man saw. Asmodeus slipped off the cane's handle and, with one well-aimed thrust, pierced the man's heart with the slender foil concealed within its antique shell.

Asmodeus smiled. He'd sleep well that night. Everything was unfolding as the Corbel had long planned. He walked home knowing that soon he'd have what had so long been denied them. The darkness would triumph.

His footsteps were the only sound in that silent and dangerous part of Barcelona.

2

JUNE 6, 2006

LIKE A LIZARD basking in the sun, Juan Givell sat on a bench on the grounds of his nursing home. He wondered if the fragmentary thoughts that blew through his mind, like aimless gusts of wind, had been remnants of a dream. Had he imagined it all? Or was it real?

He was ninety-two years old. Or at least that's what they'd told him this morning. Or was it yesterday? Juan Givell wasn't sure. His mind was like a flock of birds, flapping this way and that. At any rate, he was happy here in the sun. On his bench. In the gardens. The young nurse dressed in white had parked him there, as she did every morning.

"Will you be OK here?"

"I'll be fine, child. What's your name?"

"Eulalia."

"That's beautiful. Like the saint. The patron saint of Barcelona. She was martyred by Governor Datianus in 304 AD, during the Diocletian persecution. February 12, that's her saint's day."

His lucid moments never ceased to surprise her.

"This is my bench, isn't it?" the old man asked.

"Yep. The same one as every morning."

"It's nice here. I like it."

"I know you do. If you need anything, I won't be far."

"Thank you, child."

The nurse was about to walk away when Juan Givell tugged at her sweater. "What's your name, child?"

"Eulalia, like the saint," she said, repeating his exact words. "You know, the patron saint of Barcelona. The one who was martyred by Datianus."

"Oh, yes. That's such a beautiful tale. Beautiful and terrible."

Eulalia Pons walked away, saddened. She'd been working at the home for two years now, but she'd never get used to such conversations. Why such tragic human decline? It made no sense. It was one thing to know that these things happened, but quite another to live them day in and day out. Taking care of all those old people, some of whom couldn't find their own noses. In the time Eulalia Pons had been working at the nursing home, she'd stopped believing in God.

Juan was alone now. He was just beginning to sink back into the past when someone sat down beside him.

"Want a piece of candy? When you were little, you used to love it."

Juan looked left, toward the tall, strapping man holding out a piece of candy; he looked like a basketball player. He smiled at the giant and accepted. Taking the candy, he unwrapped it and popped it into his mouth with trembling fingers.

"Mmm. It's good."

"I know. How are you, Juan?"

"Good. Very good. Are we going to hide the secret?"

"No, Juan. That was a long time ago. You remember?"

"No."

The giant knew he was lying.

"I know you remember. Not all the time, maybe, but you remember."

"You're not Cristóbal. He's much older than me, and your beard is still thick and dark, just like it was that night, the night of the tram . . . ,"

Juan said, his speech trailing off slowly. "The tram," he repeated again. "But so much time has gone by since then."

"Not for me. I made a pact with time long ago."

"This is a dream."

"No, Juan. No dream. Not now. Maybe it was before, but not now. I'm right here, by your side."

"So we're not going to hide the secret?"

"No, Juan. Now we have to *find* it. The time has come. We have to carry out the prophecy."

Juan's mind came and went. He knew that she, his granddaughter María, had to bring the work to completion. That's why Cristóbal was here. For years he'd tried to protect her, keeping her far away from all that.

"She's all I've got. They'll kill her. If they find out, they'll kill her."

"We'll protect her."

"Like you protected the master?"

The giant made no reply.

"My granddaughter is everything to me, she's all I've got," he repeated.

The giant knew he had to seize this moment, take advantage of it before darkness descended over Juan Givell's mind once more.

"My head is like a black hole. Sometimes it just goes. Well, at least that's what I've heard . . . They say I'm losing my mind . . . but I never fully remember what they've said anyway."

"She'll come today, like every day."

"Does she always come?"

"Yes. Since she returned, she visits every afternoon."

"I know she comes. But I didn't know she came every day."

"Well, she does."

"What a good girl. So, I'm to pass it on to her then?"

"Yes. And tell her everything. Everything you can remember."

"I don't know where I hid it. You stayed outside that day. You refused to come in with me."

"I couldn't. I wasn't supposed to come in, just to protect you. You are the guardian. All I did was put you on my shoulders and take you across the river. I aid travelers on their journeys. That's my destiny. Only in that way am I a servant of the Lord."

"A fine guardian I am," Juan said skeptically. The years had been long, and his duty was nearing an end. Although he knew the cause was just, the work had taken extreme patience and faith.

Yes, a fine guardian, the tall, well-built man thought. His big, dark eyes, surrounded by tiny crow's-feet, were full of kindness. His look seemed to transcend time. Named after Saint Christopher, Cristóbal had sworn his life and services to the one truly omnipotent lord. That's why he was here, sitting with the old man who had trouble remembering what he'd promised to protect so long ago.

"She'll come. You must tell her everything you remember," the giant repeated.

Juan remained silent. "I've got it; it's right here," he said to himself, placing a hand on his chest. When he looked up, the giant was gone.

Juan remembered. He was a knight. Maybe the last one. And he had to keep the promise he'd made to Don Antonio. Don Gaudí. And the promise was there, somewhere, floating around in his head. He had to remember. He had to.

There wasn't much time.

3

LATER THAT AFTERNOON, María Givell strode through the door of the nursing home on Calle Numancia, behind Diagonal, close to the Illa shopping center. It was a quiet area. The home had grounds where the residents could stroll and enjoy the sun. She thought it a fitting place for her grandfather to spend the time he had left.

Since returning from the United States three months ago, she'd come to see her grandfather every single day. Sometimes he didn't recognize her. Other times he did. María never knew what to expect. She'd sit beside him at the window and tell him stories or read him a book until visiting hours were up. She didn't have a day job, and since she spent so little time at the Friends of Modernism Foundation—two days a week—she had no problem arranging her schedule around the visits to her grandfather. She owed it to him. She owed everything to him.

She'd lived with him ever since her mother died during childbirth. Her grandfather never knew who María's father was. Whenever she asked, he just said that her mother was as pure as the Madonna.

Her childhood had been one long, pleasant morning spent with an elderly man who protected her, read her books, told her stories, took her to Park Güell and La Sagrada Família or on day trips to Montserrat, and to the movies, which she loved. He'd always taken care of her. Not even as a teen had she caused him problems. She was a brilliant student, what some would call real bookish, complete with braces and a taciturn nature, a loner who stoically suffered her classmates' teasing.

By the time she started college, the first signs of her grandfather's illness were appearing. Then, when she graduated, he insisted she continue her studies in the United States.

"I'm not leaving you, Grandfather. Not now," she'd said.

He was stubborn. He seemed to have her entire life planned out for her.

"You cannot and will not stay here and take care of me. I'm ninety years old; my head's not so good anymore. I'll be fine in the home. And I want you to go to the United States. That's the only thing that will make me happy. Study. Finish your education. The crème de la crème are in the United States. And when you come back, you can visit me as much as you like."

And that's what she did. She never contradicted her grandfather. He'd never raised his voice to her, never punished her, and never treated her like a child. She was always treated as an equal. Children are people, not idiots, he always used to say. Children will understand anything if you explain it to them properly. And that's what he did: explained it to her, time and again. His was the best decision, María realized. New York opened her eyes to a whole other world.

Now she was twenty-six, an attractive, assertive young woman. She helped out at the foundation and was finishing up her dissertation. She was an exceptional art historian who, though not overly glamorous, would attract the glances of all who felt the magnetic pull of her beautiful green eyes. She was tall and athletic, but still surprisingly curvaceous. Yet, perhaps because of her lonely, sheltered childhood, María had a melancholy air. She had an aura about her that intrigued only the bravest and most curious people. It was as though one needed to pass a test to get close to her. And most were nowhere near up to the challenge.

"HIS ILLNESS IS advancing. He's gotten a lot worse over the past two years. I know it's not much consolation, but your grandfather has had . . . well, not many people make it to his age," the director of the home told her before she went in to see her grandfather.

María listened carefully.

"He has lucid moments, intermittent periods when the fog lifts. But they're less and less frequent now. We do everything we can, give him the best care possible. You know there's no cure for his illness."

"I should never have left him."

"What difference would it have made had you stayed? None. Look, as I said, you made the right decision. You couldn't have given him better care by yourself. A lot of people don't understand that. But that's what we're here for; it's what we do: make the waning years as pleasant as possible." He stopped justifying her decision for a moment and then, a second later, resolutely concluded, "There's not a single thing you could have done to reverse this."

"How is he today?" she asked, resigned.

"He's been a little upset these days, more excitable than usual."

"Yes, I noticed that, too, over the past few visits."

"Enjoy his lucid moments. He has very few left."

"Is he going to become a vegetable?"

The doctor couldn't lie. He wasn't going to sugarcoat his reply, as he often did with family members. María was a woman of mettle.

"It's only a question of time."

"Some days he doesn't even recognize me."

"That's normal. The day will come when he forgets you entirely. That's just the way it is; no sense in fooling ourselves."

On her way to his room, she recalled what her grandfather had said when he asked her to admit him into a home. "I've had a good life, María. A studious life. You're what I loved most in this world. My pride and joy, although I might not remember that for long. Go, study, have a good time, and when you come back, you can visit me as much as you like. I'll wait for you. And even if I don't remember your name, or mine, I want you to know that I loved you more than anything in the world." He'd repeat this again and again, relentlessly. Yes, he was ill. There was nothing she could do about it, the young woman thought before boarding a plane for America and leaving the old continent behind her. She did as he requested and left. It was what they both wanted.

She walked into his room. He sat gazing out an open window. She came up behind him slowly. She called his name affectionately, almost in a whisper, not knowing whether he'd recognize her. Maybe he was gone forever. She had to act naturally, not become emotional or do anything to startle him. She stood in front of him, careful not to block the golden rays of sunlight shining on his face.

"Hello, Grandfather. It's me, María."

He didn't answer. His far-off gaze wasn't focused on anything in the room. She sat beside him and waited. Then she took his hand.

"María?"

"Yes, Grandfather."

His granddaughter's touch had snapped him back to reality, away from the dreamlike state he so often found solace in.

"Why didn't you say anything when you walked in?"

"I didn't want to disturb you," she lied.

They were both silent.

"Do you know who I am?" María asked, after a few moments.

"Yes, child, I do. I'm not a doddering old fool all the time, just most of it," he joked.

"Would you like me to read to you?"

"No. I have some things to tell you. But first, you tell me. Are you dating anyone?"

"Yes."

"What's his name?"

"Miguel."

He started.

"Miguel! *Michael*. Of course. He couldn't have any other name," her grandfather declared loudly. "The dragon slayer. What does he do?"

"He doesn't slay dragons, Grandfather, if that's what's worrying you." María smiled.

"That's just a matter of time. You'll understand after you hear what I have to tell you. But first, tell me, what does he do? Tell me about him. And most important, does he love you?"

She waited a few seconds before saying anything. He asked the same questions every time. After taking a deep breath she gave her standard response. "Very much. He loves me very much, Grandfather." She was going to add "as much as you do," but stopped herself. "He's a mathematician. He teaches at the university and also does research."

"I know that already. He won the Fields Medal four years ago, when he was thirty-six; it's like the Nobel Prize but for math. Yes, yes, that's all fine and well, but tell me, does he *really* love you?"

María was no longer surprised by the way his memory came and went; she tried to follow the conversation.

"What does he research?"

"Well, he spends all day computing things I don't understand, trying to prove conjectures and come up with theorems on geometrization. He doesn't just hole up in the library, though. He's also really fun, and he loves music and literature. Miguel's in touch with the world, that's for sure."

"That's the way it should be. You can't be good at anything if you lose perspective. My master used to say that it's nature herself who provides the best solutions. It's just a question of knowing how to look at it all, how to see—really and truly see things, as they are. Does he know how to look at you, María? Does he truly love you? What I mean is, are you thinking of getting married, starting a family? . . . I'm old fashioned and it's hard for me to understand young people today, the way couples act, friends who just decide to get together, have no commitment to each other, go their own way, both free and independent, spending their time thinking about their careers instead of each other."

Before going to the United States, María had argued with her grandfather about the state of today's couples many times, but today it didn't bother her. Today it made her happy. She'd been expecting his condition to have deteriorated. But she saw their conversation pulling him out of his mental black hole. How long until he sank back in?

"Would you be willing to give up everything for him? And what about him? Would he give up mathematics, his career, out of love for you?"

Her grandfather turned and gazed into her eyes as he asked this. María trembled; she was happy that he was lucid. That was how she remembered him. Sharp, direct, but gentle, too. Yet the question disconcerted her. *Would* she be willing? Would *he*? Would Miguel give it all up for her? Everything? What was everything, anyway? A good job, being recognized in one's field, a nice apartment, a comfortable life, no major hardships . . . What else?

"You have to tell me the truth," the old man insisted.

"Grandfather, we . . . we don't want commitments. We like each other, we're attracted to each other, but we're adults and we're independent. Try to understand that. The world's changed a lot since you were young. Our jobs are important to us, and we respect each other. But we don't want a family right now. We love each other, but—"

"It doesn't matter. I don't want to argue about it; it's just so strange to me. That's the way young people are today." Her grandfather shook his head and turned back to the window. "Now I need to tell you a few things that might change your life forever. And I'm afraid, because only people who are truly in love can understand what I'm going to say, only those willing to give up everything for love and receive nothing in return. When you meet someone you'd do that for, when you meet someone who'd do that for *you*, the miracle will happen. I know it's out of fashion these days, but the idea of living life without ever really knowing what true love is . . . it's so sad."

María didn't know what to say. She was attracted to Miguel, they had things in common, had great sex, but they were free and uncommitted.

When it came down to the most important things, though, she had not and would not let her grandfather down. She had deep convictions. She fundamentally respected and valued all that he'd taught her.

He turned back now and contemplated his granddaughter's face once more. She could see in his eyes that he was all there. He seemed to have momentarily recovered his memory entirely, although she knew that it was just an illusion and that he could drift off again at any moment.

"Don't be sad, María. When the time comes, you'll know how to make sense of what I tell you. I'm sure you'll find someone special, very special, someone who'll have faith in you. You don't have to get married and have children, or even live together. None of that matters. But when you meet the man you really and truly love, even if he's far away, you'll always carry him in your heart; you'll love him more than life itself."

Try as she might, María couldn't hold back her emotion. She wiped the tears from her eyes with the back of her hand. Her grandfather lifted a finger and tenderly helped her wipe them away, just as he had done so many times before, when she was a child. He held his moistened finger up to the sunlight streaming in from the window.

"You see, María? The whole universe is right here. That's what the master always said. All of humanity can be found in the pure emotion of one person. In this little teardrop, I can see the whole universe: time, life, the stars. It's like a mirror. If . . ."

He drifted off for several long seconds. María fleetingly thought those may have been his last lucid moments. She felt a knot in her throat; if they were, he'd chosen such a beautiful way to say good-bye to her. But she realized she'd been wrong when he suddenly came to and asked, "Do you know who my mentor was, who the master was, María?"

"No, Grandfather, I don't."

She'd never known what he did or who the master he always talked about was. In her mind, her grandfather had always just been an old, retired man surrounded by dusty books on architecture.

"Who?" she asked, curious but still preoccupied by the thought of losing him at any moment.

"Antonio Gaudí."

She wasn't surprised to hear this, although, stopping to calculate the years, she realized her grandfather had been a child when Gaudí died. She knew that he'd admired the architect's genius his whole life; he'd passed that admiration on to her. He knew a phenomenal amount about Gaudí. Everything she knew about Gaudí came from her grandfather. When she was a girl and asked if he'd ever met him, he always said, "One day I'll tell you everything about it, child." That day seemed to have arrived.

"I need to tell you today. I remember now and I might forget in a little while. You know how my memory comes and goes. Especially goes. It's important. I know I'll die soon."

"Grandfather, don't say that."

"It's true."

His breath quickened. María took his hand. She hadn't seen passion, at least not such fiery passion, in her grandfather's eyes for so long.

"I was with Gaudí the day he was murdered."

4

MARÍA REALIZED WITH sorrow that in fact her grandfather had already lost his mind. That precious instant when he'd spoken to her about the universe contained in her tear, about love and life, was probably his last rational moment. Her grandfather had said good-bye so poetically. But now he was gone; he was speaking like a prophet, almost without seeing her, grasping at what he thought were memories, one after the other, stringing together a fantastic and truly imaginative story.

For a few moments she almost doubted herself, wanting to believe what he was saying. But no, the whole thing was impossible. He really had lost his senses, she thought with despair. He repeated over and over that she must pay close attention to everything he was telling her, while she struggled to hold back her tears.

As she listened, she began to realize, though, that all of these impossible fantasies were backed up by historical facts and dates. She was fascinated by the tale he spun about Alfonso Givell, his own grandfather, who'd lived in Riudoms and was a friend of Gaudí's. And he talked about their early days in Barcelona. How could a sick man possibly weave such a crazy tale, blending fiction and reality so convincingly? But what he said next truly disconcerted her.

"What are you talking about? Antonio Gaudí was run over by a streetcar," María retorted when her grandfather again referred to his murder.

"Exactly, child, run over at the corner of Bailén and Calle Cortes, which is now the Gran Vía. Like I said, I was there. I was only eleven or twelve years old. It was five thirty in the afternoon on June 7, 1926. And it wasn't an accident."

"Grandfather, please."

María didn't want to listen to what she heard: the newspaper stand, the killers, his escape, the secret he had to hide, the giant who helped him. It was all too much. But she had to, out of compassion. What else could she do?

"I went to the burial and I was able to hide among all the people waiting by the wall surrounding La Sagrada Família. I had to work really hard to convince the giant to let me go. I knew it was dangerous, knew they'd be there, looking for me. And I was right. But I just had to see the master, to let him know that I'd carried out his wishes. They were there, but they didn't see me. I recognized their leader immediately. I knew it was him because Gaudí made sure to include him in La Sagrada Família, sculpted in stone. Evil always has the same face. Do you remember the man? The face of the man carved into La Sagrada Família?"

"The bad guy? Grandfather, that was years ago!" María exclaimed.

"You were just a little girl and so scared of the image. But you always insisted on seeing his face."

"I remember. The anarchist with the Orsini bomb in his hand in La Sagrada Família's Portal of the Rosary," María said. And then she finished for him, "Man's temptation, the mythological monster on the man's back, both giving him strength and pushing him toward evil. I know it by heart, Grandfather."

She clearly recalled all of their visits to La Sagrada Família when she was a child. The unfinished cathedral was like a second home to her.

"Be very careful. That man really exists. Don't forget his face. Evil always has the same face. Yet it's always hiding, donning new disguises.

You mustn't trust anyone. Like I said, the man of darkness whose face is set in stone was at the funeral, searching for me amongst all the people."

Her grandfather fell silent, looking frightened, as if the man carved in stone had suddenly appeared next to María.

"So what happened?" she asked, trying to bring him back, to make him focus.

"After that, my friends hid me."

"What friends?"

"The knights of the order."

"The order?"

"Yes, the order that initiated me when I was eleven. The seven knights are in charge of keeping the great secret safe. The one that Grand Master Gaudí gave me."

"Are you telling me Gaudí was a Mason? And that you belong to some secret sect?"

"No! For God's sake, you haven't heard a word I've said! Gaudí was no Mason. Gaudí believed in Christ, in the divinity of Our Lord. He took vows of humility, obedience, chastity, and poverty. And he lived in poverty, like Saint Francis, right up to the very last day of his life. The Masons think Jesus Christ was a good man, a great leader, and a prophet. But nothing more. We believe, we *know*, that he's the Son of God."

"We?"

"Yes, we: the Knights of Moriah." He stopped then, aware perhaps of how this revelation might sound to his granddaughter.

"I am the last grand master. Gaudí was my predecessor."

That was too much for her. Pure insanity. But she didn't know what to say. María was speechless.

She'd never heard of the Knights of Moriah, but rather than becoming exasperated, she asked patiently, "Who are these Moriah knights, Grandfather? What are you talking about?"

"Are you listening to a word I say? There have been seven of us guardians, seven knights in succession, one after the other, guarding the greatest secret in Christianity. Defending it, not just from its enemies, but also from some members of the Church. *Christ's own Church!* I know there are whole groups and sects who call themselves Templars. They supposedly perform rituals, wear ornate costumes, all that esoteric medieval paraphernalia that doesn't make any sense at all. Pure theatrics. Real knights know that there is only one truth, one inner revelation that matters. We seven knights are men and women who live in this world, and we have a mission on this earth. We're anonymous, we blend in, and that's our greatest protection. We're seven souls keeping vigil, keeping the secret, and now you, María—you're the one who has to complete the mission. The sign is within you. You are the Mirror of Enigmas. It's all up to you. It's imperative that you believe me."

No. There was no way María could believe it. She hardly even recognized her grandfather; he was suddenly full of a vitality and energy she'd never seen before. He was so convinced, so passionate about what he said.

Still, she replied, "Grandfather, what do you mean you're a Knight of Moriah?"

"I'm the last grand master of the Moriah."

"So you're a monk?"

"No. We're knights. We are valiant devotees of Christ, prepared to die if necessary. For centuries we've fought evil to keep the world in balance. And we can't lose now."

"Lose to who?"

"To the worshippers of the Dark One: the Corbel. They lust for power and chaos. They're killers who profane the host, murder, and do what they can to ensure that the weak and poor are severely dealt with, all the time kneeling before Baphomet, the demon they pray to."

"Sounds like your run-of-the-mill satanic sect to me," María said halfheartedly.

"I know you don't believe me. I can't blame you. If someone came to me with a tale like this, I wouldn't believe it either, especially if it came from a sick old man whose memory is full of more holes than a moth-eaten sweater," he said mournfully. After a second he perked up, adding, "But your life depends on it. I've been protecting you since the day you were born. But they're back now. They found me. I know it. That's why it's time to fulfill our destiny."

"Who found you? What destiny?"

"The men who killed the master. The same ones who will try to kill you. Because you've been chosen. The one."

That revelation gave her chills. Why would they want to kill *her*? What had she been chosen *for*?

"Listen. We don't have much time. They murdered him. Do you understand me? They murdered him. Whoever guards the secret is in danger; it's sacred. Now you . . ."

Her grandfather faltered; he couldn't get his words out.

"They contacted Gaudí . . . young . . . said no . . . Satanic . . . Turn it around . . . Return of the Devil . . . But no . . . Temple of the poor . . . Solomon's temple . . . the true house of God . . ."

"Grandfather, I can't understand what you're saying."

María knew his mind would go black at any moment and she'd lose him. What was the danger that lay ahead?

"I was with Gaudí . . . the day they killed him . . ."

"I know that already! What else?"

She decided to let him speak, not to interrupt, and then try to make sense of it later. "He took me to see the Enchanted House."

"The house in the forest?"

"Yes . . . I lived there . . . at first . . . Then . . . studio . . . This city is like a forest, he used to say. He . . . leave a trail . . . marked with stones . . . buildings . . . lost . . . arrival . . . gave me the key . . . You have to see, you have to know how to look through the Mirror of Enigmas . . . You have it. You must."

He fell silent. His eyes had that lost, faraway look she'd come to recognize.

"Talk to me, Grandfather. I'm listening. I'm here with you, just like when I was little and you'd tell me a story."

That last word seemed to shake him from his daze. He launched into it again, without looking at her.

"That's right, child, like 'Hänsel and Gretel.'"

"You always changed the ending; there was a dragon instead of a witch," María said, managing a smile at the memory.

"That's the way it should be . . . Remember the riddle game? Guess what it is."

"What did you hide, Grandfather?"

"What did I hide?" he said, no longer hearing her.

Her grandfather sank back into silence. María waited. She knew it was a waiting game. Within that sickly body a great battle was being waged between his conscious, rational mind and his fabled dreams.

"The bone, the bone!" he suddenly shouted, trying to unbutton his shirt.

His fingers fumbled awkwardly at his neck.

"The bone, the bone," he repeated, again and again.

"I'll help you, Grandfather."

But she didn't have to. He took his granddaughter's hand and placed the object that had been hanging around his neck into her palm. Then he closed her hand, squeezing her fist tightly.

"What is it?"

"It's a bone, child. Every day, from my little cell, I show it to the dragon. He thinks I'm too thin and gives me more food; he wants to eat me up when I'm nice and plump. The bone makes him think I'm still too thin. Like in the game . . . I have to solve the riddles. And now it's yours. But first, the archangel will have to kill the beast at the third door. He'll have to kill the beast that goes with him. Take the bone; it will keep them from eating you. Remember."

And then, his voice trembling, her grandfather recited a riddle from her childhood:

Hard on top,
hard underneath.
Face of a snake
and sticks for feet.

"The tortoise?"

"That's right!" he exclaimed, pleased, and then added, "You're a clever girl. The tortoise. Your favorite one. There are two, you know. Face of a snake and sticks for feet."

When she was little he told her riddles all the time. He even built a game for them: it had a small board, like a chessboard, with a different symbol on each square. Then he'd make up a riddle she had to solve for each one. If she got it right, that meant Hänsel and Gretel killed the dragon by stuffing him in the oven, and they would escape with a great treasure.

If you drop me on the tile
you won't find me for a while.
Though you think I'm just a lizard
I am also quite a wizard.

Suddenly her mind was filled with riddles her grandfather had taught her. And the one she liked the best was:

I move from cell to cell, though free
for there's no jail that can hold me.

But what did these riddles have to do with anything?

"The bone . . . in the tortoise . . . Face of a snake . . . Sticks for feet . . . One day alpha will save you . . . In La Sagrada Família . . . the first enigma . . . then Jonas will help you . . . I have to see Jonas . . . You must say, 'On earth as it is in heaven,' and they'll reply, 'What is above is as what is below' . . . The race will begin with the tortoise . . . There's not much time . . . Just a few days . . . Don't let them catch you . . . Do not let the dragon catch you . . ."

He repeated this last sentence over and over, like a litany.

María was disconsolate. Tears again welled up in her green eyes. This man was no longer her grandfather. Darkness had enveloped his mind. María got up and turned on the light.

"Kill the beast at the third door, the race, the tortoise . . . Go soon . . . tomorrow . . . at six in the morning . . . ," Juan Givell repeated relentlessly, his eyes unchanging, lost in the deep shadows of his mind. María kissed his forehead.

"I'll be back tomorrow, Grandfather."

"Wait, wait. María, I know you'll suffer. But whatever happens, promise me you won't stop to cry when it all begins . . . There are only a few days left and you must fulfill the prophecy. Nothing must prevent you."

"Oh, Grandfather! What are you talking about?"

"Promise me," he repeated. "You won't cry . . . nothing must stop you. Nothing."

"Fine. I promise."

María walked out of the room, tightly clutching what her grandfather had given her. She didn't dare look at it right away. Her mind was still reeling over what her grandfather had told her. What had he meant? When she finally unclenched her fist, she saw it was some sort of key, made of what seemed to be bone. A key? She put it away and headed for the exit, wanting to get home as soon as she possibly could.

5

MARÍA LEFT THE nursing home and went up Calle Numancia until she got to Diagonal. She needed to take a walk, make some sort of sense of all the emotions raging wildly through her. The traffic on Diagonal was terrible. She passed the Hilton and the Corte Inglés department store. Then she reached the Caixa building, two black cubes she'd always admired, though at that moment she paid them no attention whatsoever. At the intersection in front of the department store, a constant flow of people formed a human river, almost knocking her over. She carried on aimlessly, oblivious. She sat down on a bench. She wanted a cigarette badly and almost regretted quitting.

It was getting dark.

She opened her purse. There was the key. A key. She took it out and held it in her hand, examining it. It was strange and seemed as if it wouldn't fit into any normal lock. But that key, that bone, from what she understood, didn't open a door; it opened a tortoise. A tortoise? And she had to find it soon. At six o'clock in the morning, her grandfather had said.

She stood and walked to a nearby café that she used to go to while still an undergraduate. She ordered a coffee and took a seat. The café was crowded, just as it had always been.

She tried to recall everything her grandfather had said; she wanted to record every detail, every word, in her mind. There seemed to be two tortoises and a race. She presumed he was referring to the tortoises in La Sagrada Família, though she couldn't be sure. What made no sense at all, however, was that business about killing "the beast at the third door" and "On earth as it is in heaven." And what did he mean about the sign being within her?

When her coffee arrived, she realized she was still tightly clutching the key in her right hand. She didn't put it back in her purse but instinctively slipped it into the pocket of her jeans instead.

María's mind raced back to her childhood. Her grandfather, that huge apartment on Avenida Gaudí with all those bedrooms. There was no doubt that her grandfather was obsessed with Gaudí, even going so far as to live on the street named after him. Near his masterpiece. His masterpiece! She'd gone for so many walks in and around it as a little girl, holding her grandfather's hand, looking at one of its three façades more intently than the others: the Nativity.

"This is no ordinary cathedral or church, child," her grandfather would exclaim. "This is an expiatory temple. The cathedral of the poor! The third temple. It will record our faith and take us back to its origin."

Whenever they stopped in front of La Sagrada Família, he repeated this.

What had her grandfather done for a living, she wondered. She never knew.

"What did you do when you were young, Grandfather?" she'd asked him many times when she was a girl. "Before you retired?"

"Safeguard our faith," he'd say, smiling as he stroked her hair.

An ambiguous reply that told her nothing. After a while she'd stopped asking. Maybe now she'd never know. But from that moment on she'd started watching him when he worked in his study, trying to discover what interested him most. His library was piled high with books and articles on medieval constructions, Romanesque chapels, cathedrals, architecture, and religious imagery. And he drew a lot. And wrote, too. Especially in one particular notebook. He always locked it up in the middle drawer of his desk. The notebook he guarded so carefully. The locked desk.

He'd surely been stoking the fires of his insanity for years, she thought. Then again, what if he was right? What if what he'd said was actually true? That whole series of revelations had really thrown her, especially the idea that she was the chosen one, and more important, that she was in grave danger, that she—along with the archangel?—had to kill some beast that lived at the third door. She tried to put it all together, to make sense of his last words.

She remembered the riddle game, which was based on a very unusual ending that her grandfather had invented for the fable of Hänsel and Gretel. She still had the board at home in the spare room somewhere. Her grandfather had built it for her. It had sixty-four square compartments, tiny cells, with a total of sixty symbols, and in the middle four cells was the Enchanted House, hidden under a black board. A good deal of the iconography Gaudí used in his works was contained in those little cells: the salamander, the dragon, the caduceus—a serpent coiled around a cross—the hexagon, the tortoise, the tree of life, the bull . . . triangles, circles, and other geometric shapes. She remembered all of it. It was like a chess table but much thicker, since a mechanical device was housed inside it. The board had a four-inch wooden peg at each corner, which elevated it from whatever surface it was placed upon. Her grandfather would find a symbol, or two or three, and make up a riddle for each one. Then he'd press down on the compartment, triggering a lever on the side that opened a little green window. Once the green window was open, they could begin the game. Each round grew progressively more difficult. He'd start with just one riddle for her to solve, and when she'd guessed the correct symbol, she'd press down on the cell. If she was right, the black cardboard in the middle would slide back and a light would go on, which meant the dragon was burning in the oven of the Enchanted House. Then he'd move on to a series of two, three, four, five riddles. It was always the same process. She had to solve them, figure out which symbol each one referred to, and then push down on the compartment in question, all in a certain order. And she only got one chance.

Her grandfather had just told her to play in the Enchanted House. *Why?* she now wondered. She knew exactly where it was: as a girl she'd seen it with her grandfather in Park Güell many times. María needed to get home and find that game. If it was marked green it meant that her grandfather . . . what? *Left me a message there, maybe?* she wondered. *But what riddle do I have to solve? I already have the key; I know I have to go to the tortoise, and I know where it is.* Her mind raced. What then? Was she even right?

Maybe it wasn't all true, but some of it had to be. Her grandfather had certainly not been crazy when she lived with him. She remembered him as an old man full of common sense, a man who instilled in her a great love of good books, music, and objects of beauty. A man who taught her to see. "There are many ways of seeing, and some are deceptive," he used to say. Her grandfather had passed down his moral code to her, as well as his joie de vivre and the pleasure of discovery, of curiosity, which, she now saw, was the most valuable thing she could possibly have inherited from him. "Esteem the good, love the weak, flee the evil, but hate no one." "The wise carry virtue in their hearts, the fools court vanity in theirs." Why was all of this coming back to her now?

Her grandfather couldn't be insane. There was something to his story, some riddle she didn't understand and had to figure out. She owed it to him.

María left the café and walked to the bus stop. It was completely dark by then, and the bus was taking forever to arrive. As she waited, she kept turning everything over in her mind, desperately trying to make some sense of it.

A man in black joined her at the stop. He stood a few feet away. Without knowing why, María felt uneasy. Though he pretended to look straight ahead, to the other side of Diagonal, she got the feeling he was actually keeping an eye on her. She looked at her watch. The bus was really late. She'd been waiting almost fifteen minutes. A moment later another man, also in black, approached the bus stop and stood a few feet on the other side of her. They looked like twins, she thought. And without knowing why, she recalled the carved face of the bad man sculpted into La Sagrada Família. *They look just like him. Hold on, what am I doing?* she thought. *These are just absurd fantasies,* she reasoned, trying to calm herself down. But she couldn't. They posed a threat; she could feel it. The first man, a cigarette dangling between his lips, edged toward her. She looked away. It was true; he had the same eyes as the man with the Orsini bomb, the anarchist. She wanted to run away, to flee, but she was scared. She turned her head and looked at the other man, the twin, who was edging toward her from the other side. It was as if they were synchronized, like symmetrical shadows. There was no one on the street, no one else at the bus stop. Her panic was mounting.

A sudden screeching noise startled her. It was all so fast. She had been lost in her own paranoia. Folding doors opened before her.

"You getting on?" the driver asked, not noticing her frightened face.

María quickly got on. The two men in black followed. She punched her card, glancing furtively around the bus. There were very few people. Six passengers, maybe. She didn't dare go all the way to the back. Instead she took one of the front seats, a single. There was an older woman in front of her and a very tall, well-built man with a beard behind her. He looked huge. His long legs took up the empty seat beside him, and he was reading. As she sat down, he looked up and smiled. María glanced at the title of his book. It was about Gaudí. She wanted to turn and examine the man with the book but was too afraid of drawing more attention to herself. Gaudí? Was it a coincidence?

One of the two men in black sat at the rear of the bus; the other stood by the exit door. They stared at her.

María took out her cell phone and began to dial.

THE FOIL IN Miguel's hand sliced through the air and took his opponent's breath away. Its fine, thin blade was deadly in the hands of an expert. And Miguel was an expert. Luckily for his opponent, they were just practicing; gone were the swashbuckling days of real swordfights. Miguel spun his wrist skillfully, disarming his foe and leaving the tip of the blade an inch from his chest.

"Touché!" Miguel cried.

Just then his cell phone went off. He glanced at the screen and, recognizing the number, motioned that class was over for the day. He raised his protective mask, revealing a thin, attractive face with dark, penetrating eyes. He moved confidently. He was lithe and muscular, a man with tremendous physical strength belied by his thin frame.

"Hey, María. What's up?"

Her voice was faint, almost a whisper, which made it hard to hear what she was saying, and the reception was far from perfect.

" . . . weak signal . . . Come pick me up, quick."

Miguel strode quickly over to the gym's large windows.

"What's going on?"

"Please. It's urgent. Pick me up in ten minutes at the bus stop on Balmes, by the Abacus Co-op."

The signal improved.

"Is something wrong?"

"You *have* to be waiting when I get there. It's very important."

"But you know I don't like to use the car, there's never anywhere to park."

"Just do it! Keep the car running."

"Well, in three minutes . . . ," Miguel said.

That was it. María hung up without waiting for his response. She'd been trying to conceal the fact that she was on the phone, but she couldn't tell if the two men in black had noticed. She glanced around. The huge man, his legs still taking up the majority of two seats, continued reading. A woman had gotten off when the bus stopped. One of the men in black took the empty seat. She could see the back of the man's neck, thick and muscular as a bulldog's.

Time stood still. Each second seemed interminable. She thought of her grandfather's words: she was the chosen one, and she was in grave danger.

María stood up casually, trying to remain calm. She headed toward the front exit of the bus. Both men got up, too. One came and stood on her right and the other headed to the back door. She wasn't imagining this. She was in danger.

The bus stopped, but María didn't get off. She'd pushed the call button, but she made no move to actually exit the vehicle. Neither did the two men. She looked ahead and didn't see Miguel's car. Her heart was pounding, pumping adrenaline through her veins. She wasn't sure what to do. If she moved fast enough, she could just push the guy and then hurry off.

"Anyone getting off?" the driver asked.

No one replied. Two long seconds passed. María clenched her fists tightly.

The driver prepared to close the doors and pull away, but before doing so he asked once more, "Getting off or not?"

She couldn't think. She had to act. It was a matter of seconds.

She shoved the man on her right and rushed to the front of the bus. It took him a moment to react. He lunged for María, but the tall man reading the book stood and blocked his way. The man in black shoved him.

"Hey, watch it!" The tall man feigned surprise, grabbing hold of the much smaller, stockier guy next to him.

"Let go of me, you idiot!" the stocky man shouted, hitting him.

In that instant, María jumped off the bus. She ran down Balmes, toward the sea. The two men, however, had also scrambled off as fast as they could. She was ahead of them, but she still didn't see Miguel's car. *Where the hell is he?* she thought, running. Everything was dark, and the two men were catching up to her.

Just then, a few feet away, the headlights of a car parked on the side-walk flashed on.

"Get in!"

It was Miguel.

"I told you not to turn off the engine!" she cried, slamming the door shut.

"It stalled. What's going on?"

"Drive!"

"Tell me what's wrong."

"Miguel, just *drive!*"

Still wearing his white fencing suit, Miguel glanced in the rearview mirror. A man dove onto the back of the car. Another ran after them, just a few feet behind. Miguel hit the gas, the car's wheels screeching like a wounded animal. And then they heard a sound: once, twice, three times.

"Are they *shooting* at us?"

"I think they're trying to shoot out the tires!" María exclaimed, pure adrenaline coursing through her body.

Miguel couldn't believe it. He ran a red on the corner of Balmes and Rosellón, driving right through the intersection.

"I can't believe it! We're actually being *shot* at!"

6

MIGUEL TRIED TO soothe her as they walked through the front door. But María kept saying she had to tell him something important. He sat down, took her hand, and listened intently to what María had to say.

"So you're telling me that your grandfather thinks he's a knight and belongs to some kind of order?" Miguel asked incredulously, trying to process María's chaotic, rushed story.

"That's right. He claims he's the last grand master of an ancient order called the Knights of Moriah, and that Gaudí was his predecessor," she confirmed. She sounded almost apologetic, convinced he would think it was crazy.

Miguel was baffled.

"And you *believe* all this? Your grandfather has Alzheimer's, María; you have to accept that," he said conciliatorily.

"I know, I know . . . but after everything that's happened today I don't know what to think."

"He's ill, María. Old people imagine things. He's losing his mind and you feel helpless. That's all it is," he insisted, adopting the same soothing tone and trying not to hurt her feelings.

"I know, I know," she repeated. "But how do you explain those guys on the bus?" she asked, trying to make sense of the last hour.

"A couple of thieves, or a couple of perverts after a pretty girl. I don't know why they followed you and shot at us. But I'm sure it was a mix-up. Maybe they thought you were someone else. I don't know!" Miguel exclaimed. Would a couple of perverts really try to shoot out someone's tires to get at them? Of course it was possible, Miguel thought, but it wasn't exactly an everyday occurrence. María didn't reply. He didn't know how to ease her mind. He wanted to call the police, but she wouldn't let him. First she insisted that he hear her out.

"You don't believe me, do you?"

"It's not a question of believing you. I really want to," he said, pulling her to him. "I love you. But try to understand: you can't just ask me to sit down and then tell me straight out that your grandfather belongs to an ancient order, some secret organization or some sect, and expect—"

"No, they're not like that. My grandfather isn't a lunatic, he's a knight. And there are seven of them."

Did she actually believe what she was telling him?

"OK, I admit I didn't start off explaining this well. But I'm upset," María pointed out.

"I know. Why don't we start again? I'll make some coffee, and you can tell me the whole story, calmly, from the start, and then we'll figure out what to do. For now, you just sit tight and relax for a minute, OK?"

She nodded. Miguel went to make coffee. He had a feeling it was going to be a long night. Meanwhile, María tried to organize her thoughts. When he returned, she began to explain.

"My grandfather was the grandson of Alfonso Givell, one of Gaudí's boyhood friends. They were students together at a school run by the Escolapian Fathers and then at architecture school, and from what I gather, that's where something first happened."

"*What* happened?"

"I didn't understand that part too well. But they tried to contact them, some satanic sect or something. They were just two young idealists looking for a cause, and for a few days, they toyed around with the idea of joining, but they decided not to when they realized what the group actually was."

"Presumably, that didn't go over well," Miguel said, his voice edged with sarcasm. "One doesn't just quit a satanic sect."

"No, they never forgave them for refusing to join their organization, or whatever you want to call it . . ."

Miguel saw how telling the story, making sense of it, seemed to calm María.

"Go on."

"Well, then they joined the ranks of some utopian socialists. Like I said, they were two kids bursting with idealism. They studied together in Barcelona at the Provincial School of Architecture, met a lot of people, hung out with the intellectuals of the day. Imagine, two young guys from a small town . . . well, OK, Reus isn't that small, but still."

She took a sip of coffee and continued.

"This was the end of the nineteenth century, and back then Barcelona was a thriving city, in full expansion; it was at the center of many social and political trends of the day, a refuge for fringe groups in Europe: anarchists, socialists, communists, *carbonari*, Masons—each had a huge presence in the city. When he told me all this, it occurred to me that both the Catalan *Renaixença* and later Catalan Modernism are connected with all of them."

María paused, finished her coffee, and then went on.

"It's something I've always thought indirectly tied in with my work at the foundation. You see, every artistic current feeds off of, and is intimately related to, the society in which it exists. Did you know that during the *Renaixença* of the late nineteenth century, and then during the Modernist days at the beginning of the twentieth, there were at least sixteen different secret lodges in Barcelona alone? The city was growing in every way and somehow acted as a magnet for underground movements. Tons of artists and intellectuals were associated with secret sects back then. Barcelona became more important than Lyon and was actually the esoteric capital of its time."

"María, I didn't know that people at the foundation were into all this esoteric stuff: sects, Masonry . . ."

"No, it's not that. All I'm saying is that that was the cultural environment thriving at the time of Catalan Modernism—"

"But what does any of that have to do with your grandfather?" Miguel interrupted. "He wasn't a Mason and neither was Gaudí. Or at least that's what he wanted you to believe," Miguel said.

"Yes, but he wanted me to know all of this for some reason. And it's related to his secret. I'm trying to connect all the things he told me this afternoon to the stories he used to tell me when I was little. There was a legend that said Barcelona was founded by Hercules on his way to his eleventh labor, en route to the Garden of Hesperides, in search of the fruit from the Tree of Life. The antimony orange tree!"

"Hang on. I'm lost here," Miguel said. He wanted to make sure he could follow what María was saying.

"I'm lost, too. But I'm trying to tie up loose ends." María stopped for a minute, then explained, "Gaudí built an orange tree made of antimony at the Güell Estate, with a wrought-iron dragon to protect it. Antimony is an essential element in alchemy, an ancient science that's directly related to the Gothic movement. In fact, cathedrals are considered alchemists' books of stone. The *Renaixença* was a revivalist movement that tried to make Gothic art look as though it were actually coming alive, breathing even, using German aesthetics of the time—"

"Hold on, María, slow down! You know art is not my field. I know you're a specialist, but I'm a little shaky on all this . . . I read some of the books you recommended, but what you're saying is simply bizarre. Are you now going to start in on the pseudo-theories of obscure alchemists?" he asked, playing devil's advocate and yet trying to be nice, trying not to hurt her. "Don't you see? You had one crazy conversation with your grandfather, and now you're all turned around. You're trying to turn esoteric nonsense and historical facts into a logic that doesn't add up and leads you who knows where."

Miguel tried to control himself; he lightened his tone to give her a break. Then he apologized and told her to go on. María related the rest of the conversation with her grandfather until they got to the part Miguel already knew: the day of the master's murder.

"I swear, Miguel, he was very convincing. It was like he was reliving the whole thing. He'd get caught up in the story and it was a little hard to understand what he was talking about, but then he'd get back on track and be even more convincing than he was before."

Miguel looked skeptical.

"I asked him to try to remember, to make an effort," she explained. "A stranger helped him that night. Men were following him. They were after the object Gaudí had given him."

"What was the object?"

"He couldn't remember."

"Of course he can't: that was *eighty* years ago. And he's got Alzheimer's!"

"He remembers hiding it, though."

"But not where," Miguel added, trying to make her see how absurd the whole thing was.

"Right. Not where," she admitted.

"And then his friends the Moriah, or whoever they were, hid it for him."

"Yes. Until the Spanish Civil War ended in 1939."

They fell silent. Miguel poured some more coffee.

Miguel was a mathematician, used to things like the Riemann hypothesis, and his research revolved around trying to turn conjectures into theorems. He liked fantasy and imagination and knew that without them, particularly the latter, you couldn't really excel at math. He even enjoyed literature and had no problem getting into books—if they were well written and the narrator pulled him in. But the things María had just told him were too hard to believe, regardless of the fact that he'd been shot at and chased. Plus, even though he was no expert on Gaudí, he did have his own opinions about his work. He was willing to admit that he was an amazing architect, a genius, definitely unique, sure. But he was as immoral as all things Gothic. The way Miguel saw it, cathedrals, churches, temples, they were all immoral, all built on people's fear. It was a style of architecture that served the powerful, upholding only their way of thinking. Architects in the service of absolute power. The Church was no work of God. And anyway, God was an invention, made up by men in order to take advantage of other people, namely the uneducated. It was as simple as that; there was nothing more to it. That was how he felt. And he used the rest of his brain on things that truly did help people. From a very young age, he'd realized that's what math did, throughout history. If there was a god in this world or this universe, it was math. A god that was actually useful for something, for good. A comprehensible science, if you put in the dedication, effort, and time to study it. A demonstrable science that actually could be used for good.

"As far as I know, if we leave out Gaudí's short-lived flirtation with socialism, he was a Roman Catholic, plain and simple, who spent his latter years living the life of a monk; they're still talking about beatifying him," Miguel said. He wasn't actually speaking to María but to himself, attempting to sum things up and see where it all led. "And now here we have some Templar Gaudí, or Mason, or member of some sect or something, a man who was hiding a great secret that, before dying, he gave to a young boy who's now an old man with no idea what it was or where he hid it . . ."

"Well, maybe the bone will help us clear things up. That might have been what those two thugs were after," María chimed in.

"Bone?" he asked. Miguel was nearing his limit.

"Yeah. My grandfather gave me this. He called it a bone."

Miguel stared at the strange key, flabbergasted.

"Your grandfather gave you this?"

"Yes. Maybe this key will open the door to this great secret. I believe him, Miguel. I know it sounds insane, but I believe him. Do you trust me?"

Miguel didn't know how to respond. He was silent for a few minutes, trying to process everything María had said up to that point. Then he said, "Of course I trust you. But I think we need to get some rest and talk about all of this tomorrow. I'm just asking that you put yourself in my shoes; try to understand—"

"All right, Miguel. I know it all sounds crazy. But will you come with me to La Sagrada Família tomorrow morning? I have to be there at six; that's what my grandfather said."

"Sure. No point in not giving it a try. That key *is* very intriguing . . ."

"I think it opens a tortoise," María said.

Miguel didn't answer. He'd heard enough far-fetched nonsense for one night.

"My grandfather said that the race would start with a tortoise and that there were only a few days left, and I couldn't let them catch me. It makes no sense."

They went out onto the balcony. It was almost midnight. On the other side of Paseo de Gràcia, a little to the left of the window, they could see one of Gaudí's famous buildings, La Pedrera, all lit up. It had an aura about it, otherworldly, almost unreal, and there it stood before them with its ethereal shapes and curves. Miguel couldn't stop thinking about what María had just said. He was disconcerted. Too many things had happened in too short a time.

"Doesn't it look supernatural?" she asked. Then she added, "Will you stay with me tonight? I don't want to sleep alone."

He hadn't even considered the possibility of leaving her alone that night. He might not have believed everything she'd said, but a couple of thugs had chased them, even shot at them. There was no way he was leaving her. She was upset and she needed him.

"Of course I will, María. And try not to worry. If there's one thing mathematics can confirm, it's that every problem has a solution, and it's always the most logical one," he said reassuringly.

"There's one more thing," she said hesitantly, realizing how overwhelmed he was by the events of the night.

"More? Go on, spit it out. At this rate, nothing will surprise me," he joked.

"I know you're not going to believe this, but . . . Wait there a second."

She went back to the small storage room at the end of the hall and searched the room's upper shelves. Finally her hand touched the cardboard box. She pulled it down carefully and took out the game that was inside, dusting it off as she felt her excitement grow. She looked at the side: it was marked green.

Her grandfather had left it set up for her. She was right.

When Miguel saw her reemerge with that radiant look, holding a strange-looking board game, he had no idea what to think. What was she up to? Were they supposed to play some childhood game now?

María explained. "Today, when he was delirious, my grandfather told me I had to play. He insisted."

Astonished, Miguel gawked at the wooden game she set down on the table. It had squares the size of those on a checkerboard, but each one had a different illustration on it.

"Those are the symbols Gaudí used in his architecture," she said.

Then she went on to explain the rules of the game.

"My grandfather built it for me."

Miguel could see that it was handmade, but it looked like there was some sort of mechanical device inside it. It was an amazing piece of craftsmanship.

"See? The window is green. That means the game is all set up and ready to play."

"So you think your grandfather left this prepared for you? To play the riddle game?"

"I'm not sure, but—"

Miguel was about to press down on one of the squares when she grabbed his hand.

"Don't! We only have one chance. We can only play it one time. Those are the rules. Plus, we don't have a riddle to solve yet."

"This is unbelievable." He sounded both curious and ironic at the same time. Then he asked, "So the deal is, if you guess the right symbol in answer to a riddle, the middle opens up and . . . there's a message in there?"

"Yep."

"We can solve your grandfather's puzzle right now!" Miguel exclaimed decisively. "Just get me a hammer and a screwdriver, and—"

"Good God, Miguel! You think my grandfather would be so stupid? No. We have to play. First we have to use the key. We'll go to La Sagrada Família at six in the morning and try to figure out which tortoise it opens. We have to play the game, but not tonight."

No, not right then. They were too tired, and, as María had insisted, they didn't have any riddles to answer.

"I'm scared," María said before going to bed.

Miguel hugged her tight. She buried her face in his chest, searching for warmth and protection.

"Don't worry. I'm here."

"I love you," María whispered, looking up into his eyes.

"I love you, too."

She was the chosen one? It was an idea she couldn't shake, couldn't get out of her head, and it seemed to contain a threat. She knew she was in danger. Were those around her in danger as well?

"Go on, go to bed. I'll be in shortly," Miguel softly intoned, jarring María out of her thoughts.

María went to bed, but she had trouble falling asleep, turning the revelations of the day over in her mind again and again.

Miguel couldn't sleep, either. Though his short, dark hair was increasingly speckled with gray, showing the telltale signs of premature aging, it didn't diminish the strength emanating from his lively almond-shaped eyes, which hid a curious, analytical personality. He loved to challenge himself, even if he rarely showed it. But María's story was almost too incredible a challenge.

His beloved Sherlock Holmes needed two pipes to ponder and then solve a case. Miguel could generally make do with the sound of the TV in the background. So he turned it on and sat down in front of it, paying no attention whatsoever to the images on the screen, trying instead to organize and make sense of what María had told him. Her grandfather had said there wasn't much time, that they had to visit the tortoise and unlock it. What on earth did that mean?

Álvaro Climent was on some sensationalist show dealing with all things supernatural. He was theorizing about the mystery of Atlantis. How long had it been since he'd seen his old friend? Álvaro's image made him think about his past. His boyhood enthusiasm for logic was what led him to mathematics to begin with. He recalled the passion for fencing he'd felt back then, too. It's a purely mathematical sport, his friend Álvaro had told him. He was the one who'd gotten Miguel into it. Álvaro gave up math after his first year of college and took over his father's bookstore, as well as indulging in his other curious obsessions. And now, there he was on TV, discussing Atlantis, talking about a lost civilization.

"What are you doing?" María asked. She'd just gotten back up.

"Thinking."

"While watching TV?"

"I'm not watching. I just need background noise; it helps me focus. That's an old friend of mine," he said, pointing to the screen. "We went to college together." Then he got up and turned off the set.

"I'm going back to bed."

"I'll be right in."

But he stayed up awhile longer. Miguel went to grab a book from María's shelf. Then he lay down on the sofa and tried to concentrate on the biography of Gaudí.

It was very late when he finally closed the book and went into María's bedroom. And it was even later when he finally drifted off, but only after gazing down at María's face, watching over the fitful sleep of the woman who would forever change his life.

PART II

THE MASTER

7

———

J UAN GIVELL TURNED over in bed. His mind drifted. He was tired. *Maybe she shouldn't know, or maybe she should know everything,* he thought to himself. But what *was* everything? His memory was fading. It came. It went. It disappeared and returned unannounced. He closed his eyes and saw an image of the master, striding along in his leather boots. He was holding a young boy of eleven or twelve by the hand. That boy was him. He recognized himself and his heart skipped a beat.

Juan's parents had both died of typhoid fever. His grandfather, the only family member left in Riudoms, had sent a letter to Barcelona, the capital.

One afternoon, a couple of weeks later, a strange man came to town. He had on an old, ragged coat, a black hat, and shoes so worn that you could see the wool bandages around his ankles. But his white beard, penetrating blue eyes, and sprightly gate made it clear that he was no ordinary vagabond.

Juan watched his grandfather and this stranger embrace in silence. The man stayed by the door. Grandfather didn't invite him in and he didn't take off his hat.

"You owe me now, Antón," his grandfather said.

The stranger nodded.

Grandfather had already packed a bag with a pair of rope-soled shoes, trousers, two shirts, and some bread and sausage for the road.

With tears in his eyes, he hugged the boy.

"Go on, Juan. This man is my best friend. He'll take you to the capital, he'll take care of you and make a good man out of you."

Little Juan didn't want to leave; he was trembling. He'd never been out of Riudoms before. That town was his whole world. It was where his friends Little Pep and Andreu Three Stories—called that because he always told made-up stories three at a time—lived. Andreu was the one who had told him how huge the capital was and that children who got lost there were hung from streetlamps. But he knew Andreu told tall tales, and besides, he'd never seen a streetlamp and wasn't sure they even existed.

The carriage was waiting for them. Juan clung to his grandfather, sobbing. His grandfather was all he had left in the world.

"You'll like the capital, Juanito. I went to school there, and I worked there with my friend here. That was a long time ago. Juan, don't ever forget your parents, your name, or your family. Antón here will make you his protégé; you'll help him with an important mission. He'll make a knight of you."

Juan said good-bye to his grandfather and took hold of the stranger's hand. There was a lump in his throat, but he didn't want to cry again. Why did everyone abandon him? That was when he noticed the man's eyes. They had a spark to them. There was no doubt he had a temper, but he also had very kind eyes.

"Have you ever been on a train before?"

A train! All the kids he knew dreamed of seeing a train. It was magical, mysterious, and extraordinary. Like the sea, something else he'd never seen, unless you counted the old photographs the rootless gypsy who periodically came through town kept in his cart full of trinkets and knickknacks.

The boy made no reply.

They climbed into the carriage, and seconds later, the driver shook the reins and they were off. The horses headed toward Reus. The road took them to the edge of a dense forest, which they had to cross. That was the boundary of the boy's world: he'd gone beyond the border of his old universe and left it behind. What was out there, through the forest? Suddenly, he was overcome by a sense of sorrow that only grew as he got farther from home. Juan felt like he was living out the story of the brother and sister abandoned in a forest by their father, the tale his grandfather used to tell him, the one he had liked so much. *Why does everyone abandon me?* he wondered again. *First my parents, now my grandfather.*

It didn't take them long to travel the two and a half miles from Riudoms to Reus. Day was fading to dusk; the last rays of light waned in the sky. The old man tried to strike up a conversation with the boy in an attempt to distract him, to shake him from his somber thoughts. He had to earn his confidence. After all, the boy was lost. Lost in a forest, much like he now found himself, the old man thought.

"You know, my father and grandfather were both from your town. They were cauldron makers."

"What's a cauldron maker?"

"A person who makes cauldrons."

It wasn't a very good answer, he knew, but if the boy's interest was piqued, he'd ask a question. And he did.

"And what's a cauldron?"

"A big, round metal pot you use to boil water, among other things. And they worked copper stills, too, to distill alcohol from grapes."

"What about your mother?"

"No, my mother wasn't a cauldron maker."

"No, I mean, was she from Riudoms, too?"

"No, child. My mother was from Reus. And by the way, we're almost there."

They were on the outskirts. Juan stared out at the scenery around him, afraid and excited at the same time. Then he saw lights twinkling here and there. Houses and other buildings were lit, little by little. He was used to his house in Riudoms, where candlelight was all they had. His grandfather had told him they didn't need candles in the city. He gazed at a cluster of low-built houses, each with rows of small windows, all of them brightly lit. It seemed odd that people would need that much light in those tiny rooms. Suddenly something caught his attention. The lights were moving! He rubbed his eyes, not quite understanding what he was seeing. It scared him to death. Turning quickly from the window, he covered his eyes and sought refuge against the shoulder of the master, the man who was to become his mentor.

"What's wrong, Juanito?"

"I saw the Enchanted House! The house in the forest. The one from 'Hänsel and Gretel.' I'm scared. I want to go home to my grandfather. Please, sir . . . don't leave me here!"

"You saw the Enchanted House? Where?"

"Out there! Look! I saw its lights . . . the whole house was sliding along in the dark, like a worm, but all lit up. It's the haunted house from the forest!"

The old man burst out laughing.

"No, no, no! What a thought! The Enchanted House! Heavens, if that's not the limit. Don't be afraid, Juan, that's not a house. That's the train pulling out of the station."

The old man's explanation, along with the twinkle in his amused eyes, calmed Juan. Slowly, he sat up to glance out the window again, though still not entirely convinced.

The old man told the coach driver to take them for a ride through the center of town before going to the station; they had plenty of time.

"That way you'll start getting used to seeing new things, Juan."

The boy had never been to Reus; this was the first time he'd been to any city. He stared out excitedly.

"There're so many people," he said, filled with wonder.

"Thirty thousand of them."

"Do they all live here?"

"Yes."

"Is there enough room?"

"Oh, there are a lot more people than that in Barcelona. You'll see."

As he looked in amazement, the carriage continued its tour, driving down the city's main streets toward the station. When they reached Sant Joan Street, his jaw dropped.

"Pretty, isn't it?"

"Is that from a fairy tale?" he asked innocently.

"That's Casa Rull. You see those floral motifs, the flowers there?"

"They look so real," the boy said.

"Yes, child, they do. They almost come to life. It's a beautiful house with a splendid garden."

"Who built it?"

"One of the world's greatest architects: Domènech i Montaner. Thanks to him and a few others, this place has flourished marvelously. It's a city reborn!"

Juan was left speechless once more when they reached the train station. Everything about it impressed him: the engines, the train carriages, all those illuminated windows. They really did look like houses, but they had wheels on them, which fit snuggly into the rails. He'd never guessed that this was what a train looked like. In his dreams, it was just a huge tube with lots of billowing smoke, like in the gypsy's photo.

"Are we going to ride on a train?"

"We are."

"A fast one?"

"An express. How does that sound? An express is a train that only stops at the most important stations and travels very, very quickly."

"How fast?"

"Twenty-five miles per hour. If all goes as planned, I estimate we'll get to Barcelona in about four and a half hours," he said, slightly preoccupied.

"Is something wrong, sir?"

"Why do you ask?"

"Because ever since we got to the station, you've been looking around. You seem a little nervous."

He was a very observant boy, and clever, too, the old man thought. He fumbled for an excuse.

"No, no, child. I'm just looking around to see if I know anyone before we board. I told you my mother was born here. And so was I."

They walked hand in hand through the station to the train. The old man helped the boy climb up the train car's steps. There were very few passengers on board, and he and his new master were almost alone in their carriage.

"Do you know the tale of Hänsel and Gretel?" he asked suddenly.

"Yes. My grandfather tells me that story all the time."

"Would you like me to tell it to you, too?"

"Not right now, thank you."

"I know a slightly different version. In my story, there's a dragon."

"If you don't mind, sir, I'd like to go to sleep."

"Of course, child. You sleep. We've got a long journey ahead of us."

After a little while, the boy asked, "A dragon?" Juan could no longer fight his own curiosity.

"Yes. And a sunflower, a cross, a pelican, some stone warriors, and all sorts of other marvels."

"Will you tell it to me while I'm going to sleep?"

"Of course I will, child."

And he began to tell Juan about those two children whose father and stepmother tried to abandon them in a forest.

A long time ago, in a great forest, there lived a poor woodcutter with his wife and two children. The boy was named Hänsel and the girl was named Gretel. And one year, everyone in the land went hungry; there wasn't enough bread to eat. At night, the woodcutter tormented himself with heartbreaking thoughts.

He said to his wife, who was the stepmother of his children, "What will become of us? How are we going to feed our children?"

And the woman replied, "Tomorrow, very early, you will take them to the forest and leave them, and that way we'll be free of them."

"But how could I possibly abandon my own children in the forest?"

"You fool! Would you rather all four of us starve to death? In that case, start cutting the wood for our coffins!"

She wouldn't leave him in peace until he was convinced.

But the boy had heard everything and ran to tell his sister.

"Oh no! We're lost," Gretel said.

"Don't worry," Hänsel said. "I'll find a way to save us."

When their parents took them to the forest, the boy left a trail of pebbles that showed them the way home. And that night, they returned.

Their stepmother was furious.

Every morning, the boy filled his pockets with stones, and that way he and his sister could always find their way back home.

But one morning Hänsel used bread crumbs instead of pebbles, and the birds ate them up, and they couldn't find their way back.

They came upon a house where an evil dragon lived. Whenever the dragon found little children, he killed them and cooked them and ate them up.

He locked Hänsel up in a cage, and every day the dragon said to Gretel, "Get up, lazybones! Make your brother something good to eat. When he gets fat, I'm going to eat him."

Then he'd go to the cage and say to Hänsel, "Put out your finger, let me see if you've gotten fatter."

But Hänsel always stuck out a small bone he had found, and the dragon, who couldn't see very well, was always surprised that the boy had not grown any plumper.

After four weeks, the dragon became impatient and didn't want to wait any longer.

"Gretel, come here! Bring me some water. Fat or thin, I shall eat him today."

Gretel lit the fire and put the pot on to boil.

"First we'll bake some bread," the dragon said. "I already lit the oven."

And he pushed Gretel toward the oven, intending to roast her. But she guessed his plan and said, "I don't know how to do it. How do you get in?"

"Fool!" the dragon replied. "Look! Can't you see? The door is so large, even I could fit inside."

So the dragon stuck his head in, and Gretel pushed him with all her might, then closed the door and locked it. The dragon began to scream in the most hideous way, but Gretel left him there to roast.

And then she ran to find her brother, Hänsel.

"We're free! The dragon is dead!"

So they took the dragon's treasure and decided to return home.

They came to a great river, but there was no bridge to cross it, so . . .

The words were familiar, as was the tone, and though this version of the story was a little different, the man had the same voice as his grandfather. He felt so much like Hänsel now—lost in the forest. If only he could find his way home. And so, with the train's steady rhythm and jostling, the boy slowly fell asleep.

It was night when they reached the capital. The platform was empty. But someone was waiting for them. There was a car. The boy was still asleep. Hazily, he heard the man's voice telling them not to wake him. Someone picked him up. It wasn't the old man. It was a very strong, tall man who lifted him and tenderly carried him.

A short while later, Juan was put to bed by the tall man, who seemed like a giant to him. The man had a thick black beard, long hair, and kind eyes. He pulled the covers over the child, and little Juan slept.

He lived with the master for almost a year, the first few months in a pink fairy-tale-like house, and then in his studio.

That year was to alter the course of his life, as well as define the destiny of his beloved granddaughter, María.

8

L   YING IN THE darkened room, Juan Givell stared up at the ceiling. He was trying to remember who he was, where he was. It was a very strange feeling. He was tired but fighting sleep as hard as he could. He didn't want to give in until he'd recalled a voice, an image, a scent, *something* that might reveal his identity or some part of his life. But it was no use; he gave up. And that's when the miracle happened.

All those years after the fact, amidst a tangle of disjointed memories, Juan was to recall, for the last time, that distant afternoon when the master decided to show him the way of the stars.

Juan normally stayed in the studio. But for a few days now, he'd been accompanying the man on his walks, which seemed to have no set route. He'd reach into his pocket and pull out handfuls of breadcrumbs and toss them onto the ground. Juan knew it was a signal, a sign, like in the story, a symbol he must pay attention to. He had to note where the crumbs were left and remember the place. It was just a game. The signs didn't last long, because there were always groups of pigeons waiting to devour them. Some even caught the crumbs in midair. People would stare at them, but the man didn't seem to mind and the boy thought it was fun. *Nothing like learning while you play*, the master would think.

For a few weeks now, Juan had been going with him to San Felip Neri Church in the evenings, too.

One day, before they went out, the man gave him a small sack made of cloth that closed with a drawstring and told him to put it in his pocket. Whatever was in it didn't weigh much, and it fit easily into the palm of his hand. He knew that whatever he'd just put in his pocket was very important to the master. He didn't know what was in the little sack, but he did know what he was supposed to do with it if anything happened to the man.

"You can take your hand out of your pocket, you know; it's safe there."

He didn't answer, but he smiled up at the master and took his hand out of his pocket.

"You're clever, Juan, very clever indeed. Don't forget: we're knights, and we're on a mission."

They always played at being knights, but this time Juan knew that it was more than a game. He instinctively sensed that danger, although he'd never seen it, was for real and that one day he'd have to face this peril head-on.

"If anything happens to me, Juan, don't be afraid. Don't come near me or try to help me; just run as fast as you can, OK?"

"Yes, sir."

"You have the knights' greatest secret in your pocket, and you must leave it where I told you to. You remember, don't you?"

"Yes, sir."

"Good, Juan. That's very good. There's a note for you in that little sack. Read it when the time comes."

"Is something going to happen, sir? Are we in danger?"

"Yes, Juan; I saw the men who mean us harm. They don't know it, but I saw them and I know what they're up to."

"We'll fight them!" the boy proclaimed decisively.

"No, Juan, we won't." The man knelt down and placed his hands on the boy's shoulders. "Remember. You're a knight, and it's your mission to keep the secret safe. Whatever happens, don't look back. Just run. Our people will protect you."

"Our people? There are other knights?"

"There are, young Juan. Now put on your cap or we'll be late."

"Yes, sir."

"How many times have I told you to call me 'Grandfather' and not 'sir'?"

"Yes, sir," Juan replied, taking the man's hand.

It was just as they crossed Gran Vía at Bailén that he realized they were being followed: two men with hair so short it looked like their heads were shaved, both dressed in black. Though one was taller and the other heavier, they oddly looked like twins.

He dropped a few bread crumbs and said to the boy, "Remember, Juan: the city is like a forest, and I've spent my whole life filling it with signs to show the way home, like Hänsel and Gretel. Remember the story your grandfather used to tell you, the story I told you on the train, the one I've told you so many times since then. Don't forget it; tell your grandchild. The journey won't end with you."

"Is something wrong?"

"Do you remember all the symbols?" he asked, ignoring the boy's question.

"Of course. You've told me over and over." He was about to start reciting them when the master cut him off.

"Quiet!" he shouted.

That scared Juan.

"Do you remember the way of the stars?" he asked quietly, not looking at Juan, staring straight ahead.

"I could draw it with my eyes closed," the boy replied in a whisper, realizing something terrible was happening.

The man tried to calm down. They were near Plaza Tetuán, between Calle Bailén and Girona. The black-clad men were a few feet away, trying to look casual. The man knew it was only a matter of minutes before something happened, and he had to save the boy. He glanced at his watch: five past six. The boy must not cross Calle Cortes with him. It was a wide, tree-lined boulevard with an island in the middle dividing the two-way traffic. The central part was where the streetcars ran in both directions; it had cast-iron posts with electrical conductor wires running above. That's where they'd attack him, he thought. A public place, crowded, ideal for a couple of well-trained assassins who knew how to act quickly, decisively, taking advantage of the general confusion.

Despite his reputation as a bad-tempered old man, he was possessed by the urge to hug and kiss the boy. But he couldn't risk attracting their attention. The boy had learned a lot; he knew what he had to do. At first the old man hadn't agreed with the others. How could they initiate a boy? How could they turn him into a knight, the one in charge of keeping and someday fulfilling the prophecy? That was precisely why they should do it, because he was a boy, they'd said. No one would suspect a boy. And so he'd been chosen.

But he was still just a boy, and in a few minutes, he'd be all alone.

"Juan, go over to that newsstand and buy me a paper," he said, handing the boy a coin.

"We never buy it here."

"Just do what I say, OK? Do you understand?"

He understood. He knew the moment had arrived. He took the coin. The man encircled his wrist with his fingers.

"We're lost, Juan. Remember that. Lost in the forest, and we have to get back home. Remember. That's why I've spent my life filling this city with stones, with signs, mapping it out. Remember the Enchanted House: evil lives there. You have to defeat it to get the treasure. Then and only then will we be able to go back to our people. He'll come, Juan. Remember what I've told you so many times: neither you nor I will reach the promised land; not even your children will see it. A long time will pass before the prophecy is fulfilled. But even if the temple is unfinished, I've traced the way. It will be fulfilled early in the next millennium, by one in your family, of your blood. Someone you'll call María."

The boy moved to hug him.

"No! You mustn't do that! Go! Our people will help you. The giant will find you. He'll always find you. And don't forget the tortoise. One day you might need to hide a secret."

Juan half-turned and walked to the newsstand, passing the two men on his way. He asked for a copy of the *Veu de Catalunya*, paid for it, and waited. He didn't take his eyes off the master for a second.

Juan saw the whole thing.

The master, walking slowly, crossed to one side of the road. The two men did the same, situating themselves on either side of him. The master watched a streetcar approach from Girona. Another came from the other direction. That was when Juan saw him being shoved, roughly. He lost his footing, banging his head on a metal post. He looked as though he were dizzy, off balance. Yet another shove knocked him backward; he fell back onto the tracks. The boy watched the second streetcar hit him and saw the men pounce on him, going through his clothes amidst the shouting and general confusion brought on by the staged accident. Juan wanted to thrash those evil men. But he couldn't. He had to keep his promise and do what he'd said he would.

Before he ran away, he saw the killers' faces. They searched for him but he hid; they couldn't see him. Reflected in their eyes, he saw fear, rage, and cruelty. It had all been useless. They didn't find what they wanted on his master. They had nothing.

The shouting grew louder, and passersby began to come forward. Someone said they should take the vagabond to the first-aid post on Ronda de San Pedro, but none of the three taxi drivers there appeared willing to transport a poor man who had no identification on him.

The two men headed off again, taking advantage of the mayhem, and went over to the newsstand.

"Where's the boy? The one you sold a paper to?"

"What boy?" the vendor asked.

Frustrated and angry, they began to argue with the vendor, who called a policeman over to straighten the matter out.

"Let's go," one finally said.

They took off, searching for the boy with mounting desperation.

They both knew they wouldn't find him.

They knew they were as good as dead.

9

"YOU FAILED."

"The old man didn't have it on him."

"Are you sure?"

"We searched him—thoroughly. All he had were some raisins, peanuts, and bread crumbs in one pocket."

"Bread crumbs? Peanuts? Is this some sort of joke?"

"No. We told you, he was crazy. He used to feed the pigeons, they followed him everywhere. People gawked; it was a sight to see. He dressed like a bum and no one ever recognized him."

Asmodeus was livid. He hadn't called this meeting in order to learn why some crazy old loon—one of the most reviled and most admired men in the city—lived like a pauper, dressed like a vagabond, and gave away all his belongings. No. Something had gone wrong, something he didn't understand and wanted explained. He wanted to know why the hell the old man didn't have the secret with him, when for years he'd guarded it so closely that he even slept with it.

"And that was all he had?"

"That and a copy of the Gospels. That's it. He wasn't even carrying any identification."

"We searched him—thoroughly," the other man repeated, as if begging for mercy.

"I assume he's dead."

"You can be sure of it."

"Did you bring the book?"

Their silence infuriated him further. They hadn't brought it. It hadn't even occurred to those imbeciles that perhaps the Gospels hid some sort of clue, some indication of the coveted secret. At that moment Asmodeus wanted to rip their heads off.

"Do you think I have people killed just for the fun of it?" he asked, struggling to control himself.

They made no reply. They wouldn't put it past him. They knew. Killing for sport was a pleasure that can only be comprehended and fully appreciated by those who've done it. It was like nothing else.

"The man you got rid of possessed a secret that could change the course of history, the whole world. That damned fool and his men have been trying to wipe us off the face of the earth for years. You've both put our survival at risk. We've been working for years to make sure the prophecy is not fulfilled."

"Maybe he hid it somewhere else. We could break into his studio. That'll be easy, I can assure you. We'll find it; just give us a few hours."

"There's no time for that. By now they must know who the old man on the tram tracks was; it will be impossible to get anywhere near his studio. Besides, do you really think his men are so stupid? No. That's not where the secret's hidden. Something doesn't add up."

The two men knew it. They knew exactly what it was that didn't fit. How could it be that Asmodeus himself hadn't realized it yet? They didn't really want to search the studio; they wanted to gain some time and find the kid. And if they failed, they wanted to run and hide—if there was any place on earth or in hell where they could.

When Asmodeus asked the next question, they knew it was too late.

"The boy was with him, wasn't he?"

"Yes, the boy was with him."

"He stayed behind. The old man sent him to buy the paper."

"And you didn't suspect anything? Didn't the old man always buy his paper from the kiosk in Plaza Urquinaona?"

Neither of them answered.

One finally said, "I think he knew he was going to die."

"Of course he knew, you imbeciles! He saw you and used the boy as a carrier. The boy had it on him, and you let him escape!"

"We'll find him. Next time we won't fail."

"No. There won't be a next time. I'm going to use you for something else."

"What do you mean? We're not looking for the kid, then?"

"Leave that to the others. I'll call you soon."

Asmodeus watched them go. Once he was alone, he pulled off his mask. His hard, inexpressive eyes, an ashy shade of gray, flickered like flames. Those idiots would pay for this. By choosing them, he had failed just as miserably as they.

He put his mask back on and said, "Bitru."

His loyal assistant emerged from the shadows. He'd been hiding in the crypt, behind one of the arches, listening to Asmodeus's conversation with those fools, who now, no doubt, he'd have to take care of. Bitru silently followed him into another chamber.

It had been quite some time since he'd been inside this room. It was there that he'd taken his oath to be initiated into the lodge. The baptismal font was in the shape of a pentagon, in the center of the dark room, with the Baphomet idol inside it. Above it, like a gruesome chandelier, hung a suit of armor. Blood dripped slowly from the body still inside, anointing Baphomet's head. That was the kind of death awaiting the men who had failed: agonizing, slow—maybe days—and painful; they'd be hermetically sealed into suits of armor until they took their dying breaths.

"Death is life. Fire burns in my veins, but my hand holds the dagger," Asmodeus said, watching the hanging man slowly bleed to death from within the suit of armor.

"I'm ready," Bitru said.

The crown prince's voice registered admiration, total submission, and absolute devotion. This was his God.

"He's an eleven-year-old boy. He's lost in the city, and he's scared. The city's like a forest to him, and you know what children are like . . ."

No, he didn't know. His childhood had ended at the age of three, the first time he was beaten by his father. His father was a drunk who was always covered in grime from working rail construction.

"He's scared," Asmodeus repeated, "but he has to keep the secret until the day arrives."

"That day will never arrive."

"No, Bitru, it won't. It can't. Or we'll be gone forever."

"I won't let that happen."

"I know. I know you'll do everything possible, but I don't think you'll find the boy tonight. We lost valuable time with those two imbeciles, and we lost track of the boy, too. But we have to try. We've got a lot of work to do tonight."

"I'll kill him. I'll rip out his heart with my bare hands."

"Bitru, don't be a brute. I need him alive. They'll protect him, I'm sure of that. I know them too well. They know as much as we do. Without light, there is no darkness. Do you understand, Bitru?"

"No. I could have taken care of them a long time ago. They're our enemies, they know we exist, they beat us, kill us, and—"

"And that's the way it's been for hundreds of years," Asmodeus said, cutting him off.

"But I had them in my reach! I could have blown them to pieces. It would've been easy. A perfect plan. I don't see why—"

"Bitru, Bitru, my son!" he exclaimed condescendingly. "You and your hit men and arsonists . . . You're the best, no doubt, but sometimes you're like a child. Bombs and guns are fine, but not for this. They serve another purpose: making sure the city remains dangerous. What the hell do we care about industrialists or the bourgeoisie and the fucking workers? Do I look like an anarchist to you? Like one of those 'from each according to his ability to each according to his need' fools? Like I believe in a society based on participation, a society with no coercion? Do you really think I care about 'the conquest of bread' or, for that matter, that I want to help the businessmen and the bourgeoisie continue unfettered? Why? So they can keep fucking the women who work in their factories in Pueblo Nuevo and shooting the men, who play at being anarchists and socialists and communists? No, Bitru! What I care about is chaos. Disorganization. Unrest. I want a city that's physically and socially rotten, infested with crime, paranoia, and bloodshed. That's why I let you keep throwing bombs and shooting workers, priests, and businessmen. It's not my priority right now, but it is part of the plan. Barcelona has to be a living hell."

"You mean I can keep killing?"

"Of course you can, my son. As long as you don't expose yourself too much or jeopardize us. But do it in your free time and don't be too vicious. And please, make sure there's no ideology behind it."

"I know who my master is."

"As you should, son. Never forget the hand that feeds you. You're not an anarchist like your father."

Asmodeus's last word set him off.

"I don't have any other father! You're my father!"

"I'm sorry, Bitru. I didn't mean to offend you. I just don't want you to get the wrong idea or forget what you are."

"I know. You taught me. I still remember what you said when I made my first kill, that unlucky bastard who was just trying to help."

"Your first murder?"

"Well, the *first* one doesn't count; that time it was justice. Besides, he was going to die anyway."

"But you remember what I said?"

"You said, 'You have to begin sometime, and it might as well be now,'" Bitru parroted.

Yes, Asmodeus thought with satisfaction, this was his best student. "And was I right?"

"Yes. Killing is like anything else; it's just a question of getting started. After the first one, the rest come naturally."

"Go, son, hurry. We've got much to do."

10

BITRU WAS BORN Edmundo Ros, one rainy February morning, on a narrow street in Barcelona that dead-ended onto the market. Two neighbor women assisted his mother, Juana Vidal, when she gave birth in a tiny home: an old fisherman's dwelling divided into four 375-square-foot apartments almost entirely lacking light and ventilation. She decided to name the boy Edmundo, after the character who was betrayed by his three best friends in a novel she liked so much. Juana Vidal didn't know how to read, but the parish priest did, and every afternoon he'd read a few pages to the children of the tiny, forgotten town where she was raised in Campo de Tarragona.

When she was nineteen, Juana began working as a servant in the house of some merchants on Calle del Comerç, across the street from the Borne market. They had several stalls there and owned a few grocery stores and seed shops on nearby Calle Montcada.

When she'd been there a month, the man of the house sought her out and threatened to fire her if she didn't let him have his way with her. Soon she was pregnant. His wife noticed the girl's state, and Juana confessed what had happened.

"My husband does *not* sleep with tramps," the woman replied scornfully.

And she turned her out like a stray dog.

Señor Fitó was a womanizer, he couldn't help that, but for the first time in his life, he actually cared, and besides, the girl was carrying his child. He secretly helped her out until his wife finally caught on and gave him an ultimatum.

Señor Fitó tried to find a solution. There was an employee he trusted whose son worked in railway construction at the Maquinista Terrestre y Marítima.

"He's not very bright, sir."

"But will he do it?"

"If you arrange everything, he'll marry the girl and look after the child. I know my son. He may not be smart, but if she's a good, clean girl and you help him out, it's a done deal."

Fitó promised him a monthly stipend that would more than double the salary that young Rafa Ros was earning as a mechanic at the Maquinista Terrestre y Marítima.

So they were married.

The day Edmundo was born, Ros spent the afternoon in a tavern near the port in Barcelona, eating the grilled octopus he loved, drinking red wine, and playing cards; after all, the bastard wasn't his.

Three years later the money stopped coming, and it wasn't long before he started drinking heavily and beating his wife. Juana could take it, though. Her mother had put up with the same for years. But her father had never touched his children. After beating her and locking her in a room, that pervert, Rafa, would take it out on the boy in the most unspeakable way.

Edmundo Ros lived in hell, terrified, until the morning of March 15, 1908. He was eight years old.

At that time, there was a series of terrorist attacks all over Barcelona, to mark His Majesty Don Alfonso XIII's visit. They began on the tenth, when three bombs went off on the pier, by the city walls. The next day there were more explosions at the shipyards. The man behind the terror was one Juan Rull, who was one of the governor's confidants.

On the morning of the fifteenth, Edmundo was with Ros, near the Boquería market. Ros had arranged to meet up with a couple of old buddies he was doing a job for.

"Wait for me here, bastard," Ros said to the kid, smacking him on the head.

The boy stood there alone by a flower stall on the Ramblas while Ros crossed the street, heading for the market's entrance. His two friends were waiting for him. The boy watched him take a small packet out of his pocket and give it to one of the men. The other handed him a wad of bills, which Ros smugly tucked away without counting them. Suddenly there was a deafening noise. A huge cloud of dust, smoke, and fire enveloped all three of them and some other unfortunate passersby.

A bomb had exploded.

Edmundo heard muffled cries and crossed the street as if in a dream. Everyone was trying to get away; he, on the other hand, drew closer and closer, until he too was enveloped in the cloud of smoke. He wasn't scared.

Ros was on the ground. His left arm was still wriggling, warm and bloody, a few feet from the rest of his body. The others were dead, literally disemboweled.

"Kid. Help me. It's those fucking anarchists, goddamn it. Hey . . . what are you doing? Come here. Move!"

Edmundo knelt down beside him. Smiling.

"Help me!" he shouted, slapping Edmundo with his remaining hand.

Edmundo lifted one of the paving stones loosened by the explosion.

"What are you doing?" Ros cried.

Edmundo smashed the heavy stone against Ros's head again and again, methodically, until his face had virtually melted into the ground.

That's when he saw him—Asmodeus, wearing his mask, with his cape and his cane. Asmodeus held his hand out to the boy, who instinctively kissed the man's ring. Edmundo had found his father.

Edmundo Ros never returned home to his mother.

Ten years later, half of the Orsini bombs exploding in Barcelona bore his mark. He himself had no ideals, but at seventeen he took part in the first general revolutionary strike, clashing with the soldiers in Plaza Catalunya, aiming canons at Avenida Puerta del Ángel. Months later, the workers finally gained the right to an eight-hour workday—seven for miners. That would cause an uproar, Edmundo thought.

And it did. On October 11, the king signed a royal decree establishing a mixed commission made up of both workers and employers. They were to arbitrate social issues throughout Catalunya. The commission would report to the Council of Ministers. But the big employers, already stirred up by the eight-hour workday, became increasingly belligerent. They even threatened the government, warning that they wouldn't tolerate any further rebellion.

Edmundo was one of those in charge of organizing the bosses' henchmen, at the behest of the governor of Barcelona. The war between employers and workers was on, and he trained both sides to use firearms and explosives.

Asmodeus knew the boy was the best. He'd raised him, taught him, treated him like a son. The city of Barcelona—and its constant clashes between workers and employers—was his training ground. And Edmundo had indeed found a true father, a man who gave him everything and trained him in the mysteries of the Corbel. He accepted his name change and his job, spreading chaos and disorder with every step.

He was the new prince, the one who would succeed Asmodeus, who'd have his face, who'd wear the mask of evil. Edmundo Ros, now Bitru, would be his successor—the new Asmodeus.

Bitru only asked for one thing.

Juana Vidal never saw her son again, but each week she received an envelope containing enough money to live better than the captain general of Catalunya.

11

YOUNG JUAN KNEW what he had to do, but he was terrified. He'd obeyed the master's orders and run away as fast as he could. But he was so frightened that he became disoriented and was soon lost. The few passersby out on the street all looked like the killers to him. He was sure they were after him, that they wanted to steal the secret.

But he couldn't let the master down. What's more, he was a knight, the youngest ever. A knight who knew all about the master's great work. He'd told Juan so many times. "It takes years, and the labor of many generations, to complete a creation this monumental. My successors will leave their own stamp on it, which makes no difference. The majority of it is done; it's all mapped out, and in time the plan can be carried out . . . it will be one of yours who completes it, someone you'll name María."

Yes, Juan knew what he had to do. He just needed to remember the right order; that would indicate the path he must follow. But he was very scared. Looking around, he recognized his surroundings; without realizing it his feet had taken him to the neighborhood where the studio was. That was a mistake: it was the first place the killers would look for him, he thought. But maybe it was where his master's friends would look, too.

There was something mysterious about that afternoon, June 7. It was very hot, but he felt cold. The sky was tinged with red, like spilled blood. Juan hid among the building supplies across the square from the studio and tried to think, to sort things out in his mind. He couldn't fail. He had to overcome his fear. He didn't know how long he'd been there, but night had fallen, and judging by the commotion around the studio, he realized that the old man's absence must have been noticed. He could risk going out into the open, crossing the square to get to the studio. He'd be safe there. But no, he had to carry out the master's orders, follow the path he'd been taught. Besides, he kept thinking he saw the killers prowling around, and he was sure they wouldn't be alone; others would be looking for him, too. Juan decided he had to get out of there.

He ran until he reached the woods that divided the city in half. He'd have to cross through them and get to the other side without being seen. Hiding behind trees, confusing the sound of his own footsteps with those of his pursuers, he walked and walked. But Juan misjudged his location. He'd ended up in Plaza Tetuán, close to where his master had been killed. This wasn't the right way, and without knowing how, he ended up lost in a maze of narrow streets. His heart raced wildly. Where was he? It was so dark he could barely read the street sign: CALLE DEL VIDRE.

The street led to a large, square plaza with magnificent arcades. He sat down on the ground, leaning back against a stone column. He had to focus. Running from one side of the city to the other was getting him nowhere.

He knew the right way; he'd been learning it for weeks now. Bread crumbs marking the spots he had to remember. Who would ever suspect it? The two of them were the only ones who knew; everyone else saw an old man, out with a child, randomly throwing bread to the pigeons. That's exactly what his enemies must have thought, too. They spied on him every single day. Juan remembered the way. He was about to get up when a seemingly superhuman force lifted him up into the air. He tried to scream, but a giant hand covered his mouth.

"Don't shout, child. I'm a friend."

The boy stopped struggling.

"I was a friend of your master and I'm here to help you, too. Do you understand? If so, raise one hand very slowly and I'll let you go."

Juan did as the giant ordered.

The stranger let go of him. The boy didn't know what to think. On the one hand, he instantly trusted him; he'd never seen anyone like him. The giant looked like he'd stepped out of another time. He had long hair and a thick black beard, and he was dressed like a monk. Juan saw him unsheathe a sword inside his habit. It was all very fast, but he caught a glimpse of a cedar tree on the shirt he wore underneath.

"You're a knight!"

"Quiet, child. Yes, I'm a knight."

"So am I," the boy replied. He knew now that he could trust the giant.

"I've seen them lurking around here. Even Bitru himself."

"Bitru?"

"Yes. He's the worst one, son. A cruel and merciless killer. So let's get out of here. Quietly."

It was too overwhelming, and the boy burst into tears. The giant drew him near and muffled his choking sobs.

"I saw them murder him! They pushed him and then he got run over by the tram."

"Take it easy, son. I know what they did. I'm here to help you. Exactly what did he tell you? It's very important."

"Well, I'd been going with him to mass lately instead of staying in the studio. The master told me that the city was a forest, that we're lost in it, and that he'd spent his whole life filling the forest with pebbles, signs to show the way home. That's what he said."

"Lost in the forest. Yes, like the fable," the giant said.

"My grandfather used to tell me that story when I was little, then the master, and you know it, too."

"That's right, son. You must take the same path as the one in the story; you must get lost in the forest in order to understand."

"But, sir, they killed him," the boy repeated.

"I know, son. And that's a tragedy. But I need you to be strong. You can't be sad. You're a knight, aren't you?"

"Yes, sir. A knight, like you."

"We'll protect you; we'll teach you, help you understand. But right now, you have to remember what he said. Evil people are involved, you see; they will do anything to prevent destiny from being fulfilled."

"Some mornings we'd go for walks together and he'd toss bread crumbs in the places he wanted me to remember. At each one he'd show me a symbol."

"You're a very smart boy, that's why he trusted you. Besides, who would ever suspect a child?"

"That's why he gave me this," Juan said, taking the small sack out from his pocket.

"The secret!" the giant cried, astounded. "Put it away. We have to guard that with our lives. It can't fall into Asmodeus's hands."

"Who's Asmodeus?"

"You'll recognize him when you see him. May that never happen."

The boy didn't ask any more questions. He felt inside the sack and said, "There's a piece of paper."

"You must read it. Then we'll destroy it."

Juan took out the paper and read.

Dear Juan,

Don't be afraid, my little protégé. My brothers will help you. Now it's your turn to keep the secret. You must hide it; follow the instructions. They'll help you. When you've completed your mission, you'll have to wait for the path to reappear. That will take many years, Juan. When the words of the "Our Father" come true: On earth as it is in heaven. Then your descendant will fulfill the prophecy.

"That's all it says. You can burn it now," Juan concluded, handing the giant the slip of paper.

And that's what the tall man did.

He gave the boy one hand and with the other took up his sword. They walked to the center of the plaza, to a lamppost by the fountain.

"Juan . . . Juan . . . Of course!" the giant suddenly exclaimed. *Juan el Bautista;* you're named after the Baptist. '*He must increase, but I must decrease,*'" he said, recalling the Gospels verse. "John preceded the Redeemer . . . and the old man died . . . the Book of Revelation says so, and that was the master's favorite book." The giant looked at the boy. "For years, he's been building the foundations of the new Jerusalem."

"I know," the boy replied.

The giant raised his sword and pointed.

"And there is your first clue, son: the serpent. The Ouroboros: all is one. The serpent of light that resides in the heavens, in the Milky Way. The serpent Jörmungandr in Norse mythology. The circular magnum opus: the beginning and the end that unites the conscious and the subconscious. Do you see those two serpents coiled together on the lamppost?"

"Yes, but I don't understand anything you're saying."

"The caduceus of Hermes! Alchemy. It's a very ancient art."

He realized the boy really didn't have any idea what he was talking about. Though the child was a knight, he had much to learn. He'd only just been initiated, and his time with the master had been cut short.

"We've got a long night ahead of us, Juan. We have to complete the task that's been entrusted to you. You're the only one who knows exactly where to hide the relic. It must be hidden until the day comes. After you hide it, we'll hide *you,* so they can never find you. That's *our* mission. And now, let's go to the Garden of Hesperides. The dragon awaits us, and he's your new guardian."

12

A T ABOUT TEN thirty, the caretaker of the temple, who, along with his wife, saw to room and board for the master and his apprentice, went to the rectory to find Father Gil Parés. Neither the master nor the boy had returned at the usual time, and he was very worried.

"Let's wait a little while longer," Father Parés said, barely able to hide his concern. "If they don't come back soon, we'll go to the infirmary. That's all I can think to do."

It was a warm, still night. A strange calm was in the air. There was no sound of gunfire; the anarchists and their bullets were quiet that night.

Father Parés and the caretaker finally hailed a hansom.

"I'll go; you stay here, Father. If I find anything out, I'll let you know."

The caretaker went to the infirmary on Ronda.

"At about six o'clock we treated an old man who fits the description you've given, but he had no identification. He was hit by a tram on Calle Cortes."

"Where is he? What room?" the caretaker asked.

"He's not here. The old man was in grave condition. I think they sent him to Hospital Clinic."

The caretaker started back to the rectory to pick up Father Parés, but he decided to stop at Ronda San Pedro 25, where the architect Domingo Sugrañés lived. He explained to the architect the terrible situation before they got Father Parés and continued on to the hospital.

"We've got a body that could be him. He was dead on arrival."

Their blood ran cold. The master couldn't be dead.

"Are you sure it's him?"

"All I know is that we've got an indigent old man who was run over by a tram."

"People are run over by trams every day," Sugrañés countered.

"Can we see him?" Father Parés asked.

"Of course, Father. Of course you can."

They walked into the morgue. Father Parés raised the sheet. Although he lamented the poor man's fate, he was tremendously relieved: it wasn't the master. God would forgive him that joy.

"If you like, I can contact the infirmary where he was treated. Usually the ambulance drivers decide which hospital to take the injured to," the orderly said.

"We'd appreciate that," the architect replied.

The attendant made the call.

"Yes, another vagabond was hit by a tram . . . He might be in Santa Cruz Hospital."

The three men thanked him and hurried to the next hospital.

A MAN IN a hat bumped into a group of nuns. He was dressed entirely in black, wore impeccable leather shoes, and held a cane with a carved ivory handle. One of the nuns glanced sideways at the strangely shaped ornament and shivered. The man strode past without even greeting them and continued walking down the hallway of Santa Cruz Hospital. He looked at his watch: ten to twelve.

A moment later he reached the Santo Tomás ward and approached bed 19. The old man was there. He'd received extreme unction.

The man in black stood at the foot of the bed. He stared impassively at the dying man's face. With his cane, he traced strange, unfathomable signs in the air while reciting a bizarre, otherworldly litany. The dying man grew agitated, almost convulsive. He struggled to regain consciousness, the effort consuming his last bit of strength.

"Good. Calm down. Yes, I invoked his name and you regained consciousness."

The old man whispered almost imperceptibly. A name. Then exhaustion overcame him once more.

"Yes, it's me. It's been a long time. Do you remember?" The man in black came close, almost touching the old man's face with his own. "I'm Asmodeus now." He paused and then went on. "You refused to join us. You could have had it all, but instead you chose the wrong path. You opted for the world of the weak. Look at you. You're an old beggar. You have nothing, no family, nothing left."

Asmodeus backed up and walked slowly around the bed several times like a wolf circling its prey.

"I came to see you so I could tell you in person that your plan has failed. Forty-three years of work for nothing. Half your *life*." He spit out this last word. "In a way, I admire you, you know? I've kept track of you ever since you refused to follow us, to join me. I always knew what you were planning." He paused again and then said, "We've got your young apprentice. You've failed," he repeated. "The game's over."

The old man shook his head weakly.

"Yes. We've got him."

The old man fixed Asmodeus with his blue eyes. He stared deep into his soul. And then he smiled. He knew his opponent was lying. He closed his eyes and felt at peace once more. Asmodeus would never get the secret. It was safe, and sooner or later his plan would be carried out.

"Damn lunatic! Idiot cauldron maker!" Asmodeus shouted, overcome with rage. He raised his cane and threatened the old man, hurling a string of insults. "Where's the boy?"

Asmodeus knew Gaudí would never tell. He was at death's door and wouldn't give in at the last moments of his life. After all, he'd come this far.

Asmodeus was preparing to bring his cane crashing down on the old man's head when he heard footsteps. Several people walked into the ward and approached from the far hall. He quickly regained his composure and barely had the time to utter, "May you and your God rot together."

FATHER PARÉS AND Sugrañés arrived at midnight. They were told that there was no record of the master's name in admissions.

"But have they brought in anyone who fits his description?"

The man glanced down at the registry.

"Yes, at about eight o'clock. A vagabond, run over by a tram; he's in the Santo Tomás emergency ward. Doctor Prim is the physician on duty; he should be able to give you more information."

"Thank you."

The three men headed to the Santo Tomás ward, passing a man dressed head to toe in black. They bid him good night, but the stranger made no reply.

They found bed 19.

It was him.

13

W ELL, HE'S GOT three broken ribs, but that's not the worst
of it. He also suffered a serious concussion and his heart is
very weak," said Doctor Prim.

"How long has he been unconscious?"

"Since he was admitted." The doctor asked for his name, since the
old man had no identification on him. So Father Parés told him who the
patient in his care was. The physician was astonished. It seemed impossible, but he wasn't about to doubt the word of a priest, especially one
who'd come to the hospital at that time of the night.

"No one recognized him, Father," Dr. Prim said, and then added,
"Who would have thought that such a distinguished man would dress
so raggedly?"

"He is a saint. He's taken a vow of poverty and lives by it. He even
said he wanted to die in a hospital for the poor, like anyone else without
means."

The doctor was about to say that he'd gotten his wish, but he stopped
himself. They'd have taken his sincerity as a joke made in bad taste. But
he knew it was just a matter of hours until the old man would deliver
his soul to God.

Father Parés, Sugrañés the architect, and the caretaker went home.

None of them slept for the rest of the night. At six o'clock in the morning Father Parés sent a message to Don Francisco, the ecclesiastic canon in charge of the church school, and to Father Agustín Mas, the master's spiritual adviser. They arranged to meet at quarter past eight to go to the hospital with Sugrañés.

When they reached the ward, several physicians were examining the patient, the famed Doctor Trenchs y Homs among them. They all concurred on the diagnosis: a possible fracture at the base of the skull, cerebral concussion, multiple contusions on the legs and other parts of the body, deep scratches on the cheek and left ear, and three broken ribs. His friends asked if they could move him to a private clinic.

"An ambulance ride would be risky," one of the doctors asserted.

"We'll treat him just like he was in a private clinic," his colleague announced.

"Of course. We weren't questioning your abilities for a moment," Father Parés responded.

They agreed that the patient should, at least, be moved to a private room. They hung a lithograph of Saint Joseph and a Lourdes rosary from his headboard. He started to regain consciousness and they asked him if he wanted to receive the viaticum; he nodded. Later, they thought they heard him say, "My God, my God," though they couldn't be sure.

The news spread through the city, and thousands of Barcelonans were distraught at the master's fate. At eleven o'clock in the morning the bishop of the diocese, Doctor Miralles, went to visit the illustrious patient. He sat by his bed, and though the old man tried to speak, his painful shortness of breath would not let him get a word out. Visiting, too, were his true friend Father Parés; Francisco Bonet, his nephew; the architect Buenaventura Conill; and other friends who'd come to the hospital as soon as they heard the tragic news. Señor Ribé, representing the city's mayor, offered to help in any way possible. He visited the sick man several times that day. So did Señor Milà i Camps, president of the council.

At five in the afternoon on the tenth, another strange man entered his room. His amazing height was his singular characteristic. He was wearing a habit that no one present recognized. The master, who'd been unconscious for some time, seemed to register his presence from deep in some abyss and raised an arm to the stranger, giving a little whimper that moved everyone who witnessed it.

The giant knelt by the head of the bed and put his lips to the master's right ear. No one heard what he said. No one except the master.

"The boy is safe. The mission has been accomplished. The secret is safe."

The old man closed his eyes. The giant stood and left the room, with tears in his eyes. No one said a word.

Half an hour later, the master died.

On the eleventh, his body was laid out in the chapel. Condolences poured in from the city's most distinguished citizens—Baron de Viver, the mayor; General Milans del Bosch, the civil governor; and José Miralles Sbert, the archbishop—as well as from thousands of ordinary people who silently expressed their sorrow before his remains.

On the twelfth they had a funeral procession, led by the city police on horseback. Crowds followed the cortege through the streets.

A boy waited by the cathedral entrance, surrounded by throngs of people who had congregated in silence to pay their last respects to the master. The boy waited for the hearse to appear. He knew they might recognize him, but he didn't care. He was waiting to say good-bye to his mentor.

The hearse drove past, just a few feet from where he stood. If he'd reached out his hand, his fingers would've surely grazed Gaudí's coffin.

"I did it, Master. The secret is in place. Right where you wanted it," little Juan said quietly, to himself.

Antonio Gaudí, the master, the brilliant architect, *God's architect,* was buried in the cathedral's crypt.

PART III

THE RELIC

14

MOUNT MORIAH IS where Solomon built his temple to God, almost a thousand years before the birth of Christ. It was during this period that the Trees of Moriah were founded—later called the Seven Knights of Moriah, named for the seven cedar trees that grew on the level ground where Solomon erected the temple, whose wood was used to build the Ark of the Covenant.

Their name was only spoken in hushed tones. They were cloaked in anonymity, a legend thought to belong to the distant past.

The Seven Knights became the guardians of the temple's secrets, long before the Templars existed. Their mission was to ensure the purity of that holy place. Tales of their strength and bravery were known far and wide, well beyond the Sea of Galilee. Metal tools were smelted in the forge at the temple, and that's where their swords were made. They lived on through the ages, protected by silence and secrecy. After the death of King Solomon came tragic times: from the darkness, men in the service of evil—the Corbel—launched an unstoppable war against them. They plotted from their shadowy cave near the Black Pentagon. With the invasions of Israel came Syrian and Phoenician deities who desecrated the temple. But the spirit of the Trees of Moriah lived on, triumphing over darkness. The temple was restored several times during the reigns of Ezekiel and Josiah. But finally the Babylonians, led by King Nebuchadnezzar II, came and razed the temple to the ground in 587 BC.

The Israelites were sent into exile, and the Seven Knights of Moriah worked to bring about the temple's reconstruction. Inevitably, the forces of evil continued to attack, taking their toll again and again. There were further desecrations, and death, destruction, and false idols entered the palace of the Israelites, culminating in the taking of Jerusalem by King Antioch IV, who ordered the pagan image of the Greek god Zeus to be placed in the temple. The Knights of Moriah incited the Jews to revolt in the Maccabean Rebellion, led by Judas Maccabee. The temple was restored again in 150 BC, but the expansion of the Roman Empire proved to be a continual threat. Nevertheless, Herod the Great returned it to its former magnificence in 20 BC.

The Moriah heard talk of a prophet from Nazareth who preached and performed miracles throughout Galilee. This man attracted great crowds, and his fame had spread throughout Judea. One day this prophet, who was baptized by John in the waters of the River Jordan, came to the temple with his disciples. The guardians were there, too, hidden, masked in anonymity, amongst the people. On that day, Jesus denounced the prevailing corruption of the rich. He burst into the temple and drove out the merchants and moneychangers with a whip, knocking over the pigeon sellers' stalls and creating an enormous furor. Jesus of Nazareth shouted, "It is written, my house shall be called a house of prayer, but you make it a den of thieves." The blind and the lame flocked to the temple, and he healed them.

From that moment on, the Knights of Moriah knew that he was the true Messiah and they followed him, listening to all of his sermons.

One day Jesus declared a prophecy from the Gentiles' Atrium. "You see this temple? Assuredly, I say to you, not one stone shall be left here upon another that shall not be thrown down." But he told them to fear not, because the day would come when a new building would be conceived by God, and its seven doors would always be open to the redemption of man. "That will be my true temple."

Jesus of Nazareth recognized the Seven Knights of Moriah right away and called them aside to tell them that their mission was not complete, that they had to ensure that the prophecy was fulfilled no matter how long it took, that the true house of God must one day rise once more.

One of Jesus's twelve disciples, a fisherman named Simon Peter, noticed the mysterious men. Peter, who was easily excited, believed that the guardians had been sent by the high priest and feared for his teacher. Whenever Jesus preached, he made sure to sit nearby, keeping a close eye on the seven men. If necessary, he would protect his teacher with his life.

One day, on his way to Caesarea Philippi, at the foot of Mount Hermon, in the north of Palestine, Jesus called Peter and spoke to him: "Simon Peter, do not fear. The men you so carefully watch do not wish to harm me nor hand me over to the high priest."

"But, teacher, I saw them in the temple. They are not like the other men. I believe they are under orders from Caiaphas; in fact I'd swear that—"

"Speak not, Peter. It is written that the Son of Man has come to build the true temple where all good men shall find refuge. Listen to me: they are the Seven Knights of Moriah, the temple's guardians."

"But teacher, that is just an old legend . . ."

"Simon Peter, when I am no longer with you, you shall understand these words. Many temples shall be built in my name, shrines covered in jewels and precious metals. Towers taller than that of Babel will challenge heaven, and new idols will be placed on the altars, idols more powerful than the golden calf that our people falsely worshipped when Moses came down from Mount Sinai with the Ten Commandments."

Peter, always tempestuous, raised a fist in the air and shouted, "Teacher, I will never let that happen. No one will raise a false temple in your name!"

But Christ responded sadly, "Peter, I assure you that before my father's house is rebuilt in the hearts of the humble, you will deny the true relic I reveal to you today in Caesarea Philippi."

SEVENTY YEARS AFTER Christ's crucifixion, the zealots rebelled against the Roman Empire, fulfilling the first part of the prophecy: the temple was again razed to the ground. The relic remained in Caesarea, abandoned to the fate of whoever recovered it.

For centuries, the guardians' mission had been to search tirelessly for that lost relic. Their swords, forged from the metal used to fell the seven cedars of Moriah, were passed from hand to hand, from generation to generation.

MANY YEARS LATER, in the year 1126, Draco—the dragon constellation—in the sky above Jerusalem foretold that the second part of the prophecy was to be fulfilled: a race to build the new temple. The Knights of Moriah came out of hiding to recover the relic all had scorned and take it to the New Jerusalem. They had been after it for so long. Now that the occasion had presented itself, they knew what to do.

A lone horseman rode along the dark hillside of Mount Hermon. It was a volcanic region where the sun's intensity made wheat grow faster and heartier than anywhere else. From the sea, one saw only a mass of dark land, and thus it was known as the "land of shadows." That was the source of the River Jordan, which flowed north to south.

The horseman followed the river from the Dead Sea, near Jericho, up to the Sea of Galilee and then into the mountains. It was a dark, narrow river, full of sediment. But its source was special. The crystal-clear waters were thought to flow directly from the Garden of Eden.

The lone horseman rode on, up the hillsides in the "land of shadows," headed for the source of the sacred river whose waters John had used to baptize Christ. Psalm 42—which was written there—rang through his head: "As a deer longs for flowing streams, so my soul longs for you, O God. My soul thirsts for God, for the living God. When shall I come and behold the face of God?"

The rider was on his way to meet a Sufi master, a Muslim ascetic, one of the last men to know the rules of the Order of the Knighthood of Love. It's said that he was a disciple of Al-Khidr—the Green One—the eternally youthful guide of Moses. The Sufi had relinquished his name; he was no one. His body, voice, mind, and soul were a flame in the dark cave, guarding a tiny artifact, a pitiful relic. He was the only one who had absolute, blind faith in its sanctity. He'd dedicated his life to protecting it, keeping watch day and night in the dark cave. No one had believed him; everyone had scorned the true relic, rejected it, while he, with love, with zeal, had secretly kept it safe all this time. People thought he was mad and left him alone. Neither those of his faith—followers of Mohammed—nor the Christian infidels believed him.

It was the ascetic's faith in that holy artifact that kept him alive, kept the legend alive. He knew that when he handed it over to the infidel, his life would end, and he'd turn to dust. But he had no fear of death, because it was prophesied: "One of the Trees of Moriah will come to the source of the River Jordan and shall receive the relic, that the believers may establish the New Jerusalem."

The rider dismounted, tying the reins to a blackish rock that resembled a lone head emerging from the ground. He walked up a trail, listening to the sounds of the water, the source of the Jordan. That was where he was headed. He approached the river, drank from its crystalline waters, and waited. He did not realize that the Sufi had been seated on the opposite shore, watching him, for some time. Finally, the Christian noticed the figure clad in a grayish tunic observing him impassively. He looked like a beggar. The Sufi's eyes bore through his soul and profaned all of his secrets. And that was when he knew he was one of them. There was no doubt: the horseman was a Knight of Moriah.

The rider stood, unsheathed his sword, raised it threateningly in the air, and then plunged it into the ground with both hands. The old man on the other shore walked toward him very slowly, seeming to glide. He was barefoot and agile, despite his advanced age. His hair and beard were white as snow. He crossed the narrow water and stopped before the sword; then he crouched down, ripped a strip of fabric from his wool tunic, turned, and wrapped what was hidden in his hands inside the cloth. The Sufi gave it to the knight, their eyes connecting. The relic the Knights of Moriah had been seeking for many years was finally in their possession.

The horseman rode off without looking back. He had the relic in his haversack and would take it to a port in Palestine. The race to fulfill the prophecy had begun.

IN 1230 THE Seven Knights left the relic in the care of the Paris command of the Knights Templar. At that time the Templars had just retaken Jerusalem. They were feared and their fortresses were respected; the relic would be safe there. Hundreds of years later, it would form the basis for the new temple's construction.

Sixty years later, the legend of the Knights of Moriah had nearly faded into dust at the end of an age filled with crusaders, sorcerers, and apocalyptic heretics traveling through the Holy Land. They were unpredictable times controlled by evil powers determined to destroy the relic at any cost, as determined as they had been hundreds of years before Christ, when they'd plotted to desecrate and destroy the second temple of Solomon. The enemies of the Seven Knights of Moriah lived on through the generations as well, and they'd fight with all their might to carry out their objective.

The light of just one man shone brightly in those dark times, a wise missionary named Ramon Llull who was a true alchemist of words. He'd dedicated his life to devising a method of divinely inspired reasoning, which he planned to use to convert the Islamic world to Christianity: the *ars magna*, a blend of logic and mysticism. He invented a strange device: a series of concentric disks mounted on a central axis, on which questions, answers, subjects, predicates, and the hundred names for God and all of his attributes were listed.

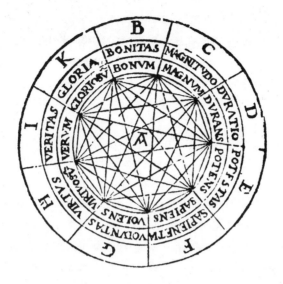

The wise Llull used this object to confront Muslim sages in a battle of symbols and reason. His name rang out in every Christian and Muslim court, and he was greatly respected by most, though on more than one occasion, while preaching in markets in the Orient he was nearly stoned to death by angry mobs who did not understand his logic. But no one knew the true secret of this traveler and tireless writer, a man who committed himself to the learning of languages in order to convince Jews and Muslims of the theological truth of his vision. Ramon Llull was one of the Seven Knights.

After the fall of Acre in 1291, the military orders lost prestige all across the old continent. Llull sent the Pope a document proposing the unification of all the orders: the Hospitallers, the Templars, the Order of Calatrava, and the Order of Santiago. Together they would form the Order of the Holy Spirit, with a single teacher of theology and a group of Arabic and Hebrew linguists, philosophers, saints, and sages who would begin their missionary work in eastern lands to convert the infidels. But events overtook them. The project failed. Philip the Handsome, king of France, poisoned by the elixir of greed he'd been forced to drink, had begun a campaign to disparage the powerful Templars, who, despite increasing economic strength in old Europe, had lost everything in the Holy Land. The threat was so urgent that the old and now tired missionary Ramon Llull called an urgent meeting with the Seven Knights. The winds of ambition fanned the embers of their legend back to life and the guardians' flame burned once more, reflecting its light on the swords of the Seven Knights.

They went to the grand master of the Knights Templar, Jacques de Molay, and demanded what was theirs. It was Ramon Llull himself who met him secretly in Paris. The Templars refused to give up the relic. Perhaps fear that the king of France would make good on his threat to turn their allies in Rome against them hardened their hearts to the truth, and they rebelled. The wise Llull realized that this could be the end; nevertheless, one of the Knights of Moriah had a powerful position in the Paris command, and he was to act at precisely the right moment.

The Knights Templar fell in October 1307. King Phillip the Handsome and his troops took Jacques de Molay prisoner and the Paris command was disbanded, the monks taken by surprise. Only one, a tall man named Cristóbal, managed to slip out through the catacombs, absconding with the relic. He took it all the way to the other side of the Pyrenees. Cristóbal crossed rivers and mountains and valleys before reaching the castle of Miravet, on the shores of the River Ebro.

The days of the Templars were all but finished, thanks to the ambitions of Pope Clement V and Phillip IV of France.

The knights prepared to fight; they'd never give up. The Templar commands fell into the hands of the monarchies, the Inquisition, and the nobles. Their castles, homes, and possessions all fell like dominoes in a matter of weeks; the Templars lost everything. Knights, monks, and teachers were taken prisoner, and tortuous trials began in which they were accused of being heretics, worshipping Baphomet. The Order of the Templars no longer existed; all that was left was the castle of Miravet, a presumably invincible bastion, which put up a fierce resistance.

Jacques de Molay, the grand master, was sentenced to death, along with other great knights of the order. Meanwhile, Miravet held on.

From his Paris cell, Molay recalled a secret meeting he'd had a few months before the fall of the order. It was about a very urgent matter, something quite delicate. Ramon Llull had shown him a sword of Moriah and demanded he hand over the relic the Templars had in their care.

The wise Llull had assured him that the relic was the greatest treasure in Christianity and that it had divine power over the Templars. In seventy years, they had spread like a spiderweb from the center of Paris, where the relic had been deposited, to the rest of Europe, bringing everything and everyone under their influence. He warned Molay that this very power would end up destroying the order, because the relic had to be taken to its rightful place. No one paid any attention to Llull, the sage from Mallorca, not even when he asked for its return as one of the Knights of Moriah. De Molay regretted not listening to Llull and the arrogance, fear, and greed that had played a large part in the Templars' downfall.

Jacques de Molay, locked up in prison, realized that Ramon Llull had predicted what would happen, had foretold this disaster. The mother church that was to have protected the Templars abandoned them. The last grand master of the order, moments before he faced death, reflected on all of this. By refusing to return the relic to its rightful owners, he had lost his honor. This was his sin, not the absurdly defamatory claims of deeds and rituals the Templars had never practiced. Jacques de Molay begged forgiveness and knelt before the cross of the Order of the Templars, a simple wooden image. Providing the cross was the only mercy the Inquisitor would grant, hours before de Molay was to be burned at the stake.

15

MIRAVET, 1836

A T THE WENTWORTH residence in the Thames Valley some
nineteen miles from London, an old Carlist general—the legendary Ramón Cabrera, known as the "Tiger of Maestrazgo"—
received a strange visitor who was said to come from far-off lands. The
extraordinarily tall man visited him every day, and the Tiger told him
the story of his life, of the brilliant military campaign he led in the
First Carlist War, earning him the highest rank and the title of count
of Morella, after he turned the walled city he had conquered into an
impenetrable fortress, now the capital of his small empire.

Ramón Cabrera was a young man from Tortosa who left the city in
search of fame and fortune. When he set off from the shore of the Ebro
he wasn't sure which way to go, so he raised his handkerchief in the air
to let God show him the way. A gust of wind fluttered it in the direction
of the mountains, the heart of Maestrazgo, Morella. Without a second
thought, he set off in that direction and joined the parties of men meeting up there to defend the usurper of the Spanish crown, Carlos María
Isidro of the House of Bourbon, brother of the deceased Fernando VII.

Fernando VII, shortly before dying without a male heir, abolished

Salic law, which prevented women from succeeding to the Spanish throne. Queen María Cristina of Naples, with the support of the Liberal Party, became regent in the name of Isabel II, the two-year-old daughter she had borne Fernando. This started the war between Fernando and his brother Carlos, leading to great strife between families, friends, and neighbors—a civil war, the worst of calamities.

The visitor listened attentively to Cabrera's adventures in the First Carlist War, which began in late 1833. Forty years had passed, but the legend of the Tiger had catapulted him to the highest echelons of power and fame. He also fought in the Second Carlist War, which earned him the title of marquis of Ter after the battle he won in Pasteral in late June 1848. He didn't take part in the Third Carlist War in 1872. By then he'd fallen out with Carlos VII, the arrogant usurper, and gone so far as to recognize Alfonso XII, the son of Isabel II.

He'd been exiled to England for many years, where he'd met his wife, Marianne Catherine Richards. They married in 1850, had children, and now he lived like a gentleman in the Wentworth residence, near London. Old and tired, removed from politics, Cabrera welcomed the chance to relive those scenes from his youth, when he was the indisputable leader of Carlism, fighting the Liberal armies and defeating María Cristina.

It had been incredible, almost miraculous. Their only weapons were courage, valor, and the mountains, which gave them stealth. They were warriors, fighting in tiny bands, continually ambushing and savaging the regular army. Wearing his white cape and using a cane, he became an expert at hand-to-hand combat. He and his volunteers—with their cry of "Avant!"—were invincible. He defeated all of the queen's generals and, in the end, was only brought down by illness, a strange affliction that had plagued him since childhood. His lands crumbled while he was confined to his bed; citadel after citadel fell like dominoes until finally, at the end of the Second Carlist War, all he could do was go into exile.

These memories weighed on him, but today, rather than wars, love affairs, battles, and adventures, he recalled a different scene, one of great shock and deep sorrow, an event that he would never reveal to his visitor or anyone else. He'd take it to the grave. It had nothing to do with the Carlist Wars, court intrigues, or party politics. He was thinking about the oath that a monk had made when he came to his tent at Miravet on the night of Good Friday, 1836, a few months after his mother had been executed by firing squad.

The episode had caused shock and sorrow, because in it he'd lost his seventeen-year-old nephew, of whom he was especially fond. After the Tiger's innocent mother was executed in Tortosa, by order of the hated General Nogueras, he had shown the boy great affection and tenderness.

At the start of Holy Week in 1836 he was planning the siege on the castle of Miravet with Torner, an instigator and native of Roquetes, which was a town near Tortosa where the last remaining men from a defeated Liberal column had taken refuge. They followed the banks of the river, crossed the imposing Barrufemes Pass, and took refuge in the fortress. It had been a Templar castle, later occupied by Hospitallers and then abandoned. It was partially destroyed but still had the defensive structures to provide strong resistance. It sat above the town of Miravet, atop a mountain with natural stone walls and steep rock that dropped down to the surging waters of the River Ebro, the green river making its way to a blue delta at the Mediterranean Sea.

There were fewer than thirty Liberals and a delegation of seven civilians. It seems that when the Tiger's troops ambushed them in Roquetes, they'd been on their way to Miravet with a secret mission. The entire column gave their lives so that this small group and their escorts could reach the castle at Miravet.

The besieged defended themselves valiantly. Torner, a local who knew the terrain, managed to scale one of the rock faces along the river. He and a group of Carlists breached the fortification. They killed five Liberals and took ten more prisoners, including a lieutenant, executing all of them immediately. The law of Talion was in full force during that fratricidal war, and no one on either side would show mercy. The remaining soldiers and the civilians were holed up in the fortress, its front gate shut and locked.

So the Tiger—on his horse Garrigó, his white cape fluttering, his Carlist beret on his head, and his cane black from the dried blood of those he'd killed—stormed the fortress with one hundred men. Don Ramón, as his volunteers called him, set up his tent on one of the nearby patios, in a cove safe from the Liberals.

That afternoon, Cabrera sent negotiators in an attempt to convince the besieged to surrender. They refused. It was suicide: sooner or later, they'd manage to enter the parade ground surrounding the fortress, and the Liberals would drop like flies. But they chose to die rather than give themselves up.

Don Ramón ordered Torner to go back and talk with them once more. It was eleven o'clock at night. When he returned, he informed Cabrera of the situation.

"They're friars. The seven civilians are all monks. Really. They're wearing habits, they have trees on their shirts, and they carry swords. The Liberal officer told me that they'll never surrender because they've come for a secret that they have to guard and deliver safely to the shrine of the Black Virgin of Montserrat. The fifteen Liberal soldiers guarding them want to surrender. The officer who accompanied me to the gate made that very clear. He said the monks are insane, they've locked themselves inside the castle, in the treasure tower, and they'll never come out. Those lunatics have no firearms, only ancient broadswords. The officer told me they'll open the gates at dawn, as soon as day breaks; he'll surrender and so will all of his soldiers, but he asked me to spare their lives. He requested that I give him an answer tonight, at exactly twelve o'clock. Lighting a torch and holding it up at the wall will be the signal. What do you say, Don Ramón?"

"Done, Torner. We'll spare their lives. You may light the torch. Monks hiding a secret they have to take to Montserrat? What is this, Torner? Are you sure of what you've told me? They truly have no firearms, just old-fashioned swords?"

"Yes, Don Ramón. The Liberal officer who explained the circumstances was as perplexed as we are. Until that moment, it seems, they knew nothing; all they'd been told was that they had to guard the delegation and protect them with their lives, accompanying them to the castle of Miravet and then on to Montserrat."

When day broke on Good Friday, Cabrera and a detachment of elite marksmen—his personal guards, which included his nephew Juan—entered the parade ground. The officer and his fifteen soldiers silently surrendered. Cabrera spoke with the man once more, interrogating him. The man confirmed everything Torner had said. Their lives were spared, but Don Ramón ordered that their fingers be cut off so they could never again serve in the military. The seven monks were still inside the castle. Cabrera could not accept what was happening; he simply couldn't believe it. "Monks guarding a secret with their lives? Taking it to Montserrat? There's something very odd about all this . . ."

The parade ground was ten feet below the gate leading to the fortress. When the seven monks, crazed or whatever they were, saw that they had been betrayed by their protectors, they immediately removed the ladder and closed the gate.

That same morning, from one of the battlements, one of the lunatic monks spoke.

"I challenge you, Cabrera. A duel. Here in the castle's parade ground. Choose your best soldier. I know you're a man of your word. All I ask is that if I win you allow us to depart."

The Tiger's response to this plan was a volley of rifle fire. At noon on that Good Friday, they tried to force their way through the castle gate from the parade ground using ladders they'd brought up from the town. The operation didn't seem risky, given that the monks hadn't appeared all morning and they hadn't taken the opportunity to fire from the fortress's side windows. Juan, Cabrera's nephew, a valiant young man who loved his uncle dearly, insisted on taking part in the next round of the siege.

There were no shots fired, no rifle, musket, shotgun, or blunderbuss.

But from the top of the castle, heavy flagstones rained down upon the men positioning the ladders. It was a totally unexpected attack; they had no time to react. Cabrera, who was several feet away, shouted desperately.

"Juan!"

His nephew died, killed by a stone that crushed his skull. Three other volunteers also lost their lives, and five more were wounded.

Don Ramón was beside himself with rage. He screamed and cried, completely distraught at his powerlessness, and held his nephew, cradling his crushed head in his arms. The boy had been pummeled and was nothing more than a mass of flesh and bones, totally unrecognizable.

They tried to scale the castle walls, but the task was impossible. Battlements and merlons collapsed upon the attackers.

By nightfall nothing had changed. The seven monks, without having fired a shot, were still locked up inside. Cabrera managed to control his initial rage. He cried long and hard over his nephew Juan's dead body and swore that he would personally slit the throats of the men responsible. And then that same voice shouted down.

"Cabrera, you'll never enter! We have plenty of food and water. I challenge you. A duel, a sword fight, here on the parade ground. Pick your best man. If we lose, at exactly twelve o'clock we'll surrender. If we win, we'll take our leave at that same time."

Cabrera shouted up from below.

"No empty words, friar—or whatever you are! I accept your challenge! I myself will fight, to the death. You have my word. If you defeat me and I die, my men will let you go. But if I win, you will surrender, and you know what awaits you. You'll pay dearly for your audacity."

"You have my word, Cabrera. Prepare the battlefield. Daylight has almost gone."

They placed a series of torches in a circle on the parade ground. The Carlists gathered round. Cabrera waited, cane in hand, his chest bare, fury clearly visible on his face. The gate opened. A man wearing a long, open tunic and white shirt emblazoned with a cedar tree slid down a rope. He was young, with blond hair and a beard. The crowd parted to let him through.

"This is my son Guillermo Nogués. Take a sword, or two if you like. Take a lance, a shield, a mace. This fight is to the death, and he'll show no mercy."

The man's voice rang out from above the wall; it was coming from a window where shadows could be seen, moving about.

"I need none of those things to avenge my nephew's death. Whoever you are, say a prayer, because you're going to die."

The monks began to pray in Latin, their words resounding on the parade ground. Cabrera's opponent crossed himself, raised his sword, and placed his fist on his forehead.

"Come on! What are you waiting for? You're going to die, damn you. I will avenge my nephew Juan Bru's death."

The duel began. The monk was agile; the blade of his heavy sword sliced the air, whistling. The Tiger moved this way and that, dodging the young monk's masterful strokes. Cabrera knew he could not let his weapon receive a blow; his wooden cane could be easily sliced in two, no matter how well it had been hardened in the embers of burning olive trees, on battlefields where he'd sown terror among the Liberal troops. His strategy was clear. He had to concentrate, maintain his reflexes, stay calm, and save vengeance for later. He needed to parry skillfully, move constantly, slip out of his opponent's reach, turning this way and that. He had to be patient, tire out his adversary, and wait for the right moment. After all, the monk was only a man, like himself; there were limits to his endurance. Then Cabrera would strike. Just one blow in the right place would be enough to defeat him. All he needed was to land that one perfect blow.

One of the monk's strokes grazed Cabrera's chest, slicing him and drawing blood. He felt the intense, burning pain of the steel blade, but he quickly overcame it. His enemy knew then that Cabrera was cornered and gave it his all, attacking relentlessly, forcing him back up against the torches, burning the Tiger's back. Cabrera, his eyes wild, knew this was it; one false move and he would surely be killed. He jumped to one side and the monk's sword tore through his thigh; it was a clean cut, not very deep, but blood poured down his leg. Cabrera felt faint, and he was limping now. But his rival's moves, after half an hour of ceaseless attack, were no longer so precise, either. It was becoming harder for him to raise the heavy sword. This was the moment. The Tiger managed to bring the cane crashing down on the monk's arm. It wasn't much, but the Carlists shouted, applauding their leader. The monk, who until this point had not hesitated for a moment, took a step back when he saw Cabrera brandish his club, windmilling the weapon threateningly above his head. This was his moment of weakness, the moment Cabrera had been waiting for. The Tiger lashed out with all his might, striking the monk's left side, and quickly repositioned when the monk turned to protect himself with his sword. He swung again, delivering a vicious blow to the forehead. A euphoric cry rang out from his men; the jubilation was shocking. The Carlists cheered wildly. Cabrera stared at the young swordsman, whose eyes were unfocused, his face dripping with sweat. He raised his arm threateningly, first to one side, then the other. The monk couldn't see clearly; the blow to his forehead had stunned him, and blood ran from his nose, staining his blond beard. He lurched back and forth, swinging wildly with his sword, thrusting forward, then turning, panting; he was lost. The Tiger had him in his clutches now, and he breathed deeply, contemplating the monk with a mix of pleasure and hatred. The wave of rage and ire, the vengeance he'd so coolly contained throughout the duel, was now unleashed.

He delighted in tormenting the monk, like a cat with a mouse in its claws. The Tiger's first blow knocked the sword to the ground, crushing his hand; the second smashed his cheek. Then he brought the cane crashing down on his shoulder, his face. Each blow broke bones; the poor boy was whimpering, groping blindly in every direction without knowing where to turn. The Carlists jeered, their laughter echoing off the fortress walls.

Anguished howls rang out from above, cries begging for mercy, but they were drowned out by the frenzied clamor of the men forming a circle around the torches. Cabrera turned, raised his cane, and blindly lashed out again. Finally, when he tired of toying with his prey, he quieted the men who stood laughing and cheering him on. An icy silence fell over the parade ground. From the castle windows came a murmur that grew louder and more intense. The monks were reciting a funeral prayer. The Tiger raised his cane with both hands above the young man who now knelt before him, vanquished, awaiting the final blow, the one that would take his life. Even in that state, the young man struggled to raise a hand and make the sign of the cross. Cabrera was overcome by hatred and a desire for revenge. Without stopping to think, he struck a monumental blow down upon the young man's skull, right on the crown of his head. Possessed, he thrashed at him again and again.

"Die! This is for Juan, my poor nephew. Your men crushed his skull. I'll do the same to you! This is my vengeance!"

Ramón Cabrera, completely beside himself, rained blow after blow on the body that now lay dead. He looked up and saw his men, standing silently.

"My son!" cried one of the monks from the window. "No! Cabrera! Please, leave him now. My son!" Those last chilling words, together with the anguished cry of the father watching in horror as Cabrera destroyed his son's face and body, took everyone's breath away.

No one moved; they all stood aghast. Cabrera, kneeling, his strength gone, kept striking the lifeless body over and over, shouting and crying in rage and anguish. He was overcome with wrath and fury.

"I want Garrigó! Bring me my horse! I'm going to rip this man to pieces," he shouted.

He tied the young monk's corpse to the horse and mounted, forcing the animal to trot and then gallop through the parade ground. Everyone watched in horror, not daring to say a word. He circled again and again until, utterly spent after having lost so much blood in the duel, he fell to the ground. From the window, the young knight's father, the same one who'd proposed the duel to begin with, shouted exhaustedly. They took Cabrera to his tent to tend to his wounds. While he was being carried, the Tiger struggled to raise himself and exclaimed, "Bring me that wretch of a body! No one touch him; he's mine. Did you hear me? He's mine! He belongs to me! I'll kill anyone who touches him."

Two orderlies immediately obeyed, dragging the body and tying it to a stake in front of Cabrera's tent, while inside, doctors stitched up the wounds on his chest and leg.

Shortly before midnight he awoke with a start. An aide helped him sit up.

"I'm fine, I'm alright now."

"The doctors said you must not move, Don Ramón."

"I'm fine, son. It's all over now."

Cabrera went to look out of his tent, pulling aside the canvas flap, and saw the mess of flesh before him. The monk's body was completely disfigured. Turning, he asked, "Have they surrendered?"

"Not yet, Don Ramón. They said they'll come out at exactly twelve o'clock. They're praying now. Can't you hear them?"

"Yes, I can."

"Would you like me to bring you something to eat?"

"No, you can go. I want to be alone."

"But, Don Ramón . . . I'm on guard duty."

"You'll do as you're told, orderly. Leave the tent. I want to be alone."

"Yes, sir."

The orderly walked away. Cabrera emerged from the tent and examined the disgraced corpse once more. In his mind, however, he saw his nephew's crushed face, his mother's face. With the tip of his boot, he flipped the body over, and something caught his attention. The little wretch was wearing a small leather sack around his neck. It was completely covered in blood. He crouched down to rip it from the body, to further offend and debase him, but something stopped him. A gust of wind raised a cloud of dust around him as the lugubrious sound of the monks' funeral hymns floated off down the riverbanks. Cabrera was overcome by exhaustion and went back inside the tent. He listened to the monks more closely now; it must have been close to twelve, the time they'd chosen to surrender, and Cabrera considered what to do with them. He was tired of death; perhaps he'd let them go. He still hadn't decided when he heard steps approaching the tent. He looked for his cane. Cabrera was sitting on a folding leather chair and had no time to stand.

"Don Ramón, take pity on me. I'm just a poor father and I've come to ask for my son's body, to give him a Christian burial."

He recognized him. It was the monk who'd proposed the duel, the father of the dead knight, an elderly man who'd come unarmed, wearing a tunic and shirt with a cedar tree imprinted on it. His hair and beard were white as snow. The old man knelt and kissed Cabrera's feet.

"You fool. You sent your own son to his death. Why?" the Tiger asked scornfully.

"He was invincible with a sword. He was the best."

"Until he met my cane. And now you've lost your son. Do you want to lose your own life as well, crazy old man? How dare you appear before me, the man who killed your son!"

The old man looked up and said, "Remember your own father, Cabrera. He is the same age as I, entering the tragic decline of old age. Take pity. I've done what no other man would: put my own life in the hands of the man who killed my only son. He was all I had in the world."

This was what the old knight said as he squeezed the Tiger's hand in his own, kissing it as tears rolled down his cheeks. The memory of his dead mother, so recently executed, overcame Ramón Cabrera, and he shuddered. He felt a desire to weep, for all of his loved ones, but especially for Juan, a strong, noble young man whom he'd loved so dearly. Cabrera had sworn to his sister that he'd protect him with his life, and now Juan was dead. He began to sob, choking at the memory of his father, who had died when Ramón was nine. Then he saw the face of his mother, brutally murdered by General Nogueras.

Cabrera and the old man, each crying for his dead, embraced next to the tent. Finally Cabrera pulled away and spoke softly to the monk.

"Take your son, old man. Leave right now; don't tempt me. Bury him. Go, while my tears are fresh and I am thinking of my loved ones, whom you've dug up from the cemetery of my mind. Now it's your turn. Bury your son; he was a noble warrior, and he fought bravely. He deserves a decent burial."

"I'll give him one, Cabrera. I want to take him to Montserrat, the sacred mountain. To the shrine of the Black Virgin. There I'll dig his grave with my own hands."

The old man turned to go, and when he was about to leave, Cabrera said, "Stop! Where did you say you're going to bury him?"

"Montserrat."

Torner's words had flashed through his mind, his report of the first talks with the monks, and then the confirmation he'd received from the Liberal officer who'd opened the gate.

"Montserrat? Isn't that where you were going on some secret mission, escorted by the Liberal garrison?"

The old man froze. He didn't know what to say. Tension filled the air. Cabrera grabbed his cane and raised it. The old man bowed his head and fell to his knees once more.

"Wait, Don Ramón. You should know the truth. My pain and anguish are sincere; I came to you for my son. But it's true, there's something else. I think I can speak openly to you. All I ask is one thing: you must take an oath of silence over what I tell you."

"You dare to make demands of me, to require an oath?"

From down on his knees, the old man spoke firmly, with no hesitation.

"I do not fear death. Kill me if you wish; my life is in your hands. You are a man of honor and you'll understand my motives. I cannot reveal anything to you if you don't swear first. You have my word."

Cabrera was surprised at his stoic manner.

"Alright, old man. Too much has already happened tonight, and I'm tired. I have no desire to kill a defenseless old man. Go ahead and speak; I swear I shall never reveal your words to anyone."

"Cabrera, my son was the bearer of the secret. It was hanging from his neck, in a small leather sack. We are the Seven Knights of Moriah, the temple mount in Jerusalem where Solomon built his temple. We were founded a thousand years before the birth of Christ, and we've endured all these years. Many years ago, the knights before us brought the most valuable relic in all Christianity from the Holy Land. The Order of the Templars served us, because we were their forefathers. So the relic was deposited in Paris under the Templars' protection. But when the order fell in 1307, it was moved here to the castle of Miravet, which held out fiercely. It's been hidden here for over five hundred years. The Seven Knights of Moriah have kept it safe here, hidden in the treasure tower. No one would ever have guessed where it was. And the relic remained there; we felt sure that this spot, so desolate and abandoned, was ideal . . .

"But this civil war, and the news that the castle was to be occupied by troops with plans to fortify and reinforce the walls, made us fear that the relic might be lost. That's why we decided to act. We had to get it back and take it to Montserrat. We knew it would be safe there. Within a few generations, at the turn of the century, it will be handed over to the great architect who will rebuild the temple. That is all."

"Old man, now that you've told me this much, I want you to tell me everything. What kind of secret are you talking about?"

"Cabrera, you can see it with your own eyes."

The Tiger recalled, for an instant, having seen the secret, the relic. He even held it in his hand, as a gust of wind whistled through the castle's battlements. The monks fell silent at just the same moment. It was exactly midnight, Good Friday, 1836. Don Ramón felt something strange in his hand, cold, warmth, something overpowering. He felt a terrible fear, and yet, simultaneously, an inexplicable impulse deep in his soul told him that he had to help that poor old man complete his mission.

So he did. Don Ramón Cabrera ordered a group of his men to accompany those monks to Montserrat, where the secret was then buried in a huge cave below the sacred mountain, beside the body of the young Knight of Moriah he had honorably killed in a duel.

PART IV

THE TORTOISE

16

I've lived in this neighborhood for more than half my life," María
said, finishing her coffee.

The morning of June 7, before walking into La Sagrada Família, where she knew the tortoise was, they stopped at a café on Calle
Marina. They could see the cathedral from the café's front window.

"My grandfather was a huge admirer of Gaudí's work. In fact, I know
this church like I do my own house. He took me here all the time,
and Park Güell, too. He always pointed out how much the pavilions
on either side of the entrance looked like the dragon's house in 'Hänsel
and Gretel.'"

Miguel listened, trying not to be judgmental. But he couldn't help
feeling that the old man had been fueling his insanity for years. When
his illness finally overtook him, he could no longer distinguish truth
from fiction. And María's words confirmed this.

"He used to say that Gaudí was ahead of his time, that he always
took risks. No one has ever designed anything like him. There's been no
one to carry on his work and his legacy. That's what he used to tell me.
Gaudí made things up as he went along, like an artist, constantly refin-
ing. He worked side by side with builders, carpenters, and metalworkers.
He used to say Gothic architecture was an imperfect art and that its

buildings were only beautiful when they were in ruins, overtaken by the forces of nature and time." She stopped and pointed to the temple, adding, "The whole thing is a blend of architecture and sculpture, a reflection of nature." Then she paused again. "You could never make a building like this nowadays. It doesn't meet any city planning standards, and apparently they never even got any permits to build what they did."

There was a long silence. It wasn't even six o'clock yet, but the bustling noises of the city were overwhelming. Miguel was still looking at the cathedral, picturing its interior. He knew it well, too. Who didn't know La Sagrada Família, arguably one of the most famous structural oddities in the world?

"Why did we stop here?"

"I want to show you something. Let's pay."

They left the café and walked toward the church without speaking. Facing east, it opened onto Calle Marina, where they stood. Even now, the building was tremendously imposing, without equal. Deep down, they both had an uneasy feeling. As they headed to the Nativity Façade, María pointed out what she'd been looking for.

"There it is: the Corbel man. See him?"

Miguel did.

"Man's temptation: the face of evil, with an Orsini bomb in his hand. Gaudí designed all of the sculptures on this façade. The collection was put together by his colleague Llorenç Matamala."

Miguel listened as he stared at the sculpture of a man with a bomb, preparing to throw it. There was something terrible about it; he felt it.

"That's him. I don't know how to explain it. The one on the bus. The two men who were following me were identical, like twins; they had the same expressions, the same appearance. That's him," she said, pointing. "Why are you so quiet?"

"Because it's ridiculous . . . We need to think clearly, and what you're saying is impossible. There must be hundreds, thousands of men who look like the guy in that sculpture. You're letting your imagination run wild."

"Oh. So was it my imagination that tried to shoot us yesterday?"

"No. All I mean is, you're trying to connect things that are unrelated. I agree, what happened yesterday was unbelievable. We're not drug lords; there's no reason why anyone should try to shoot us down right in the middle of Calle Balmes, but . . . we're talking about a sculpture here. A stereotype of evil. It's too bizarre, María."

But deep down, Miguel thought something he wasn't saying. When one of the gunmen had thrown himself onto the car as Miguel sped away, he, too, had seen something similar, something that reminded him of this stone portrait. But he chose to ignore it. He didn't want to worry María any more than necessary.

They kept walking. María had a familiar feeling as she entered the cathedral, the impression that she was walking through the very heart of a stone forest and surrounded by huge tree trunks and immensely high, almost transparent stone branches.

Miguel looked around and felt he was in a place filled with mysterious lines and spiritual light, colored reflections cast by the stained-glass windows. It was like a kaleidoscope.

From a mathematical perspective, he admired Gaudí tremendously. He may not have understood the architecture, but the math was no problem. There was an empty central area, an unreal point from which the whole structure was ordered. The temple was alive, it was organic. And that perfect, almost natural serialization that established such a dynamic order was more a mathematical concept than an architectonic one. Gaudí was an expert at fractal order, the mathematics of life: repetition of the same pattern to infinity, one that apparently challenged the laws of physics, calling into question Newton, Euclid, and Pythagoras. All of science, reduced to nothing. One tiny decimal imbalance: the number pi, 3.14159, crucial for calculating domes, circles, any natural curve. Pi hates straight lines and perfect squares. The bigger the object, the more disproportionate the imbalance, ruining all calculations. And Gaudí just adored the whole idea.

"What are you thinking about?"

"Math."

They felt both trapped by and attracted to the space. A slight change in the light turned the interior into a cascade of shadows.

"There's proof of his early political ideas, you know," María said.

"Whose?" he asked distractedly.

"Gaudí's. I just remembered this morning."

"Did your grandfather tell you about that, too?"

She went on, ignoring his last question.

"When he was a high school student in Reus, he made friends with a couple of other students, Eduard Todà and Josep Ribera. Ribera was from L'Espluga, near the monastery of Poblet, and they used to take trips out there. They dreamed of restoring it. They were full of ideas—the three of them even made blueprints and wrote up a proposal. They wanted to turn Poblet into a commune, a phalanstery or something like that. That's what the utopian socialists of the day were advocating. Anyway, the anticlericalism couldn't have been clearer."

"OK, so they were utopian socialists. What are you getting at?"

"I don't know. I was just thinking that there may be a lot of things people don't know about Gaudí, that's all."

They stopped talking and walked out through the Passion Façade.

"Come on. The tortoise is waiting."

THERE WASN'T ONE tortoise, though; there were two. María already knew that, of course. *Hard on top, hard underneath . . . Face of a snake and sticks for feet,* she thought. They each supported columns that formed an arch, framing the door to the cathedral.

"What are we supposed to do?"

"First, we have to pick one and see if this fits in it somehow," she said, taking the strange key from her pocket.

Fortunately there were no visitors that early. Miguel stood in front of María, blocking her, while she bent down to examine the tortoise on the left.

"Why that one?"

"Well, we have to start somewhere. Face of a snake. The other one doesn't have the face of a snake; it doesn't seem to have sticks for feet either, and according to the riddle, it should."

Miguel felt ridiculous, but he kept covering María while she examined the tortoise. She started feeling around, trying to find someplace where she could put the key. And then she had an idea. She put the key in one of its eyes and pushed. Nothing. She tried the other.

They heard a strange noise, like cogs beginning to move. The front of the sculpture, the head and legs, slowly opened like a drawer.

"My God!" Miguel exclaimed. He'd stopped keeping a lookout and was now watching the stone drawer as it slid out and then stopped. He had a sudden thought and glanced at his watch: it was six past six in the morning.

"Achilles and the tortoise. Zeno's paradox. The race has begun."

"What are you talking about?" María asked.

"I don't know. It's nothing, I was just thinking aloud."

There was something inside. María reached in and pulled it out, noting that at the very back of the drawer, carved into the stone, was the face of a snake. Very slowly, it closed back up. María thought about the riddle again: face of a snake. But then, what about the sticks for feet? Without thinking twice, she began to examine the tortoise on the right, trying to stick the key in one eye and then the other. Miguel watched her, perplexed; he had no idea what she was doing. The key didn't fit. *Then where are the sticks for feet?* she wondered. All they had was a box that had emerged from the tortoise.

It was a small, rectangular box made out of cedar. It was about eight inches long and five and a half wide, and it couldn't have been more than an inch and a half tall. On the lid there were raised numbers, one through nine, and on the side was what looked like a little drawer, though there was no keyhole or lock of any kind. Miguel shook the box and they heard a metallic sound. Then he inspected each side carefully, trying to find a way to open it. He pushed on some of the numbers etched in the lid.

"I'm sure there's a combination to open this. But without some sort of clue, the possibilities are endless."

"Let's get out of here," María said.

"Why?"

"We're out in the open; anyone could see us."

"Oh, like the satanic cult that's spying on us?" Miguel joked.

She made no reply. Deep down, Miguel wasn't so sure of himself, either. After seeing the tortoise open up, he didn't know what to think. He slipped the box into the inside pocket of his jacket and they left.

THAT AFTERNOON MIGUEL decided to go with María back to the nursing home. If there was anyone who could give them the combination to open the box, it was Señor Givell. But they found the old man was not at all lucid.

He didn't even acknowledge their presence.

María showed him the box, but the old man's eyes were far away.

"Do you remember? The combination? How do you open it, Grandfather?"

After a long time, he said simply, "The master's death," so quietly they almost couldn't make out the words.

"What was that, Grandfather?"

"My master's death," he repeated.

They stayed with him for over an hour. It was already getting dark when they finally decided to leave.

"My master's death," he said once more as they closed the door.

"We'll come back tomorrow," Miguel said, trying to cheer María up as he put the car in gear.

"OK, maybe we'll have more luck then," she replied, sounding unconvinced, unsure of what had to be done next.

17

THE MORNING OF June 8, Juan Givell was praying. His lucid moments were so intermittent that when consciousness overcame the abyss of nothingness, he seized on prayer; it was his only consolation.

In his room at the nursing home, his mind began to drift again. He was kneeling at the foot of his bed before a simple wooden cross.

First thing that morning his mind had been sharp, so without wasting any time, he spoke at length with Father Jonás. He told him everything, absolutely everything he could remember.

Someone knocked on the door but Juan didn't answer. He knew he was about to fall back into the abyss, knew his mind was starting to wander. The sound of knocking on wood was like an echo. It sounded so far off. The door opened.

"You have a visitor . . . It's a friend, Juan, from when you were a little boy," said the night-shift nurse before leaving.

The old man was suddenly alert. A whirlwind of images and memories flooded over him. He looked into the nurse's eyes, and she bowed her head, looking away.

She was one of them; he had no doubt. They'd found him.

He knew his time was up. He'd been waiting for this. He'd been afraid of that inhuman, murderous look for so long, the look that had stalked him since childhood. Ever since the day they'd killed the master, right there on the street.

Someone walked in and the nurse closed the door behind her, slowly, lowering her eyes submissively before the visitor.

"Asmodeus," the old man murmured, his eyes blank.

"It was only a question of time until I found you."

The old knight knew it was the end.

"I finished with you a long time ago," the old man said, as if to himself. *Evil always has the same face,* the knight recalled his teacher telling him often.

"But not with evil. You know that, don't you?"

Yes, he did.

"Take off your mask. I want to see your new face. See who you are now."

"We always have the same face. We persevere. We're immortal."

No, evil wasn't immortal. That's why he'd guarded the secret for so long. That's why this ghost was here. Because evil is afraid. Because it is in danger. Yes, it was the same face. But a different killer. They'd come for him. They were scared, the old knight thought.

"We found you, Juan. As I said, it was only a matter of time. In fact, we've known everything about you ever since the master died. We could have finished you off long ago, but we want the secret. Did you tell her?"

The old knight knelt and prayed.

"Our Father who art in heaven, hallowed be thy name. Thy kingdom come. Thy will be done, on earth as it is in heaven—"

"Heaven will do nothing for you; I've come to kill you. Did you tell the girl? Did you tell her where you hid it?" he asked, interrupting.

But the old knight kept praying.

"Did you tell Jonás?"

The name sounded vaguely familiar. Jonás?

" . . . thy will be done, on earth as it is in heaven," he continued.

The killer looked into his eyes and realized the old man had sunk back into his darkness, to a place where he couldn't hear him.

"Crazy old fool," he said angrily. "Where are you?"

But the old knight couldn't hear him.

" . . . this day our daily bread," he recited, lost in another world.

Asmodeus was too late. The knight had passed it on. Now it was her.

"You're of no use to me now," he said scornfully.

He opened the door and looked both ways: the hallway was empty. The stairwell was at the far end.

Asmodeus grabbed the old man by the arm. The knight got up and let himself be led meekly along as he finished his prayer. They walked slowly to the top step. Then the man gave him a hard rap on the back of the head and pushed his lifeless body down the stairs.

He tumbled down, rolling over and over, until he finally came to a stop at the bottom. Asmodeus strode down the stairs, pushing the old man out of his way with one foot. The old knight's face was like a newborn's. It registered no pain, only peace, as if he'd found his way. Asmodeus hated him, hated that face, hated the life that he'd extin-guished. He hated the crazy old man, hated everything he represented. His eyes exuded venom.

The nurse came back and saw what had happened. But she showed no alarm.

"Father Jonás was the last to see him," she said.

She gave him the address of the parish.

Asmodeus made a monstrous face, a mixture of disgust and resigna-tion.

He didn't say a word, just strolled out at a leisurely pace. He left like a spectral shadow.

The nurse stood by the old man. She waited there, motionless. The rest home was completely silent.

One minute. Two. And then she screamed.

18

W E'RE SO SORRY, María. This was a terrible accident." The director of the home was as comforting as he could be.

When he'd called her that morning he hadn't been sure how to break the news, so he just told her that she must come immediately, that it was urgent. She arrived fifteen minutes later, with Miguel by her side.

"Grandfather," María whimpered when she saw him.

He was laid out on a stretcher, a bloodstained sheet pulled over his body. An ambulance was waiting outside, at the home's entrance.

They'd seen it pull up when they'd gotten out of the car, and she'd feared the worst. A police car was parked beside the ambulance, a few feet away.

The judge and coroner had arrived some time ago and moved the body. It was an accident, it seemed. A tragic accident.

"It'll be OK," Miguel said, giving María a hug when he saw the tears streaming down her face.

María tried to pull herself together, to regain her composure, but she couldn't quite manage. She had to put some space between herself and the director and Miguel. She bowed her head. Both men stood there not knowing what to do. Nurses, cops, and onlookers gathered round, but

Miguel didn't notice. The director glanced over at him, trying to think of something to say. And then María returned.

"I'm OK," she said shakily.

But she wasn't.

"There was nothing we could do. He wasn't well, as you know. Lately his illness had progressed. You must have noticed on your last few visits."

"But wasn't there anyone with him? What happened?"

"We think he fell down the stairs and hit his head; that's what the coroner says." Then, by way of excuse, he added, "We do everything possible, but we can't have a nurse for each resident; please try to understand. This isn't a prison. Our guests need their space. Of course they're taken care of, but they need to feel they have a certain level of independence."

"Well, your care leaves a lot to be desired," she replied somewhat angrily.

"We have three nurses on each floor. I imagine that when the accident happened, they were all busy in other rooms. Besides—"

The director stopped himself, unsure how to say it.

"Besides what?" Miguel asked.

"The police aren't ruling out the possibility of a suicide."

"My grandfather did not commit suicide! It would never even have occurred to him!"

"Not under normal circumstances, no, but—"

"Never!" she stated firmly, the rage in her voice leaving the director momentarily speechless.

"Please try to understand. We do think it was an accident, that he fell down the stairs and hit his head. But the police . . . you know, they never discount any possibility, no matter how remote."

"My grandfather was Catholic. That possibility would never have crossed his mind, I can assure you. He was expecting a visit from me today."

The director kept his mouth shut, not wanting to point out the obvious.

"I want to see him one last time," she said, her eyes puffy, tears running down her cheeks once more.

Miguel and the director went with her to where the old man's body was. The paramedics were about to put him in the ambulance. The director signaled to them and they stopped. Beside them, with two police officers, was a short, middle-aged man taking notes on a little pad and frantically chewing a toothpick. He approached the group.

"I'm Inspector Mortimer, Agustín Mortimer, at your service. I'm so sorry for your loss," he said, removing the toothpick from his mouth.

María didn't seem to hear him. Miguel shook the hand the inspector held out. The inspector then told a policeman to lift the sheet covering the old man.

It was all too much; she buried her face in Miguel's chest.

"Don't cry; it's OK," he soothed.

"We're so sorry. This is a terrible tragedy for all of us here at the home. If there's anything you need . . . ," the director said.

She didn't reply.

"If it's alright with you, I'd like to ask you a few questions," Inspector Mortimer said.

She nodded.

"Who was the last person to see him alive?" Miguel asked the director suddenly.

"The nurse on duty, Nurse Rosario. She's an excellent professional; she's very upset by this. Someone else had called her to another room, and it seems her colleagues were all busy. All of the nurses carry pagers so the residents can contact them at any time; they have call buttons by their bedsides. That's the first thing they learn."

"I mean besides the nurse. Did he speak to anyone?" Miguel pressed.

"Let me think. Yes, of course, Father Jonás, the confessor, was the last one to see him this morning."

"Father Jonás? A confessor?" Miguel said, sounding surprised.

The name put María on guard. Jonás. What had her grandfather said about Jonás?

"We're a secular institution, but many of our residents are Catholic. So we ask Father Jonás to come. He's always willing; the man is a saint. He and Juan used to have long conversations. He was his spiritual adviser. Well, he was actually a lot more than that; they were good friends."

"And he came by this early?"

"Well, Father Jonás says mass at eight thirty. It might seem odd, but he often used to visit Juan quite early in the morning."

"Can I speak to him?" Miguel asked.

This string of questions was making Inspector Mortimer uneasy. He didn't like having his role usurped. *He* was the one who was supposed to ask the questions. Besides, all this was already in his report. Still, he didn't interrupt.

"He doesn't live here. As I said, this is a secular institute. He's in San Cristóbal Parish, in the Zona Franca neighborhood."

"He came all the way from there to hear my grandfather's confession?" asked María, who'd been following the conversation.

"Yesterday, after you left, your grandfather insisted that he come, so we called him. Father Jonás visits quite often; he's like family here."

"Could you give me his address?" Miguel asked. "He might be able to help us."

"Don't worry, we can get ahold of him; we know how to do our jobs," Mortimer said.

The inspector's irritation didn't go unnoticed. He seemed pretty hostile for someone investigating an old man's accidental death, Miguel thought.

The director, who'd been glancing back and forth between the police officer and the couple, hesitated for a moment, holding back. But he felt bad for María, so he gave her the address as if it were an apology. Mortimer glared at him, tossing his toothpick to the ground. Miguel memorized the address.

"Don't worry, we'll take care of it. Now, I'd like to ask you a few questions," Mortimer said to María.

"Would you excuse us for a minute first? I need a cigarette," Miguel said.

"Sure," answered the inspector.

They walked toward the main door, out of Mortimer and the director's line of vision.

"You don't even smoke," María said as they turned the corner.

"Can you stay here by yourself?"

"My grandfather spoke to me about a Jonás, remember?"

"Can you stay here and deal with the inspector?"

"Why?"

"Because of what you just said. I have to go see your grandfather's confessor."

"Father Jonás was supposed to help me. Do you think my grandfather might have told him something?"

"I don't know, but I need to see that priest. I have a . . ." He didn't dare finish his sentence. " . . . premonition."

He didn't like that word. He was a mathematician.

"Yeah, maybe. A premonition."

19

HE'D NEVER BEEN to the Zona Franca before. Everything he knew about the neighborhood came from literature. Las Casas Baratas was an agglomeration of hideous, square apartment buildings from the fifties and sixties that had been built to house the thousands of families who flooded in after the civil war. Spain had Europe's longest, saddest, and most wretched postwar period. When he'd read Paco Candel's novels as a teenager, both the era and the neighborhood had been indelibly stamped in Miguel's mind.

This is anti-architecture, Miguel thought. Though, of course, the building's functionality and profitability were maximal. The square and rectangular concrete towers lacked any and all aesthetic detail, and the taller they were, the more space they saved, making more money for greedy developers. They were just cells, built for laborers, *"men from Murcia with dynamite,"* Miguel thought, reminded of a verse from a famous poem. He saw where Candel had gotten the title for his book *Thirty Thousand Pesetas for a Man*, saw why those buildings had been called jails for "the other Catalans," immigrants and their descendants. *This place is* awful, he thought, driving around the block, looking for a place to park.

There it was: San Cristóbal Church, a building that looked like it had been borne of the worst social realism, built from the cheapest of construction materials. Now *that* was a church of the poor.

Finally he found a spot on Calle Ulldecona, about a hundred and fifty feet from San Cristóbal. He pulled in, parked, and was about to get out of the car when suddenly he stopped. On the other side of the street, a man dressed in black was walking toward him: shaved head, long overcoat. *The Corbel man,* he thought, knowing he was being irrational. Instead of getting out, he watched the guy, but he couldn't see his face. The man stopped, got into a black Audi, and sped off.

Miguel got out of his car, walked over to the parking meter, and took his ticket. *The Corbel man,* he repeated to himself. Then he walked the short distance to the church.

It stood in the middle of an ugly, cold-looking, rectangular cement park with a small garden. The old trees had been left, miraculously, back when bleak urban planning leveled the place. He skirted a fence and saw a few kids playing ball in the plaza on the left. The main doors of the church were locked, so Miguel went around the back. There was another, smaller door at the end of a narrow, dead-end alleyway. The park's cement walls blocked this part of the church. *It must be the sacristy,* he thought to himself. The door looked closed, so he rapped on it with his knuckles, but it gave slightly and he realized it was open.

The smell of wax and incense filled the dark room. He was momentarily blinded by the contrast between the outside sunshine and the darkness inside. Taking a step forward, he felt along the wall for a light switch, but something made him stop. Instead he waited a few seconds for his eyes to adjust to the dark. Slowly, objects took shape in the shadows. A ray of light was coming in from a crack in the wooden door, and he saw the white rectangle of the light switch. Walking over to it, he flipped it on with his elbow.

What he saw before him made him freeze in his tracks. It was too much to take in. He started trembling. He was terrified, but he had to pull himself together. He felt dizzy and nauseous all at once. He didn't think he could move, didn't think he could take one more step, toward the huge pool of blood, toward the priest's mutilated body lying before him on the ground like a shapeless sack.

Now he knew; the man in black really had been the Corbel man. There was no doubting this now.

The priest had been disemboweled, and blood was still flowing from his body. The stench of death was in the air. He looked like he'd dragged himself across the floor, trailing his guts on the ground of that small, bare-walled stone room. At the back was a round door leading to the altar. On the right was a table that held books, papers, and a computer, which was turned off. Everything had been ransacked. The doors of the armoire on the left side were open, as were the drawers, and clothes were strewn all over the floor. The opposite wall held only a crucifix.

"My God! Who would be capable of such a thing?" Miguel's legs were about to give way. He couldn't support himself, so he sank to the ground, leaning his back against the wall. He dropped his head between his knees to block out the grisly scene before him.

He tried to think. He was overwrought; he needed to distract himself somehow from the horror. Should he call the police? Get out of here as fast as possible? What was he doing here, anyway? Thankfully, María wasn't with him. Were the two deaths related? Miguel stood back up.

He had a strong urge to run, but also an instinctive need to stay. He wanted to understand. He wanted to see. But see what? He knew he might not have much time. *The police . . . Inspector Mortimer from the nursing home will surely want to talk to the priest. They can't find me here,* he thought.

His mind raced. It looked like the priest had dragged himself toward the door of the temple for a reason. The grotesque image stunned and bewildered him. It was horrible. He couldn't stop staring at Father Jonás, lying on his side. The blood was still seeping out of him. He couldn't have been dead for very long. How much time had passed since he'd seen the man in black? Ten, fifteen minutes? Twenty? Looking at the corpse, he realized its position seemed very unnatural: one arm out, fingers extended, as if he'd been trying to write something on the floor tiles. From where he stood, Miguel couldn't see, and what's more, the pool of blood was slowly expanding, taking up more and more space. If he *had* written something, it would soon be obliterated. Miguel's fear was overwhelming.

Was it possible that the man in black had killed María's grandfather as well? Was he the man who'd committed this brutal crime? Had someone at the home told the killer that Father Jonás was the last person to speak to the old man? Questions raced through his mind.

He moved forward gingerly, trying not to step in the blood. One step, another; now he'd have to go to the right. There was blood everywhere. Looking at the ground, he saw a lump of blackish flesh; he didn't even want to contemplate what it might be. He took a deep breath, looked toward the man's face, and bent over, carefully; it was very difficult to move with so much gore everywhere. "My God!" Miguel said aloud. The priest's eyes had been gouged out. *Who could do something like that?* he wondered again. Inhaling deeply through his nose and exhaling through his mouth, he tried to calm himself. Then he slowly turned and looked at the dead man's outstretched finger: it was bloodstained. He'd written something with it. What looked like a triangle. No, it wasn't a triangle, it was an upside-down V. And just above the vertex was what looked like a capital B with a long stem. Was it a Greek beta? Below the upside-down V was something else. He crouched down a little; it was blurry, and the pool of blood to the left was advancing on it like a sea of molten lava. The first sign was illegible—he could only see the bottom of it—but there were several more. He looked carefully; they were numbers, yes, now he could tell. Miguel was incredibly frightened, tremendously queasy, but he knew he had to memorize the numbers. Something, one, one, eight . . . then the next one was too hard to make out, it was just a stain . . . and then two more: two, two. He repeated it over and over. One, one, eight, then maybe a zero or a . . . no, it was impossible to tell; and then twenty-two.

He looked at the upside-down V again. Maybe it was actually an upside-down Y with a very short stem. He stared at it; the symbol reminded him of something. Something he'd held in his hand many times, back when he was a student, when he used to draw. He searched his mind, adrenaline coursing through his veins, his heart pounding. Finally he had it: a compass. It was a compass. He was sure of it. With a beta above it. Now he had to memorize the numbers: . . . 118 . . . 22. Whatever came first and fourth was illegible. He looked closer and said to himself, "The first one is bigger; it could be a symbol, or maybe a five and a letter."

The pool of blood continued spreading across the floor, flooding it, erasing everything. He had to get out of there, and he had to do it carefully. *Good God, how much blood does one body have?* he wondered. He tried to jump the pool but didn't manage to clear it, and when he took another step, his red footprint was clearly visible on the ground. By the time he reached the door he was frantic and, without realizing it, rested his hand on the door frame before rushing out.

As he strode quickly to his car, he repeated the string of numbers to himself. The children who'd been playing ball were gone. There seemed to be no one on the street at all. He rushed to his car, opened the door, and got in.

Taking a deep breath, he opened the glove compartment, where he always kept a pad of paper and pen. Leaning on the wheel, he sketched the signs and numbers the priest had drawn in his own blood. He duplicated them as well as he could. Maybe it was a message; it could be something that revealed the identity of the killer. Yes, that might be it. But what did it mean? What was Father Jonás trying to say?

He put away the paper and inserted the key into the ignition.

A police car approached on his left and then stopped a few meters ahead of him. Before ducking down he saw a toothpick fly out of the driver's window. The inspector! It was Mortimer. He hid. Indeed, it was Mortimer, his assistant, and another officer. They got out and headed toward San Cristóbal Church. Miguel waited a few seconds, until they were out of sight. Then he started his car and pulled out. As soon as he got to the corner he accelerated. That was when it hit him. *Damn it, I think I touched the door. My fingerprints must be all over the place,* he thought, panic stricken. He felt sick. And his shoes. He'd have to get rid of them.

20

EDUARDO NOGUÉS BENT to pick up the toothpick his boss had just thrown on the floor. It was the third one that day. All he needed was for Mortimer to contaminate the crime scene; it was bad enough as it was. A complete mess. This wasn't just a crime; it was an atrocity.

The forensics team had been working for a couple of hours and they'd already given their preliminary report.

"So, what do we have?" Mortimer asked. He was extremely tense.

"Anything wrong, boss? You seem a little uptight."

Eduardo Nogués was completely unflappable, the kind of guy who'd eat lunch during an autopsy. But Mortimer was in no mood for jokes. *Why the hell would the killer leave the lights on?* he wondered.

"Whoever did this was a total psycho."

"Nogués, stop trying my patience and just give me the facts."

"Well, it looks like the ol' padre here—"

"Show some respect, Nogués," Mortimer said, cutting him off.

"They disemboweled him. But they did it slow, like they enjoyed it. And they gouged his eyes out. But the priest, maybe because he *was* a priest, miraculously had time to say an 'Ave Maria.'"

"What do you mean?"

"I mean, after what they did to him, it's a miracle he was able to drag himself across the floor. He was still alive when they left, there's no doubt about that. See? That's where he started . . . ," he said, pointing.

Mortimer held his breath and swallowed. His mind seemed to be elsewhere.

Nogués was used to these moments, to his boss losing concentration, and he said, "Why don't you just take up smoking again? I highly recommend it. Chewing all those toothpicks can't be good for your teeth, believe me."

"Enough with the advice," the inspector said, before ordering him to continue.

"He got this far and . . . well, there's blood everywhere; it's like he was trying to tell us something. Maybe the photos will give us a clue. But the second guy did a good job of contaminating the evidence."

Mortimer was just about to toss another toothpick when Nogués said, "Don't do that, boss."

Mortimer paid no attention and threw the toothpick, which Nogués caught in midair.

"Second guy?" Mortimer asked curiously. "There were two?"

"Well, I don't know if they were both murderers. The footprints seem to indicate that someone got here later."

"How do we know?"

"That there were two? By the shoes. We have two different prints. The second one left very clear footprints. I'm thinking they weren't together, that someone else came in afterward, saw the stiff, and took off like a shot. Must've scared the living shit out of him."

"Speak right, Nogués. You're a real cop, not an actor on *Law and Order*."

"Sorry. It's the movies, you know? You see enough and you start talking like one."

"What about the motive. Any ideas?"

"I don't know what to think. No one caught stealing the alms box would do something like this. You think this murder could be related to the old guy at the home? The priest was his confessor, and he was the last one to speak to him."

Mortimer made no reply.

21

"YURI, YOU HAVE to do me a favor," Bru said.

Yuri said he'd be there in half an hour. Some things couldn't be discussed over the phone. Bru didn't trust that gang of lunatics he'd financed. He didn't do it because he wanted to but because, deep down, he was a man of his word. And you have to keep your promises, especially to family. But he wanted the notebook. If that diary contained any information that would give him power, he wanted it. Besides, he didn't trust Asmodeus, and he definitely didn't trust his henchmen. They were all crazy.

Jaume Bru was fifty-eight years old. That hadn't always been his name. He'd changed it when Franco died in 1975 and his politico friends convinced him that, to adapt to the times, it would be good to switch from Jaime—a Spanish name—to Jaume, the Catalan version. Personally, he didn't care one way or the other, just like he didn't care which party was in power; he was one of the city's richest men, and he backed them all.

His house—an enormous mansion—was a catalog of splendors of the past and present, a veritable compendium of his lineage. Modernist furniture, figurines, sculptures, and priceless paintings were everywhere.

His family had been patrons of the Catalan *Renaixença*. They could afford it: they had businesses in Cuba before the disaster, factories in Barcelona's Poble Nou. It was all thanks to the shameful origins of their fortune: the slave trade, until the eighteenth century. In the mid-nineteenth century they legitimized by trading in cheap labor.

When Spain lost Cuba it was a catastrophe for the Bru family business. Weakness and incompetence in Madrid's government, war with the United States—it was all a painful economic blow for them and other entrepreneurs. But the Bru family always came out on top. By the beginning of the twentieth century, Marcos Bru, his grandfather, was hiring gunmen to deal with the damn workers at his factories who'd embraced anarchy and were posing a threat to the fortune the family had amassed during World War I. His boats might not have been transporting slaves anymore, but they were certainly trading with all of the countries embroiled in the dispute. They needed merchandise, and under the flag of a neutral country, Bru supplied them all. And the Brus were totally unscrupulous. By the time World War I ended, their fortune had tripled, and they weren't about to let a bunch of agitators and malcontents jeopardize the stash they'd been hoarding for centuries. The city was theirs, because they'd bought and paid for it. They put in regular appearances at the Equestrian Circle, the Palau, the Liceo Theater, the Chamber of Commerce, the Employers' Association, and their involvement helped keep those organizations afloat and helped to showcase the Brus' class and economic splendor.

When Madrid's politicians were unable to put a stop to the violence that had erupted in Barcelona, Marcos Bru ordered Catalunya's captain general to take control of the situation.

Peace was short-lived, and even then it was incomplete. A few years later, Bru also funded the operation that would bring another general in to lead a military uprising. But he couldn't get out of Barcelona in time; he was trapped by circumstance. He'd known that would be the case. For three years he stayed locked up in his house in a Republican zone, and no one—no communist, militiaman, or anarchist—dared go near him. Marcos Bru finally emerged on January 26, 1939. He stood in the street on Avenida Diagonal like he was an ordinary citizen and raised his arm in a decisive fascist salute. Then he wept. Three years. Three long years without going outside, without walking down the streets that had been his. Marcos Bru wept with an emotion comparable only to what he felt when his beloved wife died. She was a grand woman: attractive, Catholic, and sentimental. Chorus girls, working girls, prostitutes, they were something else entirely. They were like cava—when the bottle's empty, throw it away and get another one. But his wife, she was a saint. His vices he saved for the others.

Franco's dictatorship had been brilliant for the Bru family business.

Jaume Bru's father was worthy of his lineage and got along famously with the general, who hated politics.

Jaume Bru—son of José Antonio Bru, personal friend of Generalissimo Franco and a member of his parliament—was the last of his caste. He'd been educated at the German School—his father was a Germanophile during the war and his grandfather paid to stage some of Wagner's works at the Liceo. He had finished his studies in England. His mindset and way of being and seeing the world was an exact replica of his father's; he lived up to the nickname that had been given to the men in his family for generations: the Tiger.

Jaume Bru looked out over the city and realized it was still his—not just Barcelona but four others, too. That was the way it had always been and always would be. New York, London, Paris, and Barcelona. That hadn't changed.

Jaume Bru was a clever man, and in addition to his legitimate dealings, he also kept up the family business. The fall of the iron curtain had been providential. Bru supplied young flesh to whorehouses not only in Barcelona and all over the Mediterranean coast, but to every major European city as well. His dealings with the Russian Mafia were just the logical continuation of his family's slave-trading past. Globalizing his business had been a piece of cake: Chinese, Thai, Burmese, and Japanese girls filled his brothels.

"My girls are clean, they're young, and if they have to be, they're very nasty, too. You'll like them," said Yuri, one of his associates.

"That's great, but we have to get rid of the ones that are too young; you know I only want real women. We're not a family of savages from the Russian steppes who resorted to cannibalism at the risk of starvation. My family has history; we have principles, and we've always believed in God."

"Come on, Bru, give me a break!" the Russian retorted.

"We're lords. Pigs and lords must be well bred."

"Huh?"

"Forget it; it's a Catalan expression. You wouldn't understand."

"Whatever you say. But what do you want me to do with the children?"

"Same as always until further notice. I have an idea."

It wasn't a new idea; in fact, it was a family tradition he wanted to revive. Why hadn't it occurred to him before? That was when he started the farms. He had three in Africa and one on the Catalan coast, in the Maresme. That was all he needed. They took all of the young girls and boys, and those who were healthy were fed and taken care of for years; they even received a basic education and learned the language of the country they'd be going to. It could take five to ten years for them to be introduced into the market—five for the youngest, who went into the porn industry. The lucky ones were sold into clandestine brothels.

That was how things stood when Jaume Bru walked out onto his huge terrace. He looked out over the city. It still belonged to him and a handful of others. That's what he was thinking when she walked out, shed her clothes, and dove into the pool that took up most of the terrace. Bru walked over to the edge. She swam to him, still underwater, and then emerged like an Asian mermaid, giving Bru a kiss.

"Hi, boss," Taimatsu said.

"I'm not your boss. You're your own boss and you can stop working whenever you want."

"No chance. Half my life is wrapped up in the foundation."

"I thought I was your life."

"You're the other half."

"I'm too old for you. You only love me for my money."

Taimatsu's beauty was almost feline. She looked like she was about twenty years old. Bru was almost twice her age.

"Don't be ridiculous. My uncle has more money than you. I love you because you're good, fun, sophisticated, handsome, elegant—"

"Alright, alright!"

"And besides, you own the foundation that means the world to me."

Taimatsu was the director of the Friends of Modernism Foundation, which was founded and subsidized by Bru Property Development and Contractors, SA, one of the leading businesses in the field, with subsidiaries in the Czech Republic, Hungary, Poland, and other Eastern European countries. Jaume Bru had bought a Modernist building on Calle Bruc, between Provenza and Mallorca, to serve as the foundation's future headquarters.

Taimatsu didn't know much about his other business dealings, or about her uncle Yukio's, either. Ever since she was a little girl she'd lived in a bubble. She was an art historian, an expert in Catalan modernism. She came to Catalunya for the first time when she was ten years old; her aunt and uncle had purchased a house in Cadaqués through Bru Property Development. Taimatsu assumed that had been the start of her uncle's friendship with Bru. She and her aunt and uncle spent the summer in Cadaqués; sometimes Bru would show up as if he'd been invited. And she fell in love with him. She'd moved to Barcelona two years ago to take charge of the foundation. Her uncle put up no resistance, though of course he knew nothing of the clandestine relationship between his niece and the Catalan mafioso.

Barcelona was her second love. She was absolutely spellbound by the city. She had a fabulous apartment in the trendy, bustling Gràcia neighborhood, which was full of cafés that she loved because they were always crowded with fun, interesting people. And the Verdi movie theater, which showed foreign films, was there, too, so sometimes she got to see movies in her native Japanese. Taimatsu was happy; she had a job she loved, and she lived in a city filled with the works of the best architect of all time. And her feelings for Bru just kept growing. To her, the mature, attractive man was a benefactor and the nicest man in the world. She was truly in love. To Taimatsu, he was the perfect representation of the Catalan people's drive and the Catalan bourgeoisie's love of art. They were people to admire, a society of entrepreneurial, philanthropic, educated princes who, she felt, had a connection to the Japanese idea of how life should be lived. Bru found all this quite amusing.

Yuri's arrival was announced.

"Let him wait," Bru said. "Can we have lunch together?" he asked Taimatsu.

"No. I made plans with a friend."

"Who?" He regretted the question as soon as it was out of his mouth. He knew she hated feeling controlled. But that wasn't why Bru had asked. He just wanted to know everything about her.

"María. María Givell. We just met recently, but we've become good friends. She's doing some work for the foundation. You don't know her."

Taimatsu was wrong about that; he did know her. Bru, one way or another, knew everything, or almost everything, about the people who worked for him.

"I'm a little nervous; it's almost opening night."

The Friends of Modernism Foundation was soon to be inaugurated.

"Don't worry; everything's going to be great."

"I have to go," she said, leaving after giving him a kiss.

Yuri walked in a few minutes later.

Bru shook his hand and said, "I need you to do me a favor."

22

H E WALKED IN anxiously, donned a black tunic, and approached the altar where Asmodeus awaited him. The man bowed his head before his master as a sign of submission and respect.

"What do you want?" demanded Asmodeus. "If you requested a meeting with me, it must be serious."

"It is," he concurred nervously, adding, "Bitru's gone too far. I don't like that guy. He's a bloodthirsty psychopath. Top brass wants an investigation. Things can be taken care of at the nursing home, but at the church, with the priest . . . He went too far."

Asmodeus signaled for Mortimer to remove his hood. He did, though without daring to look Asmodeus in the face. That mask was intimidating.

"Father Jonás was one of *them*. You know how this goes. They have to be disemboweled, their viscera must be removed. That's the way it's always been. They do it to us, too; you should know that by now."

"Disembowel us?" Mortimer asked in horror. He hadn't counted on that when he joined the sect. What he remembered from his initiation was the mask, in particular, and the ring with the black pentagonal stone that Asmodeus made him kiss.

"I mean they kill us, you imbecile. When they get the chance to finish one of us off, they don't think twice."

"That's not the same; it's just not the same," the inspector replied.

Asmodeus didn't want to get into an argument about the particulars of murder with a subordinate.

"Juan Givell managed to fool us, to infiltrate our organization. And we failed to recognize the traitor. We'll show them no mercy."

"But this could jeopardize the mission; the final objective is what matters, and right now we have nothing," Mortimer countered, not daring to raise his voice.

"I'm sure you'll manage to take care of things. I have faith in you; if you show progress, you'll move up."

"Well, this damn psychopath has complicated things. He had a field day with Jonás, but then when the idiot left, the priest was still alive."

"That's impossible."

"Nogués, the agent with me, said it was a miracle."

"I don't understand. Bitru isn't stupid; he uses his brain, and he's the best killer there is. Nature blessed him with that virtue. I've never—"

"Believe me, he was alive. Not for long, but he was. And there's something else."

"What is it? Out with it."

"When we got there, the light was on."

"The light? Impossible. Bitru never turns on the light, he can't stand it. Besides, this was a ritualized execution; darkness is essential. Are you sure about this?"

"Absolutely positive."

"Then—"

"It gets worse. There's proof that someone else was there."

"Well, perhaps our butcher did get a little carried away; that doesn't bother me. But he always works alone. I don't understand; everything was perfectly orchestrated. This makes no sense. Alive? And with the light on? Did you get there—"

"Yes," Mortimer cut him off. He realized immediately he should have waited for his lord and master to finish his question. "I got there half an hour after the execution, just as we planned." He paused for a moment and then continued. "Obviously, it was in that interval that someone else was there and must have turned the light on. Personally I think Bitru screwed it up."

"I see. He might be a savage, but he'd never leave a light on. So someone else must have been there right before you. Do you think they saw anything?"

"I don't know. I need to go over the photos again. The priest dragged himself across the floor, and his hand was outstretched. He might have written something that was covered by the pool of blood. Looking at the infrareds all I could see were some strange-looking marks. It's pretty blurry, but I did recognize one that could have been the symbol, with some numbers below it. I need to go back over the prints and analyze them thoroughly, but it will take a few hours."

"Do you think the priest could have given us away?"

"It's possible."

"If that's the case, Bitru made a very grave error. He should never have left without making sure that Jonás was dead. That's unbelievable. There must be some way to take care of it."

"Right now the chances of proving a connection between the old man's death and the priest's are slim. But I can't control everything. You know how we work. If anyone else starts looking into this, they'll put two and two together and we'll be on thin ice."

"You are sure someone was there, in the church, after Bitru?"

"I'm afraid so," he said quietly.

"That mathematician is smarter than I thought."

Neither of them spoke for a minute. Mortimer knew Asmodeus was watching every move the old man's granddaughter made.

"You're doing a good job; you'll be rewarded," Asmodeus said.

"He was asking a lot of questions at the home, and the director told him that Father Jonás was the last person to speak to the old man. If you want him out of the picture, that won't be hard to arrange. We've got his prints," he said, trying to make his boss happy.

"No. That's not in our interest yet. Just put some pressure on him. Besides, after what he saw, he must be afraid by now. Our mathematician is about to enter a whole new world, and I seriously doubt he's ready for it. For now we don't want either him or the girl out of the picture. I think they might prove quite useful to us. But we have to keep an eye on them. As soon as we have what we want, we'll kill them."

"I'll do what I can, don't worry. And as for Bitru, we should take him out of commission for a little while. Don't let that idiot interfere; he could ruin everything. For now, give him a few days off. It was bad enough when those morons started shooting at the girl right in the middle of Calle Balmes."

"Anything else?"

"Yes, sir. We know they went to La Sagrada Família. One of our men followed them, and they went straight to the Nativity entrance. They spent a long time staring at the Rosary door. They were looking for something."

"The portico?"

"Yes, master. Why? What's so special about that?"

Asmodeus didn't reply. He waited a moment. Images, distant conversations, and assumptions raced through his mind.

"Nothing. What did they do after that?"

"You won't believe this. Well, they were at the Nativity Façade and—"

"Get to the point."

"They found something inside—"

"Where? Inside what?"

"Inside a tortoise. One that supports the columns."

"The tortoise!" Asmodeus exclaimed, and then added quietly, "The countdown has begun."

"Come again?"

"God's work was completed in six days, and on the seventh day he rested."

"Isn't six a sacred number for the Jews?"

"It symbolizes the six directions of space. Gaudí filled Barcelona with four-armed crosses; he crowned nearly all of his buildings with them, to point in all six directions. The sixth day is the deadline. That's the time limit for the prophecy to be fulfilled."

"I don't understand."

"Never mind, I was talking to myself."

"Anyway, there was a box inside the tortoise."

"Yes, with a notebook inside it."

"A notebook? How do you know that?"

"That was the only thing Bitru got Father Jonás to confess as he was being tortured. We knew something about it already anyway. We knew the old man had a notebook where he jotted things down, copied drawings, sketched old shrines, capitals, vault keystones, cathedral structures . . ."

"That's all the old guy left? A notebook?"

"Yes, but imagine: he's losing his mind. He knows he's got a secret, and that he hid it, and that perhaps the notebook says where it is and what to do with it. But he can't quite remember."

"If he can't remember, why bother getting rid of him?"

"Because we found out that he'd improved the last time he saw his granddaughter. It's as if he'd been waiting for something, for his mind to unblock. We couldn't do away with him before; he was the only witness, the only one who could lead us to the secret. But not anymore. Now his granddaughter is the new guardian; we're sure of it."

"And we have to get the notebook?"

Why should he explain that to a subordinate? He didn't answer, and Mortimer interpreted his silence correctly.

"I see," he said. "We have to get it, but more important, we need to keep a close watch on the girl, because she's the one who'll be able to give us the information we need."

"Don't get ahead of yourself. I, personally, will give you the order when I'm ready; this is a race against the clock. And we need to buy time."

Abruptly Asmodeus fell silent. He was convinced that María, the old man's granddaughter, was the only person who'd be able to figure it out. All they had to do was follow her and the mathematician and strike when the time was right.

"You may go."

Mortimer bowed his head and left.

23

MIGUEL LEFT THE car in an underground garage. When he got up to street level, he stopped for a minute in front of the Casa del Libro bookstore, and then a few feet farther on again at the Jaime's bookstore window. But he wasn't actually looking at the books; he was completely distracted. Then he crossed Paseo de Gràcia and walked up the street. He'd arranged to meet María and Taimatsu for lunch at La Camarga. He didn't know whether or not to tell María what he'd seen, but with Taimatsu there, this certainly wasn't the best time. Besides, he wasn't planning to stay. He needed to be alone, to think and do some research. Should he tell the police he'd been at the scene of the murder? That he had some evidence that might be useful to them? But really, what did he have? A few numbers, a couple of symbols drawn in blood. Good God! What was all this about?

He kept walking up the street until he saw them sitting at a café just across from Gaudí's Casa Batlló.

Miguel tried to act naturally. He gave María a kiss, said hi to Taimatsu, sat down with them, and ordered a beer. They were having coffee.

"María told me what happened," Taimatsu said.

"It was a terrible accident," Miguel replied.

He realized María couldn't hide her pain. The tragic death of her grandfather and the events surrounding it had hit her so hard that she'd literally shrunk in her chair. She'd tried to cancel her date with Taimatsu, but she hadn't been able to get in touch with her. She'd spent most of the morning at the home, taking care of paperwork and arranging the burial. She looked dazed.

"How did it go with Father Jonás?" María asked tearfully.

"Fine. Turned out to be nothing. He just heard your grandfather's confession, that was all."

María realized he didn't want to talk about it, so she changed the subject. Miguel said they should meet up later since he couldn't stay for lunch because he had work to do.

"I'll just sit for a minute," he said.

"Before you got here we were talking about Gaudí. María was telling me that her grandfather was an expert on his work and that you're looking into the relationship between Gaudí's architecture and fractal mathematics."

What was she talking about? Miguel was at a loss.

"I told Taimatsu you were researching it," María prompted.

"What's your thesis? What kinds of things are you looking at?"

He had to think fast.

"Well . . . actually . . . I'm not sure yet. It's just an idea right now, not even that, really. More like a hunch based on the application of the natural growth principle of trees and branches that Gaudí seems to have applied to the columns of La Sagrada Família. And, um, you know, modulation, seriation, the repetition of shapes, especially helicoids and paraboloids. But I'm just starting; I don't really have anything yet."

"Well, when your 'hunch' is further developed I'd love to hear about it," Taimatsu said.

"So, why are the Japanese so obsessed with Gaudí?" Miguel asked, in part to change the subject, but also because he really did wonder why thousands of Japanese tourists came to Barcelona every year to visit the Reus architect's works.

"Well, our culture is closely related to Zen philosophy. All human activity, no matter how simple or simplistic, is a path toward *undo*: perfection. For us, Gaudí would have reached *satori*: illumination. Basically, he'd abandoned formality and embraced creation. Zen masters teach us that a finger can be used to point to the moon, but once you see the moon you shouldn't keep looking at your finger. Gaudí built houses, buildings—fingers to point to the stars, heaven, the spirit. But we keep looking at the finger. Maybe that's one of the reasons why after Gaudí, no other architect ever followed his lead."

"Very interesting theory. Too deep for a Westerner. Here we're much more superficial. But Gaudí wasn't actually the only one—"

"Don't make fun of me!"

"I'm sorry, Taimatsu, I wasn't making fun. I believe in Gaudí. His buildings are like a reflection of nature, they're like rocks, groves . . . They remind me of Japanese gardens and houses, actually. Especially the way he creates such intimate spaces, like shadows from enormous trees, full of chiaroscuro."

"You're right. Gaudí understood the importance that my culture places on the use of reflection, nature, and craftsmanship. In the West these are considered low art—crafts. In Japan it's all high art. Flower arranging—ikebana—or bonsai, for example. Or our great tradition of masks and puppet theater . . . Anyway, Gaudí improvised; he was always right there with the master builders, assistant architects and draftsmen, and especially the master artisans: the metalworkers, stonecutters, and sculptors. Though it might seem strange to you, in my culture artisans are revered as highly as artists. They're all seeking perfection in their work. So we appreciate the skill and beauty attained by often-anonymous craftsmen. And Gaudí did, too . . ."

"Maybe because he was the son of cauldron makers? I have to say, I find the Japanese conception of art a little surprising; you see it in the most unlikely things."

"You're making fun of me again, Miguel."

"No. I'm just starting to research Gaudí, you know, so I need to collect as much information as I can in order to flesh out my theory. For now, I'm interested in everything; later, I'll narrow it down. I know he evolved a lot. At one point he was very into the architect Viollet-le-Duc, who was key to the Gothic Revival. But Gaudí surpassed him; in fact, he even thought that some of the architectural solutions employed by the Gothic movement were just crutches. Natural light was really important to him. That's why he modified La Sagrada Família crypt when he took charge of the project in 1883, so it got much more natural light—which was *not* how Villar had originally planned it."

"I see you're very informed about the master!" Taimatsu said.

"Not really. Gaudí is so complex. You can't fool me; now you're the one making fun of me."

María didn't say a word, but she was surprised by how passionate Miguel seemed. She'd always thought he didn't like Gaudí at all, that he dismissed architecture as an art in the service of power.

But Miguel carried on, oblivious to the effect he was having on the two women.

"I think his work is just a question of aesthetics, that's all. Gaudí comes out of the Neo-Gothic, which was the predominant style at the time. In fact, as I'm sure you know, Villar began La Sagrada Família, the cathedral of the poor, using a conventional Neo-Gothic style. Gaudí went far beyond that. Some people criticized him; they looked down on him and accused him of using 'eclectic' architecture, a chaotic fusion of different styles. Even though he comes out of the Neo-Gothic, to a certain extent he's also influenced by Mudejar art, and a lot of his buildings have something of the Romantic, which is directly connected to nature."

"OK. I give up; your appraisal beats mine. But it's not *just* a question of aesthetics. Gaudí was very religious, especially toward the end of his life, and his architecture is a measure of his spirituality. I'm not talking about the Christian symbolism, or even hermetic symbolism. What I mean is the building itself: nature was his master. Gaudí built living buildings. His architecture is organic; it's alive."

"I think I've heard that before. Alchemists thought of the stones and metals they burned in their ovens as organic, living things, too."

They talked on, discussing different aspects of Gaudí's work and his personality, but María wasn't paying any attention. She couldn't stop thinking about her grandfather. Had he really been crazy? What if it was true? OK, maybe he wasn't a knight, but what if Gaudí really did give him a secret to hide? What could be so important that they'd kill Gaudí for it and, eighty years later, maybe her grandfather, too? Who could wait eighty years? "There are no paths," he said. "We're lost in a forest." And she was supposed to kill the beast waiting at the third gate. That was the last thing her grandfather had said to her. The beast at the third gate.

"María?" Taimatsu asked.

"Sorry. I was thinking about something else."

"María, Taimatsu was just saying something interesting: in Japan, sincerity is frowned upon. Language should always conceal something, though it should be done subtly. The Japanese find Westerners' excessive frankness troubling. Maybe that's why they like Gaudí so much. His work is so full of symbolism, things that have to be interpreted: rocks, trees—"

Taimatsu interrupted him.

"Again, they're a reflection of nature. In his architectonic language there are no straight lines; everything is sinuous, full of curves. Every detail is full of hidden meaning. He used a lot of esoteric symbols, which are sometimes virtually incomprehensible. I don't think it can all be aesthetic. It's an indirect language that has to be interpreted. You have to read the stones, the bricks, his *trencadís* style of mosaic. It's the art of suggestion, of speaking without words. That's Zen. Gaudí knew how to hide the true secret within, so each person could discover it and discover their own spirituality. His architecture, his rich symbols, are a *do*, a path toward illumination. Gaudí tells us a story, but his language never gives away the ending, the secret. He's offering the fruit so we can find out what it tastes like, what it feels like . . . What sense would it make for him to give us fruit that already had a bite taken out of it? That's the path to Zen: suggestion. The word that says nothing but contains everything. The finger pointing to the stars. We just have to look at them. I think that Gaudí's architecture is close to *suiseki.*"

María looked confused and raised her eyebrows at her friend, who explained.

"The word *suiseki* derives from *san-sui-kei-jo-seki,* which means mountain, water, landscape, feeling—"

"What is *suiseki?*"

"The art of stones. *Inochi suiseki,* art created by nature. It's very ancient, from China originally; it began about two thousand years before Christ. It came to Japan in the fifth century and quickly became very popular."

"Oh, that's right," Miguel said, making a weak attempt to recall. "I've seen a few exhibitions. They're little stones arranged like miniature landscapes."

"Yes, stones that have weathered into shapes that look like landscapes, or even the universe. A stone that calls to mind an entire landscape. A mini-cosmos."

"Is that like bonsai?" María asked, tuning in to the conversation now.

"In a way, yes," Taimatsu responded. "Bonsai is the art of growing miniature trees, and *suiseki* is like a miniature landscape. But *suiseki* is more complex and profound than bonsai, and, like I said, it's closely related to Zen, and to *sado,* the tea ceremony. The *suiseki* is a stone that's living because of the wear from the water's current; it's linked to *wasabi,* which is a very Japanese concept: looking for harmony in the universe. Gaudí's buildings, his projects, especially Park Güell, are *suiseki.* And La Pedrera, for instance, is a very clear example of what I'm talking about. It's fascinating: a building as a stone, as *suiseki,* art created by nature, like a little mirror reflecting a living landscape; for us that has very significant and evocative power."

Taimatsu was incredibly cultured, and Miguel was impressed listening to her talk. Everything she said was both profound and beautiful, but at the same time, he couldn't stop thinking that there was something else, something hidden, related to Juan Givell's story, that had trapped them in some sort of web. Killing the beast at the third gate, finding a secret—that had been María's grandfather's message; she was the chosen one. And now Father Jonás's death at San Cristóbal Church. What did Jonás know? What had he written? And how had he known that Miguel would be there? Because who else could Jonás have written that enigmatic message for, if not María? All this was flying through his mind like a shooting star through the sky. It was a disturbing series of images. San Cristóbal—Saint Christopher—patron saint of travelers. What made him think of that?

Taimatsu brought him back to the conversation, distracting him from his thoughts.

"Look where we are, for example," she said, pointing to Casa Batlló. They all turned toward the building.

"When Gaudí was working on it, his contemporaries called it the House of Bones; it looks like something out of a fairy tale, like the house in—"

"'Hänsel and Gretel'? The pavilions at the entrance of Park Güell look like the gingerbread house, too," María offered.

"Exactly! Look at the iron railings around the windows. They look like masks. Dare I say . . . Japanese masks?"

"You're right, Taimatsu! It's a style that reminds me a lot of that puppet play you took me to see: *The Love Suicides at Sonezaki.* That was such a beautiful story . . ."

"In Japan we have many types of puppet and mask theater. That play, *Sonezaki Shinju,* is performed in a style called *bunraku,* which is one of the loveliest. The puppets are very striking, and there are three people, plus a *gidayu-bushi* chanter and a musician who plays the *shamisen,* a three-stringed lute. It's the kind I like best, especially this play, which was written by Monzaemon Chikamatsu, a seventeenth- and eighteenth-century playwright often thought of as the Japanese Shakespeare. *The Love Suicides at Sonezaki* was the first *sewamono* story, which basically means it was about common people."

María recalled the story of the two lovers. The protagonists were Tokubei, a clerk in a soy shop in Osaka, and a prostitute from Sonezaki named Ohatsu. Their love, of course, was impossible. Ohatsu was desolate in Tenmaya, the brothel. Tokubei, taking advantage of the darkness, went to see her, and at midnight they left together, holding hands, unseen. They committed suicide in the Tenjim forest at dawn, and their only witness was a crow sitting on the branch of a tree. The crow's black eyes, like a dark mirror, reflected their image. The crow's savage look had stayed with María.

"Those masks scare me a little," she said.

"Why?" Miguel asked.

"Do you remember the poem 'The Mask of Evil'?"

"That's Brecht," Taimatsu said.

María recited:

> On my wall hangs a Japanese carving,
> Mask of an evil demon, painted with gold enamel.
> With sympathy I note
> The swollen vein in the brow, showing
> How exhausting it is to be evil.

Taimatsu laughed. "I think you might be getting a little carried away. I've never connected Brecht's poem to those masks."

"Well, I know it doesn't make sense temporally; all I'm saying is that they make me think of the poem."

Taimatsu didn't want to get too far off track, although she loved talking about all of the different facets of her country's theater; despite the fact that she also liked Brecht, she guided the conversation back to where she'd been heading.

"The history of Casa Batlló is interesting because in theory it was a renovation. The house itself already existed and belonged to the industrialist José Batlló. It was fairly boring when Gaudí took charge of the remodeling project in 1904. But what he did was so revolutionary that in the end it looked nothing like the original house. The main façade and the lobby, for instance, are almost new, made of Montjuïc limestone. And the wavy surface—look—was done with picks and then afterward covered with colored glass and ceramic."

"It certainly is unsurpassed; it looks like a mirror," María said.

"The idea was that the morning sun, when it hit the façade from the side, would shine, making it look iridescent, reflecting off the multicolored glass. They say that during its construction Gaudí stood on the sidewalk watching and ordered the workers to take specific shards of glass from the baskets they were in, and told them exactly where to put them."

Miguel and María had seen the house thousands of times before, but they were still astonished; people always value things more when they learn about them.

"What about the roof? All those undulations?"

"That's a headless, tailless dragon; the roof is its spine, and it ends at the cylindrical tower. It's made of big pieces of spherical and semi-cylindrical ceramic, and it changes color."

"With the light, you mean?"

"Well, yes, of course with the light, but also the color of the pieces themselves, their arrangement." Taimatsu paused and then added, "It's really interesting. The Cátedra Gaudí has a recording of Señor Batlló explaining how all the supplies were hauled up with a simple pulley, and the scaffolding was just boards and rope. They used brick, stone, and mortar."

"Do you think it would be possible to interview someone from the Cátedra Gaudí?"

"For your project on fractal mathematics?"

"Um, yeah," Miguel lied.

"Sure. When?"

"I don't know . . . As soon as possible."

Taimatsu took her phone out of her bag, walked a few steps away, and made a call. Her conversation was so brief that Miguel didn't have time to tell María anything about what had happened that morning.

"Does tomorrow at five sound OK?"

"Perfect," Miguel said. He couldn't believe how quickly Taimatsu moved.

"Great. Señor Conesa said to come to his office. We can all go to-gether."

24

A FTER LEAVING MARÍA and Taimatsu, Miguel locked himself in his office at the university. He sat in front of the computer, determined to make sense of the message Father Jonás had written in his blood. He started with some Internet searches on sects, Freemasonry, secret societies, and satanic cults. He didn't know much about symbology, but he did know that compasses were instruments used by architects, master builders, and designers, so it was no surprise that it was one of the Masons' favorite symbols.

He found several different stories explaining the meaning of the compass, and most stressed the fact that it symbolized the light of mastery and perfection. He also found references to the temple of Solomon and its architect, Hiram, who saw the secret emanating from the light of the compass—perfection. That was the thing about the Internet: it was total chaos. You start with one page and navigate from site to site until finally, if you aren't careful, you're lost—or worse, you end up finding nonsense or totally unverified information.

Miguel recalled that on top of the compass the priest had drawn what looked like a Greek beta. *What could that mean?* he wondered impatiently. Miguel's knowledge of Freemasonry was scant, because frankly, until then he'd never been interested in or concerned with

Masons. So he carefully read the most reliable-sounding definition he found:

> Freemasonry, or Masonry, is an organization defined as a philo-sophical and philanthropic brotherhood whose aims are the mate-rial and moral betterment of human beings and society, and whose structural base is formed by the lodge. Masonic lodges are normally organized administratively into Grand Lodges (sometimes called Orient Lodges).

He kept reading, taking notes, and summarizing what he'd found.

Masonic symbols were related to building and architectural tools. In addition to the compass, there were the plumb, T square, chisel, mallet, stonemason's apron, and a nine-stepped ladder symbolizing the nine steps of ascension. There was an infinite number of doctrines and rites involved, all slightly different from one another. They did all have one thing in common: their philanthropic aim, striving for individual and social betterment. The lessons Masonry taught were those of the motto of the French Revolution: liberty, equality, fraternity. In fact, those were the ideas that present-day Masonry was founded upon, al-though Masons themselves saw their roots as being further in the past, in the stonemasons and master builders of Gothic cathedrals. Their initiation ceremony and the degrees of Masonry—Entered Apprentice, Fellow Craft, Master Mason—also appeared to be fairly similar in most descriptions. All lodges had a compass as a symbol, and it was almost always crossed with a square, forming what almost looked like a Star of David. But the compass was never alone. *Why not?* Miguel wondered. Something else surprised Miguel, too, as he was trying to make sense of the chaos. All Masonic doctrines revered the Great Architect of the Universe, who was referred to as "GAU" in some rituals. GAU? . . . Gaudí? *What a bizarre coincidence,* he thought, although he was sure it was meaningless.

After a while, Miguel was disheartened and exhausted. There was so much information, and so much of it contradictory, that he found himself scrolling through pages without rhyme or reason. He'd click from one to another, adrift and overwhelmed. He was fed up, confused, and—occasionally—a little excited by some tidbit or other. But it was too big a topic to research in just a few hours. There were a million and one aspects: sects, categories, degrees, rules, rituals. It was a very intricate world, hard to understand or gain access to, veiled in an aura of secrecy that made it almost impenetrable to the uninitiated, the profane, those who were not already inside its realm. It seemed clear that Masonry's origins were based on different classical myths. Solomon's temple, cathedral builders, and before that, those who built the pyramids. But there were Templars, too, and Rosicrucians. It was an incredible mishmash, and the only thing he was sure of was that he couldn't make sense of it. It was too disorganized and ambiguous. He had nothing concrete to go on. For the moment, the drawing of the compass seemed to point to a Masonic lodge. But considering the information he had, it made no sense for the killers to be Masons. Why would an organization dedicated to universal fraternization commit the atrocious murder of Father Jonás? No. Whoever did that was a complete lunatic. If they were Masons, they were a deviant offshoot of some lodge—evil, twisted, and bearing no relation to classical Masonry. Were they just using their symbols to implicate them, or were they imbuing them with different meanings? Could it be the same organization that María's grandfather claimed had contacted Gaudí?

Miguel decided to concentrate on the number Father Jonás had written: . . . 118 . . . 22. Could it be part of a phone number? It was hard to tell. There had been some other symbol first that looked sort of like a five, but it had been bigger. Something else? A letter?

He hadn't come up with much and felt confused and discouraged. So he dove back into the Internet's sea with what he had: lodge 118 . . . 22. He waited for results. Nothing; just more confusion. Then he tried adding words to the numbers: "kabbalistic," "hermetic," "esoteric." Nothing. Pages that made no sense whatsoever, percentages, some in other languages. Finally, he turned to the books he'd checked out of the library, taking notes on Gaudí's life and work.

After several hours, Miguel was exhausted. He looked at his watch. Time had flown by.

He shut down his computer. He had to go see María. There was no way she could be alone tonight. He should be with her.

Should he tell her about Father Jonás's death tonight, when she was already so upset? What on earth was going on? What was in that damn box, anyway? What was this race that had begun?

He had to think things through before they went to meet Conesa the next day. It was all connected. He knew it, but he hadn't a clue what on earth united all of these things.

25

W E'VE GUARDED OUR secret for years, waiting for the great day to arrive. That day is nearly here. She's a clever girl; it's just a question of time. When she asks the right questions, she'll find the answers."

"We have to watch her very closely."

"Nothing must be allowed to happen to her."

"Her grandfather was one of us and he lost the secret."

"It was a mistake for him not to have shared it with us back then."

"He was the chosen one. No one could have known that in time his mind would go."

"What's done is done. Now we are close. I feel it."

"Yes, but our enemies are strong, and they are many."

"We've always had powerful enemies. The Corbel, of course. But we've lasted through the centuries. We're still here. We survived."

"But look at us now. Look *how* we survived."

"We did it the only way we could, adapting to the times, hiding in the silence of the ages."

"We're nothing compared to what we once were."

"But we still serve the same Lord, Jesus Christ. That's something many others have forgotten. We have power. We just don't use it for our benefit, like the Mafia, bankers, politicians, even priests. We use our power to continue our work, and to serve Christ."

"We can't forget, this world is a testing ground: good versus evil. The eternal struggle. And the boundary between them is a very fine line, like the blade of a knife. Fortunately, we have not been tempted to fall on the wrong side. Other brothers have, but not us. We still follow the rules of our Lord. We still defend the way of the pilgrims, of all those who venture to take the right path; our patron—Saint Christopher, the bearer of Christ—protects us, inspires us, and aids us. We are rocks, strong and hard; we are temples of resistance against temptation; we defend those humiliated and wounded by infidels."

"But now the infidels inhabit our land."

"Yes, we are surrounded by evil. Those who truly serve the Lord are few."

"That's why we must restore order. Man has not only stopped believing in God—which is a forgivable sin—he has stopped believing in himself. And that goes against God's plan: the Great Work."

"We're the last knights. We're sculpted in stone; the stones will preserve our memories, for those who know how to read them."

"Now we must pray for the soul of our brother Jonás. They found him and slaughtered him mercilessly; they gouged out his eyes, they disemboweled him. It was a ritual killing, like in ancient times. It was Bitru. He left his mark, his brutality. Jonás was prepared to withstand anything. He was an exemplary knight his whole life, loyal to the cause no matter what, even in pain, even through the heinous torture inflicted by one of the angels of darkness. Jonás knew he was going to die and he saved his strength to write a message—his last. The archangel was there. He must have the message, though he won't know how to read it; we have to help him."

"You mean he fooled Bitru and made him believe he was dead?"

"Yes. His heart stopped beating, his entrails were desecrated, but he saved his dying breath to warn us. He was the last one to speak to Juan Givell. Now we have to find the witness. We can decipher the message, but we have to act before Mortimer gets to him."

"Who is the archangel, the witness?"

"María's boyfriend, Miguel, a mathematician. We have to protect him; it's not time to reveal ourselves yet. Asmodeus will try to obtain the information at any cost. The Corbel men will take action. But we must be prudent and cautious. Miguel may not believe in us; he's a rational man, skeptical by nature. He still doesn't know this, but the guardian, the archangel, *is* acting through him."

"So . . ."

"Leave him be. If he's the one we're waiting for, he'll keep going, investigate on his own, try to get to the bottom of things, and when he does, we'll act."

"Alright. We've been sent by heaven; the great day is near."

"Precisely. The day is near. And there's very little time left."

"The day of the beast, the day of the poor. That's what Gaudí built his expiatory temple for: La Sagrada Família, the cathedral of the poor."

"The prophecy will be fulfilled. 'On earth as it is in heaven.' The skies will open; we must be alert. We'll face Asmodeus and his killers and fight to the death. If they win, darkness will rule the world. When there is no longer piety or innocence, no one to embrace poverty and achieve spiritual wealth, then all will be lost. And the angel of extermination will burn Barcelona, the new Babylon, to the ground."

"But we've waited so long. It makes no sense. This was the promised land, the Garden of Hesperides. Our grand master Ramon Llull told us when to complete the Great Work. It was all arranged; Wagner even Christianized the barbarian legend in his work."

"It was no mistake. This is the land of *Preste Juan*, John the Priest . . . The Great Work began with the awakening, the *Renaixença*. But then *they* emerged to stand in the way."

"Yes. Asmodeus. And the Great Work couldn't be completed. Barcelona, the promised land, Garden of Hesperides, became an inferno, the axis of evil, and the fury of hell was unleashed. War, death, calamity . . . the relic has been hidden for eighty years, lost in one man's memory, in his hallucinations. Now we must help the new bearer of the prophecy. She doesn't have much time."

"You protect Miguel and, if necessary, show him the next step."

There was a map; it was written, and they knew it. Social and spiritual forces combined, the bearer of Christ crossed the river of history, and the relic that had been scorned by the Pope, imams, and priests, and hidden for so long beneath the great mountain, protected by the Black Virgin, would be handed to the new architect of the poor on the day of glory. During his life he served the lords of both the earth and hell, and he ended his days wading through the river of the poor, like Cristóbal, Saint Christopher. He was the only one who knew where it was . . . Now she was the only one.

26

R AMÓN CONESA RECEIVED them the following afternoon in his office on the corner of Calle Mallorca and Pau Claris. It was a typical Ensanche neighborhood building with high ceilings, and Conesa and his partners at the architectural firm had respected the building's original structure and had not altered it much.

Conesa was about fifty years old, though he looked thirty-five. He had the appearance of a retired tennis pro and wore an elegant suit. His voice was deliberate, his manner suave, and it was obvious that things had gone well for him. He was a man who did what he liked and spoke passionately about his work. Conesa was one of the most notable members of the Cátedra Gaudí and a great admirer of the genius of Reus, the architect whose life and work he knew like the back of his hand.

He greeted the visitors cordially, asked them to sit down, and offered them a drink; all three politely refused.

"So, Taimatsu told me you're interested in looking at Gaudí's work from the perspective of fractal mathematics. That's a very interesting and very timely topic; in fact, I think it was a French mathematician of Polish origin who—"

"Yes, Mandelbrot; he was the one who defined fractals in 1975," said Miguel. "Fractal math studies the irregular shapes found in nature—

clouds, leaves, landscapes—and also infinitely repeated patterns that are reproducible on any scale."

"Gaudí thought of himself primarily as a geometrician, and nature is always present in his work, so I guess there could be parallels between his organic architecture and fractal geometry, I don't know . . ."

"Well, there are two kinds of fractals: mathematical and natural. I think Gaudí used them both in much of his work. Columns shaped like trees, helicoids, spirals . . ."

"Very interesting. A new field to be investigated."

"Yes. But I'd like to have a more holistic, but concise, vision of the master before I really get started."

"Well, I don't know if I can help you, but I'll be happy to try to answer any questions. What would you like to know?"

Miguel wasn't sure where to start. He was going to say he wanted to know everything, but that would have been too vague for someone who, in theory, should have come with some fairly concrete ideas and a list of questions that, frankly, he didn't have.

Conesa seemed to understand. He guessed that this rushed visit had taken the mathematician off guard, despite the fact that he'd been the one to request it. So without waiting for Miguel to reply, he sketched a brief biographical outline of Gaudí: his origins, his studies, his early work.

Miguel listened attentively.

Conesa wrapped up by saying, "Gaudí was a simple man. He loved his language and his land. He didn't follow preconceived theories but instead saw things unconventionally."

"Do you think you could tell me a little more about his early projects?"

"Well, in his early days Gaudí evolved in a way that was not only fascinating but also magnificent and innovative. After his very first projects he began to be influenced by Eastern work. When he was thirty years old, he read Walter Pater and John Ruskin. And while other architects of the day, like Lluís Domènech i Montaner, were inspired by the

German architecture in vogue after the Franco-Prussian War, Gaudí became more of an Orientalist, interested in what he saw as the exotic architecture of India, Persia, and Japan."

"Are you referring to things like El Capricho, at Comillas?"

"That, and the Finca Güell and Palau Güell."

"And don't forget Casa Vicens," Taimatsu added.

"Of course, of course," Conesa replied. "His magnificent use of colored ceramic tile there really gives it a Moorish feel—and then there's the catenary arch over the waterfall in the garden."

"And the interior," Taimatsu pointed out.

"That's right. Gaudí designed the furniture, and he used papier-mâché in his interior decorating. He was also lucky to have good partners, as he did with the Palau Güell: the painters Alejandro de Riquer and Alejo Clapés, and the architect Camilo Olivares."

"Is that where Juan Martorell Montells comes in?" Taimatsu asked.

"Yes, Martorell was fifty years old, and he was a very religious man, a good friend of Gaudí's—in fact, he ended up becoming his patron. He was the one who put Gaudí in touch with the Güells and the Comillas, and who recommended him for La Sagrada Família, too. Juan Martorell built churches and convents; he admired the writer and architect Viollet-le-Duc and his ideas on Gothic architecture. Gaudí, who'd worked with Martorell on some of his projects, learned about the Neo-Gothic movement popular at the time from him. Gaudí didn't like Renaissance architects; he thought of them as ordinary decorators. In fact, he said Gothic architecture was the most structural of all styles—though he also said it was imperfect and incomplete. Gaudí himself claimed that the proof that Gothic works were deficient was that they have more impact when they're dilapidated, ivy covered, or moonlit. Now, I won't bore you with the projects he undertook at that time; I'm sure you know all about those . . ."

Taimatsu, who was the specialist among them, gave them a quick rundown of Gaudí's work on convent schools in Sant Andreu del Palomar and Tarragona, the chapel he made for the parish church in San Félix de Alella, his modifications to work on the Santa Teresa convent school in Sant Gervasi, the bishop's palace in Astorga, and Casa Botines.

"What I *would* like to mention, though," Conesa continued, "is Bellesguard, in the Collserola mountains. A medieval house belonging to King Martí the Humane was there. It was his secretary, the great poet Bernat Metge, who suggested the name: *Bell Esguard,* which means "Beautiful View." To commemorate the last king of the Catalan dynasty, Gaudí planned a project inspired by fifteenth-century Catalan Gothic, which put forth new ideas and daring structural solutions. If you read Bassegoda's work, you'll see that Gaudí, who'd just been commissioned to build a majestic residence, turned that house into an homage to the king. Gaudí rebuilt the walls, which had been in ruins; diverted the road to Sant Gervasi Cemetery, which cut through the middle of the property; made a viaduct alongside the Belén stream; and built a castle that, as I said, was inspired by the Gothic, using semicircular arches, double-lancet and colonel's windows, and a needle-nosed tower with a four-armed cross and a ring of battlements. Which brings us to the period you're most interested in."

"His organic work," Miguel affirmed.

"Fractal, as you seem to like to call it."

"Gaudí's most creative period," Taimatsu noted.

"But also a series of failed projects. Or at least ones that didn't have happy endings."

"Yes, a real shame. I assume you're talking about the mission in Tangiers and the hotel in New York City," Taimatsu said.

"Mission in Tangiers?" Miguel asked, his curiosity obviously piqued, paying no attention to the other project.

"Commissioned by the marquis of Comillas," Taimatsu said.

"I have to tell you, we're skipping a period," Conesa said.

"That's OK, we'll come back to it," Miguel said, enthralled.

Conesa continued.

"In 1892, the marquis commissioned a project for the Franciscan

Catholic mission in Tangiers; there was to be a church, a hospital, and a school. Gaudí finished it all in a year, but the Franciscans thought it was too ostentatious. Plus, they didn't like the idea of the central tower being two hundred feet high."

"They didn't like the tower?"

"Well, my guess is it wasn't only that. Maybe they just didn't like his architectonic solutions."

"What kind of solutions?"

"Brilliant ones! Leaning walls, hyperboloid windows, paraboloid-of-revolution towers—none of which were built. Gaudí was crushed that the project was never realized."

"Shame. What a waste," Miguel agreed.

"No."

"No?" he inquired.

"After 1903, Gaudí used his designs for those towers on the Nativity Façade of La Sagrada Família."

"That's not unusual," Taimatsu said.

"Well, if nothing else, it's curious," Miguel added. "What about the other project, the New York one?"

"In 1908, two American businessmen came to see him about building a hotel. It was to be almost nine hundred and eighty feet high, with a catenary profile to achieve perfect equilibrium."

"And what happened? Why wasn't it built?"

"No one knows for sure. It seems Gaudí fell ill in 1909. But at any rate, both of those projects were vital to the final shape of the Expiatory Temple of La Sagrada Família. The elegance of the Tangiers project and the monumentality of the New York project both inspired Gaudí to build the definitive models of La Sagrada Família. He perfected his knowledge of ruled surfaces, like hyperboloids of revolution and hyperbolic paraboloids, and the columns in the church's nave."

"You said a minute ago that we were skipping a period."

"Yes. Before these projects, Gaudí realized that nature prized functionality over beauty. And that began what we call his naturalist period, which he developed by studying plants, animals, and mountains. He realized that there are no straight lines and no planes in nature, just an infinite variety of curves."

"Are you saying he didn't use blueprints?"

"I'm saying he went straight to the three dimensional, using models."

"Casa Batlló," María said. Though she knew as much as Conesa, she'd hardly said a word throughout the conversation.

"And Casa Milà," Conesa added.

"So in your opinion, those would be the ultimate expressions of his naturalist architecture?"

"Mine and that of every other specialist there is. One example from Casa Batlló would be the organic shape of the glazed pottery, and in the case of Casa Milà, the clifflike shape, a symbol of sea and land. You can also see it in the stained-glass windows of the Mallorca Cathedral and the Resurrection of Christ on Montserrat."

"Park Güell is a good example of that naturalism, too," Miguel added.

"Indeed. Gaudí adapted the curves of the paths to the topography, designed viaducts so as not to level the natural land, used the original stone from the area without even planing it down, and made use of rubble from a cave; that was where he got the colored rocks that are all over the park. As I said, this all emerged from his keen interest in nature."

"And that's extraordinary for an architect, someone accustomed to compasses and T squares," Taimatsu added.

"But he came not from a family of architects but a family of cauldron makers and coppersmiths. His father had a workshop in what's now Plaza Prim de Reus, right on the corner where the banking firm sits today. His grandfather Francisco was a cauldron maker, too, in Riudoms, a town about two and a half miles from Reus. The architect Juan Bassegoda believes that as a child, Gaudí got his sense of space right there in that workshop, seeing helicoidal serpentine tubes and warped cauldrons. He thinks he always pictured things three dimensionally and not the way architecture students are taught, supplementing two planes with the help of perspective and descriptive geometry. Gaudí, though he never bragged about it, always felt his ability to see and conceive of things spatially was a gift from God."

"So the way he worked is atypical for architects?" Miguel asked.

"Very much so. From the pyramids to I. M. Pei's new entrance to the Louvre, architects have always worked the same way: with a compass and square, projecting two-dimensional images and then using standard polyhedrons—cubes, tetrahedrons, octahedrons, icosahedrons, et cetera—to create three-dimensional forms. But Gaudí was able to observe the world and realize that those regular shapes don't exist naturally, or, if they do, only very rarely."

"In effect, he questioned the view of the elements that Plato proposed in *Timaeus,* which identifies geometric shapes with the four elements: fire, air, water, and earth," Taimatsu explained.

"And the quintessence. I see you've read your Bassegoda!"

"And García Gabarró, the first Spanish architect to write a doctoral dissertation on Gaudí's use of organic forms. But you explain it better than I do—please, continue."

"Well, according to Bassegoda," Conesa said, smiling at Taimatsu, "Gaudí saw, for example, that there was no column better than a tree trunk or the bones of the human skeleton. And that no cupola is as perfect as the human skull. And that by observing mountains you could learn to achieve perfect structural stability."

"Simple," María said.

"Simple, yes. Simplicity is genius. But first you have to visualize it, and then you have to be able to utilize it in construction. I want to show you something."

Conesa took out an envelope of photos and spread them out over the table in pairs.

"Look at this."

He pointed to one picture of La Sagrada Família and another of a plant.

"This is a *Sedum acre*, also known as stonecrop, from near Reus."

Taimatsu and María had seen the photos before. But Miguel was blown away. The plant looked like an exact replica of La Sagrada Familía towers.

Conesa continued with his series of photographs.

The next pair showed the model for the Glory Façade alongside a cave in Nerja, in the province of Málaga; they were virtually identical.

Next came a drawing of the church at Colonia Güell and a picture of Mont Blanc: they looked the same.

After that, a chimney on Casa Milà and a sea snail. Then a forest in Campo de Tarragona and the columns of La Sagrada Família.

Conesa kept going, showing more photos that demonstrated striking similarities between the Reus architect's work and different natural forms. Miguel, María, and Taimatsu, seeing the images and listening to Conesa, grew increasingly excited.

"As you can see, the work of architects who follow Euclidean geometry bears no resemblance to these forms whatsoever. But Gaudí discovered thousands of structures in the three kingdoms of nature and went on to use them in his work. That's no secret, but it's also important to note that he was very tuned in to, and had great respect for, popular architecture—after all, he was from Campo de Tarragona. Catalan stone huts, for instance, are perfectly adapted to their natural surroundings."

"So basically, you're saying the solutions Gaudí provides are geological, botanical, and zoological."

"He saw how the laws of gravity and nature create parabolic and catenary profiles in leaves, branches, and treetops. Eucalyptus trunks and some creepers are helicoidal. A lily is a helicoid, and a femur is a ruled hyperboloid. I hope I'm not boring you and that this is making sense."

Miguel might not have understood the terminology, but he got the gist. It was brilliant of Gaudí to have used those shapes to make his buildings stronger and more structurally sound. But despite how magnificent it was, that was just the tip of the iceberg, Miguel thought. He wanted to know why.

"Why?"

The question surprised Conesa.

"To continue God's work," he replied simply, without a moment's hesitation.

"Was Gaudí a Mason?"

Miguel had spoken too hastily. Maybe now the prominent authority would change his opinion of him. But it was too late; he'd already asked.

"Would a Mason use a simple line to project his works? Would a Mason scorn a T square and compass, two of the three Masonic lights? I can't see Gaudí following the directives of a secret society whose God uses a compass to draw the earth. No, I don't think he was a Mason. Gaudí was a high priest of architecture, an architecture that followed the laws of God by turning to look back at His great work: nature. He built fountains, birds' nests, anthills, stalactites, mountains, trees, rocks, plants; Gaudí turned them into towers, vaults, cupolas, columns, pillars. Gaudí said that originality meant going back to the source, and that beauty is the brilliance of the truth. And for him, the truth was represented by the Son of God."

"Is it possible that his work derived from something occult, some sort of mysterious plan?"

"I don't know what you mean by 'mysterious plan.' I suppose poets, writers, and other artists are always after some transcendental idea to form the framework of their oeuvre. Gaudí, to my way of thinking, was attempting to sublimate the spirit. What he was building was simply the house of God."

"Are you referring to La Sagrada Família?"

"To the *Expiatory* Temple of La Sagrada Família. Don't forget that part—'expiatory.' It's a temple of redemption, one he spent half his life building. No, Gaudí was no Mason or medieval builder. Gaudí believed in man's salvation through Christ, and he felt true devotion to the María, the Virgin Mary. In fact, the frieze in La Pedrera includes the invocation to the Virgin."

"*Ave gratia plena Dominus tecum,*" Taimatsu recited.

Conesa nodded.

"He was even going to put in a statue of the Virgin del Rosario, flanked by Miguel and Gabriel—the archangels Michael and Gabriel," their host concluded.

"But he didn't?"

"The life-size sculpture was cast in plaster; but that was in 1909, and with all the violence during the Tragic Week, Señor Milà didn't dare exhibit the sculptures. However, that's not the point. What I'm saying is that Gaudí was deeply religious and dedicated the last part of his life to his work, living like a monk in the temple."

"Tell me about the temple's genesis."

"The first stone was laid in 1882, on the day of San José—Saint Joseph's Day. He got the idea when the First Vatican Council proclaimed San José the patron saint of the universal church. A bookseller named José María Bocabella founded the Association of San José Devotees. Their aim was to apply the Catholic Church's social doctrine to Catalan workers. Bocabella bought what would be the equivalent of one square block of the Ensanche neighborhood, with the idea of building an expiatory temple. The architect Villar designed it for free. Then, for a whole series of reasons, Villar stepped down and Gaudí took over in 1883. Gaudí didn't like Villar's design, but it was impossible to change the church's major axis. As I said, Gaudí spent forty-three years working on it, over half his lifetime. Before he died, he finished the model of the temple and the Nativity Façade, and he made the symbols he wanted to use throughout it very clear."

"But don't you think that many of those symbols, and not only in La Sagrada Família, are somehow—"

"Esoteric?" Conesa interrupted, a hint of irony in his voice.

Miguel made no reply; he didn't want to come off the wrong way. He was a mathematician, and for that very reason, he didn't want to overlook any possibility, no matter how absurd it might seem.

"People have written all sorts of things about him. I've read—with no proof on the author's part, of course—that Gaudí was an alchemist searching for the philosopher's stone; I've read that he was an anticlerical leftist in his youth . . ."

"Let's go back to the symbols."

"The way I see it, those that are not Christian images are strictly decorative."

"Couldn't they conceal some type of message?"

"I don't know what you mean by that."

"Well, for instance, what about the *Amanita muscaria?*"

"The mushrooms? Are you referring to all those stories about Gaudí high on drugs?"

"Yes."

"Good Lord! That's complete nonsense! Have you ever stopped to look at Casa Calvet?"

"What should I be looking at?"

"At the proliferation of mushrooms on the façade, for example. He did that to please his client, Señor Calvet, who was a mycologist. So as you can see, the truth is quite simple, and it refutes both that story and a lot of other nonsense that's been written."

"What about the serpent?" Taimatsu asked.

"What serpent?"

"There's a Valencia-tile serpent's head in Park Güell."

"I'm sure it symbolizes Nehushtan, the bronze serpent on Moses's crook."

"The mystic rose?" the young woman inquired.

Taimatsu knew the symbolism of all of these items, but she was curious about Conesa's opinion and she wanted Miguel to hear it from a renowned specialist.

"Symbol of the virginity of María, queen of heaven and mother of Jesus Christ. It's on La Pedrera."

"The labyrinth?" she pressed on.

"In medieval cathedrals they're known as 'chemins à Jerusalén'; they were seen as a substitute for the pilgrimage to the Holy Land when the faithful went through them on their knees while praying. The one at Chartres Cathedral is forty feet wide with a path six hundred and fifty-five feet long."

"The lizard?"

"The rising sun of justice: Our Lord Jesus Christ. Symbol of death and resurrection."

"The tortoise?"

"Saint Ambrosius said you could make a seven-stringed musical instrument of its shell whose sound would delight the soul. It represents peaceful strength and the search for protection against outside enemies. The stone tortoises, like the ones on the Nativity Façade that bear all the weight on their backs, for example, guarantee stability in the world. There are two."

"The pelican on La Sagrada Família?"

"In alchemy there's a type of vessel called a retort that's shaped like a pelican, and it's also an image for the philosopher's stone, which, when submerged in molten lead, melts and transforms into gold."

"Plus, the Rosicrucian knights were known as 'Knights of the Pelican,'" Miguel said.

"Not bad, but I prefer the relationship it has to the image of Christ's sacrifice. In the *Bestiary* there's a medieval hymn that includes the words *'Pie pelicane, Jesu Domine.'* Which means, essentially, 'Pious pelican, Lord Jesus.' And it mentions that pelicans eat only what is strictly necessary for survival, 'like the hermit, who eats only bread and does not live to eat, but eats to live.' Doesn't that sound like the last stage of Gaudí's life—a hermit locked up in his studio finishing his great work?"

They all fell silent for a moment, reflecting on Conesa's words. But then Taimatsu resumed her interrogation.

"The rainbow?"

"Yes, the rainbow can be found on Casa Vicens. Gaudí's idea was that if the water spraying out of the marble-basined fountain hit an elliptical reticule, like a spiderweb, it would create warped sheets that would break down into the colors of the rainbow when the sun's rays hit them."

"Well, that's the technical explanation, but—"

"In Genesis 9:11, the Covenant of the Rainbow, God says that there will be no more floods. It's a divine symbol, a benevolent one. The Judge of the World is often represented enthroned on the rainbow at the end of time. In the Middle Ages, in Christian symbolism, the three main colors of the rainbow were seen as images: blue, the flood; red, the fire of the world; and green, the new land. The seven colors represent the seven sacraments and the seven gifts of the Holy Spirit. And they also represent María, the Virgin Mary, who unites heaven and earth."

Miguel and his two companions were astonished at how knowledgeable and erudite Conesa was. Seven colors, seven knights. *Strange coincidence,* thought Miguel.

"What about the number six?" he asked.

"That's a very interesting number in Gaudí's symbolic language. The Sabbath is on the sixth day for Jews. God took six days to create the world. Saint Ambrosius thought the number six represented perfect harmony. And of course, there are the six directions in space: north, south, east, west, up, and down."

"Which brings us back to Gaudí's four-armed crosses," Miguel said.

Taimatsu kept firing questions.

"The forest?"

"Certainly a widespread symbol. In folk legends and stories, the forest tends to be inhabited by dangerous, enigmatic beings—witches, dragons, demons, giants, dwarfs, lions, bears—all the dangers adolescents have to face during their initiation into adulthood, like a rite of passage or test of maturity that has to be passed in order to leave childhood behind. The light that appears in these stories, shining through the trees, is hope. And what, if not hope, is a temple? The light shining on the path of darkness, inciting us to look up to the heavens, so we can be transformed, converted."

"The cross?"

"Of course the cross is prevalent in Gaudí's work. From a Christian perspective, clearly it represents Christ's crucifixion. It's the most universal symbol there is, and not just in Christianity. Originally it signified spatial orientation: left, right, up, down. But in addition to the quaternity, it also denotes the number five. In many cultures, the cosmos is represented by a cross. In the Bible, paradise was represented with a cross, too, for the four rivers that flow there. In Gaudí's work I think its symbolism is quite clear: it means suffering, death, and the hope for Christ's resurrection."

"The number thirty-three?"

"The age of Jesus Christ, of course. But also the number of cantos in the *Divine Comedy* and the number of steps on the 'mystic ladder.'"

Taimatsu was going to ask about the symbolism of this ladder, but another question popped out of her mouth instead, one she'd had in her mind for some time now.

"The athanor?"

Conesa burst out laughing.

"I'm sorry," he excused himself, "it's just that the athanor is one of the elements used to talk about Gaudí the alchemist. But notwithstanding, the athanor is both a fusion oven and a bread-baking oven. If you follow Jung, he believed that fire—a lit oven—represented life force; unlit, because of its womblike shape, it represented maternity. So if we go back to the children's tales, say 'Hänsel and Gretel,' for instance—"

María pricked up her ears on hearing this fairy tale mentioned.

"—the oven they use to burn the witch that wants to eat them represents the bonfire that purifies and destroys evil, leaving no material trace of it. And if we look to the Bible, the Book of Daniel tells us that only those chosen by the Lord can withstand fire, like the three boys Nebuchadnezzar threw into the furnace for refusing to bow down to an idol. But honestly, in my opinion, Gaudí uses the oven to pay homage to his origins—his father and grandfather the cauldron makers. That's all."

"Why was the staircase removed from Park Güell and replaced with a cosmic egg? In alchemy, as I'm sure you know, the philosopher's egg is what later becomes the wise men's stone—"

"The philosopher's stone, you mean," Conesa corrected.

"Yes, exactly."

"I have no idea why it was removed, but Gaudí's symbolism has nothing to do with that. Gaudí was no alchemist," he concluded, giving a comforting chuckle.

"An Easter egg, maybe? A symbol of spring?" Miguel asked.

"It could be for Easter. But what I think is that, considering how deeply religious Gaudí was, it was just another representation of Christ. By way of Christian analogy, the chick that hatches from the egg is Christ's resurrection. The white shell symbolizes purity and perfection. Nothing magical or esoteric about it," Conesa said, wrapping up.

"You don't see Christianity as magical or esoteric?" Miguel asked.

His comment wounded María. She was a firm believer.

"That depends on your individual belief; I'm not going to go into that. I won't start doubting electricity just because I can't see it," Conesa retorted, feeling his Catholic faith was being mocked.

"I'm sorry; I didn't mean to imply—"

"I know. You have nothing to be sorry for."

Taimatsu tried to refocus the conversation with her relentless questioning.

"What about the staircases? Gaudí's work is full of them."

"So are all architects' works," Conesa replied.

"But Gaudí's are the ones I'm interested in. The mystic ladder, with seven rungs, is a symbol of thirty-degree Masons within their, uh, organization."

"Yes, and in the Middle Ages each step symbolized one of the liberal arts."

"Grammar, rhetoric, logic, arithmetic, geometry, music, and astronomy. There's the number seven again," Miguel said to himself, attentive to the conversation.

"And justice, kindness, humility, loyalty, work, courtesy, and generosity," Taimatsu added.

"Yes, but Gaudí wasn't a Mason," Conesa insisted. "In Christianity, which—I repeat—is what he believed in, the ladder or stairway symbolizes the union between heaven and earth. Do you remember Jacob's vision?"

"Sure, from Genesis. Jacob had a dream in which he saw a ladder with angels going up and down it," María said.

"Yes. Though I think it represents Christ's ascension."

"With a dragon at the bottom?" Miguel asked, thinking of Park Güell.

"Well, I'm just conjecturing now, but what you're talking about could be a ladder of asceticism, whose first step is the dragon of sin, which has to be trampled. That would keep it within the realm of Christianity."

The three of them thought it was a brilliant interpretation. Conesa continued.

"But I still think, personally, that the ladders have a more Byzantine meaning, with María—the Virgin—being the 'ladder of heaven' that God descends when he comes down to earth through Jesus Christ, and that allows men to ascend to heaven."

"You're invincible," Miguel conceded.

"The beast at the third gate?" María asked suddenly, before the architect could even catch his breath.

Conesa hesitated, repeating the phrase.

"Hold on . . . Yes. I know. It refers to the dragon. I'm afraid it's the dragon again, my friend."

"The dragon at Park Güell?"

"No, the one at *Finca* Güell. Gaudí's patron bought thirty hectares of land between Les Corts and Sarrià. The land had originally been two separate properties: Can Feliu and Can Cuyàs de la Riera. When Eusebio Güell died, it was divided up. One section of it is now the gardens and palace of Pedralbes, which is part of the royal household; other plots were acquired by the university and used for the campus—in fact, the Cátedra Gaudí is housed in one of the pavilions there. Anyway, Gaudí built three gates in the wall surrounding it. One of them is by the Les Corts cemetery. The second one was demolished when they built the Faculty of Pharmacy, but was later rebuilt. The third is the main gate, the one on Paseo Manuel Girona, where, as you know, there's a dragon."

"The dragon in chains," Miguel said.

"Tied to a brick pillar with the antimony orange tree on top of it."

"And what does that mean?"

"That's Ladon, the dragon that protects the golden fruit in the Garden of Hesperides."

The Garden of Hesperides, the city of Barcelona. The dragon watching over it, María and Miguel thought simultaneously, shooting each other a complicit glance.

"We could go on and on," Conesa continued. "But the way I see it, there is nothing esoteric, occult, or mysterious about Gaudí. He wasn't a Mason, an alchemist, a Templar, a Rosicrucian, or a *carbonari*. All that nonsense is fine for novels, but the reality is quite different. The painter and architect Josep Francesc Ràfols said that Gaudí would always be incomprehensible if not seen through faith."

"The writer Josep Pla analyzes his work using a terrestrial interpretation of Catholic liturgical symbols, turning his abstractions into real, physical objects," Taimatsu said.

"Gaudí was a true Mediterranean. He was from Campo de Tarragona; his symbolism definitely isn't esoteric in the slightest," Conesa said by way of conclusion.

María, who'd been silent through most of the conversation, now spoke.

"My grandfather was a great admirer of Gaudí; he said several fires destroyed a large part of his legacy."

"He's right. That was during the Spanish Civil War. Gaudí had drawn up a will in Ramón Cantó's notary office, and it was lost in 1936, along with the rest of his legal documents, all destroyed."

"How do we know he had a will?" Miguel asked.

"Because both the Notarial School of Barcelona and the National Archives have records of it."

"But there were other fires, too," María pressed.

"Yes. Gaudí's files and desk were burned in a fire at La Sagrada Família in 1936."

"Doesn't that seem like a lot?"

"Well, keep in mind this was during the civil war. Many churches were burned. On July nineteenth of the same year, the crypt of La Sagrada Família was sacked and set on fire by a group of extremists. They desecrated the bookseller Bocabella's grave, and they would have done the same to Gaudí's if Ricardo Opisso, an old colleague, hadn't stopped them. Months later, Gaudí's tomb was opened by the police because they thought it was being used to conceal arms. It was left open until January 1939, when General Franco's troops entered the city, but even they only sealed it provisionally, and it wasn't until the end of that year that the tomb was definitively sealed after they'd ensured that the body inside was actually Gaudí's."

"That's quite a story."

"Plenty of terrible things happened during the war. It was tragic.

His study in La Sagrada Família was next to the priest's quarters, above the storehouse. It was divided into three parts: the draftsmen's area, an office, and the photo lab. The ceiling was covered in plaster models of the temple. Imagine all of the things that were lost in that fire."

"How is any of this known?"

"You mean what his study was like? We have pictures that were taken ten years earlier, just after he died."

"What did he use the photo lab for?"

"Well, it seems he'd set up one central light and four mirrors that let him see the photographed image from five different perspectives: from straight on, and the four reflected versions. He was a total genius who relied on many simple solutions."

"Doesn't it seem odd that all this was lost?" Miguel asked.

"It was wartime. Do you think it was some evil spell? Powerful enemies jealous of his brilliance?"

"Well, I just don't think we should overlook any possibilities."

"My friend, Gaudí had no enemies. He was a saint. He lived with his father and niece in different places, including Park Güell, until they died. Then a year before his own death, he moved into La Sagrada Família and poured his heart and soul into the project. Some say he lived with a child. I don't know. But what's certain is that Doctor Santaló and the sculptor Llorenç Matamala were the only ones to visit him occasionally, on Sundays. He lived humbly, simply, like a monk. The caretaker's wife prepared his meals. He had no enemies aside from the stupidity and violence of an uncivilized war that destroyed part of his legacy."

27

OW ARE YOU going to tell me what this is all about?"
Taimatsu asked as soon as they left Ramón Conesa's office.
She had the feeling her friends had not been entirely forth-coming with her.

María and Miguel glanced at each other, and María nodded.

"OK," Miguel said. "But not here. It's a long story."

"Let's go to my place," María said.

Taimatsu glanced back and forth between the two of them. Never in a million years could she have imagined what they were about to tell her.

"Taimatsu, you don't have to get involved in this; it's not too late. It could be dangerous," Miguel said.

"I want to. We're friends, aren't we?" she replied, speaking to María and looking for confirmation.

But María didn't reply.

"Besides, I'm an expert on this period, and I love Gaudí," she concluded, smiling.

"Well, the information we have isn't ever going into a doctoral dissertation," he stated.

"Well then, we'll write a good novel," she retorted jokingly.

"Taimatsu, this is really crazy stuff. If this were a novel, the reader would have to seriously suspend disbelief. In fact, I think maybe we should go to the police."

Taimatsu didn't want to discuss literary theory or the genesis of the popular novel; that wasn't her thing. "Miguel, all you're doing is making me more curious. Please, I'm dying to know. Just tell me!"

So Miguel gave her a brief rundown of the story that ended with Father Jonás's murder.

"Murder? My God, this is getting interesting!"

"Brutal murder. Let's go to María's. We'll fill you in on all the details while we walk. But I want to show you something first."

They stopped in the middle of the street. Taimatsu couldn't hide her curiosity.

"Before he died, Father Jonás wrote this on the floor, in his own blood."

Miguel took out the drawing he'd made of the message. María looked frightened. She was trembling, just as she had the day before when she'd seen it for the first time. Miguel comforted her.

"What's wrong?" Taimatsu asked.

Falteringly, María responded, "My grandfather mentioned Father Jonás the day before he died . . . He said that Jonás had to tell me something . . ."

"So then, what it says on that piece of paper—"

"Yes. This is the message," Miguel replied, interrupting anxiously. "But we don't know how to decipher it."

Taimatsu looked at it carefully, repeating, "The letter beta from the Greek alphabet . . . A compass and part of another sign with a number: 118 . . . 22 . . . Well, I have no idea what it means."

They kept walking and brought her up to speed on everything that had taken place.

María was terrified. Father Jonás's death had convinced her that she'd been right about her grandfather having been murdered. Her poor grandfather. And she'd been chosen, but she had no idea what for. She did know that it meant her life was now in danger and she didn't have much time.

"Don't be scared, María, we're all in this together," Taimatsu said, comforting her.

"Yeah, together against murderers who wouldn't think twice about killing me. I can't let you get involved."

"It's too late. I already am," Taimatsu replied.

Miguel didn't say anything. He just gave María his hand, which she held tightly as they walked.

When they got to her house they went straight to the study and sat down at the table. Turning on the lamp, they showed Taimatsu the box they'd found inside the tortoise.

"We don't know how to open it," María said.

"And we don't want to force it," Miguel explained.

"Because that could destroy whatever's inside," María finished.

Taimatsu took the box and ran her fingers over the raised numbers on the lid.

"What did your grandfather say when you showed him the box?"

"Nothing; he was completely out of it."

"Well, actually, he just kept repeating the same sentence over and over," Miguel recalled.

"What was that?"

"'The master's death.' He kept repeating it," María said.

Taimatsu held the box, looking pensive, for a few minutes, and then her eyes lit up. Using the index finger of her right hand, she pressed down softly on four of the numbers.

And the box opened.

Miguel and María were astonished.

"How did you do that?" they cried in unison.

"It's . . . elementary. He told you himself: the master's death. One, nine, two, six: 1926 is the year Gaudí was killed," Taimatsu said with a triumphant smile, handing María the box.

It wasn't that they were disappointed, but the little blue notebook with a couple of thirty-two-page pads of paper wasn't exactly what they'd been expecting. And the medallion on a leather cord wasn't overly impressive, either. It didn't look very old and was about the size of a two-euro coin, with the letter alpha on the front and a bird engraved on the back.

And that's all the cedar box contained.

María put the medallion on while Miguel leafed through the notebook, trying to find some meaningful phrase. There were drawings done in pencil, and some others were in color. From what he could tell, María's grandfather had been a decent artist.

"It looks to me like your grandfather spent a lot of time copying miniatures from medieval books."

"They must mean something. What else is there?"

"Writing—longer texts, some with dates. Looks like memoirs. And some short phrases, aphorisms, some in Latin," he said, flipping quickly through the pages.

"Let's read it," Taimatsu proposed.

Suddenly María burst into tears. She'd been holding her pent-up emotions in for hours, but she couldn't contain them any longer.

Miguel held her.

"Do you want to go lie down?"

"No. I'm fine. I want to know what's in there, too," she said, wiping away her tears with the back of her hand. "I'm fine," she repeated.

Feeling both excited and uneasy, the three of them prepared to read María's grandfather's diary. They decided to take notes, analyzing as they went.

María, hands trembling, opened it to the first page and began to read.

THE DIARY

Now, at the end of my sinner's life, gray and decrepit like the world, I await the moment when I'll finally be lost forever in the bottomless abyss of my memory, which grows more and more silent. So with what little light I

have left in this room, in this beloved residence, while my tired, sickly body
can still support me, I have resolved to record the shocking and terrible
events I witnessed as a child, to prevent the Antichrist's arrival and so that
you, my dear, may fulfill the prophecy that was announced to me.

Lord grant me the grace to give faithful testimony to the events that
occurred in this city; I cannot draw a veil over her name: Barcelona.

In order to better understand what I was involved in, you must try to
envision what was going on in those decades just as I saw it at the time, by
living through it, just as I relive it now. I pray my memory is able to make
sense and tie up the loose ends of so many confusing facts.

I'm going to tell you about the master, whose sometimes excessive
intellectual pride God forgave. At the time it was only normal that boys of
my age looked up to older and wiser men, and he gave his secret to me to
give to you, so that you could fulfill the prophecy entrusted to the members
of our family. I'm going to write some of this in code; I hope you'll be able
to decipher it so you can carry out the mission for the greater glory of Our
Lord Jesus Christ and to give the needy their just rewards.

I arrived in Barcelona during turbulent times. For some the city was a
living hell, for others, a playground. Three years before I got here, Primo
de Rivera, captain general of Catalunya, had proclaimed himself leader
of a military directorate, which the king of Spain simply accepted. In
Barcelona, the conservatives were in favor of what they called "peace and
order." They liked the general and not only supported his military uprising
but actively participated in its genesis. Primo de Rivera fraternized with
them and promised sufficient regional autonomy—to be overseen by him
and his officers—to enable burghers to keep doing business and hold on
to their wealth. It was unconstitutional; the government knew about the
plot but did nothing to suppress it. Conservatives all over Spain wanted
it, favored it, and worked to make it succeed. Primo de Rivera issued his
manifesto from Barcelona. The general had the unwavering support of
General Sanjurjo, Aragón's second in command, and of General Milans
del Bosch, leader of King Alfonso XIII's military household. He didn't have
the backing of all of the captains general, but he was convinced that once

the coup had taken place—considering the support he'd already garnered and the people who were already cheering him on—they'd come on board. And they did.

The only people not on his side were the workers. But after all, the military coup was against them—against the people. So what did they matter? They represented disorder; they had to be put in their place. Someone had to silence their demands regardless of their validity. One of their leaders predicted what was coming, saw everything that was going on: Salvador Seguí, who was known as the Noi del Sucre, the Sugar Boy. He planned for a general strike if the coup occurred and also tried to put an end to the terrorism of the anarcho-syndicalist trade union, the CNT. He didn't succeed. Seguí knew that with the way both sides were acting, their only achievement would be the long-term oppression of the working class. The Noi del Sucre was murdered one March evening while he was walking with a friend on Calle Sant Rafael. A gangster shot him in the back of the head while others fired guns to distract people as the killer made his getaway. Five months later the military revolt started. The general was in Barcelona and issued a manifesto, announcing that, in light of the need to save the country from the danger posed by professional politicians, he was forming a provisional military directory in Madrid. It would rule until things settled down and order was restored. Spain, he said, had to avert the chaos threatening to bring it down.

At five in the morning one day in mid-September, the cavalry emerged from the headquarters in Montesa, charged with enforcing the edict that declared a state of war. The edict gave civil command of the provinces of Barcelona, Lérida, Girona, and Tarragona to their respective military governors, who would each give their own independent orders. When Vallés i Pujals, president of the council, was interviewed by journalists about the situation, he replied, "We accept the established power, and we will obey."

At four in the morning, when the newspapers first published the captain general's manifesto, people snatched up every copy from the newsstands. Editions sold out all morning long, one after another. But the city looked the same as it had before. The only change was the soldiers on guard at the telegraph office, phone company, tax office, and other administrative centers.

That day—and those that followed—the general promised to maintain order, assuring the normal functioning of the various ministries and official bodies without intervention from any political party. He took advantage of the people's panic, gaining their trust by promising peace, guaranteeing order, and swearing to safeguard the nation.

He dissolved the Cortes, declared a state of war throughout the country, and suppressed public rights and freedoms. It didn't take long—one month—for town councils to be dismantled and new central and provincial governments to be established. Civil service exams for administrative positions were abolished. Soon after, calm was restored— that had been one of the captain general's great promises to the Catalan conservatives. The only unions spared were the Catholic ones and the Sindicato Libre; trade union organizations were banned and their leaders were harshly repressed, driven underground, or exiled.

Primo de Rivera didn't keep his promise to the conservatives about regional autonomy for Catalunya. But they were more concerned with maintaining their wealth and waiting it out. The general seemed to be doing everything else he'd promised, so they put up no active opposition.

I arrived in Barcelona on a cold winter night. The master picked me up in Riudoms and we took the train from Reus to Barcelona, where a carriage awaited us at the station.

That was how I came to live in the Enchanted House in Park Güell with the master. Shortly thereafter we moved to his studio in the Expiatory Temple of La Sagrada Família.

Back then, Barcelona's urban fabric was going through major changes because of the World Expo, which was three years away. Most of the construction took place in the Barrio Gótico, on Tibidabo and Montjuïc, in the zoo, and in La Sagrada Família, a monumental religious architectonic project that the master had been working on for years.

Later I discovered that the master and my grandfather had studied together and were close friends; when Antonio Gaudí and the other Knights of Moriah realized he would need a protégé, someone to help him complete his mission, my grandfather entrusted me to him.

Life in the studio was better than I'd imagined it would be when I first left home. Gaudí treated me like a grandson. After school I'd watch him work until he went to mass. Then I'd have dinner with the caretaker and his wife while I waited for him to return. When he did, he'd keep working while I watched, explaining the intricacies of what he was doing. Sometimes in the evenings he'd read La Veu de Catalunya and tell me about the news.

I remember some funny stories, and his comments.

"Look, it says here that a Scottish man has invented a radio you can see."

There was a scientist named John Baird who'd just presented a mechanical device that transmitted images to the Royal Institution. It was a strange apparatus that used a tube to transform electronic impulses into pictures that could be projected onto a screen.

The master liked to keep up on technical innovations.

"Son, in twenty years we'll be on the moon," he said once.

"The moon? Why, master?"

"It says here that a man named Robert Goddard launched a rocket that runs on liquid fuel from his farmhouse in Massachusetts into space."

"That means we're going to the moon?"

"It's just a question of time, Juanito. I'm telling you, in twenty years, we'll be on the moon!"

One night during Carnival the master received a terrifying visitor.

Gaudí was drawing on papyrus, which was spread out over a wooden board that had been raised up to eye level. He was using pencil, and from time to time he'd stand back to get the full effect. I was beside him, just watching. He'd come back from mass, and after we had dinner, he'd returned to his work.

"What are you doing, master?"

"Bedtime, Juanito."

"But I like watching you draw, Grandfather."

Gaudí smiled. Sometimes I'd accidentally call him that, and he seemed to like it.

"It's very pretty. What is it?"

"I'm drawing everything that will go on the Passion Façade of La Sagrada Família."

I was seated on a stool to his left, a few feet behind him, and fully intended not to bother him. But then the master stopped working and got out a drawing from among his papers and notebooks. He spread it out on top of what he'd been doing and said to me, "This temple, son, will be the work of many generations. That means that I must set down guidelines so it can be finished exactly as I've planned. But even if it isn't completed, what must be will be."

"What do you mean, master?"

"This temple is the end of the road. It's a Bible for the people; it announces the arrival of the New Jerusalem. The poor need Jesus Christ and the prophecy must be fulfilled."

"I don't understand."

"We live in turbulent times, but soon that will change. It's time to go home. It is written; it's all in the stars. Our Lord is waiting."

The master seemed to be talking to himself.

"Man, my little one, moves in a two-dimensional world, and angels in three dimensions. It's time to end the suffering in the world. Come, come here."

I went to him. Pointing at the drawing, he said to me, "The whole doctrine, the plan of La Sagrada Família, is all right here."

The drawing clarified the temple's symbolism. It was a synoptic chart and took up less than a page. The master began to enumerate all the things it encompassed:

The three members of the Holy Trinity and their connection to the three Christian virtues and the first three commandments.

The seven sacraments and their connection to the seven petitions of the Our Father.

The seven days of creation.

The seven commandments of Mosaic law.

The seven gifts of the Holy Spirit.

The seven cardinal virtues.

The seven cardinal sins.

The seven works of mercy.

"Seven times seven?" I asked.

The master smiled and his eyes lit up. I'd obviously picked up on something the significance of which I couldn't comprehend.

I remember that day very well. We were alone in the studio. Bells rang in the distance, distracting me for a minute. Like always, I stopped to count the chimes to see what time it was. I don't know exactly what happened, but I lost count on the last toll. Then I looked up at the master. His expression surprised me. His head was tilted up and his eyes were open wide. I was about to ask him what was wrong when he suddenly put his finger to his lips, to tell me not to speak. Seeing the alarm on his face, I realized we were in danger. I'd never seen him like that before. The sound of that last bell toll was still echoing in the air when I heard breathing that sounded close by. I put my guard up. I thought it could be a cat, or maybe a dog, that had gotten trapped. But it sounded strangely human and inhuman at the same time. The breathing was coming from the other side of the studio, where it was dark, where the statues and plaster casts were all piled up. The master was looking in that direction, staring hard. It was like he was paralyzed. My eyes searched the back of the room and stopped at a silhouette. Shocked, I realized I saw a statue that had never been there before, I was sure. I looked back at the master again, and his stillness and the look on his face made me feel strange, bewildered. I was scared. What was going on?

I don't know if I was just imagining it, but when I looked back at the dark silhouette I felt its icy presence envelop me, felt its breath go right through me, course through my body like a thick, invisible mist. I shivered.

I was frozen. The master was there with me, but it seemed like he was one of those lifeless statues, too. I couldn't do anything. I felt totally alone, so vulnerable that I became dizzy. Before me a bottomless pit was opening. My body, my veins, were freezing; I sensed that this thing before me was not of this world. And that made me tremble. I could hear its death rattle, hear it whistling, whispering, calling my name. I struggled and fought to get it out of me, to muffle the voice that both repelled and enchanted me. I remember that was the first time I ever felt—almost tasted—such a strange, absurd fear that I can't put it into words. Fear of the dark, or even death, was nothing compared to the indescribable panic that overtook me, at something totally unknown. The ringing of that last bell, its metallic echo, had gotten caught in the air and was dying so slowly that it dragged me with it into the darkness. I felt horror, sheer terror, at the supernatural being there, in the study, suffocating me, pressing down on my chest. I cried silently, hearing my heart beat in my eardrums. I wanted to scream and run away, and yet I knew that I, too, had become a statue.

And then the dark silhouette, whose face was covered by a mask, took a step forward. His footstep rang out in my ears like a drumbeat. He kept walking forward.

The master's ragged voice saved me from my panic, from sheer abandon.

"Out!" he bellowed, and then began speaking in Latin that I couldn't understand.

The silhouette stopped.

"Juanito, come get behind me, quickly!" he shouted.

I still don't know how I managed to do it, but I reacted. I didn't have the strength to jump or even walk—my arms and legs were numb—but I let my body fall to the ground and dragged myself across the floor, hiding behind the master as best I could, beneath a long table covered with designs.

I couldn't understand what they were saying, but I knew a terrible battle was being waged. Both of them stood there facing each other, hurling insults in a strange language, their words like swords slicing through the air. The master's voice said a prayer, and the man in the mask seemed to writhe in pain. I covered my ears against his terrible cries. His mask turned bright red, glowing so intensely that I had to turn away. I'm not sure how long this went on; all I know is that suddenly the strangled feeling left me and the last bell finally stopped ringing.

My whole body was trembling; I couldn't control it. With a huge effort, I finally managed to ask the master if he was alright.

He was exhausted and looked like he'd aged several years: hunched over, panting, his arms slack at his side. I didn't dare come out of my hiding place; I was looking all around. After a long time, when his breathing had returned to normal, he spoke to me.

"He's gone. He won't be back. But the mission must be fulfilled. We don't have much time."

He sat down. His eyes were closed and he was having trouble breathing. I scrambled out from beneath the table to curl up on his lap and began to cry, frightened.

"It's all over now, Juanito. Don't be scared. I promise you he won't come back."

"Master, he . . . he was calling me by my name. I couldn't do anything. Who was that?"

"Little Juan, you have to be strong. Soon you shall learn to defend yourself."

"I . . . I'm scared. That wasn't human. I know it wasn't."

"Trust me. One day you'll defeat him. You can do it."

"But, master, that wasn't a man, it was, it was . . . Is that why it was hiding its face?"

"That doesn't matter. I know what he looks like. Evil always has the same face . . . don't ever forget that. I sculpted him in stone. Look!" he said, showing me a picture.

It was of a sculpture on one of the corbels on the Rosary door of the Nativity Façade. The Temptation of Man, taking an Orsini bomb from the devil. That and The Temptation of Woman were two of the master's *favorite sculptures. At the Paris exposition of 1910 he'd displayed two plaster models of them in the Grand Palais.*

"One day that man came and told me that he was the very image of evil I was searching for, the model. He wasn't wearing a mask and at first I didn't recognize him. But later I realized who it was. I should have killed him at the time, but I felt old and tired. That man has followed me for years, challenging me, trying everything he can to stop me from completing my work. And that day he dared to present himself to be photographed, after so many years."

I knew that was something the master did, took pictures. It was a hobby that scared me to death, and I never went with him. Gaudí, in his photo lab, would develop pictures of all sorts of people so he could use them as models for his figures: saints, angels, evangelists, prophets. He even went to see the director of the maternity and foundling hospital in Les Corts, to photograph dying children and corpses. Sometimes his models were people he knew. His King David, for instance, was actually a builder named Ramón Artigas.

I didn't say anything. I let the master rest, thinking that he'd tell me what was going on later if he wanted to.

Which he did. This is what he said.

"I want to tell you something, and I'm going to treat you as if you're older than you are because I know you'll be able to understand everything I say," he began. "Your grandfather and I studied together in architecture school. We were very young, just eighteen, and we were in love with Barcelona. We made friends with another student named Luis Zequeira, who was less than brilliant. I later learned that his father was a great man who didn't deserve a son like Luis. His mother was the daughter of an editor who had socialized with people in the dictatorship, playing politics in an attempt to recover his wealth; he'd neglected his business and gone bankrupt. Fortunately for him, Primo de Rivera helped him out. He started a press that published pornographic material to be distributed to all the barracks in Spain. But that's another story, Juanito. Anyway, Zequeira was a womanizer and a very charming young man. He told us that he and a few friends often met up in the basement under the Seven Doors mansion to take part in secret rituals. Your grandfather and I were young and confused; we hadn't developed the ideals we hold now. We wanted to see things, to learn, experiment. One day he convinced us to go with him. We went to a couple of meetings, and at first they seemed innocent enough. But the more we went, the more your grandfather and I began to see that those hooded men were real fanatics. One night—the last one; we never went back after that—we saw something so awful that I'm not going to describe it. It would terrify you.

Anyway, back then there were sixteen Masonic lodges in Barcelona, and they belonged to seven sects. A lot of artists and intellectuals were associated with these secret societies. But Luis Zequeira didn't belong to any of those. He wasn't a Mason. He belonged to a satanic cult. We didn't know that at first. It wasn't until we were in that room that we realized what was going on. They were Corbel men, though they liked to call themselves the Cavalry of Judas. On the altar where they conducted their ceremonies, beside an inverted compass and black square, they'd engraved CJ, which, as you can see, are the initials of Jesus Christ backward. They were killers who attacked people, murdered, defiled, carried out horrible rituals I cannot possibly explain, invoked demons, and worshipped the devil and an idol named Baphomet. You might wonder what on earth we were doing there. But as I said, at first we didn't realize what they were about. Or at least I didn't. I thought it was just another secret society; there were so many in Barcelona at the time. I thought their mission was to understand the world, to know God, and that they believed that all of nature was presented to us as a gradual revelation that leads us to the Being of Beings. Clearly, what they really did had nothing to do with any of that.

When Luis Zequeira contacted us, your grandfather was the one who dragged me along and convinced me to go to those first meetings. It wasn't until much later that I understood his interest.

Your grandfather was an infiltrator.

Time passed and we never mentioned any of that business. But Zequeira never forgave us for not joining his organization. And I always had the feeling I was being spied on.

A long while later, out of our love of architecture, your grandfather and I joined an association that organized excursions to ruins, buildings, cathedrals, and the like. We wrote reports, did research, and made plans to restore buildings, like San Esteban Church in Granollers. We visited all sorts of places.

One night in Montserrat, he finally told me everything.

Your grandfather was a knight, one of the Seven Knights of Moriah, who took their name from the mountain where Solomon built his temple. They were entrusted with the mission of keeping Christianity's greatest secret safe throughout the ages. I know this may be hard for you to believe, though you're a boy, and curiosity, fantasy, and adventure are part of your world. It's true, Juan, your grandfather is a knight. He already was one when I first met him, when we almost joined the Corbel men. For centuries, the Corbel has tried to ensure that the Moriah never fulfill their mission. That's why he planned to join the Corbel, as a spy. As I said, he told me all this one night in Montserrat. And then he told me about the seven knights who guard the secret, and I joined them.

The secret was eventually revealed to me, and in time, I became the grand master.

From then on, all of my work, everything I've built in this city, has been guided by a plan. I know that, like Moses, I will not reach the promised land. But at least the groundwork has been laid, so the prophecy can be fulfilled. Like the Baptist, I will bear witness, and in many years, it is written, one of your descendants, whom you'll call María, will close the circle.

That was what Gaudí revealed to me after the confrontation with that strange visitor.

Then we left the studio. It was a cold night, and we roamed the streets of the city without a word until we reached La Pedrera.

There, with the stone warriors as our only witnesses, Antonio Gaudí named me a Knight of Moriah.

I was chosen to guard the secret until the day I was to hand it over to you. During that time, in the morning we'd go out for seemingly aimless walks. He'd toss bread crumbs onto the ground, and my job was to recognize the signs at those spots.

After the master was murdered, the knights hid me, trained me, and shared their secrets with me, and in time, I became their grand master: the leader of the seven knights chosen to protect the secret. A secret that I had and that I hid, and that they never asked me about, because their mission was to protect me and thereby protect the secret, which guaranteed that the prophecy would be fulfilled.

Only once did I ever decide to make myself known. Ten long years had passed, and the tragic events of the time drove me to take a risk. My fellow knights tried to dissuade me, but I'd have killed them with my sword had they tried to stop me.

Bitru and his men set fire to the master's legacy and desecrated his grave. My blood cried out for vengeance.

Their organization is simple: one leader receives the name Asmodeus, and his second in command, named Bitru, is the crown prince. When Bitru moves up, he becomes the new Asmodeus and another man becomes the new Bitru. Their names are as old as the world itself; they're two of hell's most ominous demons. Sometimes it's impossible to tell them apart. Their actions are so perfidious that they have the same face: the face of evil. That's what they aspire to. They say Medusa was the mother of the first Asmodeus.

We knew some of the Corbel men used to meet up at a dive on Paralelo called El Paradís. Music halls, as they were called back then, had been fashionable for some time. They were places where people from all walks of life gathered to indulge in every vice imaginable. Some had been closed down by the government several times: the Bataclán, the Royal Concert, Pompeya, and the Apolo Concert Hall were infamous.

I walked into El Paradís looking like a vagabond, like I'd just emerged from the shadows. I had to find him. Bitru had become the new Asmodeus, after so many years. His predecessor, Luis Zequeira, had just died of syphilis, and the Prince of Darkness took his name and assumed leadership of the Corbel.

I walked in trying to look nonchalant, but my eyes were flashing like a wolf's. El Paradís was filled with hustlers, pimps, whores, and all sorts of other seedy types. There he was, sitting at a table by the stage with four prostitutes and two of his cohorts. He wasn't hard to recognize. I walked toward him, overcome by a murderous rage, and when I was just a few steps away he saw me. At first he looked surprised; then, as he recognized me, his eyes glimmered with hatred. He reached into his cloak, pulled out his gun, and took aim. That was all he was able to do. I rushed him, unsheathing my sword as I leapt. My first stroke sliced his hand clean off; it fell on the table, discharging his gun. The bullet pierced the heart of one of the prostitutes. My second blow severed his head, and it fell with a thud onto the table, knocking over glasses and rolling to a stop beside a bottle of champagne. The music ceased; the silence was deafening. I watched his body fall backward in the chair and then drove my sword furiously into his heart.

I stormed out, taking advantage of the general commotion, and slipped into the night without looking at anyone. His death served no purpose; his Bitru replaced him almost immediately.

If you've read this far, my little one, that means you solved the riddle and found the notebook.

> Hard on top,
> hard underneath.
> Face of a snake
> and sticks for feet.

Remember how much you liked riddles when you were little?

> I move from cell to cell, though free
> For there's no jail that can hold me.

The bee one was your favorite.

This notebook could fall into the Corbel's hands, so I have to take measures.

But I trust you'll be able to solve my simple riddles, uncover the secret, and realize what you must do with it to fulfill the prophecy.

This is something that you, my lovely girl, must discover on your own. It is written.

First the archangel's faith must be restored. To realize the plan, he has to believe in you.

You must kill the beast at the third gate in order to be renewed. This is the first step. The map is within him. The treasure is there, too, though only in part.

The secret has been within you since the day you were born. We are all children of the stars—everything is.

Do not forget the Our Father: "On earth as it is in heaven."

The countdown began in the year 1126 in the Holy Land, when the relic was found.

In 1926 Gaudí gave it to me before he was killed.

Now, in 2006, María, I give it to you, to fulfill the prophecy. Read with your heart and not with your head, and you'll find the truth on the last door that closes behind me.

María had read it all aloud. Miguel and Taimatsu had been taking notes as they listened. Miguel, used to math equations, was struck by the dates: Gaudí's death in 1926, and the start of the countdown, which according to the diary was 1126. Eight hundred years apart, and eighty years between Gaudí's death and the present. So perhaps there was some connection, a simple progression: eight times a hundred, and eight times ten.

María turned the page and then exclaimed, attracting Miguel and Taimatsu's attention once more.

"Hey, here they are!"

The notebook held several lines of text that looked like riddles.

They each bore the name of a Greek letter printed in larger writing, as a heading.

"My grandfather was a big fan of riddles, but these . . . I don't recognize any of these."

María showed them to Miguel and Taimatsu, and together they read:

ALPHA

Between palm trees and carnations spins the soul of the sun.

BETA

Light brings it to life, though it doesn't have a hundred feet, to turn on the oven of the night that illuminates the fruits of the Garden of Hesperides.

GAMMA

Add up the number on a staircase with no steps to see the sign the four sides enclose.

DELTA

Your mother is the water; your father is the fire. You are not a ship and you travel in time, sunk in the foundations of the new city that the warriors contemplate.

EPSILON

Not even the fires of Saint Elmo can light up your eyes, lost in the darkness.

ZETA

Wise insanity, even if you see it, won't be found above the cypress.

ETA

In the first letter of this palace the Magi saw the cross and the heart of the immaculate Virgin Mary's light.

*You have to play the game, María, like when you were a girl. There's
not much time. Use your instincts.*

From that point the notebook became an ever more chaotic mess
of drawings, outlines, random phrases, and bizarre geometric sketches.
There appeared to be no order to it at all. There were even some notes
and drawings superimposed over one another. María leafed through several pages, saddened by the thought that behind this writing lay her
grandfather's madness, his desperation. She couldn't go on; her eyes
welled up with tears and she ran into the kitchen.

"Do you two want anything to drink?" she called from the next
room.

Miguel and Taimatsu didn't respond. They respected her pain and
just waited for her to return. A few minutes later, she did.

"I'm fine," she said with a smile in response to Miguel's concerned
look. "Should we go on?"

Her eyes were red and she had a glass of water in her hand.

They continued scanning the notebook. Toward the end was a copy
of a medieval miniature, or perhaps an icon, of a monk with a dog's face,
and a name written beneath it: *Marmaritae.* Under that was an unfinished sentence that began, "M . . . will protect you in the cam . . ." Then
came something illegible and an ink stain that the author had used to
draw a two-headed figure.

Taimatsu was spellbound by the miniature.

"A monk with a dog's face . . . I don't understand. I think in Egyptian
mythology Anubis, the god of the dead, has a dog's face, too, but I'm not
sure. We should look it up," she said.

"But this drawing looks religious," Miguel said, intrigued by the
detail.

"What did you find?" María asked. She'd stopped paying attention
and had missed out on their discovery.

"A medieval miniature. See? And an incomplete sentence: 'M . . .

will protect you in the cam . . .' I think your grandfather must have been trying to tell us something. The 'M,' I'm guessing, is you. But do you recognize this drawing?"

"No. But that's odd—the figure is wearing an Orthodox cross; how strange. I think it's called the Cross of Lorraine, very similar to the Caravaca cross. Anyway, in the Middle Ages miniatures like that were pretty common: drawings of monsters and whatnot. Ancient deities. There's a kind of syncretism that blends obscure legends and old pagan beliefs with Christian mythology."

"Let's look on the Internet. We might find something interesting," Miguel said decisively.

It didn't take long. After a simple search they found a page with the picture of a monk with a dog's head symbolizing Saint Christopher—*San Cristóbal*—patron saint of travelers and drivers. From what it said, in Greek Orthodox iconography Saint Christopher originally came from an African tribe of giants or monsters called Marmaritae. The drawings were of cynocephali, from the Greek for "head of a dog."

Something jogged María's memory.

"Oh! I remember. I read something about this once, years ago. Let me think. It was a popular myth in the Middle Ages, when the cathedrals were being built. My grandfather really admired this famous alchemist named Fulcanelli; he was always talking about him. When I was a teenager he made me read *The Mystery of the Cathedrals*."

"And what does it say about Saint Christopher?"

"Well, like I said, it was a popular story in the Middle Ages, especially when cathedrals were first being built, and it blends fiction and reality. Personally, I prefer the myth. There was supposed to be an enormous young Canaanite, a real giant, who wanted to serve the most powerful king in the world. One day, after he'd been the subordinate of a certain emperor for some time, he came across a demon and asked him who he was. The devil said he was a servant of Satan, the Prince of Darkness, the most powerful being there was. So the young man became one of his servants, too, because Satan was much more powerful than the emperor. The devil and the handsome giant were walking down the road, and they came to an intersection where there was a cross. The devil ran away, because he was afraid of the cross. And Saint Christopher, seeing the devil's fear, chose to serve God, because there was no doubt that he was the most powerful king of all, certainly much more powerful than the devil. He knelt before the cross and asked God to tell him what he could do for him. God told him that nearby was a river, and that because he was so tall and so strong, he should help travelers cross the river so they wouldn't get caught in the current. And from that moment on, Saint Christopher served the Lord, carrying all the travelers on his shoulders, transporting them across the river. One day a little boy asked him to take him to the other shore. Saint Christopher put him on his shoulders, and when he was halfway across, the boy's weight seemed to grow so much that the giant couldn't move. 'Who are you, that you weigh so much?' he asked. 'I am the Christ Child,' Jesus replied, and at that moment, Saint Christopher was able to get out of the water and kneel before the Son of God. That's the story I read in *The Mystery of the Cathedrals*."

Miguel went to find *The Mystery of the Cathedrals*, which was somewhere on María's bookshelf. He wanted to see if he could find anything, despite the fact that he didn't know what he was looking for and that this whole thing seemed so utterly insane.

Taimatsu said good-bye. She was tired and the foundation's opening was going to require all her energy. Plus she had to go to Paris for a traveling exhibition; she'd been asked to do some consulting there. Before she left, she asked María if she could scan a few of the notebook's most intriguing pages: the one with the cynocephali and a few others, including a drawing that reminded her of Mount Fujiyama, the highest mountain in Japan—although the drawing was labeled Mount Hermon, in the north of Israel near Caesarea Philippi. There was also an enigmatic phrase that she said she'd think about when she had more time: "At the foot of Mount Hermon, in Caesarea Philippi. The Third Living Being of Celestial Worship: 16, 18."

She made two sets of photocopies on María's printer and gave one to her friend.

"You never know!" she said.

28

As soon as she got home, Taimatsu went into her study and took out the photocopies she'd made of María's grandfather's diary and the note with the strange message Miguel found at Father Jonás's parish.

Taimatsu couldn't sleep. The whole thing was so incredible that she just couldn't drift off. She had a true scholarly mystery on her hands. Possibly the secret to unlocking the work of the man she admired most in the world: Antonio Gaudí. Who could sleep with a bombshell like that?

So she studied the papers carefully until the phone rang. She picked up.

"It's Yasunari," said the voice on the other end of the line curtly.

"Yasu!" she cried, surprised but happy. Instinctively she glanced at the clock. It was late. What was he doing calling at that time? Was something wrong?

"I need to see you."

"Now?"

"Now."

"Where are you?"

"Downstairs."

"Downstairs! What are you doing here?"

Yasu didn't reply.

"Well, come on up." She buzzed him in.

Taimatsu had just enough time to slip the papers into her desk drawer before the doorbell rang. She opened the door.

Yasu wasn't very affectionate when he walked in. She was surprised by her cousin's sternness. They'd always been more like siblings than cousins. He was like a big brother who'd always protected her when she was a child. She reminded him of that.

"That's why I'm here," Yasu said. "I'm protecting you."

At first Taimatsu wondered, what was he going to protect her from? Yasu couldn't know anything about this business she'd just gotten involved in. That was impossible. She waited for him to explain himself.

"My father is very worried about you; you're going out with a man twice your age. A Westerner."

"Good God, Yasu, you scared me!" she exclaimed, realizing that the secret she and her friends had on their hands had nothing to do with her cousin's visit.

"You should be scared. That man is no good for you."

"If you knew him you wouldn't say that."

Yasu bit his tongue. He did know him, well. But he wasn't about to go into that. He'd come to tell her to leave him. That was all. Taimatsu had to respect the judgment of her elders.

"Yasu, this is a different world. Times have changed. We're not in Japan. Besides, I'm telling you, if you knew him you'd change your mind."

"My father is very upset. Really, Taimatsu; he's no good for you. Tell me you'll at least think about it."

I'm in love, Yasu. Really in love. That was what she wanted to say. But she didn't dare.

"Alright. I'll think about it."

"Really?"

"Really."

"When we were little you used to try to fool me."

"But you could always tell, and besides, you were on my side."

"Not this time, Taimatsu; I can't be on your side this time. I love you too much."

"Now you're scaring me."

"The man you've chosen is no good. He doesn't deserve you, Taimatsu. I can assure you."

"Can't you tell me more than that?"

"No. All I can say is you should have faith in me, like always."

And without another word, Yasu left, closing the front door behind him.

Taimatsu was speechless, confused, and tired. But that didn't stop her from going back to her desk to examine the notes about Gaudí. This was a problem she could solve, and she fully intended to do so.

PART V

THE BEAST
AT THE
THIRD GATE

29

BITRU, IT'S NOT your methods I'm questioning. Our enemies fear us for a reason. But you made mistakes—mistakes that we can't afford," Asmodeus said.

Bitru shifted uncomfortably. He was the prince, destined to succeed him. But he knew his mentor would not stand for errors.

"Mistakes?"

"You left him alive."

That declaration made Bitru break out in a cold sweat.

"That's impossible!"

"Bitru, don't raise your voice. You must be humble; that's what we taught you. You must honor your name. Others bore it before you and served nobly. One day you'll take my place and receive the ring."

Bitru bit his tongue and bowed his head.

"The priest was alive when you left. You must never underestimate your victims. You know they are strong; they're trained to withstand pain and torture."

Yes, Bitru knew all of that. But he'd done a good job. He'd carried out the ritual just as he'd been taught.

"That's impossible. He was dead. Dead," he repeated.

"No, Bitru. He was alive. And the light was on. Someone was there after you."

"How do you know all that?"

"Mortimer," he replied succinctly.

Bitru hated that name. He didn't like the cop at all.

"When he got there the light was on, and he found evidence that someone had been there after you. Tell me: you didn't see anything? Think hard."

"I did my job well," Bitru replied.

"I know that; I know how you work. That's why this is so strange. We think the priest dragged himself across the floor and left a message in his own blood. What we don't know is what he wrote or whether the other person saw it."

"Who was it?"

"The girl's boyfriend."

"The archangel?"

"Yes, though he doesn't know it yet. And he might not know how to decipher the message, either. But we're going to lend a hand with that."

"What do you mean?"

"They're going to find something that doesn't belong to them. And once they do, we'll step in. We have to let them investigate, but we also need to keep a close watch, not let them out of our sight."

"OK. I'll keep an eye on them."

"No, Bitru. You need to take it easy. I've got something else in mind for you. For now, I want you to go meditate, bare your soul, and pray."

"I followed the ritual exactly."

"I'm sure you did, son, I'm sure you did. But now you should go. Mortimer will take care of the mathematician."

Bitru realized the meeting was over, so he kissed the stone on Asmodeus's ring and left the room.

Asmodeus was now alone. He had to think. He'd give them time to look over the notebook; eventually it would be his. Then he'd have two teams investigating: his own and his enemies'.

Mistakes had been made in the past. There was even a time when they thought that if they didn't have the secret in their possession, they should destroy everything, just burn it all down. So they did.

Asmodeus was the last on a long list, and he'd be the one to get what they'd been after for so many centuries.

These were troubled times; it was hard to find new recruits who weren't psychopaths, totally insane, bored rich kids, or just ordinary killers. Crime and terror were fine, but there was much more to it. The Corbel always worked according to a plan. They weren't simply murderers. Asmodeus felt that the power that had driven him and his kind throughout the ages was losing ground. When murder is random, when evil has no master plan, what's the sense? Banality had taken over. Tragic times, Asmodeus thought. Theirs was a fight against the power of God, a fight for the furies of hell. Everything else was just petty crime.

He hadn't worked his whole life just to be an assassin. No, he'd worked for the glories of Baphomet, to spread his empire across the face of the earth.

He thought about what his predecessor had told him.

A brilliant past. His days as Bitru, the best of all. But they'd ended with a head rolling across a table in some dive on Paralelo.

Barcelona's convents were burning. Priests, nuns, and monks were put to death. On July 19, 1936, taking advantage of the outbreak of the civil war—a national atrocity that was to last a long time—they decided to defile, sack, and set fire to the crypt of La Sagrada Família. Bitru was an expert when it came to whipping a mob into a frenzy.

They profaned the bookseller Bocabella's grave in addition to Gaudí's. But they found nothing inside. They thought the boy had hidden the secret, but it didn't hurt to check the old man's remains just in case. Then Bitru burned all of the master's models, plans, and designs.

Before the military uprising they'd had a lot of leads. But then the boy disappeared. No trace of him anywhere.

The Corbel sided with the insurrection, but their coup failed in Barcelona. They had to wait for General Franco to arrive in order to get back inside the temple. But the general with a million deaths on his hands called himself a Catholic, and he ordered that Gaudí's grave be provisionally covered. Then he decided to seal it permanently, after the temple's project director, a man named Quintana, and some others who'd known Gaudí certified that the body was his.

That was when the boy showed up, seeking revenge. He'd become a man and had been trained by the guardian knights; he was one of them. He sought out Asmodeus and killed him. Then he disappeared again, for years.

Decades later, they found him. The Corbel was unwavering. They'd searched ceaselessly. It wouldn't have done any good to kidnap and torture him to try to get the secret out of him. He'd been trained to withstand pain. So they waited.

But they waited too long.

The boy became an old man and lost his mind. And now his granddaughter was their only hope.

She'd reveal the secret.

Without knowing it, María would work for them.

30

MARÍA WALKED BEHIND the casket, lost in her thoughts. She remembered the ritual when she was a little girl and her grandfather took her on day trips. The destinations changed—the cities, landscapes, buildings, and monuments—but the places always told the same story. Now here she was on his final journey, with Miguel by her side, along with two old people she didn't know from the home, the director, and two nurses. Taimatsu hadn't arrived yet. She was probably busy getting ready for the foundation's opening.

The hearse drove slowly down the Montjuïc Cemetery lanes, and María reminisced, remembering. It was as if that final trip evoked every memory that bound her to her grandfather. The good times and the bad all came rushing at her at once, hundreds of thousands of anecdotes, conversations, and situations all crowded her memory, trampling one another to pay their last respects.

One spring morning they'd visited Montserrat. It was a bright, sunny day; the sky was an intense blue, and a light breeze fluttered through the trees on the sacred mountain. They were near the cross of Saint Michael—*Sant Miquel*—high up on the mountain. They'd ridden up on the funicular. She was having trouble following her grandfather along the trails around the northern part of the monastery. Growing in the cracks of some rocks, they'd found some *Jasonia saxatilis*, an herb commonly known as "rock tea." That day her grandfather had told her about Gaudí—strange things about fabulous hidden treasures; some of them, he said, were even in Montserrat, hidden beneath the mountain. Very odd. What made her remember that now? A forgotten conversation from when she was a little girl, something she hadn't recalled until now, walking behind the hearse that was just stopping at one of the aisles. María was startled to see the open funeral niche. It was the last empty one on that row; the rest had all been sealed and decorated with wilted flowers, photos, crosses, and epitaphs. Miguel gave her arm a light squeeze. It was time to say good-bye, her last farewell.

She wanted to cry but couldn't. She got a strange feeling that energy was flowing from her grandfather's coffin to her, and a voice had stirred her memory of that trip to Montserrat, of their conversation about Gaudí and about death. Suddenly she recalled what he'd said word for word. She had just turned nine and didn't understand any of it at the time. She had her whole life ahead of her and could not comprehend the inevitability of death, neither hers nor her grandfather's—maybe that was why she'd forgotten his words until just now. "María, in the marble of the last door that closes behind me, you'll find a map of the way of the stars." Yes, that was what he'd said. She was used to her grandfather's riddles, puzzles, and brainteasers. But sometimes he still spoke in ways that were incomprehensible to her. Now María found herself wondering how that memory could possibly be so clear to her now, when just a few days ago it had been entirely forgotten. How was that possible?

She wanted to talk to Miguel, to tell him about it. She was sure he'd uncover a clue in it somehow, some message to help make sense of the chases, the deaths, the secret. The secret. All of this pounded in her head, and she couldn't cry; she had to wait for the last door to close to discover the meaning.

Miguel helped the undertakers load the coffin into its slot. Then they took the heavy marble tombstone and set it in place, sealing it shut. This took a few minutes, but when they were done, the undertakers left. María was standing slightly apart, and when she looked up she saw that Miguel had a strange expression on his face. He was reading the inscription. *The message on the last door*, María thought. Everyone stood clustered in a group, reading it. Suddenly it hit María: her grandfather was sending her a final message from the grave. She knew it might contain one of the pieces she needed to solve the puzzle.

Videmus nunc per speculum in aenigmate: tunc autem facie ad faciem.
Nunc cognosco ex parte: tunc autem cognoscam sicut et cognitus sum.

I CORINTHIANS 13:12

"He chose the epitaph himself," the home's director explained.

"Thank you," María said, nodding.

She read the epitaph carefully. It was from Saint Paul's epistle to the Corinthians. Miguel wrote it down on a piece of paper. Finally María cried, tears streaming down her face. Miguel put his arm around her. Everyone offered their condolences and politely took their leave. The couple stood there in silence for some time, staring at the sealed tomb. When she felt calm, María whispered to her boyfriend, "I think my grandfather is sending us one last message."

"So do I; I'm sure it's a clue."

She kept her voice low.

"I can translate it. 'Now we see the enigma through a mirror. Later we'll meet truth face to face.' The face . . . The face of God."

"The mirror. María, that symbol keeps cropping up. 'On earth as it is in heaven.' Reflections. The sea, the water is a huge reflection of the sky . . ."

"And fire."

"Fire?"

"Yes, Miguel, fire is the mirror of the stars."

"Duality. Fire and water. Sea and stars. Heaven and earth. Stone and air. One and zero. It's all a binary system. Our whole world, all of civilization, the logic of science, all of it's based on that model. Open and closed. One and zero. Infinite series, chains of ones and zeros. Combinatorial. With that language, the language of computers, we can describe anything in the world."

"Open and closed doors. The final door has closed for my grandfather, but for us, the next one is opening."

When she said that, they both fell silent. María thought about the sentence on the tombstone. "The enigma seen through the mirror . . . The face of God without a mask . . . The truth . . . The mask hides the face . . . The world is an infinite reflection of mirrors . . . That's the enigma . . . The infinite is the mask of the world."

It was almost afternoon. They were alone, time was marching on, and Miguel motioned for them to go.

"You go, Miguel. Get the car and wait for me at the gate. I want to be alone for a little while."

"OK. Don't be too long."

María lingered there. The noise of nearby traffic on the coastal road at the foot of the mountain wafted into her mind. She breathed deeply, and when she repeated the epitaph aloud, a light breeze picked up. Miguel had been gone for a few minutes. She glanced around. Her grandfather's slot was at the end of one of the aisles, at an intersection with other niche-lined aisles, all identical. It was totally deserted.

She'd made a promise to her grandfather, but she couldn't keep it. She was alone and wept until she'd stripped away the pain that had been strangling her heart since the moment she saw his lifeless body at the home. She allowed herself to sob until she couldn't see; one memory led to another, and each one brought more tears.

"I'm sorry, Grandfather. I know I promised I wouldn't cry until I'd finished whatever it is I'm supposed to do. Forgive me," she said, drying her eyes.

The rustling breeze was like the raspy whisper of a dying man, an immense, agonizing echo penetrating the silence of the graves. María felt a devastating calm impose itself after the last gust of wind, and in the next instant she suddenly felt uneasy. At the end of an aisle that turned right, she thought she saw something by a grave covered with withered flowers. Maybe it was just a reflection, a glimmer of afternoon sunlight shining down on the cemetery of Montjuïc—the Jewish Mountain—reflected off the sea. The light took on strange tones, casting golden hues onto the marble and the glass of some of the niches. María walked to where the other aisle branched off, where a sculpture of an angel stood, surrounded by benches. She saw more aisles heading off in all directions, all identical. It was a labyrinth of graves. She took one of the aisles, crossed another aisle, and right at that instant, out of the corner of her eye, she glimpsed a sudden movement. She stopped, anxious, then turned her head slowly and saw it: the mask. She was sure of it; it was there, watching her from the other side of the aisle, at the end of the path.

Her heart beat fiercely in her chest. She knew Miguel was in the car, waiting at the gate, so she screamed.

"Miguel!"

She felt a hand on her shoulder and started. Turning, she breathed a sigh of relief.

"Taimatsu, you came!"

After the conversation with her cousin, she'd stayed up very late and then overslept.

"I'm so sorry I'm late. Miguel's waiting for you at the gate; he told me you were still here. But . . . what's wrong? You look so scared. Take it easy."

María closed her eyes and breathed deeply. Then she looked up at her grandfather's grave and at her friend beside her. "I'm sorry, Taimatsu. I got scared. I don't know what came over me. I saw a man with a mask. He was watching me and he looked familiar."

"OK, it's OK now. It's all over. Let's go. Miguel's waiting for us in the car. Do you feel better?"

"Yeah," she said, looking both ways.

She walked back, holding on to Taimatsu's arm. They heard a car horn.

"That's Miguel."

"Let's go."

They left the cemetery. Miguel was waiting impatiently by the car.

"What happened?"

"Nothing. Did you see anyone come or go while I was in there?"

"No. Why?"

Taimatsu answered for her.

"She thinks she saw a man wearing a mask. She got lost in the graves."

María didn't know what to think; she knew only that she was relieved to be with two people she trusted. Was it really her imagination playing tricks on her in her emotional state? She didn't think so.

31

IGUEL DROPPED MARÍA off at home. She was upset and needed to rest and be alone after the funeral. In the meantime, he decided to go to the Library of Catalunya before heading back to her place.

When Miguel got to the library, he tried to focus. What was he doing there? What information was he looking for? He took out the notes he'd copied from María's grandfather's notebook. He reread the riddles carefully and realized he'd have to leave them for María; she was the expert.

Given that he'd said he was a knight in an order older than the Templars, maybe the best place to start would be with information on them, the Templars: who they were, when they were founded, their bylaws, and in particular, any myths and legends about them.

He found, however, that although there was plenty of information about military orders, there was absolutely nothing about the Knights of Moriah—not a single word.

He didn't want to waste time with sensationalistic books lacking in historical accuracy. So looking over the information he'd extracted, Miguel decided to go back to the era of the Crusades.

He reread his notes. On one of the pages, after hearing the contents of María's grandfather's diary, he'd written three dates: 1126, 1926, and 2006, along with a note that the race had begun in the Holy Land. Then Miguel recalled that the day before he died, María's grandfather had told her that the race began with the tortoise. Tortoise? Race? He took out a pencil and wrote, "Zeno. Zeno's paradox." It was as if intuition guided his hand. He wondered whether it made any sense to look for a connection between the dates he'd jotted down and Zeno's paradox. He thought again about what María had said. "Grandfather told me that the race begins with the tortoise and that there's not much time." It wasn't a lot to go on; in fact, it wasn't anything. But for Miguel, the race and the tortoise led to the most famous paradox in history: the fastest man on earth, Achilles, races a tortoise, the slowest animal. What if that was some sort of coded message from María's grandfather? The whole business was so absurd that he decided not to discount any possibilities, no matter how remote. He wasn't sure about anything, but without knowing where to begin, he decided to just start looking, guided by instinct.

Zeno of Elea, the pre-Socratic philosopher and member of Parmenides' school, was renowned for his paradoxes. He used them to try to prove that we're fooled by our senses and that truth can only be found in reason. Miguel was familiar with them: the arrow that never reaches its target, the stadium, and Achilles and the tortoise. That was the most famous one of all. All of these were different takes on the same idea: that motion is illusory, that a moving object can never reach a goal or finish line because space can be subdivided infinitely. The paradoxes were based on progressively decreasing series. But there were two ways to solve this type of problem: mathematically and physically. Throughout history, philosophers and mathematicians had found multiple solutions to this, and almost all of them dealt with infinite sums that produced finite results. Infinity—or infinite series and convergence—was an unknown concept in antiquity. But Miguel was more interested in a physical solution.

His mind raced. The starting point was the year 1126, and the finish line was 2006. That was a total of 880 years. Achilles, who runs ten times faster than his opponent, gives the tortoise an advantage. Achilles begins at the starting point, 1126, and the tortoise in 1926—i.e., with an 800-point lead. The race begins and they both set off at the same time. When the tortoise advances 80 and is at 2006, Achilles is at 1926; he's gone ten times farther, i.e., 800. The turtle's next step, following the mathematical progression, would take him to 8. Following Zeno's paradox, you'd just keep dividing the space between them, so when Achilles reached 8, the tortoise would be at .08, and so on ad infinitum. And that's the paradox: Achilles never catches up to the tortoise because he's always back at the previous subdivision. Zeno stopped time. But in the universe of Achilles and the tortoise, infinite space was all there was. Just one coordinate. That was the mistake. At any rate, Miguel kept working on the empirical solution, the one based on physics. In the real world, when a moving object travels there are two coordinates at work: time and space. Therefore, if Achilles runs ten times faster than the tortoise, he'll always catch him.

Miguel pictured the runners advancing by leaps. That way, he saw that Achilles would catch up to the tortoise on its third leap, and that was where they were now . . . Then he remembered another important fact: María's grandfather had said there were only a few days left. He thought, *The mathematical progression goes eight hundred, eighty, eight. That means . . . Achilles will catch up to us before the ninth day. Our tortoise started his race on June 7 at six in the morning when we found the box with the notebook and medallion in it. Four days have gone by since the tortoise made its first move at La Sagrada Família: the first was Wednesday the seventh, the second was Thursday the eighth, the third was Friday the ninth, and today is Saturday the tenth. So theoretically we only have four days left. That's the time limit. But . . . what do we have to do by then?*

It was late. Miguel looked around him. There was hardly anyone there, only three people left. Over the past few hours a lot of people had been through the library. They'd come in, stayed for a while, and left. Now he realized one of them had been in the reading room almost as long as he had. He was a monk of some sort, whose presence wasn't so odd given the historical reputation of the library on all matters related to Christianity. Miguel couldn't tell if he was Franciscan or from some other order. He wasn't very up on that sort of thing. The guy was old, though it was impossible to guess his age. Miguel got up to leave.

Once out on the street he decided to take a stroll to clear his head before catching a taxi back to María's. Though he felt unsure about everything, he still wanted to tell her what he'd discovered: the numerical progression, the relationship between 1126, 1926, and 2006, i.e., 800, 80, 8. It was just too much to be a coincidence. Was there something to it? *Eight days?* he wondered, uncomprehending. And, strangely, María's grandfather had died on Thursday, June eighth. He knew that might not mean anything, but he still wanted to tell her what he'd discovered.

Miguel walked down Calle Hospital. The street was crowded; businesses were still open, and though there was a lot going on, he could tell he was being followed. It was the monk from the library. He decided to zigzag, turning here and there, and the monk did the same. When he got to where Plaza San Agustín hit Jerusalén, Miguel stopped on the corner. The street was empty. He waited, clenching his fists, trying to calm himself. If his suspicions were right and the man was armed, there was nothing he could do. Even stopping would have been a mistake. The best thing to do would be to keep going until he hit the Ramblas, stop a cab, and get out of there. But Miguel wanted to know what was going on, and his curiosity was stronger than the fear that had begun to creep into his mind.

The monk tailing him didn't have time to react. The second he turned the corner, Miguel jumped him, shoving him to the ground.

"Who are you? Why are you following me?"

"I've come to help you. Believe me. Please."

Miguel didn't give him a chance to get up; he kept a tight grip on the guy.

"Why should I believe you?"

"Because I was a friend of Father Jonás. Because I can help you decipher the message, and because you and María are in grave danger."

Miguel let up his grip, and the monk suddenly used it to his advantage, throwing Miguel to the ground. Now the tables were turned.

"On earth as it is in heaven?" Miguel asked, recalling the phrase María had told him.

"What is above is as what is below," the old man said, showing him a medallion. One side of it was engraved with a letter.

"That's a beta," Miguel said.

It looked identical to the one María had.

"We each have a different letter. Seven medallions."

"She has the alpha."

"Precisely. She's alpha now. Look, we don't have much time and I have a lot to explain. We know that Juan Givell, María's grandfather, revealed part of the plan to Father Jonás."

"Which part?"

"A message that only we can decipher and that she must interpret. Letters, symbols, perhaps an evangelical quotation. And we know you were there before the police arrived."

Miguel hesitated.

"Marmaritae, Saint Christopher . . . He'll protect you in the—"

"How could you possibly know that?" Miguel cut him off, recalling the phrase from the notebook and the medieval miniature of the monk with the dog's face. He knew he had to trust this man. It was too much to be coincidence.

They stood up.

"Yes, I was there," Miguel said. "I saw what Father Jonás wrote in his own blood. He drew the letter beta, with a large compass and a series of numbers: one, one, eight . . . twenty-two, though there was another symbol before the numbers."

"Are you sure?"

"Completely. The beta was on top, and the compass was underneath it with the numbers."

"The message means one thing in that order and something entirely different if you reverse it." The old man paused. "I think Jonás has revealed where the secret is."

"Where? And what is it? What do we have to do with it? How much time do we have?"

"Let's start with your last question. It has to occur on the perfect day, with the perfect number and the word. You'll find it on the first pages of Genesis, when it all began. The master crowned many of his buildings with a number that has to be interpreted. It should be easy for you to work out. You're a mathematician. But you have to do it yourself, I can't tell you anything else about it . . . I wouldn't know what to say, anyway. Just that the race begins with the tortoise."

"Do you know Zeno's paradox? With Achilles and the tortoise? I think that in María's grandfather's notebook—"

"Yes. Juan Givell liked riddles and games like that. But don't take it too seriously; don't get caught up in the numbers. You just need to understand the message, the idea. It could be a false trail. Remember, the tortoise's advantage is not one of time or space—"

"I don't understand; what do you mean?"

"What I mean is that Achilles will never catch the tortoise as long as it is clever enough to keep dividing space. To get lost in infinity. Do you see? You must understand that concept."

"So get Achilles on the tortoise's turf? Play on home ground? Work with infinity?"

"Exactly, my friend. That's what Juan Givell was talking about. Numbers can play tricks on you; people become obsessed with them and stop thinking rationally, lose perspective, lose sight of the big picture. Numbers can be a trick—the worst kind." Then the monk fell silent.

Miguel's mind was racing at a dizzying speed. A chaos of numbers swirled in his head. A progression: 800, 80, 8. How does one enter infinity? It's impossible! All those ideas swam in his brain in a vicious circle, like a prison he couldn't escape. Numbers were Miguel's strength; he was used to concrete, definable limits. He was familiar, of course, with the mathematical concept of infinity. But the very notion had always made him uneasy; it was disconcerting. It had even occurred to him that it was like a loophole, a way to cheat; it bordered the very limits of reason. Because what's beyond infinity? Nothing. Infinity. And what *was* it really, anyway? Feeling desperate, he thought of María, envisioning her smiling face. They were such a perfect match, an ideal couple. Both of them had their own lives; they were free and independent. And then he had a thought. How *much* did he love her? How deep was his love? Infinite? How can you love someone infinitely? Beyond life and death? Miguel had never thought about these things before. And that moment of uneasiness and the uncertainty he felt when the concept of infinity was introduced into math problems made him tremble now, thinking about it in emotional terms. He felt he was teetering on the edge of an abyss and knew that he could take another step and go farther, but that would mean altering his entire way of thinking, his reality. His heart pounded. And then, without knowing how or why, he thought about the conversation with Ramón Conesa. It was like a bolt of lightning; in his mind he saw María and then the perfect number. The number of creation. The number of life, when everything began. Just for an instant.

"Hey! You drifted off there for a minute. Listen to me, we don't have much time and I think we're being followed. Let's focus on Father Jonás's message," the monk continued. "Beta is the place, and the compass is the exact spot where it's hidden; the third line confirms that we're talking about the relic."

Miguel had no idea what the monk was talking about.

"You'll find other messages in the notebook, and together you have to interpret the symbols and put them in order."

"Put the letters in order?"

"Yes."

"But we don't know what the symbols stand for, or how to solve the riddles."

"You're in great danger. The Corbel will fight with all their strength to stop you from completing this. Their symbol is the upside-down pentagram."

Miguel felt completely lost. Then the old man gave him a clue.

"Beta corresponds to Park Güell. That's where you have to look for the compass, and inside it you'll find hidden—"

He couldn't continue. The man collapsed; Miguel caught his fall.

"Hidden what? What's wrong?" Miguel asked, trying to hold him up.

Then he saw the blood pouring from his chest. It was a bullet hole, but Miguel hadn't even heard a shot fired. He looked up, but he couldn't see anyone. With one hand the monk clutched at Miguel's shirt, and with the other he pressed down on his wound.

"We don't have . . . time . . . ," he said falteringly. "It must all happen on the great day . . . the perfect number."

He was struggling to breathe; he was covered in blood. Using his failing strength to clutch Miguel's hand, he said, almost in a whisper, "Mer . . . ak, Mer . . . ak."

"What? I don't understand."

But the monk couldn't reply; he was dead.

Miguel sat there for a few moments without knowing what to do. He knelt beside the old man's lifeless body. It wasn't horror he felt but something surreal, that this could not possibly be happening. Why hadn't whoever shot the monk also put a bullet through him? Why was he still alive? It made no sense. Then he heard the sound of footsteps, laughter. A young couple, arm in arm, playful, had begun walking down the alley.

They stopped, staring in disbelief. A dead guy, covered in blood, and another man, sweaty and scared to death, kneeling beside him.

Miguel felt for the medallion the monk had around his neck and saw that his shirt had what looked like a tree on it. He found the medallion and yanked it off. Next, unthinkingly, he crossed the dead man's arms over his chest. Then he got up and ran as fast as he could toward Calle del Carmen.

32

MARÍA DECIDED TO take a long walk. She needed some fresh air and open space and to be surrounded by people. Maybe that way they wouldn't try anything. She wandered aimlessly around the Bulevar Rosa and then went into a café to kill some time. She didn't want to think. But memories flooded her mind and made her eyes well up with tears. Her grandfather had never hurt anyone. She remembered him as a peaceful man, relaxed, friendly, and he'd been murdered. After a while she realized she'd better go back home; Miguel would be there any minute. She hadn't seen him since the funeral that morning.

He'd said he'd meet her at her house after he'd been to the library.

Her front door was open. She stepped in fearfully.

"Miguel?" she called.

No one answered.

The place was a mess. Someone had been there and turned everything upside down.

Despite the silence, she sensed a presence. It wasn't Miguel, she thought to herself. She walked down the hall, taking slow baby steps, trying to calm herself and overcome the strange feeling she had.

Then María heard a soft crunching sound.

My God, they're here! she thought, terrified. But she couldn't make herself stop; her curiosity trumped her fear and she kept walking. Just then the front door closed behind her, and from behind it appeared a masked figure dressed in black.

"The notebook," the stranger commanded, holding out a gloved hand.

She backed up slowly as he advanced.

"Give me the notebook," the dark figure repeated.

María was trembling; she swallowed hard and replied, "It's in the dining room, on the table."

From within his cane, the masked man extracted a long, thin foil. He didn't believe her. "Turn around very slowly and walk to the dining room. I'll be right behind you. If you try anything, I won't hesitate to kill you. If you give me the notebook, you'll be fine."

María thought she was going to die. She was certain that with or without the notebook, this man would kill her. She felt his breath on her back. They were walking down the hall when a key turned in the lock.

"Not a sound," the masked man whispered.

It was all so fast. Miguel opened the door. María screamed in terror, a piercing shriek.

He realized what was going on the moment he walked in and reacted instantly. Snatching an umbrella from the stand in the entryway, Miguel confronted his opponent while María ran to the back of the room and started hurling every object she could find at the man in the mask.

Their fight was chaotic, and in the end, the masked man slipped out the open door, ducking the torrent of objects raining down on him and dodging his opponent's jabs. He made it out into the hallway, then ran down the stairs as fast as he could. Miguel raced after him.

When he got down to the street, the man had disappeared.

"Are you OK?" Miguel asked, as soon as he got back upstairs.

María burst into tears. He held her, letting her get it all out.

"He wanted the notebook."

Miguel didn't reply. How could he tell her now that they'd just killed another man?

"They destroyed the puzzle game," she said, pointing to the broken box, its pieces and symbols strewn all over the floor. Some were still attached to the board. One of the wooden legs was broken in half. María picked up one of the sixty-four cells, the one for the tortoise, which had been broken off. When she was little, this had been one of her favorites. Her grandfather knew that; that's why he'd given her the key. Then she recalled the riddle and shouted, "Miguel, I've got it! There are *two* turtles, or tortoises, or whatever . . . 'Face of a snake and sticks for feet.' 'Face of a snake' was in La Sagrada Família. You saw the face inside the drawer when the stone turtle opened. And this one is—"

"Sticks for feet?"

"Exactly! The game board has four wooden legs. This is the second one! It's got 'sticks for feet'!"

María examined the tiny compartment, thinking, *Hard on top and hard underneath.* She turned it over.

"Look! The message from the second turtle!"

It was her grandfather's writing; she recognized it. She read aloud: "Clever girl, María. You'll find the real game in the Enchanted House."

Miguel was disconcerted. This was a game between María and her grandfather, one they played in life and now after his death. It seemed people who didn't live by pure reason had a different sort of mathematics. María squeezed the little cell in her hands. She had to collect her thoughts, think back to her childhood, recall her thoughts and dreams and the long walks she'd taken with her grandfather.

After a few minutes of silence, she announced, "I think it's time to pay a visit to the dragon."

"First I have to tell you something about Zeno and the tortoise, and what happened when I came out of the library."

So he told her about the knight's death and showed her the medallion. This most recent murder and the monk's revelations complicated matters. Miguel tried to soothe both María and himself.

"Let's try to keep our cool."

He had to focus and tell her what he'd found out.

"I think I know exactly how many days we have to fulfill the prophecy. The countdown started on Wednesday, June 7, when the drawer opened. Remember what your grandfather said. 'The race begins with the tortoise; there are only a few days left.'"

"I remember."

"OK, well, at the library I was totally lost. I didn't know what to look up, or where. And then, going back over the notes I took, I saw the dates 1126, 1926, and—"

"2006?"

"Exactly. A progression: eight hundred, eighty, and the next one would be—"

"Eight?"

"Yep."

"So we have eight days?"

"No. See, I was convinced it was related to Zeno's paradox. The tortoise has the advantage and Achilles can never catch him."

"Now that you mention it, my grandfather loved all that stuff, I remember. He told me about the paradoxes once, though I liked riddles better . . ."

"When I left the library, the monk—before he was shot—gave me a clue that made me think about you, about our relationship . . ."

Miguel looked at María, stared at her, not able to say what he really wanted to. She shook him from his stupor.

"A clue?"

"Yeah. He mentioned the perfect number."

"Perfect number? Miguel, please, you know I'm pretty shaky when it comes to math."

"Perfect numbers are numbers equal to the sum of their factors. Euclid came up with the formula for discovering perfect numbers. In antiquity only four of them were known, but now thirty-nine have been discovered. In fact, the last one was discovered in 2001 by Michael Cameron.

You'd need a piece of paper almost thirty-three thousand feet long just to write it out. They're interesting numbers, also called Mersenne prime numbers, in honor of the Franciscan monk who came up with several theories about them—"

"Pardon me for interrupting, but what on earth are you talking about? I'm lost."

"Sorry, María. The important thing is, the first perfect number is six! Genesis: the world was created in six days, and on the seventh day, God rested. Remember what Conesa told us. Gaudí crowned almost all of his buildings with four-armed crosses."

"That point in six directions," María finished.

"Exactly. I think six days is the limit, starting from when the race began, and that was with the tortoise in La Sagrada Família. It's been four days since then, which means we only have two days left. We have until six in the morning on Tuesday the thirteenth."

"To find what?"

"That's what we have to figure out. In science they say what matters most is not the answers but asking the right questions. What are we looking for? Where is it? What do we need to do when we find it? And why? We don't have much time. But the monk is going to give me a clue. If we're together—"

Miguel was about to say "If we love each other infinitely," but he didn't. María looked at him, smiling; she understood what his silence meant. But Miguel had to take that step himself, to leap into the unknown. He tried to hide his feelings and simply added, "I think if we're together, Achilles won't catch the tortoise."

"Let's go see the dragon," María said.

33

N IGHT WAS FALLING over La Pedrera, where the Moriah were
meeting.

It was a mysterious building, one of Gaudí's last nonre-
ligious projects. By the time he built it, the master architect had quite
a reputation. He'd experimented with new shapes and materials, and
he'd been using architectonic imagery for years. He'd also brought his
assistant Josep Maria Jujol and other architects on board as part of his
team, and he allowed them to add their creative input to the secret
mathematics of his structures. Some accused him of eclecticism, of em-
ploying a sort of "natural baroque," using excessive vegetal designs in
his buildings. They were all over the city, and the cathedral of the poor,
La Sagrada Família, was the culmination of it all. The whole of it was
an allegory.

Gaudí, in addition to his reflective and inventive handling of technical and architectonic questions, developed a symbolic language.
Correctly interpreted, it spelled out his secret mission. Some wonder
if Gaudí found the inspiration for La Pedrera in Ovid's *Metamorphoses*.
Three frescoes in the foyer are suggestive of the poem, and the undulating waves on the front of the building seem to reflect Ovid's work,
too: the way the light plays on it, making it look like living skin or the

surging sea in a storm, the world beneath the sea or a cluster of clouds over the horizon. Gaudí's vision culminated in the realization that light plays the most vital role in life and that its incessant reflection and multiplication changes nature. He applied this belief to the interior of La Sagrada Família.

Like the seventeenth-century playwright Calderón de la Barca, whom he so admired, Gaudí believed that "life is a dream." That's why he concluded that the roof was the ideal place to stage both sacramental and dramatic plays. "Everything is transformed; that which appears to be one thing is another. Stone is bone; wall is column; columns are painted; life's a dream." The building's roof is organic; life is represented by an incessant play of light and shape. There were tall chimneys, like stone warriors standing guard; they corresponded to the stars in the constellation Leo, the sun, the light.

AND THIS WAS where the Seven Knights of Moriah met to ensure that everything was carried out according to the plan.

There were only four of them left now. They knew they were the last and that they'd soon disappear forever, but they were prepared to die. The order was reaching the end of its days. The secret would soon be unveiled and the prophecy fulfilled.

Their meetings followed ancestral protocol and were always the same; no one imposed his or her beliefs. Everyone spoke and everyone listened. In recent days, brothers Juan, Jonás, and David had all lost their lives. Now three knights awaited the arrival of the missing member, Cristóbal.

Soon a giant with a curly black beard appeared from behind one of the immense stone men, which held a cross that spun over Paseo de Gràcia, symbolizing the consecration of bread and sublime metamorphosis.

As Cristóbal approached the group, Sister Magdalena spoke.

"I think we must intervene, reveal the plan, tell them the steps they need to take. It will make things so much easier. The Corbel is lying in wait, and they know as much as we do."

"We can't do that," Cristóbal replied. "María has to find her own way; the answer lies within her. All we can do is protect her. She must discover the truth on her own, with no help from anyone else. Our mission is not revelation but protection."

Brother Joaquín, standing beside one of the stone warriors, spoke next.

"It's true. Brother Cristóbal is right. I think Brother Jonás might have gone too far."

"No. That was part of the plan," Cristóbal said.

Joaquín took a few steps forward, so he was at the center of the group. He was tall and thin, and a light breeze blew his dark habit against his body.

"Brothers, Sister, we need unanimity. Back in the master's day we asked La Sapinière to intervene; he trusted them completely. Remember the way of the Rosary, the hundred and fifty beads that the master built into the labyrinth. We must pray and await better times; let the secret remain where it is. For our safety, for the safety of the world . . ."

Joaquín had brought up a controversial topic amongst the knights. They all knew that La Sapinière was the code name of a small secret society created by Pope Pius X called Sodalitium Pianum. The supreme pontiff had used every means he could to combat the expansion of Masonic lodges and other secret societies in Europe at the turn of the last century. Monsignor Beaujeu was the one in charge of organizing La Sapinière for the Holy Father. It was a complex espionage network and intelligence agency at the service of the Vatican, and their most valuable weapon was the secret code they used to communicate. They undertook all sorts of missions: infiltrating lodges and clandestine organizations, and indoctrinating new members, undermining the status quo, and spreading false rumors. The master had been devoted to Pius X, and a picture of the Holy Father had hung in the bedroom of his house in Park Güell.

Maybe it was direct intervention by La Sapinière, or maybe it was just its influence, but the master accepted his destiny. Danger was lurking, and the relic had to remain hidden: that was what they claimed. It was an idea that, eighty years later, was being put forward once again there on the roof of La Pedrera.

Brother Sebastián, assistant bishop of the Barcelona diocese, felt an icy-cold jab in his chest. History was repeating itself. The Vatican, the power of Rome, would always fight to maintain its supremacy. A new church could mean the end of its mandate. A new city of God would put an end to two thousand years of silence and intrigue in the service of earthly power. The Church would fight tooth and nail to keep the secret hidden forever. After all, it could not put its continuity—the stability of Rome—at risk. Terrifying thoughts flooded his brain. His mind leapt through time, recalling Operation Flying Fish, when Exocet missiles were sold to the Argentine dictatorship during the Falklands-Malvinas War. The dictatorship had carried out the mission using Bellatrix, a company headquartered in Panama and endorsed by the Vatican bank and their financial network: corruption, Mafia connections, money laundering. Support of the Somoza dictatorship in Nicaragua and the Duvalier dictatorship in Haiti. He was aware of all this and knew where it led: back to 1945. The organization was called Vatican Corridor, and their aim was to run Operation Convent, which helped distinguished members of the Nazi party escape to various Latin American countries. Among them were Hans Fischböck, an SS general; Adolf Eichmann, the man behind the "Final Solution," the plan to exterminate millions of Jews; and Josef Mengele, the Auschwitz doctor.

Years later, the mandate was clear again: eliminate any sign of modernization from within the Church. La Sapinière, aided by the CIA, fought liberation theology fiercely.

Brother Sebastián shuddered to recall these things; he had to stop the Vatican from using a secret organization to intervene and dismantle the plan laid out by the master. But the worst thing was Brother Joaquín explicitly mentioning La Sapinière. To what degree was the

Vatican's secret organization in charge of internal affairs involved in all this?

"No. I refuse. The Vatican cannot stick their noses in this. Besides, it's the end of the road for Rome. They'll do whatever they can to hold on to their power. They'll do anything to stop the church of the poor from being born. We all know their position on modernization and renovation. We saw what happened with liberation theology."

"That's heresy. Brother Sebastián, I think you misunderstood me. If that's what you think, then let me ask you, what are you doing working in such a high post at the very heart of the Church?"

"Joaquín, there's no way to bring about change from outside the Church. It is from within that new hope will flourish—"

"What if it fails? Are we going to jeopardize the Church? The good and the bad? I'm not defending Rome; I know mistakes have been made. It's true. But we've learned from them. The most important thing is to keep faith in Christ alive. If the secret falls into the wrong hands, if the Corbel gets hold of it, we're lost. We know that. That's why I say it's wiser to keep it hidden until better times come along. As Knights of Moriah we must continue to be vigilant until that time arrives."

"That time will *never* arrive. That hope will *never* be fulfilled. Rome is not interested in it in the slightest. You're well aware of that, Brother Joaquín. The Vatican is not willing to modernize; they think they would lose power. Christians lost their faith in the Vatican a long time ago. Power corrupts."

"That's heresy, Brother Sebastián!" he repeated.

Sebastián pondered for a few minutes and then repeated a speech they were all familiar with.

"Humanity's salvation lies in the birth of Christ and his Passion. The temple of the poor has two façades, the Nativity and the Passion. The new church is founded on the Apocalypse, where it says the church is a leafy tree beneath which fountains flow . . . 'Blessed are they that wash their robes, that they may have a right to the tree of life and to enter by the gates of the city. Outside are the dogs and sorcerers, the unchaste, the killers, the idolaters, and all those who love and practice falsehood.' Does Brother Joaquín think that the Vatican will enter the new city of God and take the reins of this new power?"

"Beneath the foundations of the Church lies the—"

"*Christ* is the cornerstone! The stone the builders rejected," Sebastián said, cutting him off.

Sebastián and Joaquín continued arguing, growing increasingly vehement. The others listened attentively. In a way they were both right. Magdalena sided with Sebastián. She didn't think La Sapinière should be called in. Cristóbal didn't speak for quite some time, listening to his companions.

Finally, he said, "We'll continue to protect the chosen one. We'll follow her wherever she goes and give her our help. The plan must be carried out. We cannot betray our teacher. It is written. The race began eight hundred years ago and now we have only two days left."

The meeting was adjourned. From that moment on, they each knew what they had to do.

At all costs.

34

"NOGUÉS, WHAT DO we have?"

"Another stiff."

"I can see that," Mortimer replied, chewing furiously on his toothpick.

"Shot in the back. Nine-caliber."

Mortimer didn't respond.

Nogués loosened the knot tying the dead monk's cassock closed.

"Know anything about monks?"

"No."

"Looks like some kind of Franciscan, or else the old guy was in a Halloween costume. This is really strange. You think this one has anything to do with the priest at San Cristóbal Church?" Nogués tugged the habit open as he spoke.

"I don't know, Nogués. Does he have any ID?"

"Nope."

His shirt bore a large image of a cypress tree.

"That's some kind of symbol, like the Templars and all that," Nogués said. "Old knights wear them. What's this all about?"

"Well, looks like we've got someone who wants to kill priests and Franciscan monks on our hands."

"Do Franciscans usually carry swords?" Nogués asked, discovering the weapon the monk had hidden inside his cassock.

"Question the couple who found the body."

"Already did, boss. Before you got here. Seems there was a guy with him."

"Did they give you a description?"

"They were pretty shaken up, but the girl's got a good eye. Her description fits the mathematician."

"The mathematician?"

"Yeah, you know. The boyfriend of the girl whose grandfather died at the home."

Mortimer bent down over the body and began fiddling with the monk's shirt.

"Looking for something?"

Nogués watched Mortimer examine some bruises on the victim's neck.

"Yeah. The dead guy was wearing something around his neck. Whoever it was snatched it off him. It must have been worth something. Judging by the marks, I'd say the chain was pretty thick."

Mortimer couldn't hide his displeasure, and Nogués picked up on it.

"We should question the mathematician and his girlfriend. Maybe it's just a coincidence, but—"

"Yeah. We'll question them. But not yet," Mortimer replied tersely. "Not yet."

35

THEY DECIDED TO take a taxi and within a few minutes were able to flag one down.

They got in. "To Pedralbes. The Finca Güell pavilions," Miguel said.

María didn't say a word. She had a hunch. Maybe it was just a coincidence, but the taxi driver looked a lot like the big guy from the bus, the one who'd stood up to block the way of the thugs who tried to shoot them on Calle Balmes. He was so tall his head almost touched the roof of the car. He was big and strong, with a wide face and black beard, and although his hair was unkempt, he was friendly and smiling. Hanging from his rearview mirror was a figure both Miguel and María recognized immediately. A medallion of San Cristóbal—Saint Christopher. The driver saw them looking at it and said, "He's our patron saint, travelers and drivers. Shame the Pope decided to take his feast day off the Church calendar. But we still worship him, us drivers. We even have an association, a brotherhood."

"You don't say?" Miguel responded.

"Yeah, it's really old. Founded over five hundred years ago."

"Back when the cathedrals were being built?"

"Exactly. They've taken his image out of some cathedrals, though. But he's still at the one in Sevilla, and on the way to Santiago . . ."

The taxi driver seemed chatty, like he wanted to lecture them, so they let him. They just sat back and listened.

"It's an old tradition. With the number of accidents on the roads, I can't understand how the Pope could have removed Christopher from the saints calendar," he repeated. "Doesn't make any sense. Well, I mean, of course on one level it does . . ."

Then he fell silent. But he was smiling, as if with that last unfinished sentence he'd left a door open. Miguel held back, but María took the bait. She wanted to see where this would lead.

"What do you mean?"

"Oh, nothing. I'm just rambling. I hope I'm not bothering you."

"No, not at all! Please, continue."

"Well, in the brotherhood, we organize a lot of cultural activities. We're always learning; we take field trips, have people come give us talks. We're really interested in medieval legends about Christopher. The other day, for example, we had a history professor speak to us about the way to Santiago, you know, the pilgrim's route, because pilgrims are devout followers of Saint Christopher. Anyway, he told us the whole experience is symbolic: the journey, the pilgrimage—traveling the road to Santiago is like a rebirth. That's what he said, like dying and being born again. Like killing the dragon. Imagine! Who would've thought? We see images of Michael and James—San Miguel and San Jaime—slaying the dragon all the time, and it turns out it's all just symbolic. Of course, nobody cares about those stories anymore. Finding people like you is a miracle! I tell you, I see different people all day long and nobody seems to care about those stories. People live too fast nowadays. No one's willing to slay the dragon, so to speak. I'm just talking nonsense, you'll have to excuse me," he said.

"No, I agree with you," María said, squeezing Miguel's hand.

"Alright, here we are!"

"Could you wait for us for a little while?"

"You know what? I like you two; I won't even charge you for the time." The driver took a card out of the glove compartment and handed it to them, adding, "Here. If you ever need my services, don't hesitate to call." Miguel took the card. "Go on, I'll wait right here."

They got out of the taxi, which had parked on the corner of Calle Manuel Antonio, and walked toward the iron gates surrounding Finca Güell. They crossed the street. It was late and the place was deserted. Miguel turned around; the taxi was still there, parked by the sidewalk.

"What are you thinking, María?"

"That driver. He's the same guy from the bus."

"What do you mean?"

"It's him. I'm sure of it. He was reading a book on Gaudí and he got up and blocked the Corbel men so they couldn't get me. He stalled them until I had enough time to jump off."

"Let's go straight to the third gate and not waste any time; the dragon awaits us," Miguel said.

For a few minutes they just stood there, contemplating the impressive wrought-iron gate. There was Ladon the dragon, his jaws wide open, so fierce he looked alive. *So, I'm supposed to kill you, huh?* Miguel thought to himself. *But how? What am I supposed to do? How do I slay an iron monster? What do I do?* These thoughts were all bubbling up inside him. He needed to believe. In order to kill the dragon, he had to believe. He had to understand that what was really being asked of him was that he have complete faith in her. It was a rite of passage, a transformation. He had to get past his incredulity, to be reborn, become another, see things with new eyes. That was all there was to it. That was what he had to realize. After everything that had happened, how could he not believe? People were dying all around him, and he was caught up in a scheme that was sheer madness. Nothing was certain, Miguel thought.

He looked up at the sky and stared at the starry night. Through the Barcelona smog he could make out the North Star and Ursa Major and

Ursa Minor, which once formed part of Draco, the dragon constellation. *Another dragon,* Miguel thought. *Up in the heavens. What is above
as is what is below. Kill the dragon, be reborn. What's going on? Why am I
trembling?* He turned and gazed back at María. She was crying. Tears ran
silently down her cheeks.

"What's the matter?"

"Don't you see? It's my grandfather's message. This is the beginning.
If we start this journey, we have to be reborn, we have to believe. I know
it's hard for you, but that's the way it is. Otherwise we can't go on . . ."

"The dragon's at the gate . . ."

"Yes, it's Hänsel and Gretel's trail. The one that disappears in the
forest. Don't you see? We have to follow the signs, find the treasure, find
our way home."

"Please, María. I don't know what to think. This is all so . . . I just
don't know what to do. What is the dragon hiding? Your grandfather
wrote something about a map. Part of a map that had another missing
piece, that was inside you. What is it that I'm supposed to see?"

Miguel ran his hand over the dragon, fingering the chains, its jaws,
the pointed balls on the chains. He tried to engrave the image in his
mind.

"That's up to you. You're alone with your dragon. Don't you see?
There's nothing else to it; that's all there is. No mystery. You don't need
your sword to slay it."

"I have to thrust the sword into myself instead. Is that what you're
saying? To slay my own fears."

"I've made up my mind, Miguel. I'll go on alone. Like Virgil, you can
stand at the gates, or you can . . . believe."

Suddenly he understood. He loved her. He loved María more than
he could imagine. He couldn't possibly leave her now, leave her alone.
He loved her.

"Do you believe in me?"

"I love you."

He felt so small, and yet at the same time he felt enormous there beneath the stars, beside that monster that seemed to be saying: you've found the love of your life; are you going to leave her now?

Miguel, so rational, so skeptical, was afraid. Afraid of his own emotions. But there she was before him: María.

He stared at the dragon, his dragon, into its open jaws, and said, "I love you. I'm here with you now and I always will be, if you want me to be."

María looked at his face. It was transformed.

They embraced and kissed. And the dragon watched over that new Garden of Hesperides.

They were alone, like Hänsel and Gretel. But they knew that together they'd find their way out of the forest.

Neither of them noticed that the taxi driver had started the cab's engine and was slowly pulling away.

Miguel held on to María, looking over her shoulder at the dragon until its image was etched in his mind.

Something was happening. They weren't sure what exactly, but a transformation had begun.

PART VI

GAMMA

36

GUESTS STARTED ARRIVING at the Friends of Modernism Foundation on Sunday evening.

The building, located on Calle Bruc, had been designed by an unknown architect. It might have been built in 1901, but the exact date was unknown. It was a beautiful, symmetrical multifamily apartment house with a main, central door on the ground floor. The entryway was spacious and the walls were decorated with Eastern-looking geometric drawings. The lobby still had the original buzzer panel. The balconies were wrought iron and the front of the building was decorated with floral motifs and interesting merlons crowning the roof; it was very attractive and had a certain charm.

Bru had bought the entire ground floor—which had been a motorcycle shop—and three apartments on the second floor for an astronomical price, so that his protégée Taimatsu could use it as the foundation's headquarters.

María and Miguel arrived just as the mayor was finishing his speech on a little stage that had been erected, with long tables on either side.

Everyone who was anyone in town had come to the opening. Miguel and María stayed near the entrance to hear Taimatsu and the Ministry of Culture's director speak.

Then the party began, and the best cava from Bru's bodega was poured.

Taimatsu was radiant, seeing to all of her acquaintances while Bru socialized with guests from the world of business and finance.

María went to congratulate Taimatsu as Miguel made his way through the crowds in search of a couple glasses of cava.

"Having a good time?"

Miguel turned. A smiling Álvaro Climent held out his hand.

"Álvaro! Wow, it's been a long time!" he exclaimed on running into the old friend who, just a few days ago, he'd seen on television.

They greeted each other effusively. They had gone to school together, but Álvaro had stopped studying math after his first year of college, opting for history instead. He ran the family business now, a small bookstore on Calle Freixures, a place where Miguel had often enjoyed exploring the shelves. Álvaro was always being invited to appear on talk shows, usually sensational programs about unsolved mysteries or esoteric topics.

"I just came to hear the politicians speak about the foundation's goals, the importance of Modernism, institutional support for private initiatives in culture and all that. So how long has it been?"

"Ten years?"

"At least. You haven't changed. I've kept tabs on you, you know. When are you expecting the Nobel?" he joked.

"Very funny. Álvaro, you look exactly the same; you must have found an algorithm to stop time."

"How could I stop time's arrow before it leaves the bow? No, I'm more interested in the algorithm of garlic. Though recently I've also discovered the walnut theory . . ."

"So you're still into your crazy diets."

"Listen to me, Miguel. Give up beans, I'm telling you. Pythagoras never touched them. A field of beans is a mathematician's hell—"

"So are you still into all that esoteric stuff, still an unsolved mystery fanatic? I've seen you on TV a few times . . ."

"The bookstore's going well, and that gives me the freedom to do what I want. I've become a real authority! Hey, do you have plans when this is over? Why don't you stop by the bookstore and we'll have a chat, go to dinner?"

"I'm not alone. I'm here with—" He was going to say "a friend" but stopped himself.

"Your girlfriend? Well, that's new! Who'd have guessed? The mathematician and former national fencing champion, in love!"

"Well, we haven't been going out that long. But, yeah, I am. I'm in love," Miguel replied.

"That's fantastic. Is she here?"

"Come on, I'll introduce you."

They walked over to María, who was standing by Taimatsu and a few foundation colleagues. María broke away from the group.

Miguel introduced them.

María recognized Álvaro; she'd seen him on TV, too.

"I tell you, this TV business is great; everybody recognizes you."

"You two seem like a good combination: a mathematician and an art historian. Are you working on anything together?"

They were taken aback by his question.

"Well, uh, you could say that."

So Miguel went on to give a succinct explanation of his theory of fractal mathematics and how they related to Modernist architecture.

"Looking at any architect in particular?"

"Gaudí."

"Ah. A very interesting guy, and enigmatic, too. A true Mason."

"Gaudí wasn't a Mason!" María exclaimed, perhaps too fervently.

Álvaro Climent saw that he'd touched a nerve but continued anyway.

"Well, I'm not saying he was a grand master, but as far as I know, Gaudí's connections to Masonry are well established. He worked with Josep and Eduard Fontseré, two brothers who were renowned Masons. Plus, he used to visit the Poblet monastery regularly, where

Wharton's tomb is—or was. The poor wretch ended up broke, serving King Felipe V in a Lérida regiment."

"So? What does that prove?" María asked.

"Well, those are just details. But I can give you more. For example, the writer Luis Carandell is of the opinion that Park Güell was planned as a Masonic city, a sort of giant lodge financed by its patron," the bookseller stated.

"And yet Juan Bassegoda, the architect and director of the Gaudí Real Cátedra, thinks just the opposite. It's true that Gaudí upheld the ideals of socialism when he was younger, but Catholicism—which was a constant in his life—distanced him from Masonry. Besides, Bassegoda says that if he had been a Mason, his name would have appeared on at least *one* of the lists of the dozens of lodges that existed in Barcelona," she responded.

"But everyone knows that when you join them, you get a code name."

Just then Taimatsu approached the group.

"I hate to interrupt, but I need you, María," she said.

María excused herself, said good-bye to Álvaro, and walked off with Taimatsu.

The two men were alone again.

"It's true, Miguel, you're in love. It's a miracle. You—always so indifferent when it came to women, only interested in your theorems and calculations. You've finally fallen into Aphrodite's arms."

"Don't make fun of me."

"I'm not. I'm happy for you. Besides, she's pretty and she seems to have her head on straight. Hey, seriously, why don't you both stop by the bookstore? I have to go now, but we could meet around nine, say. Just knock. I'll be inside. I pretty much live there."

Miguel didn't promise anything but said he'd ask María.

"I'm sure this party won't go on too much longer," Álvaro said.

Miguel stood there alone, looking for María. He spotted her amidst a group of people with Taimatsu. He decided not to go over there yet;

he liked watching her. María was radiant. Truly, there was no denying it. He was in love with her. Even his friend had picked up on it. Álvaro was a strange guy, but he was happy to bump into him after all this time. They'd met as teenagers; they went to the same high school, and back then they'd been inseparable. They'd had the same group of friends who'd meet up all the time to go out, go to the movies, or study together. Álvaro had always been a voracious reader, and he was really into occult things that hadn't interested Miguel much. His father's bookstore was well stocked with those sorts of books because they always sold. Then when Álvaro had stopped studying math, they lost touch. Miguel was thinking of all this as he stood there watching María. The dragon. That's what had done it: the dragon. But what had actually *happened*? Nothing. Everything. He realized he was a changed man. The dragon had awakened him. Up until that moment, what had he really felt for María? Attraction? They had a mature relationship that gave both of them independence. He loved her, he was comfortable with her, he looked forward to seeing her, but they'd never even considered living together, much less committing themselves to anything deeper than that. They figured they'd just carry on like that until one of them got bored and moved on, or they'd keep seeing each other, making love, having fun. But that was it. Any change in either one of their lives could have put an end to the relationship—if he moved to another university or got a grant to go do research someplace else, or if she decided to relocate for her career. It had all been perfectly clear right up until that moment. Their commitment had been to the here and now. But all that had changed. Now he couldn't live without her. Now he understood what people meant when they said faith is trust, not knowledge. Standing there in front of that dragon, part of him died. Now he was going to live out his future in a whole new way. And María was the future.

From the other side of the room María was looking at him, too. They were alone. No one else existed. They knew it.

37

DO YOU THINK he's trustworthy?" María asked.

"I think he might be able to help us. I arranged to meet him at his bookstore."

"But can we trust him?"

"He's a friend. I've known him for years. And he's an expert on sects and esotericism. Like I said, he has a secondhand bookstore. He spends his whole life there."

"There and on television."

"Yeah, well," he said by way of excuse, "still, I think he's the man we need to help us solve your grandfather's puzzles . . . But if you're not comfortable with this, we won't do it."

"Have you told him anything?"

"No. And we don't have to tell him everything. Just the essentials."

María didn't respond. They'd left the party and walked up Calle Bruc toward Avenida Diagonal, then turned left onto Calle Provenza.

"Is the car parked nearby?"

"On the corner of Paseo de Gràcia, just a little past La Pedrera."

María was lost in thought as they walked. She wasn't at all sure how this guy was supposed to help them. She clutched her purse tightly. Since the masked man's visit she didn't dare leave the notebook at

home. It held the key, somewhere among its riddles, notes, and drawings.

"María, I've seen two murders and I'm sure your grandfather's death
was no accident."

"I know. He was murdered, too. I'm sure of it."

"I am, too. I can't believe the police haven't even questioned me yet.
They'll probably arrest me soon."

"*Arrest* you?" she exclaimed, frightened.

"Think about it. My prints are all over the place. Two people saw me
with the . . . the dead Knight of Moriah. María, they'll put two and two
together pretty quickly. If they haven't already, that is. And what can I
tell them?"

"We can't tell them anything. We have to find . . ."

"Find what?"

"Whatever it is that my grandfather hid. That's a mystery that we
have to solve ourselves."

"But we don't even know what we're looking for!"

"Or what we have to do when we find it," María added.

"I think when we find it we'll know what to do."

"Should we show him the notebook?"

"Who?"

"Your friend."

"I think we should tell him what's absolutely necessary, nothing
more."

"What about the murders?"

"Well, for now let's just mention Father Jonás, and I think we should
show him the medallions, too."

"What about my grandfather's story?"

"Yeah, I think so. If we don't tell him that, how can he possibly
help us?"

"OK."

They got to the underground parking lot entrance and started down
a staircase. At the bottom of the stairs, Miguel inserted his card into the

machine and took his ticket. They went through the stairwell door into the lot and looked for the car; there wasn't much light. It was deserted. They were alone, and María was frightened; she instinctively grabbed Miguel's arm.

"What's wrong?"

"I'm scared."

"Actually, me, too."

María and Miguel felt like they were being watched. They stopped and looked around, but there was no one there. Finally they found the car, parked at an angle. They picked up the pace, and when they were just a few feet away, headlights suddenly flashed on, blinding them. It was all very fast. A man emerged from among the cars parked behind them. He had a gun. They didn't say a word, didn't know what to do. Another man got out of the car that had its headlights trained on them. He also had a gun.

"Stop or we'll shoot!"

The men shoved them down against a car hood.

"Nice and easy; don't turn around and no one gets hurt."

They obeyed.

One of the men started to frisk them.

"What do you want? Don't hurt her," Miguel said.

"Shut up!"

Miguel noticed that they both had Eastern European accents.

"Where's the notebook? We know you have it," one of them demanded.

Neither of them answered. Miguel felt an intense pain in his right side. He'd been hit hard and it took the wind out of him for a minute.

"I have it, I have it! Leave him alone!" María cried, holding up her bag without turning around and without getting up off the car hood.

They snatched the purse from her. She heard its contents spill onto the floor. When her cell hit the ground, the battery fell out.

"On your knees!" one of them shouted.

They obeyed. They could feel the men's breath right behind them. Miguel thought that was it. Those guys would blow their brains out, right there, no two ways about it. As soon as they found the diary.

"Got it!" said one, stooping to pick it up off the floor.

But he didn't.

Miguel heard a sound that was very familiar: the swish of a blade slicing through the air.

Then came a cry of pain and a body falling. Several shots rang out. Miguel grabbed María and pushed her in between two parked cars.

"Don't move!"

"What's going on?"

Miguel looked up. One of the men who'd attacked them was lying on the floor in a pool of blood; he'd been decapitated. He heard more shots and instinctively crouched down. He didn't dare raise his head. He could hear someone running, swearing in an Eastern European language. Then a car started and peeled out in front of them.

Then the sound of footsteps, running to the exit.

"What happened?"

"Someone just saved us; whoever it was killed one of those guys, and the other one took off. I saw the guy who helped us going toward the exit. How could he have escaped without getting hit by all those bullets?"

"He's dead," María said, staring at the headless body lying on the ground.

"Yeah, he is. But your grandfather's notebook is gone. His buddy took off with it."

"They were going to kill us," she said, unable to hide her panic.

"I have no doubt about that. Right in this parking lot, like a couple of dogs. If it weren't for our mysterious friend—"

"One of the seven knights?"

"Well, someone who handles a sword like an Olympic champion."

"Let's get out of here," María said.

"We should call the police."

"Please, let's just go. No police. Let's get out of here before someone sees us."

They got into the car and pulled out silently.

"This is all so strange. Those two were not Corbel."

"You think there are other people involved in this?"

"Well, the Corbel certainly didn't hire them; they could do that kind of thing on their own, no problem."

"What do we do now?"

"First we need a strong cup of coffee. Then we'll go to my friend's store. I can't think of anything else to do. All I know is we only have one day left. One day and we still don't even know what we're looking for! It's a good thing Taimatsu photocopied the notebook."

"Miguel, I'm really scared," María said.

"So am I, my love. So am I."

But what he couldn't say was that he was frightened for her; he couldn't upset her any more than she already was. Miguel was convinced that for María to be saved, the prophecy had to be fulfilled—and there wasn't much time left.

38

J AUME BRU AND Taimatsu didn't wait for the last guests to go before they left the foundation. They were eager to get back to the magnate's house; they were both overflowing with nervous energy and couldn't wait to make love. Bru had never seen Taimatsu so happy. The opening was a huge success and she was radiant with joy. He'd always admired her joie de vivre, the passion life seemed to inspire in her, the way she lived each moment to the fullest. Taimatsu was so happy she couldn't have hidden it if she tried. For her, the world as it was was the best possible reality. It was perfect, and she didn't want to spoil it. She had a way of warding off all pain, anything unpleasant. She hadn't come into this world to suffer but to make a splash through hard work, through her profession. The world was her oyster, and she couldn't understand why some people were determined to mess it up. Why would she be suspicious of what her uncle did? Or the businesses Bru ran? She was incapable of seeing anything shady about him. But Bru wasn't just shady; he was evil. And he enjoyed it. Taimatsu was his antithesis, and maybe that's why he'd fallen so hopelessly in love with her. He had first seen her when she was a fourteen-year-old girl hunting for shells on the beach in Cadaqués. That was so long ago. And he, who had always had such an urgent need to possess the women in his life immediately, had waited. He waited for his little Japanese angel to grow up, patiently, like a schoolboy, visiting her aunt and uncle from time to time just so he could see her.

When he first realized he loved her, he was furious. He couldn't let himself be carried away by such a weak, frivolous emotion. He had all the women he wanted; he picked them up and dropped them at will, like objects. And that was what made him so angry: he didn't want to possess Taimatsu, or protect her, or be her friend, or even love her. So what the hell did he want from her? What he felt was horrible. Two words came to mind: "unconditional" and "destiny."

At any rate, he'd lost his mind—or that's what he tried to convince himself of. But that madness didn't make him feel defenseless or miserable. In fact, it was a release. That amazing insanity made him feel alive, like a fire fueled by the wind. He surrendered himself to a fantasy life he'd never known he could have and floated through a comfortable haze that made him view Taimatsu as perfection, a musical piece written by a genius and played by a virtuoso.

And he, so jaded and rotten, had actually been touched by another person. He'd seen the way she looked at him, like no one ever had. She thought he was noble. Of course, he knew better; he never had been and never would be noble. But seeing such admiration, such naïveté in her eyes, disarmed him. And she loved him, too.

From then on, not a day had gone by when he wasn't aware that he needed her, needed to think about her. And he did. For twelve years while he waited for her. And now, finally, they were together.

He made love to her as soon as they got back to his place, slowly and masterfully, like a sculptor. She'd taught him how. The art of love is leisurely; it's an art of appreciation. It had nothing to do with his sexual exploits with whores. With Taimatsu he discovered a new way of making love, with emotion. It was as if they were dancing together in bed, touching, kissing, caressing, discovering each other, and Bru almost lamented the moment of penetration. For the first time in his life he'd given up that base, animal urgency, given it up for an absolute calm, one of limitless pleasure. It was then that he felt capable of surrendering everything and running away with her to some deserted island. He wanted to say things he'd never even thought before, like "I love you madly" or "I'm an evil, murderous man, but I'm willing to give it all up to be with you anywhere and love you for the rest of my days. It's enough for me just to look at you, to see you smile, to stroke your hair, hear your voice, and have you by my side forever." He'd actually said something to that effect once, though he did feel utterly ridiculous. He didn't care. She was his world, and he was ready to travel the length of it if she'd let him.

"You're crazy, Jaume," Taimatsu had said, smiling and hugging him.

Yes, he was crazy. But if that delicious madness was love, then he was prepared to give everything he had for it. Taimatsu was immortality.

"I have to go," Taimatsu said.

"Already? But it's so early!"

"I have work."

"Work? What work? It's far too late to work!"

"Which is it? So early or far too late?"

Bru smiled.

"Alright, go if you want to. I know you will, anyway."

"I love you."

"I don't love you."

"You don't?"

"No. I adore you."

Taimatsu got dressed as Bru contentedly looked on.

The phone rang. It was Yuri. He was waiting.

"Did you get it?" he asked.

"Yeah. But one of my guys is dead."

"Five minutes. Give me five minutes."

And he hung up.

What did he care if some damn Russian was dead?

39

I N T H E E N D they told Álvaro everything, holding nothing back. Miguel was sure his friend would be able to help them, although María wasn't entirely convinced. They didn't have anything to go on; they'd made no progress whatsoever. In fact, all they knew was that the race began with the tortoise, and from that moment on, they had six days to complete some sort of plan, the prophecy. And five of those six days had already passed; there was only one left. They didn't have a moment to waste. Time was running out. And people were getting killed. They had to get down to business—now. They'd already lost the notebook and the game. Luckily they had the photocopies Taimatsu had made.

They'd been at the bookstore for half an hour. It was a small place on a dark, narrow street called Calle Freixures. The place gave María the creeps.

The shop itself was quite spacious, once you were inside. It was Álvaro's sanctuary: a windowless room whose four walls were covered from floor to ceiling with wooden shelves full of books. Many of them had pages torn out, and they were all jumbled together in no particular order. A small door at the back, opposite the entrance, opened onto a narrow corridor that led to a bathroom and another tiny room, also windowless, which Álvaro used as a storeroom. That was where he had his desk—it was made of some sort of black stained wood and covered with piles of books, manuscripts, old maps, parchments, and loose pages in search of the books they belonged to. There was a computer on one side and, in a corner, a dented globe with metal rings showing the trajectories of the five planets. Beside the desk sat a sagging sofa and a small table piled with magazines yellowed with age, plastic cups, uneaten food, and empty potato chip bags. In another corner stood a refrigerator and, above it, a small shelf that barely supported the weight of a microwave and a coffeemaker.

"Excuse the mess. I pretty much live here."

Álvaro picked up dirty glasses, empty bags, and leftover food. He opened the fridge and took out three beers. And since they couldn't all fit on the sofa, he went to get a folding chair from the front of the shop.

At some point during their long explanation, María began to feel uneasy. But Miguel had faith in his old friend. They talked about Gaudí, Templars, Knights of Moriah, Masons, and a whole range of other subjects. It was late by the time Álvaro finally began to speak. He seemed very familiar with the architect's relationship to various mysterious characters. Amongst the things Álvaro told them, they both paid special attention to his report of Gaudí's unusual trip to Occitania. He'd gone with the Conservation Society and his close friend, the poet Joan Maragall. The society, founded at the end of the nineteenth century, had several well-known and eccentric members: Lluís Domènech i Montaner, Francisco Ferrer y Guardia, Anselmo Lorenzo, and Eliseo Reclús, an anarchist geographer and Mason.

"Fulcanelli, the last real alchemist—I assume you know him—came to Barcelona several times. His birth name was Jean-Julien Champagne, of course. He was born in a small rural community about twelve miles north of Paris, a place called Villiers-le-Bel. He died in Paris in 1932, utterly destitute. Anyway, as I was saying, he came to Barcelona several times, but that's not where Gaudí met him. They met through their mutual friend, the architect Eugène Emmanuel Viollet-le-Duc, in Occitania. Gaudí preserved Viollet-le-Duc's works until his death; as I'm sure you know, Viollet-le-Duc was famous for his restoration of Gothic cathedrals, and Gaudí admired him greatly. I have no doubt that the three of them were masters of *art cot*."

"*Art cot?*" Miguel asked.

"Yes, they knew it well. The lost language. Fulcanelli the alchemist interpreted the words that had been carved in stone. Gaudí wanted to take things further, which wound up putting distance between them just when Gaudí began dedicating his life to La Sagrada Família."

Miguel thought his friend was going off on a tangent, so before letting him continue, he interrupted and said flat out, "Well, that's all fine. But what are we looking for? What do you think Gaudí left María's grandfather? If you have any idea, that is. We don't have much time."

Álvaro thought for a minute. There wasn't much light in the room, just a floor lamp on one side: an antique, with a serpent coiled around it, a caduceus. That and some of the other unusual decorations struck María as rather odd.

Slowly, as if it were a ritual, Álvaro stood, opened the refrigerator, and looked at Miguel and María's expectant faces. Each time the bookseller went to get fresh beers, the light from the floor lamp temporarily blinded them. He took out three cans and then turned to them abruptly. He was smiling, his eyes gleaming. He closed the fridge, nodding, and he said ceremoniously, "The Omphalos. I'm sure of it."

"The what?"

"The cornerstone. The navel of the world. That's what Gaudí gave your grandfather. Why? Now, *that* I couldn't say."

"Could you, uh, expand a little?" Miguel asked.

"In many cultures, the stone symbolizes divine power."

"Sure, it's used to make weapons and utensils. But what's so divine about that?" Miguel replied, puzzled.

"The Stone Age was the first phase of human culture. But that's not what I'm referring to. There are religious buildings made of huge stone blocks—menhirs, dolmens, stone circles and avenues—dating back to about 6000 BC. In the ancient Orient, stones signified divine presence, and people made liquid offerings to them."

"Blood?"

"And oil. Stone was used for the altar: the Beth-El, or House of God."

"OK, let's say all that's true. I'm not doubting your knowledge. But it's just mythology, cerebral fabrications, things that men—"

"Would you let me continue?" the bookseller interrupted brusquely.

Miguel started, and Álvaro, speaking slowly, went on.

"Exodus 20:25 says, 'And if thou wilt make me an altar of stone, thou shalt not build it of hewn stone, for if thou lift up thy tool upon it, thou hast polluted it.'"

"Great, now we know the origin of the altar. So is that what we're looking for?"

"No! Don't be so impatient."

"Miguel, let him talk. He's obviously going somewhere with this, so let's hear him out," María insisted, keenly interested in everything Álvaro was saying.

"Be patient, my friend. What I'm saying is that stones have been a constant source of symbolism throughout human history and in every culture. And interpreting them correctly will give us the key to what we're looking for. Now, I don't know how and where. But, for example, stones play a role in ancient coronation ceremonies. In ancient Ireland, there was a 'Stone of Knowledge' in Tara. There were also two stones that were so close together you couldn't put your hand between them. If they accepted a man as future king, the stones parted before him so that he could pass between them. The legend of King Arthur, the Excalibur sword, the sword in the stone . . . Some prehistoric dolmens in Britain were thought to be charged with a special energy, and sterile women sat on them in order to receive the power of fertility from the bones of mother earth. The heat from those stones symbolized life force, and they thought it would bring them many descendants. What I'm saying is that some cultures imbued stones with the power to store the earth's force and transmit it to humans. Now, let's jump forward in time. In Freemasonry, the rough stone that has not been shaped represents the apprentice. Becoming a cut stone, one that belongs in the great Temple of Humanity, is the goal. This symbolism dates back to medieval cathedrals, where stonemasonry was of vital importance. In fact, vault keystones often bore the mark of the master stonemason. And in alchemy, the so-called philosopher's stone or stone of knowledge, the *lapis philosophorum,* represents the ultimate goal of converting inexpensive metal into gold."

"But that's not what we're looking for."

"No. That wasn't Gaudí's secret."

The bookseller paused.

"The oracle at Delphi was the most important sanctuary of the ancient world, situated in a place considered sacred since time immemorial."

"Yes, it was dedicated to Apollo, who stood for eternal youth, beauty, harmony, and balance. He was often called Phoebus: 'luminous,'" María added.

"Well, I see you're up on your Greek mythology!" Álvaro exclaimed, obviously impressed. "So, as I was saying, Delphi was where the Omphalos was, the stone representing the navel of the earth, the very center."

"Protected by a dangerous creature."

"A python, which is where we get the name Pythia, the great sorceress and prophet of Delphi. And Apollo, in order to get the stone, had to kill the python with his two golden arrows." The bookseller paused. "You two will have to fight a monster to get what you're looking for as well."

"The Omphalos?" Miguel asked, unsure.

"Yes. But the one belonging to *our* tradition."

"OK, now I'm really lost. What do you mean 'our tradition'? There's another one?"

"Yes, Miguel. It's in the Gospels. Matthew 16:18, to be exact. That's

where it explains what the church is, as an institution. That verse paves
the way for the Passion, when Jesus reveals to his disciples what their
mission on earth shall be. Don't you remember? Christ asked, 'Who
am I?' Some said he was a prophet. But only Simon, the son of Jonas,
answered correctly. It all happened in Caesarea Philippi, at the foot of
Mount Hermon."

"In one of the pages Taimatsu photocopied, there was something
about Mount Hermon and Caesarea Philippi," Miguel said.

"It's a volcanic region in the north of what's now Israel."

"But what happened there? What do the Gospels say?"

Álvaro's expression changed.

"Simon Peter was the only disciple who said to Jesus, 'You are the
Messiah; the Son of the living God.' And Jesus said, 'Thou art Peter,
and upon this rock I will build my church; and the gates of hell shall
not prevail against it.'"

"You're saying Christ gave Peter a stone to build the church? I'm
sorry, Álvaro, but I think that's viewed as symbolic—"

"Words, words, words. The art of language is like a mask, covering
up the truth. But the word hides the stone, and that's where the secret
lies. That's one of the mysteries Fulcanelli revealed in his book. You
have to destroy the word to discover the truth. The Church, as an institution, has allowed and even encouraged a number of myths: legends
about the Holy Grail, relics of Christ, nails, the holy shroud . . . If we
added up all the pieces of wood supposedly taken from true cross that
are venerated in cathedrals, churches, and shrines all over the world,
we'd have enough to build a house. The lance of Longinus; an infinite
number of saints' relics; angels that are worshipped, observed, paraded
around in processions; et cetera, et cetera . . . And the Vatican puts
up no opposition. They allow these many displays even though they're
almost pagan. But they've done a very good job of protecting their *real*
secret for centuries: the stone, which is where their power lies. That's
where their strength comes from, and it's all over Europe, branching
out, spreading. Temples, sanctuaries, shrines, cathedrals. The greatest

secret in all of Christianity is the closest one to us, the one right before our eyes, but it's been protected, masked by words. Who would ever guess that—"

"A simple stone . . . ," María said, astonished, interrupting Álvaro.

"Yes. The one Jesus touched with his very hand. 'Upon this rock I will build my church.' And that's the way it was. The center of the world."

María noticed that as he went on, the bookseller's tone of voice changed.

"The very foundations of our faith and of Western civilization: the holy stone. In Rome the powers that be made sure to hide Jesus's secret. It's stated openly in the Gospels, in plain language: no parables, no rambling. Yet no one got it, and Peter built a church founded on the wrong thing, and Christianity was grown out of hatred and blood. If people had known about the relic and realized his mistake, the Church would never have ruled. Two thousand years of power on earth. No state, no empire—with the exception of Egypt—has managed to survive for so long. Even now—with no army, no nuclear power, just the word—from a tiny city, the Vatican continues to spread all over the world. They've been able to keep the secret hidden, despite the fact that it's right there in front of us, despite the fact that we can almost reach out and touch it. The word enshrouds it. Even in Mecca, there's the eastern cornerstone of the Kaaba, the famous black stone—another mistake that has led to bloodshed throughout the world. The orthodox version says that Abraham and his son Ishmael left it in Mecca after the flood; but some people say it was a Sufi sect that deposited it where it now sits, where all Muslims pray to it."

"Álvaro, this is all well and good, but it's just another legend. Let's just say that it's true, that the stone from Caesarea Philippi at the foot of Mount Hermon, the sacred mountain, was hidden. Then we'd have to attribute certain properties to the stone Jesus touched, properties that are—"

"Supernatural? What does 'supernatural' really mean? Anything science, reason, or math hasn't yet discovered?" Álvaro asked with a hint of irony.

"Those are ways to explain things. They're all we have."

"Sure. The Inquisition knew all about that. So did Galileo. There's a long list of scientists who were burned at the stake. But a so-called mythological explanation is just as meaningless. The real question is, what do we mean by supernatural? The world, nature, life itself, everything is full of mysteries to be revealed; it's all supernatural. It's a paradox. What do we really know for certain? Do you think it makes sense to mathematically predict the end of the universe? Renowned scientists and astronomers say that the universe will disappear in a calculable number of years: a certain number elevated to a specific power. Then the Great Entropy will be upon us: perfect equilibrium. There will be no celestial bodies, no planets, no stars, nothing. The entire cosmos, just one big proton soup. Do you think that makes sense, Miguel? I think dissolution, the road to nothingness, is the most supernatural theory around, yet science and scientists claim it's proven, knowable."

Miguel didn't want to argue with Álvaro; he was just playing devil's advocate anyway. His friend kept talking.

"As the legend goes, the stone from Caesarea Philippi was forgotten; no one cared about it. Peter built the church of Jesus Christ on a symbolic stone. The great architects of all religions ignored the true stone, and for a long time it was lost, until some knights who'd been searching for it finally found it—"

"The Knights of Moriah," María whispered.

"Exactly."

Álvaro got up and, his back to them, staring off at some point on the ceiling, spoke on.

"The Seven Knights of Moriah, the ancient guardians of Solomon's temple. They witnessed the scandal of Jesus of Nazareth when he drove out the merchants and money changers. The Moriah followed him, and he revealed the prophecy to them, revealed that the ancient temple would be destroyed and—"

"The new church would be built," Miguel interrupted.

"Exactly. The true plan of Christ. Jesus revealed the mission to his disciples in Caesarea Philippi; he gave Peter the relic. He told him he'd build his church on that stone; you see? Jesus knew that impulsive Simon wouldn't understand the real message at that time, though he was the only one to say that Jesus was the true Messiah. It was a tense period. They were simple people, fishermen, who hadn't yet received the gifts of the Holy Spirit. They didn't realize that a stone could hold such power. If he'd given them a jewel or weapons, maybe, but not a stone. Jesus always spoke using parables, examples, and Peter thought his teacher's words were just symbolic. He thought Jesus wanted to communicate the need to create a church that was solid as a rock, but he never thought that the rock itself had the power."

"So what you're saying is that the stone—"

"I think you get the idea, Miguel. How were they going to know back then that their beloved teacher was giving Peter the true cornerstone? How could they even imagine that an ordinary rock was a treasure, the groundwork, the very foundation of a new temple?"

María interrupted.

"Let me see if I've got this straight. Are you saying that *no one* understood, not a single person, none of the disciples, not even Peter himself?"

Álvaro gave her a sarcastic smile. "That's what they say. The stone remained in Caesarea Philippi. Jesus knew it would. He knew that those simple men, his disciples, were still not ready, that they wouldn't be able to interpret a message contained in such a humble object as a stone. For them, the Messiah was power, he was everything. Christ knew that they'd spread his message on the earth and prepare the world for the true arrival, which would come with the building of the real temple—two thousand years after he was crucified. The disciples, and Peter himself, bore that weight. Maybe it was asking too much; the world wasn't ready."

"What about the Knights of Moriah? What happened to them?" Miguel asked.

Álvaro turned to him abruptly.

"Yes, them. The legendary Knights of Moriah. They searched for centuries. They knew they had to be alert, to keep the flame alive for over a thousand years. Jesus told them about the plan and they knew when they'd find the secret. When the armies of the cross entered Jerusalem—"

"The Crusaders," said María, surprised.

"Yes, they even had a date: 1126. A Sufi ascetic found it, perhaps through divine revelation; they say an angel guided him to the exact spot and pointed to the stone with a sword of fire. At any rate, the Sufi guarded it until the Moriah arrived. Then, they say, the stone made its way to Europe; it's even believed that the Templars aided the Moriah at some point. But the knights with crosses on their chests disappeared. And the relic was forgotten somewhere, south of Catalunya. Finally it was transferred to the sacred mountain, Montserrat. Gaudí found it— or, to be more exact, it was given to him—when he began construction on the temple. Gaudí became one of the Knights of Moriah. His mission was to place the stone someplace in the new church. The keystone of the vault? No one knows. That's what Gaudí gave your grandfather before he died. That, my friends, is what you're looking for. Where would your grandfather hide it?"

Álvaro stared at María, his piercing eyes flickering like flames as he spoke.

"I'd like to believe you, but . . . this is all so absurd. Christianity, Rome, spreading the Gospel, power—all founded on nothing. An empire built on nothing? War, death, calamity, centuries of people of different religions killing one another: Christians, Muslims, Jews. Power, corruption . . . That just couldn't, it just can't, be the true church of Christ, his message of love and humility. How can thousands of men and women be killed in the name of a God who preached love, peace, and understanding?" María spoke from the heart. But Álvaro interrupted her.

"I know it's mind-boggling. I know. It's almost too much to take in. But in Islam, one of the most popular religions on earth, there are also scientists, practical, brilliant men and women; Islam includes wise men, intelligent people, skeptics. And they worship a stone, the Kaaba, the symbol of their power, the center of the Muslim world. It's even a precept to make a pilgrimage there at least once in a lifetime. And that's a stone. Legend? Mystery? Fantasy? Imagination? I'll leave that up to you. You asked me, and I'm telling you what I know. Of all the relics in Christianity, this one makes the most sense. Oh—and one more thing . . ."

After a tense silence, he spoke again.

"Some people say it's the Holy Grail; others believe it's the true Gospel written by Jesus Christ. But everyone's looking for the same thing: power. I'm sure there are people who'd kill to get their hands on that stone."

40

JAUME BRU WAITED. Asmodeus wouldn't be long. It was already late, but he'd told the help that he was expecting a visitor and to send him in as soon as he arrived. He put some music on to make the wait more pleasurable, poured himself a brandy, and reclined comfortably on his favorite sofa.

Bru thought about his father. He remembered there'd been a time when he actually loved his father. But he wouldn't stand for any show of affection and never offered any sign of tenderness. He'd beaten Jaume when he tried to get close. His father taught him that love was for weaklings. A man should love no one but himself.

His father had driven his mother insane, literally. She'd ended up in an asylum. And Bru was forbidden to visit her.

"She's crazy, and lunatics are not of this world. Forget about her; you have no mother."

But he did. And sometimes he'd sneak out to visit her, but she didn't recognize him. He was twenty years old when she died, forsaken in a padded room.

"Bury her," was all his father said when he received the call informing him that she'd passed away. Then he hung up. Jaume wasn't even allowed to go to the funeral.

He never had any friends, either.

"Friends make you weak. You have to listen to their problems, put yourself in their shoes, do things together, congratulate them, send presents when they have children, listen to their opinions about politics. You should only have associates and people who serve you."

While he was at school in London, his father sent him money. That was it. He never called, never went to visit him. When he graduated and returned home, his father wasn't there. He walked into his room and found two prostitutes with a note: "Have a good time."

So that was what he did. He didn't dare contradict his father.

But Bru Senior was right. That Spartan existence had made him stronger. All this was running through his head when he opened his eyes and saw the figure before him.

"How did you get in?"

The masked man didn't answer. Instead, he said, "You shouldn't have acted of your own accord."

"What's behind that mask? You're ridiculous. Take it off; we're alone here. One day I'd like to see your face, though I'm sure you're no Adonis."

"You owe me. You shouldn't have acted of your own accord," he repeated.

"I owe *you*? Who pays you? Don't get confused, now. You owe *me*. I'm the one who finances you and your merry band of morons. And I had to take care of getting that damn notebook because of your men's incompetence."

"What do you know about the notebook?"

Bru didn't deign to answer.

"And what about your little Japanese girl? What does she know about it?"

"You leave her out of it. And she's not mine. Be careful, you hear me? Leave her out of this or I'll rip your heart to shreds and feed it to the dogs."

Bru got up and took the notebook from a bookshelf.

"Here."

The masked man took it.

"Take the service elevator. I don't want any of the help seeing you. They'll think the house is haunted. And next time, knock before entering."

There wouldn't be a next time, the masked man thought, walking away. He knew he would never set foot in that apartment again, and he would also make sure that someone very special to Bru didn't, either. Vengeance was one of his specialties.

41

TAIMATSU HAD BEEN trying to put the pieces together for some time. Sitting there in the study of her small apartment, concentrating, she got up occasionally to look for some book or other. She had the photocopies of the diary spread out on the table, and her computer screen flickered with several open Web pages.

Since leaving her friends and reading the photocopies carefully, a vague idea had begun to form in her head. Taimatsu was trying to flesh it out, make sense of it. The key to whatever they were looking for was in those documents somewhere. And she'd gotten a hunch after that night, after her cousin's visit.

She thought about the numbers and symbols Father Jonás had written in his own blood before he died. Miguel was obsessed with them. She remembered what he'd said perfectly. Before the first number was a larger symbol of some sort. Miguel thought maybe it was a five. But all he could see was the curved bottom. Taimatsu considered this. "A five? No, I think he's wrong about that. It might be some sort of sign or letter. A letter that looks like a five. A capital letter? A backward 'C'? What sense would that make? No."

Miguel was quite sure the letter or sign curved and continued up higher, though he couldn't see that part. She thought of the most sinuous letter of the alphabet, the letter "S." S 118 22. "Hmm. Maybe. Let's see what Google has to say."

At first she didn't find anything, just statistics, catalogs, regulatory codes. She thought for a minute. "I need another term . . . OK, Father Jonás is murdered, and he writes something like 'S 118 22' inside a big upside-down V. Could it be a biblical reference?"

Taimatsu's heart jumped when she saw what came up after she added "Bible" to her search terms. One thing stood out. "Of course! It's a psalm! *PS 118:22!*" She typed in "PS 118:22" and the text she was looking for appeared on the screen. "The stone which the builders rejected is become the head of the corner." She wondered if this was what Father Jonás had been referring to before he died. The "P" would have been obliterated by the blood, so only part of the "S" and the numbers remained. But what did it mean? It didn't make any sense. She kept searching the Internet, looking for explanations of the psalm, copying and pasting paragraphs she found into an open document. There was a ton of information online, but she wanted to be selective; it was too easy to be swallowed up by the deluge of data. Some pages she came across discussed the Acts of the Apostles, the Letters of Peter and Paul—San Pedro and San Pablo—and of course Jesus himself. After searching for a while, trying not to lose her way in the forest of information, she found the following explanation on the home page of a Catholic organization:

> The symbolism of the rock or stone was more than a play on words with Peter's name; it came from Old Testament tradition and even earlier. Isaiah 28:16 says, 'Behold, I lay in Zion for a foundation a stone, a tried stone, a precious corner stone, a sure foundation . . .'

That gave Taimatsu something to go on; she began forming a hypothesis. She couldn't cry victory yet, but she had an idea. She flipped through her photocopies to find the drawing of a mountain. She remembered it because when she first saw it, it had reminded her of Mount

Fujiyama. There it was! She found it. Yes, the drawing, and below it, the enigmatic caption: "At the foot of Mount Hermon, in Caesarea Philippi. The Third Living Creature of Heavenly Worship: 16:18."

Now she pulled out her encyclopedia to find some information on Mount Hermon. It was the tallest mountain in Palestine. And, like Fujiyama, it was volcanic; that must have been what initially drew her attention. Geologists said it was the oldest rock in Canaan, where the River Jordan had its source. The Bible spoke of it as a celestial place of ascension, giving it a special significance, a mythical characteristic for the three great monotheistic religions: Judaism, Islam, and Christianity. And Caesarea Philippi was at the foot of Mount Hermon. She'd found a connection, so she decided to keep looking. "OK, let's see what this 'Third Living Creature of Heavenly Worship' refers to."

Taimatsu moved faster now, consulting dictionaries and her copy of the Bible, but after a little while she gave up and went back to the Internet. She typed "heavenly worship" into a search engine, and it didn't take long to come up with several pages from the Apocalypse of Saint John. Celestial worship, specifically, was in the fourth chapter. She read in silence from the start, and when she got to verse seven, she found what she was looking for.

> And the first living creature was like a lion, and the second living creature like a calf, and the third living creature had the face, as it were, of a man, and the fourth living creature was like an eagle flying.

After reading that, she had no trouble understanding that those four living creatures who each had a symbol were the Evangelists. The first creature, the lion, was Mark; the second, the calf, was Luke; the fourth, the eagle, was Juan, or John; and the third—the man—was Mateo: Matthew. Taimatsu now knew that the man, the third living creature of heavenly worship, was the evangelist Saint Matthew. It was a breakthrough. She just had to figure out how that tied in to Mount

Hermon, Caesarea Philippi, and the numbers 16 and 18 at the end of the sentence.

And just like that, she knew: Matthew 16:18. It was from the Gospel of Saint Matthew. She found chapter 16 in the New Testament and began to read; when she got to verse 13, her heart skipped a beat.

13 When Jesus came into the coasts of Caesarea Philippi, he asked his disciples, saying, Whom do men say that I the Son of man am?

14 And they said, Some say that thou art John the Baptist; some, Elias; and others, Jeremias, or one of the prophets.

15 He saith unto them, But whom say ye that I am?

16 And Simon Peter answered and said, Thou art the Christ, the Son of the living God.

17 And Jesus answered and said unto him, Blessed art thou, Simon Barjona: for flesh and blood hath not revealed it unto thee, but my Father which is in heaven.

18 And I say also unto thee, That thou art Peter, and upon this rock I will build my church; and the gates of hell shall not prevail against it.

19 And I will give unto thee the keys of the kingdom of heaven: and whatsoever thou shalt bind on earth shall be bound in heaven: and whatsoever thou shalt loose on earth shall be loosed in heaven.

According to the clock on her computer it was three in the morning. Taimatsu didn't know how many hours she'd been working, but she'd finally found it. She went back over all her notes—Psalm 118:22, the stone that the builders rejected, the reference to Isaiah. "Behold, I lay in Zion for a foundation a stone, a tried stone, a precious corner stone, a sure foundation . . ." Mount Hermon, Caesarea Philippi, the third living creature, Saint Matthew. All of it pointed to . . . "A stone!" Taimatsu cried, sitting alone in her study. What was more, the other Evangelists didn't mention this episode. Saint Matthew was the only one who spoke of Caesarea Philippi. The stone. "Gaudí gave María's grandfather a stone. That's the secret, the relic, the key to it all. Yes! Maybe it was the one Christ touched when he said, 'upon this rock I will build my church.' A stone that Jesus himself, the Son of God, had touched when he announced the creation of the church! Unbelievable. A simple rock, the foundation of the church!"

She couldn't contain herself; her mind was racing, she had to keep going. Thoughts charged through her brain, all jumbled together. Thinking of the Japanese art of *suiseki*, she wondered what the little stone looked like. A tiny fragment, a piece of life, marvel of marvels. Gaudí had it, and he'd been planning to use it to crown his work. The keystone of a life dedicated to mystical architecture, whose culmination was a piece of rock cast off by the great monotheistic religions. And who were the *people* who were cast off? The poor, the dispossessed, the miserable, those who had nothing. Gaudí was planning to put it someplace. The temple. The temple! "I've got it. I'm sure. It has to be! But then he died and María's grandfather hid it . . ."

Taimatsu wasn't Catholic, but she knew her Christian art history, its structures and how to interpret them. She was ecstatic. She'd discovered the secret, she had no doubt; she knew this was of vital importance for María and Miguel—now they would know what they were looking for. So without waiting another second, she opened her e-mail to send María a message. When she typed in her password—"hypostyle"—she had a gut feeling: Park Güell. As an expert in Modernism, she was very familiar with the park; in fact, she'd chosen her password because of the park's hypostyle chamber—the room with eighty-six Doric columns supporting the large patio where the famous undulating dragon bench was. Taimatsu thought of the Ramses II hypostyle hall she'd visited with Bru. After the pyramids, she felt it was the most important and spectacular piece of Egyptian architecture. And then she saw clearly that in a way, Gaudí, a Christian with a mystical calling, had introduced this Egyptian idea into his work symbolically. La Sagrada Família was a temple open to the public. But Park Güell, because of its complex use of symbols, was clearly restricted to initiates. The proof was in the columns in the hypostyle chamber that supported the terrace, the dragon, and the benches. In restricted temples ancient Egyptians always built a hypostyle hall with a flat ceiling supported by columns. It was a passageway, a transit area leading to the inner sanctum, which only the pharaoh and a few priests had access to.

Taimatsu's mind filled with images of the park, references, books, documents she'd read. Suddenly she looked up. "The compass! In the park they'd made some alterations. I seem to recall there was initially a compass on the main staircase. Yes, of course; it was removed. The same thing happened with the cosmic egg, which was replaced with the athanor at the end of the stairs. The compass! Father Jonás drew a compass in his message, just above the reference to the psalm. That means the stone is in Park Güell, in the exact spot where the . . ."

Completely overexcited, she hurriedly composed her e-mail to María. She had to get it all down.

It's a stone; I'm positive. The key is in the Gospel of Saint Matthew 16:18. Father Jonás drew a compass above the reference to Psalm 118:22. It's in Park Güell. They made several alterations there, but on the main staircase there used to be a compass

She started. The man with the mask was in her apartment, in her study, right behind her. She heard him breathing.

"Don't move an inch."

Taimatsu couldn't finish her sentence, although the most important part, the information María and Miguel needed, was already written.

Asmodeus approached her slowly.

Taimatsu's hands were still poised over the keyboard. She was terrified. She knew she couldn't write another word. The cursor blinked on the screen. Gathering up her courage, she moved one finger to hit "Enter," sending the message. But her words were still on the screen. In order to keep the masked man from seeing them and discovering the secret, she quickly yanked the power cord, unplugging the computer. At the same time, a cane came crashing down on her hand, destroying the keyboard. Then he brought it down on her head. She collapsed but didn't lose consciousness and heard the horrifying man shouting.

"You think that matters? Sooner or later they'd have figured it out anyway. This is all going according to plan."

She felt intense pain when he brought the cane down on her knees, and Taimatsu heard the sound of bones snapping. Then he whacked her elbows and yanked her violently by the hair. She cried and tried to scream, but she couldn't. Another blow to her shoulder, close to her neck, made her lose consciousness.

When she awoke, her head was spinning and all of her limbs hurt; it was like having jagged glass snakes slithering inside her legs and arms, shredding her connective tissue. She was tied to a Modernist chair that Bru had given her. A Gaudí design. She couldn't see a thing, since her desk lamp was pointed right in her face. But she heard him, whispering in her ear.

"Now. You're going to be a good girl. And you're going to tell me what those markings on the map of Barcelona mean, those circles. And you're going to tell me where the stone is."

Taimatsu looked down at her arms, and the sheer horror of what she saw took her breath away. Thin metal wires had been thrust into her wrists and ran all the way up to her shoulders, beneath her skin. They were connected to an electric cord and battery that she couldn't see. She looked down: the same had been done to her legs. She struggled and tried to scream, in a state of total panic. A punch in the face put an end to that. Then she felt a strong electric shock—short, but so intense that her voice broke.

"Oh my God, what are you doing? Please! I don't know anything!"

Taimatsu let out a sharp, irrepressible cry. Tenderly, the masked man wiped her tears with an immaculate white handkerchief perfumed with orange-blossom water.

"Be a good girl, now. All I want you to do is tell me what you know. That's all. If you don't answer me, I'm going to push the little button again, and an electrical current will run through your arms and legs. Don't worry, it's not high voltage. No, no. That would be outrageous. No. This current will enter your body slowly, very slowly, and burn your internal tissue, your muscles, tendons, veins, capillaries, everything. You see? You'll be burned from the inside, darling. I'll roast you alive. But you won't die right away. You'll suffer, I guarantee that. You'll feel fire inside you. Some people who've experienced this say it's the worst pain a human can endure without losing consciousness; of course, that's the point, my dear girl."

"Please. I don't know anything. I don't want to die like this. Please! Have mercy."

Taimatsu didn't want to feel that sick tingling sensation again; it was as if her limbs were asleep and she had pins and needles *inside* her arms and legs. The intensity increased slowly until it became incredibly painful, almost unbearable.

But the masked man pushed the button again. Taimatsu, after a few moments, screamed in rage, and then in desperation. Nausea, vomiting, and unbelievably intense pain followed. Then spasms—sharp, uncontrollable movements. Taimatsu felt as if millions of insects were eating her alive.

The masked man wiped her lips tenderly.

"You know, this contraption is based on a very simple principle. The idea is, stimulate the greatest possible number of nerve endings, excite them mercilessly. Endless poisoned needles, piercing your body, boring into it. Do you feel like a decomposing corpse? Like millions of worms are devouring your flesh?"

"You're insane," she whimpered.

"Yes, well, that may be. But that's not the matter at hand. You don't understand, darling. I want you to live and yet experience death, feel your own disintegration. The pain of worms devouring you. My friend Doctor Mengele, the Auschwitz doctor, who invented this little contraption and the marvelous concept behind it, he tested it on hundreds of little Jewish children, even newborns still connected to their mothers before their umbilical cord was cut. Isn't that amazing? Genius. His medical team carried out the experiments on the mother and newborn at the same time. Doctor Mengele believed that this was the sublime moment, when birth and death meet, when they're one. The beginning and the end. It's a question of reversing biological time, going backward. From death to birth. You see? Now, you're a big girl, so you won't turn into a baby literally, but you'll regress mentally to a state of childhood, maybe even back to your mother's womb. Who knows, but I can't wait to find out."

"My God, you really are totally insane!" Taimatsu shouted. Despite the intense pain, she couldn't believe this was actually happening to her; it was too nightmarish. "Please. I'll tell you everything I know, all of it. I'll do anything you want me to. But please, just stop. Take pity on me, please!" she cried, full of rage.

The masked man looked into her eyes.

"You think I want your body? No. I want your soul. I'm going to penetrate your spirit. That's what the experiment leads to, according to Doctor Mengele's notebooks. Which, by the way, are much more interesting than the one you're trying to interpret. Now, you're going to tell me everything, aren't you?"

"Yes. Everything, everything I know. I swear. I don't care if you kill me, but please just don't push that button again."

"Then be a good girl and tell me what I want to know. Where is it?"

"I don't know. That's the truth. Please believe me. But I do know what it's about."

"So do I, you idiot! What I want to know is where that damn stone is!"

Taimatsu started to talk. She told him everything about what she, María, and Miguel had discovered, everything their investigations had led to.

"I know it's in Park Güell, and if you give me a little time I might be able to figure out exactly where."

"You're out of time. Your friends will do it for you."

"I can't take any more," Taimatsu implored.

"I know, sweetheart, I know. That's the point."

Then came three long hours of indescribable suffering. Moaning, wailing, begging, vomiting. There were intervals, little breaks when she spoke excitedly; she even believed she'd made him change his mind, that he was going to show compassion. Of course it was a bluff. Those breaks were just more of his evil, his perversity, his game. He was really enjoying himself.

"It doesn't make any sense for you to do this to me."

"It makes a lot more sense than you can know."

And just when she least expected it, the pain returned, the suffering.

"Easy now, don't worry. I know it hurts. But this time it won't last as long, you'll see. I'm inside you now, darling. I'm inside you."

And they'd go back through the whole process again, the same thing repeated over and over. She was crumbling, both physically and psychologically. She screamed and shouted and cried like a little girl. The masked man pushed the button and then he'd wipe the sweat from her brow and speak to her tenderly. At times Taimatsu thought there were actually two different men, one very kind one, and the other a demon. She was delirious. The humiliation, the depravity of his words, his behavior—it couldn't be human. Pain lacerated her extremities, but she could no longer scream; her voice was slowly dying, along with her body. But she kept speaking, responding to his questions and awaiting the next terrible moment.

During one of the breaks, her mind flitted to her home, to Japan, and Mount Fujiyama and Mount Hermon, the two mountains superimposed over each other. She wished she were a samurai so she could disembowel herself, commit hara-kiri. Taimatsu had no strength left; she couldn't take any more. But the masked man was patient; he moved slowly, calmly, and even stroked her hair, her cheeks.

"Come on, just a little more. You're doing so well. You're a very brave girl. Can't you feel me inside you now?"

"You're insane, you're totally insane." Taimatsu couldn't tell if she was speaking out loud or not.

And the torture continued.

Finally, when day began to break, the masked man violently yanked the wires out of her body all at once. She could no longer feel pain. She could tell the wires were leaving her arms and legs, and she rested. Taimatsu struggled to breathe, choking loudly. But at least it was over, she thought.

"It's really a shame. There's no turning back now, little girl. I know you told me the truth. I'm convinced. Would you like to start again?"

Taimatsu weakly shook her head, her eyes rolling back. She couldn't speak; she could only babble. Asmodeus stroked her and kissed her forehead, placing the metallic lips of his mask against her skin. Her mouth was open, panting, and her eyes were unfocused. A few drops of blood fell from the holes in her wrists and ankles. The masked man wiped them primly with his handkerchief.

"I'm sorry. The internal damage is so serious that you can't be saved. You're going to die, little girl, and then you'll rest. Here, kiss my ring, it will comfort you, and then have a little drink."

Without wanting to, she opened her bruised, swollen lips, and the man in the mask rammed the bottle down her throat before she could close her mouth. When it was empty, he pulled it out and stuffed in a handkerchief soaked in the same liquid: orange-blossom alcohol.

"Just relax; this will only take a moment. We have to finish the show."

He lit the handkerchief and stepped back.

A bluish flame shot out of Taimatsu's mouth. Her chest and stomach rippled for a few seconds, and the color under her skin changed suddenly. Her bowels were on fire, her stomach, her throat. The pain was intense; the burning lasted a few unbearable moments, and she remained conscious through this final horror. The man in the mask looked out the window. It was getting light quickly. He'd have liked to keep her alive a bit longer; she might have held out another hour. But he had to go. He picked up his cane and brought it down on her clavicle. Then she lost consciousness, mercifully, with one last, ghastly wail.

Taimatsu would never wake up again.

42

I FEEL TERRIBLE."

"María, we can't turn back now. This is important; we can't lose sight of that. I'm skeptical by nature; you know that. I had a lot of doubts about getting involved in this, but it's too late to give up now," Miguel said, laying the stack of photocopies on the table.

Miguel had practically moved in to María's place. He had no intention of leaving her alone even for a minute.

"Too many people have died: my grandfather, Father Jonás . . . Besides, I've gotten the people I love most mixed up in this whole business. Even Taimatsu could be in danger, thanks to me. I'd never forgive myself if anything happened to either of you. It just seems like we're not getting anywhere. The notebook, the riddles—we don't know anything. We haven't made any progress at all. I feel like we entered a maze and we can't get out, no one can get out, not my grandfather—"

"That's not true. We know what we're looking for now. A stone. We just have to figure out where it is. You're forgetting something, María. Remember what it said in the notebook: 'Read with your heart and not with your head and you'll find the truth on the last door that closes behind me.' The epitaph on your grandfather's grave. I think that's the key to everything."

"Now we see the enigma through a mirror . . ."

"That's right, María. We're trapped in the mirror's reflection; infinity is the worst of all labyrinths. Please, listen. I'm more and more convinced of this: your grandfather couldn't speak openly; he had to hide the secret. But he understood it, and he understood it through Gaudí. This is bigger than both of us; too many people want to see it fail. They'll do anything to stop it."

"I don't know what you're talking about, Miguel."

"Well, I don't have the answers. But I think the key to finding our way out of the maze, the labyrinth, the enigma . . . is you. María, you're the only one who can do it. We have to think, we have to find the way."

"The way of the stars."

"Come again?"

"The notebook is full of references to stars. They pave the way. Hänsel and Gretel found their way home because they figured out, like ancient mariners, that each star is the key to opening a new door. The real treasure is the path itself. We came from the stars and that's where we're headed, too . . . What are you thinking?"

"I'm just turning it all over in my mind. Wait a second. OK, we know that Gaudí used hyperbolic paraboloid arches in his constructions, which are uncommon in architecture because they're considered unattractive. Yet Einstein, in his theory of relativity, said the whole universe was a hyperbolic paraboloid. Gaudí put that into practice in his work; he set up a relationship between what's above and what's below. Gaudí built his scale models as funicular models."

"I think *funiculum* is Latin for 'rope' or 'string.' A string model. Yes, Conesa mentioned something about that."

"A funicular model," Miguel continued, "was a design tool Gaudí used to calculate equilibrium in his structures, the same way the ancients discovered geometry and mathematics—"

"With string."

"That's right. Gaudí would tie both ends of a string to the ceiling, so it was hanging in the air. Then he'd hang weights from it; they were the charges. The intensity, the direction of these charges on the string creates a funicular curve, a paraboloid that contains its own equation. We know that once Gaudí had worked out the complex equilibrium of weights in his string models, he used tissue paper to bulk them out. And he took pictures and then inverted them, which gave him a projection of one or more images of the building he wanted to build. That simple. But more than anything, Gaudí learned from observing nature—not external structures, but internal ones. In nature, in the genetic code of all living creatures is a growth model based on the parabolic arch. In animals, in their bones, tendons, and muscles, and in vegetables, in wood fibers, tissues, every living cell forms a complex system that establishes a dynamic equilibrium. It's completely different from the static balance you get with scales. Nature is always changing and always has to adjust its balance, constantly locating its center of gravity. Every living creature's organic architecture is based on this model, an amalgamation of geometry, physics, and mechanics. Everything has a purpose, it's all rational. There's nothing left over and nothing missing; each piece makes sense. Gaudí learned that, and he applied it. The internal architecture of life—that was his geometric model, a fusion of the static and the aesthetic; his architectonic shapes are a reflection, a mirror of nature. Maybe it's just a coincidence, but his conception of architecture, and even the master's unusual way of working—it all has a strange symmetry."

"What are you getting at?"

"Reflections. It's all about reflections. His architecture as an immense mirror of the universe, of creation, of reality. Even his models. On earth as it is in heaven . . ."

"What is above is as what is below. The symmetry of mirrors! Now we see the enigma through a mirror. Saint Paul's letter to the Corinthians."

"It must all be connected somehow . . . Architecture as the sublime art, a human reflection, a mirror of the divine. I think your grandfather gave you the ultimate answer in his epitaph, the one that's within you, María. Even your name. Did you know María means 'mirror of heaven'?"

Miguel had an idea. It was just a hunch, a shot in the dark on that moonless night. But he wanted to see where it took them. A summer storm had caused several blackouts throughout the city, mostly affecting public streetlights. It was just a glitch, and it would be fixed soon—or at least that was what the authorities claimed. Barcelona was a different city in the dark; you could see so many more stars than usual, even from Paseo de Gràcia.

"María, let's go to Montjuïc, I need to check something. I can't explain it right now. Come on."

So she went with him. They drove up the hill and a few minutes later parked on a level area that revealed Barcelona beneath them. Most of the city was black. Houses and buildings were brightly lit, but that was it; the streetlights were all out. It was dark enough to show more stars in the sky than they'd ever seen before.

They didn't get out of the car; they simply looked into each other's eyes and were overwhelmed by love for each other. They'd been trying with no luck to find a way out of this maze, but they were lost; they only had each other to hold on to. They hugged. María was distraught, but Miguel's presence soothed her. She wanted to make love to him, she needed to make love to him. Miguel kissed her tenderly on the lips.

María and Miguel undressed each other in the car, their bodies trembling with the desire of a couple of teenagers. They made love urgently, passionately, forgetting everything. Time had stopped, everything had stopped—even the starry sky above Barcelona seemed stuck in time. María rested her head on Miguel's chest when it was over, and he stroked her back; as he stared up at the sky, a million thoughts ran through his head. Then Ursa Major, the constellation, caught his eye; it was directly above Barcelona. His eyelids closed, but in his mind he could see the bright shining outline of the Chariot, the stars making up Ursa Major. He leaned his head on her neck and slowly opened his eyes. María's back was white as snow, shining in the dark night. Miguel looked up and down the length of her body, running his fingers over the freckles that covered it, those same freckles he'd discovered the day he realized how much he loved her. Suddenly he started and then pulled away to get a better look. "What's wrong, Miguel?"

"María, these freckles on your back . . ."

"What's the matter with them? I've always had freckles, as a kid I had even more, you know—"

"I can't believe it."

"Believe what? What's going on?"

"It's Ursa Major, María. On your back. The freckles are shaped just like Ursa Major . . . on your skin. Look at the sky."

María sat up and looked out the front windshield: Ursa Major was directly above the city.

"This can't be; it's impossible," he said.

"*What* is? Tell me!"

"It's *you*, María. You're the key. Now I understand. There's a map on your back. Ursa Major. Your grandfather knew that. He told you, but we didn't understand what he was talking about."

"It's probably just a coincidence. What does that have to do with—"

"'On earth as it is in heaven.' Don't you see? Get out of the car, I want to look at something. And if I'm right, I think we could be on our way to solving this mystery—"

"But Miguel, I'm naked!"

"Well, put your clothes on! Hurry."

They got dressed. Miguel spread a map of Barcelona over the hood of the car and circled Gaudí's most important works on it. Then he connected the dots.

"This is amazing! Gaudí's most important works in Barcelona make the shape of the constellation Ursa Major. Look up at the sky, María. It's like an enormous mirror. On earth as it is in heaven."

"But—"

"It all makes so much more sense now. We just have to figure out one last thing. Remember what that man said, one of the seven knights; he had a medallion with the letter beta, and he interpreted Father Jonás's message. Remember?"

"Merak. Wasn't that what he said right before he died?"

"Exactly. I have a hunch. If that name is related to Ursa Major, I'll be totally convinced. I think we can solve the seven riddles in your grandfather's notebook."

María was overwhelmed. Miguel's eyes lit up.

"We have to go back home—now!"

They jumped into the car and drove as fast as the speed limit allowed, without saying a word. Fifteen minutes later they were in front of the computer, and in almost no time, Miguel found what he wanted.

"We've got it."

María was standing beside him and read, "Dubhe, Merak, Phecda, Megrez, Alioth, Mizar/Alcor, Alkaid . . . The names of the stars in Ursa Major. And in addition, the brightest stars were ordered using the Greek alphabet."

"Merak . . . Merak corresponded to the letter beta!"

"I don't get it."

"When I left the library, the monk talked about Father Jonás and started to interpret the message before he was shot in the back . . ."

"Yeah . . ."

"When he died he was repeating that, right beside me. Merak. It's unbelievable. Don't you see? Merak is one of the seven stars in Ursa Major. And each star is associated with a letter from the Greek alphabet, and each of the seven knights has a letter: alpha, beta, gamma, delta, epsilon, zeta, and eta. You see?"

"The riddles? Yes! There are seven riddles and they each have a Greek letter."

"It can't be a coincidence, María. It just can't. Ursa Major is on your back; you're the reflection of heaven. Gaudí built his buildings in Barcelona following the same constellation etched on your skin . . . And in that constellation every star has a name—"

"And a letter of the Greek alphabet. Seven in all. It all adds up. That's just like my grandfather! I'm sure the seven riddles correspond to the seven stars. Seven is God's special number—it represents completion, perfection, salvation. But—"

"We have the clues we need to solve the riddles. And now we know where to find them. You were the map."

"Half the map. Remember?" María clarified.

"You're right; the dragon is the other half. That's what the notebook said."

Miguel started rifling through the bookshelf.

"What are you doing?"

Without responding he pulled out a book of photos of Gaudí's work and looked for a picture of the dragon at Finca Güell, and suddenly it all made sense.

"My God! It was right there and we didn't see it. The dragon was telling us what we wanted to know!" Miguel said, getting excited. He took a red pencil and drew lines across the dragon photo.

"What was right where?"

"The dragon at the third gate is the same shape as the stars in the Dragon constellation and Hercules. His tail is Ursa Minor; the pointed balls indicate the positions of the stars," he said, showing her the drawing.

"You're right!" she exclaimed, flabbergasted.

"And you're the part of the map that was missing: Ursa Major. Look."

He picked up the map of Barcelona and map of the stars where he'd traced the constellation.

"'On earth as it is in heaven.' 'What is above is as what is below.' 'Now we see the enigma through a mirror.' These are all codes, and they add up perfectly. It couldn't be clearer. The star Dubhe is alpha; Merak is beta; Phecda is gamma; Megrez is delta . . . There's the Chariot, and the three oxen that are pulling it are Alioth, which corresponds to epsilon; Mizar/Alcor, which is zeta; and finally Alkaid, the letter eta . . ."

Miguel took the city map with Gaudí's buildings circled on it and assigned each one its corresponding star and letter.

Suddenly María got it.

"This is absolutely unbelievable! So Casa Vicens is alpha; beta is Park Güell; gamma is La Sagrada Família; delta is La Pedrera . . ."

Miguel finished for her.

"And then epsilon is Casa Battló, zeta is Casa Calvet, and eta is Palacio Güell . . ."

"The seven letters of the Greek alphabet each correspond to a specific building and a star."

"I think we know how to solve the puzzles now—"

"And we only have one day left to do it."

THEY WANTED TO call Taimatsu immediately and tell her everything. They'd unraveled it, figured out how it all tied together; they might be able to solve the seven riddles. But it was so late that they didn't want to bother her. They knew she was catching the first flight to Paris, so they decided to call in the morning. Even though Taimatsu was going to be gone for a few days, they knew she'd be excited to hear what they'd discovered; besides, she knew so much about Gaudí that her expertise would surely come in handy, presuming María and Miguel were right.

María went to get the photocopies her friend had made. She found the one with the riddles, made another copy, and wrote the name of the corresponding building beside each letter.

ALPHA
Casa Vicens
Between palm trees and carnations spins the soul of the sun.

BETA
Park Güell
Light brings it to life, though it doesn't have a hundred feet, to turn on the oven of the night that illuminates the fruits of the Garden of Hesperides.

GAMMA
La Sagrada Família
Add up the number on a staircase with no steps to see the sign the four sides enclose.

DELTA
La Pedrera
Your mother is the water; your father is the fire. You are not a ship and you travel in time, sunk in the foundations of the new city that the warriors contemplate.

EPSILON
Casa Batlló
Not even the fires of Saint Elmo can light up your eyes, lost in the darkness.

ZETA
Casa Calvet
Wise insanity, even if you see it, won't be found above the cypress.

ETA
Palacio Güell
In the first letter of this palace the Magi saw the cross and the heart of the immaculate Virgin Mary's light.

"We've got a lot to do; in order to solve each riddle, we'll be racing all over Barcelona looking for the stars that make up Ursa Major in each of Gaudí's works."

"But first we've got to think; we need some information on the buildings."

"We can't waste any time."

43

D
AWN BROKE AND they were still contemplating the riddles.
Miguel looked at his watch. It was six o'clock. Twenty-four
hours. That was all they had left.

But why visit each building? Why was María's grandfather having
them go from one to the next? Would that lead them to the stone? It
was obvious they had to get going; they'd already spent hours studying
the photocopies, thinking through the riddles.

"We need to hurry," Miguel said, sticking the photocopy of the riddle
page in his pocket.

María didn't reply.

Miguel turned and saw that she'd fallen asleep on the table.

He was about to wake her when his cell phone rang.

"It's Álvaro. I need you two to stop by the bookstore. It's urgent."

"Now?"

"Now."

"What's this about?"

"Not over the phone. I've been investigating and I think I have
something."

"OK. We'll be there in an hour."

"Make it half an hour. And don't be late."

Álvaro Climent hung up. Miguel looked at his watch. It was six fifteen. Now they had less than twenty-four hours to go.

Miguel woke María with a kiss on her neck.

"We have to go. Álvaro called; he's got something important to
tell us."

After they made their way downstairs, they discovered that a
police car was parked at the apartment building's front door. The officer told them that Mortimer wanted to see them down at the station
on Vía Layetana. Miguel was about to refuse, but he realized it would
be smarter to take care of this as soon as possible and then go see
Álvaro.

"You've got a lot of explaining to do," Mortimer said after leading
them into a small office on the second floor.

"What do you want to know?" Miguel asked.

"Everything," Mortimer responded. His tone was less than concilia-
tory.

Nogués looked on in silence.

The interrogation was long and tedious. María and Miguel were as
evasive as possible. They didn't trust that man. Besides, what could they
say? If they told him the truth, they'd be locked up in an insane asylum,
not a jail cell.

"Are you aware that concealing evidence during a police investigation is a crime?" Mortimer asked, after thirty minutes of grilling them.

"We have nothing to tell you. We don't even know how we're mixed
up in all this. Or what it's about."

"For someone who doesn't know what it's about, you've managed to
find yourself at every crime scene. So stop bullshitting me and tell me
what you know."

"Do you think I had something to do with those murders?"

"No. We think that you know something that could shed some light
on them, and that you can help us with our investigation, so why don't
you just tell us what you know?" Nogués inquired in a much friendlier
tone than his boss.

"My grandfather was murdered; you should be out investigating who did it," María said.

"Yeah, yeah, I know; it's our job. But if you stopped withholding information, you'd make it a lot easier; then we could see the connection between all those deaths. What makes you so sure your grandfather was murdered, anyway?"

"He would never kill himself. I know that for a fact."

The questioning continued, but María and Miguel stood their ground.

"Are you aware that we could lock you up?" Mortimer asked Miguel.

He didn't answer.

"You're free to go," Mortimer finally concluded with a resigned sigh.

After they'd left, Nogués opened a folder he had on the table.

"They're clean. Just two average citizens. We've looked into their bank accounts, we've tailed them. Nothing out of the ordinary. They don't belong to any sects or political parties. They spend money like everyone else, they're liberals, they pay their taxes. We've checked outstanding records. She's a historian; he's a prestigious mathematician and professor at the university—a total brainiac, headed for a Nobel. No vices that we know of. The last movie they rented was *Jules et Jim*."

"What's that?"

"Old French film. Love story."

Nogués kept flipping through the file. Mortimer glanced sidelong at the ring mark on Nogués's finger; he never wore his ring to work. He tried to convince himself that his doubts were unfounded—he had long had a nagging sensation about him, though it was dispelled whenever he heard him speak.

"There is one weird thing. When the mathematician was younger, he was the Spanish fencing champion."

"Fencing?"

"Yep."

"OK, so they're model citizens—just straight-up wage slaves who pay their taxes like everyone else."

"Average joes, I'm telling you."

"Well then we're fucked. We've got nothing to go on."

Mortimer left and Nogúes sat down to read through the file again, alone. This was certainly the strangest case he'd ever laid eyes on. What kind of mess had those two lovebirds gotten themselves mixed up in? If they were playing detective, they weren't doing it very well. It didn't look good at all, Nogués thought. He decided to go over the police files they had at the station on satanic cults. The last body they'd found, the one in the parking lot, had really thrown him for a loop. What was a Ukrainian doing caught up in this? It had to be connected. That wasn't some Eastern European gang out settling scores. Those guys just took each other out in a hail of bullets; they didn't go cutting heads off with swords. That was what he was thinking about when his boss walked back in.

"We've got two more."

"Two more? This is some morning."

"Some guy burned alive in a bookstore and a Japanese girl."

"Was she burned alive, too?"

"Yeah, but from the inside."

"Where do we go first?"

"You go to the bookstore. I'll take care of the girl."

44

B RU WENT INTO shock when the police gave him the news over the phone. When he got to Taimatsu's house, she was already gone; an ambulance had taken her to Hospital del Mar.

He drove himself there and double-parked by the ocean. Once inside, he introduced himself as a friend of the girl and was led to the morgue. When he saw her, he wanted to die. He identified her. It took tremendous effort not to weep openly and collapse in a heap in front of those people. Bru hadn't cried since he was a boy. Not even when his mother died. The hatred he felt toward his father at that time was even more intense than the pain he felt at his mother's death. He left the hospital and wandered blindly down the seaside promenade to Barceloneta beach. He wanted to jump into the sea, swim and swim to the point of exhaustion, go out deeper and deeper, and then sink down to the bottom until he felt no pain. But he had something to do first. They'd pay for their savagery. Every last one of them.

45

POLICE TAPE RESTRICTED access to Calle Freixures from the corner of Sant Pere Més Baix. A fire truck was just finishing up. There was thick black smoke everywhere.

Miguel and María approached the yellow tape. A police officer headed them off.

"What happened?" Miguel asked.

"Bookstore burned down."

"Anyone inside?"

"The owner. Please, I need you to leave. I'm not authorized to divulge any information."

"We know him; we're friends of his."

"You *were* friends; he's dead. The ambulance already took away his body."

They stepped back. Miguel peered down the street. He thought he could see Mortimer's assistant in the group of officers and fire fighters gathered at the shop's entrance.

"We'd better get out of here. We can't risk having Nogués see us," Miguel said.

"He was murdered."

"I know. This was not some random fire. When he called he seemed agitated. He said he'd discovered something and wanted to give us some information."

"Now what do we do?"

"We need to get out of here. We've got a lot to do . . . before they kill us, too."

46

THE VISITORS WERE announced and Bru ordered them to be shown in. He'd been expecting them. Bru knew they wouldn't take long to turn up and settle scores. He didn't care. He was almost wishing for it. Only Yasunari came in; the other two Japanese men waited outside.

Yasunari and Bru stared at each other without hatred. On the drive over to Bru's house, Yasunari had envisioned a thousand and one ways to torture and kill him. But his father had been very clear: Bru was to die with all the dignity Taimatsu had not been afforded. He owed it to her. Yasunari disagreed; she'd been made to suffer horribly. But when he saw the beaten look on Bru's face, he realized he'd been wrong. Bru had loved Taimatsu. Bru no longer cared about this world, and his only desire was to be reunited with Taimatsu, if there was a place beyond this world where he could find her.

"It's time," Yasunari said, holding out a case containing a samurai sword.

"I know; just give me one minute." Bru snatched up the phone and dialed a number.

"Yuri. Kill them all. Every last one. You know where they meet. I don't care how much it costs. I'll pay you double whatever you ask. Kill them like dogs, show no mercy."

He hung up. He sank down in his chair, letting his head and arms fall onto the table.

"Taimatsu, Taimatsu," he whimpered.

When he raised his head, his eyes clouded over by tears, he saw Yasunari as if through a steamy mirror, standing before him, sword case in hand.

"It's time," Yasunari said, holding it out to him.

"Yes, it's time."

Bru opened the middle drawer of his desk.

"This is how we do it here."

He put his right hand in, pulled out a gun, aimed it at his head, and executed himself.

47

SOME DAYS *it just doesn't pay to get out of bed,* Nogués thought. This was one of them. A girl brutally murdered, a bookseller incinerated, and now a shoot-out in Plaza de Palacio.

They got to the scene four minutes after receiving the call from headquarters. There were three other officers with them. When they got out of the car, the perps were long gone. On the way over, he had tried to get in touch with Mortimer on his cell. Where the hell was he? Nogués hadn't seen him since he left to investigate the Japanese girl's murder.

Business owners and employees were gathered under the plaza's arcades, as was a large crowd of onlookers.

"I was the one who called, sir," a man said as soon as he saw him.

He was a young guy wearing dark clothes, and he owned an electrical appliance shop, no doubt half stocked with merchandise that local pickpockets swiped off of tourists. But that wasn't what Nogués was there for.

"A lot of shooting, sir, a whole lot . . . The shop was full and I heard a lot of shooting," he repeated resolutely, pointing to a doorway between a fleabag hostel and a trinket shop. "Then they came running out, chief. Men. Six, eight—"

"Well, which was it—six or eight?"

"Eight. Eight men," another man confirmed.

"They took off in two different cars, parked over there," the man said, pointing to the chains hanging in front of the Nautical School on the other side of the street.

Nogués and the officers walked into the building with their weapons drawn. There was an open door below the elevator. After going through it, they descended bloodstained stairs and, at the bottom, found their way into the building's basement.

"Police!" Nogués shouted.

There was no sound.

At the bottom of the staircase they found a cellar with many corridors and winding paths. The officers kept going, covering one another, until they reached a spacious room. At one end of it, despite the darkness, Nogués glimpsed what looked to be an altar; it was black marble, shaped like a hexagon. They took out their flashlights, but before he had time to turn his on, Nogués's right foot thumped against something soft. He cast his light on it. It was the body of a hooded man, lying in a pool of blood. One of the other cops found the light switch. When he flipped it on, Nogués and his officers couldn't believe what they saw. More than a dozen dead bodies were all over the room; each seemed to have been shot.

"What the . . ."

"Jesus, this looks like a war zone," one of the cops said.

Nogués didn't reply; he edged his way forward as he pulled on his gloves. What the fuck had happened here?

"Don't touch anything until forensics gets here," he ordered.

One of his men already had.

"This guy looks Russian, boss."

The officer had searched the only body dressed in a suit. He was going through his wallet.

"Ukrainian," he corrected, handing Nogués the documentation.

"They're all dead," another officer added.

"Make a report of everything and then go wait outside. And don't touch anything else!"

The officers spread out and started to inspect the basement. Nogués didn't move. He counted the bodies: seventeen, including the Ukrainian.

"Jesus Christ!" he exclaimed, unable to contain himself.

"No more bodies, boss. But you should come take a look at this. There's some kind of torture contraption in there hanging from the ceiling, with a sculpture underneath it. It's really freaky."

"Some kind of idol," another agent added.

"Wait for me outside," Nogués ordered.

When he was alone he looked around. He wandered among the bodies looking for some kind of clue. It was clear that a bunch of lunatics was using this room as a meeting place, to worship the devil or whoever the fuck they worshipped; it sure looked like some kind of satanic cult. Then in the middle of their little party, the Ukrainians burst in and shot them like dogs. Most of the bodies had entry wounds in their backs and lay facedown. When the Ukrainians got there and started shooting, the hooded freaks must have run any which way they could, but it didn't do them any good. Only one of the perps had died, from a couple of bullet wounds to the chest. The rest escaped once they'd finished their business. But why?

Then he saw it, on the ground, in a corner by the altar: a toothpick. He crouched down, pulled out a pen, and used it to lift one end of the stick off the ground, slipping it into a plastic evidence bag. Then he put the bag into his jacket pocket.

Nogués opened his phone and dialed a number. He waited. After two seconds, he heard a familiar ringtone a few feet from where he stood. Nogués looked left and walked toward the sound. The ring sounded closer and closer. He flipped over the fourth body.

"Oh my god," he said to himself, unable to believe who lay at his feet.

48

MIGUEL AND MARÍA got off the metro at Fontana thinking, *Another death.* Álvaro had been murdered, and they feared they'd be next on the list. They ran up Mayor de Gracia toward Plaza Trilla. They crossed over to the left, went down Calle Carolines, and walked as far as number 18. They caught sight of the beautiful building long before they reached it. It was a shame it was hidden away on that narrow street, Miguel thought. The pair crossed over to get a better look.

Casa Vicens was Gaudí's first building. A Moorish-inspired work, it stood right in the middle of Gracia, built back when the neighborhood was its own separate municipality, not part of Barcelona. The façade was decorated with ceramic tile, and the horizontal lines of the ground-floor and second-floor levels contrasted starkly with the vertical lines of the flat roof.

The first thing to catch their eye was the wrought-iron fence, its grill-work decorated with dwarf-palm-tree leaves called *fulles de margalló.*

"Palm trees, Miguel. We found the palm trees . . ."

"'Between palm trees and carnations spins the soul of the sun,'" Miguel recited.

"Now we have to look for the carnations."

Miguel glanced up and down the street. *It's like they're invisible; they're here but we can't see them,* he thought.

"What's wrong?"

"They're here; I can feel it."

"But they won't make a move until we find what they want."

"I'm not so sure," he replied uneasily. "If they kill us now, the race is over and they win," he said.

"But they wouldn't get what they've spent centuries searching for."

"You might be right; still, we can't be too careful."

They crossed the street again and approached the building, poring over every inch of the façade.

The house, Gaudí's first important commission, had an impressive garden that stretched all the way to Avenida del Príncipe de Asturias. It also had a remarkable fountain, flower beds, and a pavilion on the corner.

"I think Park Güell now has a part of the garden fence that was removed when they renovated. In fact, the house's current appearance is quite different from the way Gaudí originally planned it," María said, still staring at it. "I hope the renovations didn't eliminate the clues."

They were both anxious and excited, with all five senses concentrating hard on the construction before them. They were searching for carnations but couldn't find any. Miguel consulted the notes he'd taken the night before. He saw that on the plot of land where Casa Vicens was built there had been flowers called *clavells de moro*, or Moorish carnations, also known as yellow zinnias. Gaudí had decided to incorporate them into the tiles he used to decorate the front of the building.

"Here they are! We've got the carnations, María. They're the yellow flowers on the tiles. *Clavells de moro*, the flowers that used to grow on the site before construction started," he said as soon as he spotted them.

María pondered for a moment. "My grandfather liked word games. Sometimes difficult ones."

"So, what do you think about the spinning-soul-of-the-sun part?"

"I think it's a sunflower. Sunflowers are heliotropic; they always turn to face the sun."

"Of course! That makes perfect sense. The sunflower of the soul."

"I bet in Gaudí's personal iconography, sunflowers are related to the soul."

They kept searching. Miguel wondered what the point of this scavenger hunt could be; there had to be a reason for it. He looked at the lizard and the little wrought-iron dragon on one of the windows. It seemed to threaten the passersby below. The fence on the left was open, and there was a car parked behind it. María walked in. There were large palm trees there, and it was dark and shady. That was where the balcony was. Her heart pounded; her excitement was growing, but she still hadn't found the sunflowers. Then she looked up and froze.

"Miguel, Miguel . . ."

"What is it?"

Her head was raised.

"Sunflowers!"

There they were, on a frieze above a veranda, facing what would have once been the old garden, along with the quaint inscriptions, LITTLE SUN, LET US SEE, OH, THE SUMMER SHADE, and FROM THE DARKNESS OF HOME, LONG LIVE THE FIRE OF LOVE.

"Sunflowers! The representation of the soul," Miguel noted triumphantly.

"OK, we have alpha, the first star in Ursa Major. It's the sunflower. Let's go to Park Güell to find beta."

They retraced their steps to the Fontana metro so they could take it one stop down the green line, to Lesseps. The train car was packed and María pressed up against Miguel, trying to block out the rest of the passengers. He'd made her nervous back at Casa Vicens. Now she was thinking how easy it would be for someone to try something there on the metro: they could be knifed. In the confusion the killer could easily make a getaway before their lifeless bodies hit the floor. Just then the lights went out and María screamed.

"What's wrong?" Miguel cried, alarmed. The lights came back on and the passengers closest to them stared disdainfully.

"Nothing, nothing. It's nothing."

"Calm down, María," he said, giving her a hug and trying to soothe her while still keeping an eye out for anything suspicious.

They got off at their stop and zigzagged through the streets until they reached the park's entrance on Calle Olot.

They stood at the main gate, which was flanked by two pavilions. The one on the right was originally intended for the concierge, and the one on the left was supposed to have been a lobby. It was crowned with a fifty-six-foot tower topped with the architect's characteristic four-arm cross. Beyond them lay the park, with its little plazas, roads, viaducts, bridges, staircases, and grottoes.

"The star Merak," María said, recalling, "the riddle said, 'Beta. Light brings it to life, though it doesn't have a hundred feet to turn on the oven of the night that illuminates the fruits of the Garden of Hesperides.'"

They walked past the small plaza on one side of the main entryway and headed toward the enormous double-sided staircase leading up to the Greek theater. A layer of clouds covered the sun.

"Are you OK?"

"I'm fine, really. Let's keep going."

Climbing the stairs, the two of them said simultaneously, "The lizard?"

Miguel stopped in front of the spectacular colored mosaic reptile to explain.

"For alchemists it symbolizes fire. And there's the athanor up there, the oven where the great work is carried out: the philosopher's stone. 'Turn on the oven of the night that illuminates the fruits of the Garden of Hesperides,'" he recited, and then added, "María, it has to be the lizard."

"I know, but there's something that doesn't quite fit. I don't know. I think maybe we should keep looking. There's something I can't put my finger on . . . It's just too . . . easy. Besides, it says, 'Light brings it to life, though it doesn't have a hundred feet.'"

They spent a long time searching. Before them lay Gaudí's most ambitious project and, no doubt, his most important secular work: a suburb, a garden city, protected and defended by the fence and two unique entry pavilions. It was intended to be an imitation of the garden city being built in England at the time—an entire community on fifty acres.

"The park's imagery is really fascinating. At first, Gaudí planned seven gates, like the mythical city of Thebes. But in the end, his planned community failed. Gaudí was the only one who lived here . . . for twenty years," Miguel concluded, though María already knew all of that.

"My grandfather and I must have come here thousands of times when I was a little girl. How could I have guessed he'd actually *lived* here, with the master? It's as if I've been preparing for this moment my whole life."

They were very near the Torre Rosa, the house where Gaudí had lived from 1906 until 1925, a year before he died. Little Juan Givell, just eleven years old when he arrived with the master from Riudoms, had moved in there and lived in the house with him until they both moved to the studio in La Sagrada Família. It wasn't Gaudí but his assistant Francesc Berenguer who built the Torre Rosa, which was intended to be a prototype for the dwellings that would comprise the unique suburb, the Park Güell garden city. It was named for Gaudí's devotion to the Virgin del Roser. The house was bought in 1963 by the Friends of Gaudí Association and then converted into the Gaudí Museum, which now displayed the architect's furniture and drawings.

"Hänsel and Gretel break free and burn the witch in the oven, and then they go home with a great treasure," María said.

She couldn't get that out of her head.

"Come on, we've still got a lot to do," Miguel said.

Although there was something that didn't quite fit, they decided to provisionally accept the lizard as the second symbol, corresponding to beta and Park Güell.

As they were getting ready to leave, the sky cleared up and the sun came out, shining directly down on the broken ceramic tiles and making them glimmer with an almost blinding intensity. María turned and looked up at the huge plaza above, the scaly crest of the undulating dragon benches. The play of light created an optical illusion; for a moment, it looked as if the dragon had moved. Miguel called to María from a few feet ahead.

"María, we should really go. What's the matter?"

"Wait a second, Miguel, I think we made a mistake."

The light had brought the dragon, whose scales were made using Gaudí's own personal *trencadis* mosaic style, to life. María noticed something else, too. The dragon was above the hypostyle chamber, the park's Doric temple comprised of eighty-six columns; the original plan had called for one hundred. It was to have been the garden city's market. María smiled and exclaimed, "I *knew* my grandfather wouldn't have made it so easy. He always said sometimes the truth is so close we can't see it. Beta isn't the lizard, Miguel!"

"What is it, then?"

"The dragon. The igneous dragon. Look!" she said, pointing to the benches. "Look how the sunlight plays on its back. Light brings it to life. And it's not a centipede—there aren't a hundred 'feet' beneath it, only eighty-six columns holding it up."

"The dragon isn't a centipede—"

"Because it's only got eighty-six feet," María concluded. "The dragon is beta."

49

THEY DECIDED TO walk to the next star, gamma, which corresponded to La Sagrada Família. They took Calle Sant Josep de la Muntanya and turned down Travessera de Dalt, walking along Mare de Déu de Montserrat until they got to Cartagena, then finally continued down until they hit Avenida Gaudí. It was quite a walk, but they were so excited that they didn't notice it. At the end of Avenida Gaudí stood the temple.

The riddle said:

GAMMA

Add up the number on a staircase with no steps to see the sign the four sides enclose.

They didn't think they needed to go inside. Up until now, the other riddles had been solved by contemplating the outside of the buildings. They didn't see why La Sagrada Família should be an exception. They wandered around for the rest of the afternoon, inspecting and scrutinizing every nook and cranny of the façades with no luck. While Miguel kept searching, María decided to call Taimatsu. Maybe her friend could give them some answers, a key to their race against the clock. She was sure they were being followed. They needed her help. María phoned several times but only got her voice mail.

"It seems weird that she wouldn't answer. You don't think anything's happened to her, do you?"

"Taimatsu's in Paris by now. I'm sure she'll call us once she's settled into her hotel. Don't worry. We need to concentrate on finding a ladder with no rungs: the symbol enclosed by four sides."

María nodded and, after a while, shook her head and raised her eyebrows.

"What?"

"Nothing. I was just thinking, a symbol enclosed by four sides . . ."

Miguel knew what she meant before she finished.

"A sign enclosed by four sides is inside a quadrilateral."

"You mean a square?"

"Well, yeah, or a rhombus, rectangle, or trapezoid. But I like the square better. And besides, I know where to find one . . ."

They crossed the nave and stood right in front of the Passion Façade, which opened out onto Calle Cerdeña. The sculptures there were the work of Subirachs, but the design, the idea, and the imagery had been mapped out by Gaudí before he died.

The Passion Façade faced west and represented the passion and death of Jesus Christ. It had three doorways and a porch with six columns and four bell towers, dedicated to the Christian virtues. Subirachs's sculptures were all naked, sharp edged, hard, and geometrical.

María took Miguel's hand. She was scared, and her heart was pounding. It didn't take long to reach the main door. Engraved on the lintel was a symbol representing the four elements: two triangles joined at the base, forming a diamond. A rhombus. They stared at it. But it wasn't just a rhombus, it was two joined triangles, another clear example of reflection and symmetry. On the right stood two groups of sculptures representing scenes from the passion, Christ on the cross. Above and below, on two levels, a group of women were crying; to the left was a man bearing what looked to be an odd-shaped cross—from below it resembled a carpenter's square.

At his feet, facing the main entrance, stood a geometric pillar at a ninety-degree angle, the labyrinth behind it.

María stood in front of the lintel above the main door, while Miguel glanced furtively this way and that. She had an idea, something she couldn't shake. If what is above is as what is below, couldn't it also be that what is on the left is as what is on the right?

"In the east as it is in the west . . ."

Miguel walked over to her.

"Here's the magic square. I know Albrecht Durer's famous etching *Melancholy*, where there's another magic square. A cryptogram. The sum of each column and each row is thirty-four."

The cryptogram was on the wall in front of them.

"Yeah, but on this one, each row adds up to thirty-three. Whether you go right or left, up or down, diagonally—it doesn't matter. Get it?"

"That's what's enclosed! It's in all four sides! This is the ladder with no steps! You have to count the number."

"I did, thirty-three," Miguel said, adding, "But this is a symbol. Wait. What's the symbol of Christ, who was crucified at thirty-three?"

"The Passion. A cross!"

"The four-armed cross is characteristic of Gaudí; there's one crowning almost every one of his buildings. This square encloses a cross that goes in four directions, each one adding up to thirty-three."

"A three-dimensional cross."

"Exactly, María. I think we've got our third symbol."

Now they had the sunflower, the dragon, and the four-armed cross, which were the signs for alpha, beta, and gamma. They only needed four more riddles to finish the puzzle. But they had to hurry. Although they hadn't seen them, they knew the Corbel was lurking. And they only had a few hours left.

50

THEY WERE ALREADY close to Casa Milà, more commonly known as La Pedrera, which was delta. María called Taimatsu again, but her friend still wasn't answering. Miguel tried to reassure her as they rushed down the street. There was no time to stop.

"She went to Paris for work; maybe her flight was delayed and she hasn't made it to the hotel yet. You know her; she takes her job very seriously. She gets completely caught up in a project and forgets about the rest of the world."

Miguel was suddenly uneasy, and María picked up on it.

"What?"

"Nothing."

"Come on, you can't fool me."

He decided to tell her.

"Do you realize we've solved three riddles in broad daylight with no trouble whatsoever?"

María glanced around. No sign of anyone suspicious.

"They're watching us, María. I know they are."

"But they'll wait for us to solve all the riddles, until we've got the stone. Then they'll kill us."

"Well, they haven't managed yet. And I'm not going to let anything happen to you."

"They're assassins, Miguel. Murderers."

"Let's not think about that right now; we're so close. Let's just concentrate on the next riddle."

"Delta, La Pedrera."

DELTA

Your mother is the water; your father is the fire. You are not a ship
and you travel in time, sunk in the foundations of the new city
that the warriors contemplate.

"I think I might know what it is; I have an idea," María said.

"You got it *already?*" Miguel asked, shocked.

"I'm not sure. The key is to figure out how the building in question fits into the picture. For this one, the symbol refers to the entire building. Do you remember the conversation we had with Taimatsu about all those Japanese arts?"

"Sure. Bonsai, ikebana, puppet theater . . . but I don't see how any of that ties in. I don't get it."

"Don't be so impatient. We need to look at La Pedrera from up close."

The building they'd seen so many times from her apartment window was now swarming with tourists snapping away with their cameras. They studied the building, repeating the riddle to themselves, until finally María said, "I think what Taimatsu said makes sense."

"What are you talking about? I still don't understand."

"*Suiseki.*"

"The art of stones?"

"Exactly. Remember what she told us about it? Don't you see? It's a stone! A building whose walls are rough stone, undulating curves, and even the name—La Pedrera—means 'the stone quarry.'"

"OK. So . . . it could be a cliff, or a rock, I guess."

"Now let me ask you, what might be buried in the foundations of a city?"

"A stone? The first stone."

"That's right, Miguel. A stone."

"Of course, and the warriors on the roof are contemplating—"

"La Sagrada Família. The new city."

"So it's a rough stone. A *suiseki*. The stone alchemists use for the Great Work."

"That means we have the fourth symbol."

"So the Big Dipper section of Ursa Major is complete: sunflower, dragon, four-armed cross, and stone."

As they ran down Paseo de Gràcia toward epsilon, at number 43, María tripped and stumbled.

"Are you OK?"

"I'm fine. I just tripped. Let's keep going."

Casa Batlló was right beside Casa Amatller, a beautiful building with a Flemish-inspired terraced façade built by the architect Josep Puig i Cadafalch. The two works, side by side, made one of the most beautiful and remarkable ensembles in the city; seeing them was like visiting another planet. Miguel pulled out his notes and read.

EPSILON

Not even the fires of Saint Elmo can light up your eyes, lost in the darkness.

María divided the façade and second-floor terrace into sections, trying to visually separate them from the rest. She placed her hands on either side of her eyes to limit her field of vision. Miguel watched her, intrigued. He would have liked to be the one to come up with the answer, but there was no doubt that his girlfriend was the riddle expert. Thinking about Taimatsu again, something occurred to María: that play about the suicide lovers by Sonezaki. She thought of the crow's eyes, black and shiny, reflecting the image of the dead lovers.

"What could it be?" Miguel wondered.

María had already guessed the answer. It was obvious. The secret lay in making the connection between the riddle and the building. And right now she could see it clearly; it was right before her eyes, on the façade. Just to make sure, she asked Miguel.

"Where do the fires of Saint Elmo appear?"

"In cemeteries, for one. The 'fire' is actually just the bones' phosphorus emanating from graves in the form of vapor."

"And this used to be known as the House of Bones, remember? Taimatsu told us," María said, adding, "good, now we have Saint Elmo's fire."

"Bones," Miguel replied pensively.

"A fire that can't illuminate eyes lost in the darkness," she prodded, hoping he'd come up with the answer she had in mind.

"Dark eyes?"

"Well, maybe, but your eyes are black and they're not lost in the darkness, Miguel."

"Empty eyes?"

"A face with empty eyes. What's that?"

"A dead person? A skull?"

"Look at the front of the building."

"María, I'm drawing a blank. What are you getting at?"

"Remember the conversation with Taimatsu, when we talked about puppet theater in Japan?"

"The balconies! Of course. They're masks! That was so easy; everybody knows that."

"Not even the fires of Saint Elmo can light up the eyes of a mask, because there are no eyes, only darkness, just black holes."

"You already knew that, didn't you?"

"Well, I just wanted to double-check. So—now we've got another one. Epsilon is a mask."

51

ZETA

Wise insanity, even if you see it, won't be found above the cypress.

THEY READ THE riddle when they got to Casa Calvet, which was on Calle Caspe. It was five in the afternoon. They had thirteen hours left, and they still didn't really know where the riddle would ultimately lead them. Miguel was worried. But there was no sense being defeatist; better to just focus on the building.

The house had belonged to Señor Calvet, a rich textile merchant and militant member of Solidaritat Catalana, who, like Gaudí, had a great love for the Catalan language and Catalunya.

Specialists often said this was the least representative of Gaudí's buildings, and though that might be true of the façade, the architect's style was certainly stamped on the interior.

María looked up at the cypress above the main entrance.

"You know what? When I first read this riddle, I thought of the cypress on La Sagrada Família."

"Yeah, me, too. It made me think of the Portal of Charity on the Nativity Façade, with the white doves symbolizing purity. The cypress represents hospitality as well as spiritual elevation, because it reaches up toward heaven. And its roots grow straight down toward the earth's core, symbolizing the underworld. That's why it's associated with cemeteries. But the key to solving the riddle lies in finding something on the building."

"Look above the cypress, at the wrought-iron railing. Mushrooms. They're mushrooms, Miguel."

"You're right. Señor Calvet was a mushroom aficionado, remember? A mycologist. And in Catalunya foraging for mushrooms is a tradition. Maybe that's what it refers to. Sure, because mushrooms grow under trees in the forest. That's why the riddle says you won't find it *above* the cypress."

"It could be a mushroom. The *Amanita muscaria* is the mushroom most representative of Gaudí."

"It's on the buildings at the entrance to Park Güell," he said. "And some people claim he consumed *Amanita muscaria*, too. Lots of Modernist artists did, in those days. It's a hallucinogen."

"That's just a myth. Besides, remember what Conesa told us. But the riddle says—"

"María, I think I've got it. We just have to figure one thing out."

"What?"

"I want to know what he means by—"

"Wise insanity?"

"For now, let's just say it is the *Amanita muscaria*. The mushroom where gnomes and dwarves live in fables. And the mushroom of crazy people. In fact, here in Catalunya it's known as *ou de foll*, the crazy person's egg. It looks like an orange egg, like its sister the *Amanita caesarea*, which is edible—and delicious. It was the caesars' favorite mushroom; that's why it's referred to as *ou de reig*, the kings' egg."

"I've never seen this side of you before, Miguel. A mushroom specialist!"

"Well, my father was the expert; I just used to go foraging with him."

"In any event, zeta is a mushroom."

IT WAS LATE by the time they got to Palacio Güell, the last building of Ursa Major, the one that corresponded to eta. Gaudí built it for his patron, Eusebio Güell y Bacigalupi. In addition to serving as a home for Güell and his family, Gaudí conceived of it as a venue for the social functions, cultural events, and soirees that his benefactor enjoyed so much. Gaudí presented the count with a whole slew of different designs, and the Catalan magnate chose the same one that Gaudí himself preferred. The façade on the first two floors was marble clad over masonry. Two perfectly symmetrical parabolic arches led to the palace's main entrance.

They read the riddle.

ETA

In the first letter of this palace the Magi saw the cross and the
heart of the immaculate Virgin Mary's light.

"This has got to be the hardest riddle—it seems so impenetrable," Miguel said.

They were standing beneath the Catalan coat of arms, which had a hawk on the top; it was very unique. The story went that when it was being hung, Gaudí asked a passerby how it looked, and the man told him it was awful. And that was when the architect made up his mind: it was staying put.

Miguel walked up to the main gates and examined the wrought-iron letters. An "E" on one and a "G" on the other.

"María, these are Eusebio Güell's initials: EG. So the first letter of this place is an E. The Magi saw the cross and the heart of the immaculate Virgin Mary's light. So I'd say it refers to the 'E,' which could be for 'estrella,' star. The Magi's star is the Star of Bethlehem, represented by the five-point star."

"But that's not the only possibility. The first letter could just be 'P,' for 'palace.'"

María was thinking aloud.

"The Magi saw the cross and the heart of Mary's light. The Magi were supposed to be kings, and where does a king live?"

"In a palace: Palacio Güell."

"I think if we assume it's 'P' for 'palace,' then we should find a connection between the Magi's star and letter 'P.'"

Suddenly it hit Miguel like a bolt of lightning.

"María, the chrismon is one of the ultimate symbols of Christianity; it's the Chi-Rho, the monogram of Christianity. Builders used them in churches, temples, and shrines. It's on communion wafers: a 'P,' for *pater* or 'father,' with an 'X' superimposed on it, symbolizing the son, Jesus. There's an alpha on one side and an omega on the other, meaning the beginning and the end. That one image contains everything. I think maybe the 'E' of 'Eusebio' could stand for 'Eucharist.'"

"Host wafers represent the Eucharist with a chrismon. A circle. Yes, that could be it—and circles are also female symbols. Hmm. Maybe."

But María wasn't convinced. Again, she felt sure her grandfather wouldn't have made it so easy. When she was a girl, she remembered, when he gave her riddles, one was always a trick, something to make her think. It was just like him—and he could be doing it now.

Though they'd been at it all day and they'd solved the riddles so far without any serious difficulty, that was exactly what made her uneasy. That just wasn't like her grandfather. Miguel, meanwhile, kept thinking, searching, and trying to find some connection.

"Gaudí often used letters and initials as symbols. There are 'G's for 'Gaudí' or 'Güell' in many of his works."

"And 'P's, too. Not just for 'palace,' but for 'Park Güell,' too."

"That's right. Look, I have a picture here."

Miguel took out his book on Gaudí, which showed photos of the architect's most characteristic buildings. He looked up Park Güell, and there it was. He was stunned.

"Look. The park's initial, 'P.'"

Indeed, there it was. And there was a five-point star—the star of Bethlehem—as well as an inverted pentagon, also known as a black pentagon, in the center. María stared at it and said, "Miguel, the three wise men saw the heart of light, the center of the five-point star."

"It's actually a pentagram, also called a pentacle or pentalpha. It's pure fractal geometry—a pentagon inside a pentagon inside a pentagon, and so on to infinity. We should find out if pentagons are associated with the Virgin Mary in any way. Normally pentagrams are linked to satanic cults, and I think the Church actually condemned them. María, we have three options: Eucharist, pentagon, or pentagram—the five-pointed star."

"No, just two—the star with a pentagon inside it, and the Eucharist, a circle. My grandfather did this intentionally, I'm sure, to make the seventh riddle trickier."

52

ARÍA AND MIGUEL decided to go back home for a little
while. They both needed to rest for a minute after spending
all day running from one building to the next, trying to
solve the riddles. They just had to stop and take it all in. María called
Taimatsu again. She was getting really worried now; it was late and
Taimatsu still wasn't answering her cell. Meanwhile, Miguel went to
search the Internet for information on pentagrams.

"María, listen to what I just found.

The golden ratio is found in the pentagram, a pagan symbol later
used by the Catholic Church to represent the Virgin Mary and by
Leonardo da Vinci in the Vitruvian man.

"And I found another page about English literature that mentions a
medieval Arthurian romance called *Sir Gawain and the Green Knight*,
which refers to pentangles. It says,

This five-pointed star can be drawn without lifting pen from paper,
and according to the author of the poem, the English called it the
'endless knot,' which has clearly esoteric connotations; it is also

considered a symbol of Solomon. It represents the five senses, five fingers (meaning dexterity), the five wounds of Christ, the five joys of the Virgin Mary (Gawain had an image of the Queen of Heaven on his shield), and the five virtues of knighthood (compassion, frankness, fellowship, purity, and courtesy). The number five, an odd number, is the number of perfection, and the pentagon can be inscribed in a circle, representing a cycle's completion.

When he finished reading, Miguel said, "Now I'm even more confused than before. So which is it: circle, star, or pentagon?"

"Hmm? I'm sorry, Miguel, I wasn't paying attention. I'm really worried about Taimatsu. I've been calling her all day and she still hasn't picked up. We should go over to her place, or to the foundation or something. Maybe we should call Bru, that businessman."

"At eleven o'clock at night? All right. I'll log off and we'll go."

"Wait, let me just check my e-mail first. I want to send her a quick message. Maybe she lost her phone or something."

María opened her e-mail and saw she had a new message. It was from Taimatsu. She checked the time it had been sent: three in the morning. Twenty hours ago.

"Come look at this."

They both read from the screen.

It's a stone; I'm positive. The key is in the Gospel of Saint Matthew 16:18. Father Jonás drew a compass above the reference to Psalm 118:22. It's in Park Güell. They made several alterations to it, but on the main staircase there used to be a compass.

53

T HEY LEFT TAIMATSU's building and raced straight to Hospital
del Mar. A neighbor had told them what happened after they
tried buzzing her apartment several times.

"They took her away in an ambulance this morning," she said.
"What a terrible way to go."

María was inconsolable in the taxi on the way to the hospital; it was
as if she were living a nightmare. She couldn't believe her friend was
dead. Though why not? It wasn't the first time. Those murderers had
started with her grandfather, and they wouldn't stop until they got their
hands on the stone, and on María and Miguel.

"They'll kill us both," María said. "As soon as they've got the stone,
they'll kill us."

Miguel didn't reply. He felt helpless, but at the same time he was so
furious he wanted to take on those psychopaths. He had no intention
of being killed or letting them hurt María; he fully intended to beat
them.

When they got to the hospital, they went to reception, where they
got confirmation of the terrible tragedy.

María burst into tears. Miguel wrapped his arms around her.

"Come on. Let's sit down. This has gone way too far. But you have to be strong."

"Miguel, it's all my fault. I know it is. What did they *do* to her?"

"Come on, we have to get out of here," he said.

He'd just seen a familiar face at the end of the hall. It was Nogués, Mortimer's assistant, talking to a hospital employee.

"María, we have to go. Now," he repeated, pointing.

"I can't. I can't do this."

"Yes, you can. If we don't go through with this now, it will all have been for nothing. Do you think Taimatsu would have wanted us to give up now when we're so close?"

"Taimatsu's dead."

"Yes, but we're not. We can't bring her back, but we can finish this. And if we don't, Taimatsu and your grandfather will have given their lives for nothing. Remember what your grandfather said: don't cry. Keep going. We know they're merciless. Fine, then we'll show them no mercy. But first we have to finish solving the riddles. Let's go!"

Nogués watched them leave but did nothing to stop them. He just pulled out his phone.

They decided to go back home, regroup, and plan their next move. They went to the taxi stand in front of the hospital.

Another car followed close behind.

54

WHEN THEY GOT back, they didn't turn on any lights. They could feel danger closing in. María took a deep breath and tried to pull herself together. Miguel was right: they had to finish this. It was a race against the clock and they were almost out of time. At least now they knew they had to go to Park Güell. Taimatsu's e-mail confirmed what the bookseller had suspected. Maybe he'd come to the same realization before he was killed. The secret was there, somewhere, and the game was waiting for them in the Enchanted House's oven, whatever that meant.

They made some strong coffee—it was going to be a long night. Miguel looked out the window.

"They're here. I saw them."

María jumped.

"They're out there?"

"I don't see them right now, but I bet they're watching the door."

"Do you have the number of that taxi driver? The guy who took us to the dragon gate at Finca Güell? Remember? He gave us his number before we got out."

Miguel had no idea what María was thinking, but he knew they'd have to go back out there unprotected.

"I'm sure that taxi driver can help us," she said.

"How do you know? At this stage, I don't trust anyone."

"I just know. He's one of the seven knights, Miguel. I'm sure of it."

"You're sure?"

"Tell him what's happening. He'll know what to do."

"How can you be certain? Why should I tell a taxi driver all of this?"

"We can trust him; I know we can."

Miguel made the call, but he couldn't tell if it was the same driver or not. He didn't say that they were being followed, but just said they needed a taxi urgently and asked him to wait downstairs with his engine running. The cabbie didn't ask any questions. He just said he'd be there in half an hour.

"Half an hour?" Miguel exclaimed, flustered. It seemed like an eternity.

The cab driver waited a moment and then said, "On earth as it is in heaven."

"What's going on?" María asked.

Miguel glanced over at her and replied, "What is above is as what is below."

She understood instantly. She'd been right. He was an ally, one of the Knights of Moriah.

"You're right. He's on our side. He'll be here in half an hour."

"We have to go back to Park Güell. We know where to look now, and we've solved almost every riddle."

"We should stop at La Sagrada Família on the way. The key to all of this lies in La Sagrada Família. Not only is it a compendium of every architectonic innovation Gaudí developed in his secular work, but he also turned it into a book with a message."

"One that has to be read with the heart."

"This is incredible. I think I'm getting it now. The four-armed crosses Gaudí put on almost all his buildings are spatial crosses, pointing in all six directions—"

"And what's above us? Stars."

"Exactly. María, Gaudí built a huge temple above the city. A temple of stars. But why? What are we supposed to do with the stone? The key to understanding it is in La Sagrada Família. The cathedral of the poor. A book of stone, like the Gothic cathedrals."

Miguel turned on his laptop as he spoke.

"Phecda, the star that goes with gamma, is the one for La Sagrada Família."

"Miguel, I think we've got something here."

"Maybe. Phecda is aligned with Megrez and points toward Regulus, the brightest star in Leo, which marks the lion's heart."

"The sign of Christ the Redeemer. The king, Regulus, the sun . . ."

"Leo: where the great work will be carried out. The universal force, ray of light. The son of the sun, the Redeemer. Within each seed is a ray of light that we call life, because the sun gives life. That's the power of Christ. The word 'Christ' comes from the Greek and means not only 'anointed' but also 'light.' The Savior is the Christian strength inside each of us that not only redeems us, but saves and exalts us when it unites with the father, the sun."

"OK, I think that makes sense, María. But I still don't understand what we're supposed to do with the stone."

"Place it in La Sagrada Família, in a position aligned with Megrez, pointing to Leo, the Sun . . . Christ the King and Redeemer."

"So in the temple there must be something, a symbol, some way for us to know what the exact spot is. I think Guillaume de Paris, the master builder of Notre Dame, chose a specific spot there to hide his philosopher's stone, too."

"We have to find the Caesarea Philippi stone, Miguel. The one Christ touched with his own hands. The cornerstone that the builders rejected and that will be used . . . for what?"

"I don't know. But I think we're going to find out very soon. La Sagrada Família is the temple of the poor. This all fits, I know it does. We've got five hours left. We have to do this tonight, or Achilles will catch up to us and we lose the race."

María was listening and searching the web at the same time.

"Miguel, this is amazing. The pyramids in Egypt are aligned with Megrez and Phecda, pointing toward Leo, too. They delineate the cosmic meridian. The fixed stars."

A car pulled up in front of the apartment building. Miguel glanced at his watch. It had been exactly half an hour. The car pulled up to the curb and waited.

"Let's go. He's here."

They ran out; the cabbie opened the door for them and quickly sped away.

"We're going to La Sagrada Família. Though I guess you already know that."

María looked at the driver's face in the rearview mirror; he smiled. Yes, it was him, the guy who'd helped her on the bus, and probably the one who'd saved them in the parking lot when her grandfather's notebook was stolen.

"Can you help us?" Miguel asked. "We've worked out most of this puzzle and we figured out what the symbols are, but we still don't know exactly where to find the secret. It should be somewhere on the Park Güell staircase, where there used to be a compass."

"I doubt I'd be much help with that. But I'll protect you. That's my mission. There have been renovations to Park Güell, you know."

Miguel turned to María. "Doesn't La Sagrada Família have a labyrinth somewhere?"

"Yes, in the Portal of Passion, right in front of the magic square, where we found gamma, the four-armed cross."

"Gaudí knew exactly what he was doing. He made a labyrinth of symbols, a chaotic hallucination. That's why he put *Amanita muscaria* on the buildings at the park's entrance. He knew people would come looking for the stone. But you're the only one who can find it, María, because you're the only one with the key to the entire enigma: the map on your body. We can't forget the 'Our Father,' the alchemists' golden rule."

"I don't understand what you mean."

"We have to climb up and look at the stars. Ascend. We've been lost, too, turning in circles, deceived by reason, deluded by our senses; reality is just a reflection. Now we know that in order to see the truth we have to ascend to a higher level of consciousness, one that can see through tricks of reason and illusion. This is the mirror of enigmas, like in Borges. And what do we use to climb up?"

"A ladder? Or staircase?"

"Exactly. It's one of the Masonic symbols, but it's also a Christian symbol, and that's how Gaudí used it."

"There's a staircase on the Portal of Passion."

"Yes, and it leads to the labyrinth. But La Sagrada Família is just a book of instructions. What we really need to find is the one at Merak, which is beta: Park Güell."

"There's more than one staircase at Park Güell."

"I know. There's a main one, but it's not the *only* one. It could be any of them. Our search is narrowing. In the Portal of Passion we have to figure out which staircase it is, which way it's facing. We have to find a sign, some clue to lead us to the right one. And we don't have any time to waste."

"Wait a minute," the driver said.

They both stopped expectantly. María and Miguel knew that anything one of the seven knights told them would be extremely helpful. They'd almost gotten to La Sagrada Família.

"You need to know that our enemies have controlled Park Güell for a long time now. We've always known about the labyrinth. You're right, Miguel. But they've been searching it for years."

"So they know! They deciphered Jonás's message!"

"Asmodeus is a very smart man; they know many things. You can't trust anyone. He forced Taimatsu to tell him everything before he killed her. In my opinion, if you already know what the symbols are, you should just trust your own judgment.

"Remember the gamma riddle, the one for La Sagrada Família: 'Add up the number on a staircase with no steps to see the sign the four sides enclose.'"

"Thirty-three. Thirty-three steps. The staircase at Park Güell."

Miguel's eyes opened wide. "Let's go back to the park. It *has* to be there."

A black car followed them, though they were too excited to notice.

They got to the park and, with the cab driver's help, scaled a wall to get in. He told them he'd be waiting.

Once inside, Miguel said, "María, I think they're here, too. We have to move fast."

They headed straight for the main entrance and climbed the stair-case holding hands, counting steps as they went, their hearts pounding. Different images raced through their minds: the lizard, fire, the dragon. It was as if their ascension were spiritual as well as physical. When they reached the top, they both whispered, "Thirty-three steps."

The alchemist's oven—the athanor—was right in front of them, the one Gaudí might have reproduced by copying it from a medallion of Notre Dame. This changed things; now they knew they'd followed the right path. But something still didn't fit. The symbols, the riddles, made Miguel's head swim.

"Wait a minute. The magic square is a staircase with no steps, and there's a labyrinth right in front of it. Two mirrors facing each other: the trickiest kind of labyrinth." He nodded and then said, "It's not here! This is another one of your grandfather's red herrings. Father Jonás knew that, and he died for it."

"So where do we go?"

"To the house Gaudí lived in."

They heard muffled sounds all around them. Miguel saw two men who looked like they had guns and another who seemed to be giving orders as they slowly climbed the stairs behind them. They hid on the other half of the divided staircase, pressing themselves up against the athanor. María and Miguel slowly and silently descended and followed the path leading off to the right, toward the Enchanted House. Soon they reached it. It was completely dark. Miguel tried to find a way in, and María crouched by the door. When she turned the handle, she was surprised to find it open.

"Miguel," she hissed.

"What is it? Hang on—I think I'm going to have to break a window."

She crawled over to him and whispered, "No. The door's open."

"It's open? Let's go, then! Why would it be open, though? We'd better be very careful; I'm pretty sure they know as much as we do, and they're right behind us."

Keeping as low as they could, they crept in. Miguel knew the kitchen was now a storeroom behind the tiny gift shop at the entrance. And indeed, they saw a chimney along the back wall, where Gaudí's kitchen must have been.

They searched the whole house, going upstairs to the top floors without finding anything. Finally they went down to the basement, where the pantry used to be. That door was open, too. Miguel swept his flashlight around the room. It looked like it was used to store junk. There were cardboard boxes and wooden crates tied shut with rope, a couple of wardrobes, and, at the very back by a small window, a floor vent with smaller cabinets and cupboards piled on top of it. Moonlight shone in through the small window, and they saw a squat, dark piece of furniture with four legs. Miguel shone the flashlight on it to get a better look.

"María, that's the stove!"

She approached it slowly. It was an old coal-burning stove. There didn't seem to be anything special about it; it was pretty typical of those from the time when Gaudí had lived. When he moved, the new owner must have taken it out of the kitchen. On its front was a door to shovel in the coal, and on one side there was a small oven under two iron grilles.

"There's nothing here," Miguel said, disappointed.

María didn't reply. Her mind was racing as Miguel scanned up and down repeatedly with his flashlight, not finding anything. She kept thinking of the fable: Hänsel and Gretel burning the witch, the dragon. She knew this wasn't a red herring; they were right about this. She was sure.

"Wait a minute. I think I know where the game is hidden," she said.

She opened her purse and pulled out the small mirror she kept with her lipstick.

"I want to check something."

They both squatted down in front of the stove and María held her little mirror faceup underneath it. Miguel shone the flashlight down at the floor.

At first they couldn't see much of anything; it just looked rough and uneven. Then Miguel stuck his head underneath the stove. Holding the flashlight in one hand, he used the other to feel around, fingering the stove's bumps and curves.

"María, I don't believe it! It's here! The game is here under the stove!"

"I knew it!" she cried triumphantly.

The board was stuck upside-down onto the bottom of the stove, the raised compartments facing down.

"This can't be a coincidence. The symmetry of the mirrors! It all fits. 'What is above is as what is below.'" Miguel hugged María and then said, "Now you have to play."

"I know."

María crouched down as Miguel shone his flashlight on the board. They wiped off some of the sixty-four squares with a tissue. Each square contained one of the symbols Gaudí used in his architecture.

She felt completely calm when she pressed down on the first one: the sunflower. The compartment sank slowly; she was right.

"Look, there's the dragon," Miguel said, pointing.

"Wait. We have to be sure it's right. There could be more besides the lizard. Remember, we only get one chance; we can't afford to make a mistake. It has to be an igneous dragon, with fire coming out of its mouth."

She was right—there was more than one dragon, in addition to the lizard: a coiled snake with wings, and another one eating its tail—the Ouroboros. But finally they saw it, diagonal from the sunflower: a fire-breathing dragon. That was the one they were looking for. María pushed it down and the cell sank about half an inch.

She had no problem finding the next one, the four-armed cross, though it took her a minute to locate the unpolished stone. Next she pressed down on the mask, and then the *Amanita muscaria*. It was all working so far; each compartment slowly lowered.

There was only one left to finish the game. Miguel aimed the flashlight down on the board. They found both symbols—the host wafer with a chrismon, representing the Eucharist, and a pentagon. They were right next to each other. María hesitated. She knew she had to pick one or the other.

"Trust your gut."

"Miguel, I have to think about this. I bet I can figure out what my grandfather's trick was. Imagine someone else had solved all the riddles the way we did. They stole the notebook last night, and they're smarter than we realized, so they've probably made it this far, too. But this last one . . ."

"There are two possible answers, the chrismon and the pentagon. And they have to choose the right one, or it's all over."

"That might not matter to them, though. Getting it wrong could be the easiest way to make Gaudí's plan fail."

"But who would possibly give up after coming so close? No, they'd either keep going or wait for us to solve it for them. They're taunting us, María. And they'll kill us as soon as we get the last one. Because *they* know what they have to do with the stone; they've known for centuries."

"Exactly. Put yourself in their shoes, Miguel. They use the pentagon in their rituals. And the chrismon is the symbol of Christianity, the Eucharist, the message of Christ. It contains everything."

"They'd have discarded their own symbol and chosen the chrismon; that's what seems most logical to me."

"No, Miguel. They've already gone over it like I just did. They hesitated, they doubted. One mistake and who knows what might happen. This mission is too important. One false move and we won't live to tell about it. That's how the secret is protected. Our lives depend on this, Miguel."

"On believing in our answer?"

"That's the purpose of the last enigma. That's why we're here."

Miguel suddenly understood, and shivered. Turning off the flashlight, he whispered, "María, the door was open when we got here. It was too easy for us to get in."

"I know. They were here before us. They searched the place but didn't find anything. But now they have the notebook and we've solved the riddles. It's only the last sign that has them so full of doubt that they can't continue. They're not willing to risk guessing the wrong answer, because they know this is their only chance."

"They're waiting for us to—for *you* to—"

"Yeah. They are."

"They're out there, just waiting."

"Waiting for us to do it for them."

Miguel felt his cell phone vibrate, reached into his pocket, and pulled it out.

"It's the taxi driver."

He answered.

"We're in the Torre Rosa and I know we're being watched. They'll kill us as soon as we come out. We need your help . . . OK . . . No, not yet . . . In a few minutes. If you make it to the house, when you come in, you know which room we're in. We'll be waiting for you here."

"What did he say?"

"He's going to help us get out of here."

"What do we do?"

"He'll protect us. He's on his way."

"Are you sure it was really him?"

"I don't know, María. I don't know if we can trust anyone but ourselves, to be honest with you. But this is the moment of truth. You have to choose one of those two symbols."

He felt completely overwhelmed and took her in his arms.

"María, I want you to know that—"

"I know," she said, smiling.

He hugged her and stroked her tenderly.

"No, you don't. I want you to know that I love you. I love you like I've never loved anyone in my whole life. You've suffered so much, and—"

"You, too," she said, cutting him off with a kiss.

"We're almost there. And we did it together. After all that work, all that effort, we're really almost there."

"But they're going to kill us."

"No, they are not. We can get through this, María. Believe me, I'm going to grow old with you. I can feel it. We're going to have children together."

"You're crazy!"

"Maybe, but I love you, María. I'm telling you, I can see it now. We're almost there. I know we are. Now, let's finish."

He stepped back. María touched the chrismon with her finger, but then she hesitated; she moved it to the pentagon, but she didn't dare press either one.

"You have to choose. We can't wait. And I can't help you with this. Come on, I know you can do it."

Finally, her throat dry, her hand trembling, she closed her eyes and chose the pentagon, the symbol used by the dark side. It was their sign, and she was sure that's why they'd hesitated.

Miguel held his breath. Even if María was wrong and the secret was lost forever, he loved her like he'd never loved anyone.

The compartment sank down. They heard a metallic click that sounded like something inside the stove had been activated. Suddenly, a spring-action drawer slid open from the lower part of the stove's rim.

Miguel shone his light inside, and there it was: a small cloth, enfolding the relic. María slipped her hand in and pulled it out.

She unwrapped it right there and they stared at the stone. There was nothing supernatural about it. It was just an ordinary-looking, blackish stone. This was the stone Jesus Christ had touched in Caesarea Philippi, the same one he gave Peter, his disciple, when he declared, "On this rock I will build my church."

They contemplated it for a few moments and then noticed some markings on the cloth. Miguel shone the flashlight down and they examined it carefully. It was Ursa Major, each star bearing a letter from the Greek alphabet. But gamma, the letter corresponding to La Sagrada Família, was much larger than the rest, and on top of it was a symbol they both recognized immediately.

"A pelican! I understand now. The stone has to be deposited in the pelican at La Sagrada Família," Miguel said. "The pelican symbolizes Christ and the Rosicrucians. The blood-red rose! That's where we have to put the stone: in the temple of the poor."

Something was written on the lower part of the cloth—a sentence they both recognized, from Paul's letter to the Corinthians.

VIDEMUS NUNC PER SPECULUM IN AENIGMATE: TUNC AUTEM FACIE
AD FACIEM. NUNC COGNOSCO EX PARTE: TUNC AUTEM COGNOSCAM
SICUT ET COGNITUS SUM.

"'Now we see the enigma through a mirror; later we'll see it face to face,'" María said. "My grandfather's epitaph!"

"Yes, María; I think this must be the same message Gaudí himself received, and his interpretation of it was to build his great temple in the image of heaven!"

"What do you mean?"

Miguel didn't have time to reply. They heard a noise. There was someone in the house. Miguel turned his flashlight off. María wrapped the stone back up in its cloth and grasped it tightly.

"Is that the taxi driver?" she whispered.

"I don't know. Let's hope so, because he's the only one who can help us get out of here alive. If it's one of the Corbel, he'll come straight here. But I didn't tell the driver what part of the house we were in. So let's see what he does."

"They only let us get this far so we could solve the last riddle for them," María said.

"If that's our guardian angel, he'll be waiting at the door."

They let a few minutes go by and then Miguel snuck silently upstairs, alone. He saw a silhouette waiting by the door and he whispered, "On earth as it is in heaven."

"What is above is as what is below," the man responded.

"We have to protect her," Miguel said.

"I know. We can't be too careful. She's in grave danger until the mission is completed."

He felt sure it was the taxi driver. The man was tall and strong, though Miguel couldn't see his face. He showed Miguel the medallion he wore around his neck.

"Epsilon."

"That's my letter. Our enemies are everywhere now. I got in without being seen, but it's going to be much harder to get all three of us out. Do you know where to go?"

The man looked at Miguel, who responded with another question.

"How do we get out of here?"

"The others will be here any minute. They'll protect us while we make our escape."

"How many of you are there?"

"Five," he said, and then added quickly, "we know what to do; we're prepared. As soon as they give us the signal, we'll make our move."

"OK," Miguel said, edging away.

"Where are you going?"

"To get María. I have to tell her the plan."

"Don't be long."

Miguel hurried back downstairs, his flashlight trained on the ground. He walked into the junk room and saw María waiting for him anxiously at the far end. As he scanned back and forth with the flashlight, he thought he saw something strange—some kind of reflection. María saw it, too.

"Miguel, behind the door!"

He turned and shone the light onto the wall behind the door. On the wall was a large oval that looked like a mirror, about five feet tall, with something engraved on its rim. María was as surprised as he was to see it; neither of them had noticed it before. In silence they read:

VIDEMUS NUNC PER SPECULUM IN AENIGMATE: TUNC AUTEM FACIE AD FACIEM. NUNC COGNOSCO EX PARTE: TUNC AUTEM COGNOSCAM SICUT ET COGNITUS SUM.

"That's my grandfather's epitaph again, Miguel. This is the last door! It's the same as what's printed on the cloth protecting the stone."

"This wasn't here before. We must've triggered it when we solved the puzzle. It must be connected to all of this somehow; there's got to be some sort of mechanism—"

They heard footsteps. Someone was coming down the stairs. Miguel grabbed María's arm.

"Is it the taxi driver?"

"No. It's one of them. The guy showed me a medallion, so I thought he was one of the knights at first. But when I asked him how many of them had come to help us, I knew he was an impostor."

"What did he say?"

"Five. That's impossible. There were only seven altogether, and including him, that leaves four. The Corbel killed the rest of them—including your grandfather."

"So what do we do now?"

"Follow your grandfather's instructions before that guy finds us. This must be the way out. It's like *Alice in Wonderland*," he said, pointing to the opening before them.

He pushed against the metallic oval, and it opened. As soon as they'd stepped through it, the disk clicked shut behind them. There was no turning back now. The door was sealed. Miguel shone his flashlight ahead of them and they saw stairs. María was scared. They walked down the stairs, hearing muffled shouting and banging on the metal behind them.

The underground tunnel was three feet wide and about six feet tall. Shining the light ahead of them, they could see it veered to the right.

"María, the message on the cloth with the stone . . . when the drawer in the stove opened, I heard a strange sound. But we were so engrossed in the game I didn't really stop to think about it—"

"Gaudí planned the whole thing . . ."

"Exactly. This is the secret passageway. And when the drawer on the stove opened, it activated the mechanism that opened this last door. Your grandfather told you about this, too, María. This is the last door. It all makes sense."

55

WHO COULD HAVE guessed there was a crypt beneath Park Güell? Did Gaudí build it, or was it natural, something that was already there? Both Gaudí and his patron Eusebio Güell had shown great interest in purchasing the land. Though it was long gone, at one time there had been a hexagonal mosaic at the park's entrance to commemorate the purchase, listing when and where the transaction had taken place: "Reus, 1898." The same inscription, along with champagne bottles, was found at Palacio Güell, too.

They purchased that rugged land—a hill near Tibidabo, facing the sea—in Reus, at the Hotel Londres. The owner was Salvador Samá, marquis of Marianao, and the property had a name: Can Muntaner de Dalt. Gaudí and Güell were ecstatic. Work on the garden city began in 1900. From the start, the architect refused to level the mountain, opting instead to respect the land's natural contours, to adapt his work to it.

Miguel thought about that as he shone his flashlight on the immense fossils decorating the crypt. He and María both wondered the same thing: were they sculptures or natural formations? Either way, they were exceptionally strange and beautiful. There were prehistoric animal skeletons and large shells with stalactites coiling down from inside them, ending in five-petaled flowers that looked like stars. Everything was petrified, but they were comprised of different shades that blended together harmoniously. An enormous hanging tortoise shell formed what looked like a chapel, right in the center of the grandiose hall. They walked beneath it, aiming the flashlight up at the ceiling, and then froze, staring—inside the shell there seemed to be thousands of transparent veins with water circulating through them. Looking left and right, they saw that the walls were dripping. Then they noticed that the floor was decorated with countless petrified fish, whose bodies made a mosaic. As they passed under the shell they were surprised by how loud the water was; it was awe inspiring. From the ceiling of the next chamber hung the skeleton of a strange, grandiose animal, its wings folded like a mummy's arms. Water cascaded off it, giving the surreal, ghostly impression that it was moving, that it had a life of its own. Beneath it was a small lake, its waters silvery from the rocks surrounding it, its surface reflecting the underside of the antediluvian creature. They wondered if it could be an enormous bat. Gaudí had used a few on his buildings. María thought of the one beneath the cross on the weathervane at Palacio Güell, symbolizing Christ's power over evil and darkness. But this was some deformed creature, a fusion of more than one thing. It reminded Miguel of one of the funicular models Gaudí used for the Güell crypt.

They couldn't afford to stop and stare; they were on a mission, and time was running out. They had less than two hours left. So they rushed through other galleries filled with numerous fossilized animals embedded in the walls, floors, and ceilings, all looking so natural, perfectly adapted to their stone surroundings, creating amazing baroque spaces, great halls, even buildings that shared their space with majestic gardens populated by stone trees whose branches formed canopies throughout the caverns. There were endless varieties of leaves, plants, exotic fruits, and fossilized birds. Other caves had impossibly steep and curved staircases made of bones that gleamed like marble. Capitals, cornices, and skeletons from extinct species formed huge paraboloids overhanging like balconies high up on the walls. There were rows of leaning columns and canopies inlaid with what looked like dark glass. In other places, larger fossils were suspended from the ceiling, intertwined in a jungle of lianas, like petrified roots in an immense forest. One of the rooms gave them the impression that they were in the belly of a sea creature. Hundreds of animals, shells, fish, and other small creatures were trapped in the floor, on the ceiling, and along the curved walls, like a gigantic mosaic. Miguel shone his flashlight in every direction, making them feel tiny by comparison. They were uneasy when they came upon a whimsical sculpture that seemed to simply emerge from the wall, creating a platform of stylized skeletons, sharp as needles, in animal shapes; it appeared to be suspended in midair. Then the cavern suddenly narrowed and they went through a passageway made of very tall columns at precarious angles; though they stood firm, their equilibrium seemed to defy all laws of physics. Next they reached a work whose architectural beauty was breathtaking. It was a sanctuary, a cathedral of life, built of life. This left them with no doubt; it exceeded all human capabilities. Not even Gaudí could have created something of such unbelievable magnificence. It was like a fossilized cemetery. Perhaps it was the very place where Gaudí was first mesmerized by nature, his own grand master.

As she walked, staring up at the cavern's ceiling and the bizarre fossils on the wall, María couldn't stop thinking about Hesiod's cosmogony. In his legend of the creation, Gaia—Mother Earth—gave birth to Uranus and then lay with him to create the Cyclops and the Titans. One of them was the indomitable Cronos—Time—who cut off his father's genitals with a scythe his mother had made. The cave they were crossing now could have been the center of life, the Omphalos, the womb of the world, where the seed of Uranus had fallen, creating the new world; evolution simply followed its already set course.

Cronos was a tyrant who devoured Gaia's children. But when she gave birth to Zeus, to save him from death, she gave Cronos a rock swaddled in diapers. Zeus killed his father and ended the tyranny, and he was the start of the world. Zeus, the god who ruled Olympus with thunder and lightning. María realized it was a stone that had saved Zeus from death.

Miguel wasn't thinking about Greek mythology at all. To him, that phantasmagoria was like an H. P. Lovecraft dream. He thought of one of the books he'd read as a child: *At the Mountains of Madness*. What came to mind was an underground palace, a huge warehouse of bones and shells, an unknown jungle of gigantic ferns, a forest of Mesozoic mushrooms, petrified cicadas, Tertiary palms and angiosperms, extinct species of cetaceans, Eozoons, Silurians, and Ordovicians—a door to the secrets of the earth and bygone eras.

At the end of the long, increasingly narrow corridor, they saw an oval opening in the wall and headed toward it. Miguel shone his light through the darkness and they saw there was a deformed spiral staircase heading up. They climbed to the top and came out into a perfectly round room. The flashlight's batteries were low by this time, but there was enough light for them to see what looked like a two-foot circle on the wall with a large metal ring in the center of it.

"María, I think this is the way out. Hold the flashlight for a second."

He tried to yank the ring, but it was impossible. Finally, he realized that although he couldn't pull it toward him, he could move it sideways. He tugged as hard as he could, and the stone disk slid to one side.

"Let's go."

María was the first one through, still holding the flashlight. Miguel followed right behind. They seemed to be inside a sewer pipe. Though it wasn't tall, at least they could stand. They shone the flashlight in every direction.

"We have to find a way out."

Before they'd taken even three steps, they were startled to hear a sound behind them. The disk Miguel had moved slid back into place, sealing the hole they'd come through, camouflaging it perfectly in the wall behind them.

They kept going. Soon they reached some rusty stairs.

"This way," Miguel said.

They came up onto the street from a manhole on the corner of an alley that led to Travessera de Dalt. They'd lost all sense of time and had no idea how long they'd been underground. One look at their watches told them there was less than an hour until dawn—less than an hour to fulfill the prophecy.

56

W E HAVE TO get to gamma, La Sagrada Família," María said, feeling the weight of the stone in her hand.

There was hardly any traffic at that hour, and they raced toward the temple, stopping from time to time to make sure no one was following them. It was a long trek, but finally they made it to the cathedral of the poor.

They were both utterly exhausted; the lack of sleep was beginning to take its toll.

Miguel kissed María tenderly and said, "I can't come with you for this part. You have to fulfill the prophecy on your own. Find the pelican; it will tell you where to place the stone."

"The pelican?"

"Yes, María; I finally figured it out on our way over. The crow in Notre Dame Cathedral indicated where Guillaume de Paris had hidden the philosopher's stone. In alchemy the crow symbolizes corruption, the corruption of man, who searches for the stone out of greed. But the pelican is the bird of the Rosicrucians, the bird that rips open its own chest to feed its young. Don't you see? It's the symbol of the Sacred Heart of Jesus! The Lion Heart, the Redeemer! That's where you have to put the stone that the builders rejected. You have to be the one to do it, and we're almost out of time; it's nearly dawn."

There was nobody around. Miguel helped María scale the fence, and he stayed outside as she approached the Nativity Façade. She tried the door. It was open; she slipped in. Just then she heard tires screech out on the street. There was shouting, and she momentarily panicked. She thought of Miguel. Her heart pounded furiously. She had to carry on. She crossed the temple with the rock in her hand, frightened and disoriented, but propelled by a force. She thought she heard voices, a sort of low, deep chanting, and looked up. Through the apse, dawn's first light filtered through the stained-glass windows and was reflected throughout the temple onto a series of columns, making them look almost translucent. She thought about the enchanted forest. María felt faint and clutched the stone tightly. She had to find the pelican.

She waded through that forest until finally she fell to her knees.

"My God, I can't go any farther. I can't," she said to herself. Something seemed to break in her. She was exhausted, but also confused. Something was different in her. Something in her began to change.

Suddenly, from behind her, she heard a deep voice.

"María, don't worry. You're here; you made it. I've been waiting for you. You're the chosen one . . ."

She hesitated. It was such a seductive voice. *Finally*, she thought, and turned to face it. The man was dressed in a frayed gray habit, his head covered and his hands hidden inside the cassock's billowing sleeves. He advanced slowly toward her.

"Have no fear, María. You're safe here. No one can hurt you."

The hooded man stood before her now and took his hands from his sleeves. A ray of light, perhaps the first light of dawn, seemed to illuminate his hands. Was it a reflection?

"We guided you here to complete the work. Who do you think opened the doors for you?"

María heard the muffled sounds of the city waking outside, and she thought of Miguel's words: the Rosicrucian, the pelican's bleeding heart was a symbol of Christ. It's where she had to deposit the stone.

"Look at my hands."

María approached the hooded man slowly. She was tired, so tired, but she was convinced that this was where the cornerstone belonged. She saw his hands stained with blood, his fingers curled into what looked like a red rose. She wasn't sure whether what she was looking at was real or just a delusion.

"This is the pelican's chest, the red rose you're looking for, where the stone belongs."

She had no doubt now and continued to slowly approach the monk. But then a voice, a shout, grew louder, ringing out through the temple, through the rays of light. The hooded man looked up. That was when María saw his face and trembled. What she saw in his black eyes terrified her. She felt Taimatsu there with her, warning her. She recalled the Sonezaki story of the lovers who got lost in the forest and in the first light of dawn committed suicide, the crow their only witness. And in his eyes—the eyes of the man forming a rose with his bloody hands—that image was reflected.

María saw her and Miguel's death reflected in the monk's black eyes. It was a moment of sheer terror. *They* were the lovers lost in the forest— she and Miguel.

She realized that the monk was the crow. She knew he was there to kill her and felt a sharp pain in her chest. She couldn't breathe, but she heard Miguel's voice, and the voice of her beloved grandfather, and her friend Taimatsu, who had reminded her of that story of the crow, the bird of corruption. "María, have faith. Run."

The shouting got closer. It was Miguel, coming to help her, she was sure of it. She jumped to life and stepped back. The monk, furious, ripped off his hood. Though terror clouded her vision, she recognized him: the Corbel man. He was speaking in a strange language as he raised his cane. She ran as fast as she could and hid, crouching down behind a column, petrified. The monk leapt silently forward. He landed just behind her, a macabre smile on his face. María didn't even know he was there; she was still huddled behind the column, clutching the stone in her fist. Overtaken by panic, she trembled, trying to hide from a killer she could no longer see. Instinctively she turned, and she saw the monk's black eyes, his enormous face wearing an expression of pure hatred. From within his cane, he extracted a thin foil that he now held poised over her head. It was a sword of some type. A sword sliced through the air just above it. María moved to one side and saw the taxi driver. It was the giant—her guardian—wearing a great red cross on his chest. He stopped the blow that would have severed her head.

The two men turned to face each other. The clanging of metal echoed throughout the temple, and the men jumped agilely from side to side with unbelievable strength.

"You shouldn't have come. Now I'll have to finish you first, before I cut off her head."

"I've been waiting a long time, Asmodeus. This is the end for you."

"Your prophecy will never come to pass. You chose the wrong lord, and you're going to pay for that now."

"I chose the only Lord who deserves to be served. And his coming is near."

"I'm here to stop that."

Their blades sliced through the air, clanging against stone when they missed; the sound of it was deafening. Still leaping this way and that, they thrust and stabbed at each other. María curled up into a ball against the column, watching the duel, knowing that by its end, one of them would be commending his soul to God or the devil. She knew, too, that her life depended on the outcome of that duel.

Asmodeus delivered a blow to the taxi driver's shoulder, and blood flowed from the gash. The giant needed both hands to hold his sword, and now he could only just manage to raise it, to fend off his enemy's blows. Asmodeus laughed, backing his adversary into the column where María still cowered, trembling with fear. When he was only a few steps away, the giant could no longer hold out, and with his enemy's next blow, the sword fell from his hands.

He was disarmed. He knelt and looked at María, as if to ask forgiveness for his defeat, then made the sign of the cross. Asmodeus severed his head with a single blow, laughing triumphantly as he did.

María wept, terrified. He approached her, muttering, "I'll send you to the devil as well!"

He positioned the tip of his sword just a few inches from her chest.

"I'm going to sink this blade into your heart and destroy the rock forever. The Omphalos."

His triumphant words rang out through the temple.

Asmodeus saw Miguel running toward them from the nave.

"Let her go!" he cried.

It was too late.

"I opened all the doors so you'd do the work. I could have murdered you a long time ago, like I did your grandfather and your friend Taimatsu. But I wanted you to show me the way. You showed me everything, and now I will kill you. The time has come for my lord to rule. And for you to die."

Asmodeus lunged at María, sinking his sword into her. She fell back. The stone she'd been grasping so tightly fell to the ground. Blood poured slowly from her chest.

"María! María!" Miguel cried. He was only a few feet away.

"And now it's your turn," Asmodeus said.

Miguel used both hands to pick up the sword of the monk Asmodeus had just killed. An uncontrollable fury shook him, but he had to focus, to control himself. Rage would be of no help if he really wanted to kill that bastard. He was an excellent swordsman, but this weapon was too heavy for him and he couldn't handle it with his usual dexterity. He looked down at María; she lay motionless, her eyes closed, her chest bleeding. Miguel feared the worst. He turned to his opponent and couldn't believe what he saw.

"You!"

Miguel recognized Álvaro. Despite the sickening expression on his face that made him look just like the sculpture of the man with the Orsini bomb, that lunatic was Álvaro, his old friend, the bookseller. But that was impossible! He'd died in the fire at the bookstore.

Álvaro Climent guessed what was racing through his old friend's mind.

"Bitru was the one they found in the bookstore. That was his last mission."

"But why are you involved in this? I never would have suspected you—"

"You still don't get it, do you? I serve my lord just like they serve theirs," he said, nodding toward Cristóbal. "You've always been a doubter, needing science to justify things. But I discovered something far better that makes the world go round: horror. I am not going to die, my friend. My master has given me a job to do, and that's to make sure the prophecy is not fulfilled. I'm here to destroy that damn stone and slaughter the Seven Knights of Moriah once and for all. They've been waiting for this for centuries—for their prophecy, for the second coming of Christ. I've been chosen to stop it. I'm here to prepare for my lord's reign. A world of terror and panic, a world of insecurity and savagery. The devil's world."

Asmodeus laughed; he sounded insane. Then, pointing to María with his sword, he gestured for Miguel to approach his beloved.

"Go on. Say good-bye. After I'm through with you I'm going to cut off her head and take it as a trophy."

"Never! I'll kill you first!" Miguel replied, kneeling down, putting his arms around María, and pulling her to his chest.

Asmodeus smiled sardonically.

"I've been patient; you led me here. I had many chances to kill you, but instead I paved the way so you'd do the work for me. I couldn't have made it this far. You did a very good job with Zeno's paradox. But Achilles is here now. I caught up to you."

Asmodeus kept talking, but Miguel wasn't paying attention. He was staring at María's chest, the red stain slowly spreading. He embraced her as he opened her shirt. In the middle of her chest was the alpha medallion, covered in blood and cracked down the middle. *Alpha will save your life,* he recalled. Then he put two fingers to her neck and realized she wasn't dead: her heart was still beating. Her grandfather's medallion *had* saved her life. He tried to hide his joy. Achilles hadn't caught the tortoise yet. María was not dead yet.

Asmodeus approached slowly, still speaking, the blade in his hand. Just then María opened her eyes, and Miguel pulled her to him quickly and looked up at Asmodeus.

"Yes, my friend, I have exceptional aim. And the worst thing is, you don't even know what the stone is for."

"No, but I have a feeling you're about to tell me."

"That's right. I'm going to tell you because you're about to die, and you deserve to know why. You already know where the stone came from, but you don't know where it goes. Gaudí spent years retracing the seven stars, Ursa Major, in Barcelona and erecting a temple of the poor, La Sagrada Família. Bocabella, the bookseller who bought the temple's land, was in on the secret, and so was Güell, his damn benefactor. Gaudí created this map of the heavens to guide the Redeemer back, to bring on Christ's second coming, man's salvation. That's what the stone is for. It was to be placed in a specific spot in La Sagrada Família, and when it was, the Redeemer would be born again. The Word would become flesh once more, and, thirty-three years later, when La Sagrada Família was finished, he would enter Barcelona, the New Jerusalem. And the reign of Jesus Christ would change the face of the earth."

Miguel couldn't believe what he was hearing. But it all added up; everything made perfect sense. Following the trail of clues, like the pebbles in "Hänsel and Gretel," they would find the treasure and lead all of humanity to salvation. The answer to the seven riddles was the completion of the prophecy.

"Believe me, it's written. Gaudí, a man with a leftist past, a man who the Masons wanted in their ranks and who we tempted with no luck, built a monument to his faith. The Nativity Façade with its three doors—Faith, Hope, and Charity—what do you think they're for? That's where the poor and the faithful would enter. Gaudí wrote it all down. We knew, and he confirmed it. Gaudí wrote that man's salvation lay in the life and death of Christ: the Nativity and the Passion. That's why the temple has two façades, one dedicated to each."

Asmodeus paused, and when he began speaking again his voice was triumphant. "For years, we've fought to stop the coming of Christ. The Templars knew about it, and with the Pope's help, we destroyed them. The Catharists knew it, too, and we killed them. Liberation theology intuited it, and they were discredited. For years, I have battled as As-modeus, serving the powers of evil and fighting the Knights of Moriah, the seven knights charged with keeping the secret safe and ensuring the prophecy was fulfilled. And you're the last one. María—Mary—didn't you even realize she bears the name of the woman God used to create Christ, his own reflection? Doesn't that mean anything to you? María, the mirror of heaven. And what is creation but a reflection of divine essence? Well, I'm the one destined to break the mirror and establish a very different reign, that of the dark mirror of death and misfortune. I killed your God by impeding his return, and now I'll open the doors to my lord."

Miguel looked at the forest of columns and recited a sentence he had written in his notes.

"The Church is a leafy tree, beneath which fountains flow."

"Yes, and this is it, the cathedral of the poor. Now prepare to die."

He charged furiously, the sword in his hands, planning to impale them both. Miguel anticipated this and shoved María hard to one side, saying, "Wake up, María! Run. Fulfill your destiny."

Miguel managed to dodge the blow. Asmodeus's sword clanged against the ground, the metal echoing loudly. He was livid, staring at Miguel and María, who were on either side of him, unsure of who to attack first. She snatched up the stone and ran while Miguel blocked Asmodeus's way, brandishing Cristóbal's sword.

Dazed, María ran through the forest of columns, her chest throbbing painfully. She had to find the pelican—it had once stood in the Nativity Portico but now sat forgotten in the corridor of La Sagrada Família museum.

Meanwhile, Miguel leapt forward, wielding the sword with both hands, and managed to strike Asmodeus's arm, below his left shoulder. This was the arm that held his blade, and the gash was sufficient to encumber him. Like an injured animal, Asmodeus groaned furiously and shoved Miguel back. He tried to fend off his opponent's blows, holding the weapon with both hands.

María had disappeared, but Asmodeus knew where she was going and pursued her. A few minutes and it would all be over. Time had almost run out. Now they heard other voices inside the temple.

"Freeze! Police!" It was Nogués, chasing them through the columns.

María had crossed a short wooden bridge and was rushing through the museum—through models, old photographs, designs, and drawings showing all of the plans for the temple. She heard voices growing closer. And then she saw it, on her left, its wings spread. The only thing separating her from the pelican, just a few feet away, was a blue cord hanging between two metal poles. She stepped over it, took the stone from its sack, and reached out.

Asmodeus reached her. Miguel was following close behind. María stretched her arm out, reaching toward the pelican's chest, and just then sunlight shone in through the temple's stained-glass windows. A beam of light seemed to illuminate the stone pelican.

"No!" cried Asmodeus frantically, rushing to stand before the pelican and block her way.

The same light seemed to pierce him like a fiery sword. He let out a horrific cry, which rang out through La Sagrada Família's towers. Asmodeus's body seemed to smolder in flames.

Nogués stood beside Miguel; together, they watched in silence as Asmodeus's life evaporated in front of them.

María put the stone in its rightful place and collapsed.

"Is she dead?" Nogués asked.

"I don't know," Miguel replied, taking her in his arms. He now knew that she was everything to him. It had been a long, long time since he cried; he couldn't remember the last time. But now it took every bit of strength he had to hold back the tears stinging his eyes. Images of her, of the past few days, raced through his mind. He was not a believer, but what he'd been through with María had opened a door to something he didn't fully understand. He'd have given anything, everything, his life, for her. But now he could only gaze at her face, which almost seemed to be smiling. His love for her was so immense; it was a feeling that came from the deepest, truest part of him.

Alpha, beta, gamma, delta, epsilon, zeta, and eta all began to glow at once, creating an intense light throughout the city. From the highest point in the city, startled onlookers came outside to contemplate the two identical constellations, the one above the city and the one below the Barcelona sky, whose seven buildings showed heaven the way home.

Nogués and Miguel, with María in his arms, went outside. They walked away from the Nativity Façade and toward Avenida Gaudí. They turned to look back at the temple. La Sagrada Família was like a golden flame, and the church bells rang. They'd never heard that sound. People came out onto their balconies and down into the street. In a matter of minutes, Avenida Gaudí was swarming with astonished crowds.

"What's going on?" Nogués asked.

What could Miguel tell him? The truth?

Miguel, with María in his arms, stood in front of the temple. He was now certain it was made in the image of the heavens. The cathedral of the poor. The third temple. Solomon's third temple.

Then he looked at María's face. And to him, it was the face of the Madonna.

57

AFRICA, 2006

One night the Chariot of Heaven will stop on top of the mountain of Phecda and a Traveler will descend, and she will bring light to the hut where the child will be born.

THIS LEGEND, KEPT alive by the elders, was passed down from generation to generation. But over the years, hunger, terrible drought, and AIDS had decimated the population. There were few who still sat beside the village fire to listen—starving children, women, and people who were old by forty. Their faces reflected neither hope, nor desolation, nor impotence; they reflected nothing, because there was nothing, they had nothing—only a myth to keep them alive.

Each night they told the same tale, pointing to the sky. The littlest ones stared up into the stars, their eyes wide, holding their breath, waiting in silence, longing for the miracle. But for years the Chariot followed its course without ever stopping on the mountain and then disappeared over the horizon. Some people thought it was nothing but a story, a way to keep the memory of their people alive throughout the generations. And then the Chariot finally stopped on the mountain of Phecda, the rocky peak worn away by the wind.

That night something happened. The elders got up, still staring at the sky. They couldn't believe their eyes. They whispered to one another. Women began to sing and dance around the fire. They had no doubt—the other stars were still moving. But there was the Chariot. The time had come. Their faces lit up in excitement. The littlest ones scrambled down from their mothers' laps and ran, searching for the Traveler. The prophecy was going to be fulfilled.

One of the elders asked quietly if anyone was missing. He was told that one of the women was about to give birth. He raised his cane to quiet all present. Two midwives were with the mother-to-be. They had always helped bring new life into the world. The elder gave precise instructions. Four men, the village's best men, ran in four directions to bring news of the miracle. One of them would inform the three missionaries.

The children's shouting grew louder, as did that of the woman in labor. And then, in the distance, they saw her approach—the Traveler, who would come to announce the prophecy. In her hands was the light of a star. Children surrounded her, joyful in their innocence. The elders came forward and pointed to the hut with their canes. Everyone waited outside, sitting around the hut.

The Traveler went in. Busy helping the woman give birth, the midwives did not look up. The Traveler moved a rock on the floor and deposited a stone beneath it, burying it in the earth just as the first rays of sunlight fell on that remote, isolated place. The baby's cries caused uncontainable jubilation in the villagers waiting outside. Drummers began their rhythms and did not stop for three days and three nights.

The newborn, swathed in clean cloths, was placed on the stone. The Traveler stood contemplating the child. Only when the three men from the mission entered did she react. One of them, a very tall man, spoke her language and asked her who she was.

"I've come from far away . . ."

"We have known of you for centuries," the man, whose name was Cristóbal, told her. The Traveler acknowledged him as though she had always known him. Their paths had always been connected.

Another of the men went out to the jeep and returned with some presents.

"From the mission," he told the mother.

"For the child," they added.

"You can come with us; you've completed your task," Cristóbal said.

"Yes, it's time to go home," the Traveler replied.

The prophecy had been fulfilled. In thirty-three years that child—born in the heart of Africa, in a poor, forsaken village at the foot of Mount Phecda, a place ravished by hunger and poverty—would enter the cathedral of the poor and forever change the world.

ACKNOWLEDGMENTS

First of all, we would like to thank Ramón Conesa from the Carmen Balcells Agency, who had faith in this story from the start.

To our wives, who put up with endless hours of solitude while we worked on this.

To our children, in the hopes that they come to see, like Albert Camus did, that people have more qualities to be admired than they do to be scorned.

To Raquel Gisbert, our editor, and to Antonio Quintanilla.

And to the following authors and media who made this book possible through their works and studies:

Consol Bancells; Joan Bassegoda Nonell; Hans Biedermann; Jorge Luis Borges; Bertolt Brecht; José Calvo Poyato; Francesc Candel; Josep Maria Carandell; Xavi Casinos; Saint John of the Cross; Revista de Occidente's *Diccionario de Historia de España*; Umberto Eco; Carlos Flores; Fulcanelli; Gustavo García Gabarró; the Brothers Grimm; Xavier Güell; Hesiod; Homer; Horace; Lovecraft; Ernest Milá; Howard Phillips; Oriol Pi de Cabanyes; Isidre Puig-Boada; Javier Sierra; Junichiro Tanizaki; Manuel Tuñón de Lara; *La Vanguardia*; Oscar Wilde.